MURDER AT MULLINGS

An intriguing 1930s country house murder mystery: first in the brand-new Florence Norris series.

When there's a brutal murder at Mullings, ancestral home of the wealthy Stodmarsh family, housekeeper Florence Norris and local publican George Bird are determined to protect their nearest and dearest from suspicion. Could there be a connection with the mysterious 'ornamental hermit' who lives on the estate? It's up to Florence to find out.

Previous titles from Dorothy Cannell

The Ellie Haskell Mysteries
THE THIN WOMAN
DOWN THE GARDEN PATH
THE WIDOW'S CLUB
MUM'S THE WORD
FEMMES FATAL
HOW TO MURDER YOUR MOTHER-IN-LAW
THE SPRING CLEANING MURDERS
THE TROUBLE WITH HARRIET
BRIDESMAIDS REVISITED
THE IMPORTANCE OF BEING ERNESTINE
WITHERING HEIGHTS
GOODBYE, MS CHIPS
SHE SHOOTS TO CONQUER

The Florence Norris Mysteries
MURDER AT MULLINGS *

Other Titles
SEA GLASS SUMMER *

* available from Severn House

MURDER AT MULLINGS

Dorothy Cannell

Severn House Large Print
London & New York

This first large print edition published 2014
in Great Britain and the USA by
SEVERN HOUSE PUBLISHERS LTD of
19 Cedar Road, Sutton, Surrey, England, SM2 5DA.
First world regular print edition published 2014 by
Severn House Publishers Ltd., London and New York.

British Library Cataloguing in Publication Data

Cannell, Dorothy author.
  Murder at Mullings. -- (The Florence Norris mysteries)
  1. Murder--Investigation--Fiction. 2. Hermits--Fiction.
  3. Detective and mystery stories. 4. Large type books.
  I. Title II. Series
  813.5'4-dc23

  ISBN-13: 9780727897480

Severn House Publishers support the Forest Stewardship Council™
[FSC™], the leading international forest certification organisation. All
our titles that are printed on FSC certified paper carry the FSC logo.

Printed and bound in Great Britain by
T J International, Padstow, Cornwall.

For my granddaughter, Hope Thomas,
who brings sunshine to the cloudiest day.

ACKNOWLEDGEMENTS

To Joe Maron, who inspired this book by
telling me about ornamental hermits.

ONE

When Florie Wilks arrived at Mullings to work as a kitchen maid, she saw herself stepping not only into a world of grandeur, but one poised thrillingly on the ledge between reality and the sort of transporting fiction she loved. She couldn't count the number of such books she'd devoured at the risk of being told by her furious father that the next time she wasted a tallow candle staying up half the night reading he'd send her to live with nasty Aunt Aggie.

Carrying her small bundle of possessions on arrival day, she passed through the iron gates and was waved on by the lodge keeper towards the servants' entrance. Alas for her wide-eyed dreams, she was soon to discover that bricks and mortar, coupled with extensive acreage, do not always make for a world abounding in heroes and heroines.

With its velvet lawns, formal gardens, expansive woodlands, serenading waterfalls and productive home farm, Mullings was the acknowledged great house of Dovecote Hatch. Nonetheless, it had long been the conviction of the neighbouring gentry that the Stodmarsh family, which had inhabited the estate from one generation to the next since its beginnings, must

9

be counted hereditarily a sadly dull lot. In the broad scheme of things, this view had validity. England had long flourished or floundered without members of the Stodmarsh family being accorded honors for valor or hanged for villainy. Within an hour of her arrival, Florie was to discover that throughout the generations not one riotous scandal or harrowing melodrama had occurred within the boundaries of Mullings to wend its way into local, let alone national, lore. She was promptly informed by the housekeeper that there were no tales to be told of unfaithful wives tossed off the roof, no insane persons locked in turrets, no duels fought with either swords or pistols in the murky first light of dawn, no daughters gambled away into wedlock with debauched old men by their profligate fathers' reverses at the gaming table. A pity the same could not be said of other leading families who she wouldn't name!

In the view of those who gladly boasted of their rollicking forebears' escapades, the Stodmarshes' failure to live life to the hilt would have been their affair, had their mopish propriety not cast a pall over any social event in which they participated. The men did not foxhunt, revere their tailors or know a damn thing about poker. They handled the running of their properties themselves without the aid of an estate manager, and even when young their conversation was jeeringly found to be middle-aged, running the gamut from farming to the need to repair the church roof. As for the Stodmarsh females, it was a source of much drawing room tittering and

10

chortling that they were either petulant pansies or dismal dahlias not worth being plucked.

Had Florie heard these comments, she would have thought them very unkind (even though she would have been disappointed that the Stodmarsh women were not considered as beauties scattering male conquests like silk scarves in their wake). Just the sort of thing nasty Aunt Aggie would say in different words: 'All of a bunch, squint-eyed or saggy-bottomed, take your pick.'

There was one meagre mercy. The critics – chief of whom were the Blakes of The Manor in Large Middlington, the Stafford-Reids of Hidden Meadows in Small Middlington, and the Palfretts of Chimneys in Kingsbury Knox – could not accuse the Stodmarshes of viewing themselves as scholarly. An announced familiarity with Virgil, an impassioned interest in the history of the Belgian Congo, or even – God forbid – the ability to haltingly list all the kings and queens of England from Ethelred the Unready to present times would only have served to shove them higher up the ladder of the most crushing bores the glory of Britain had ever produced. Leave the pontificating to politicians and parsons! The Blakes in particular believed the increasing association of brains with success in trade made displaying more than a modicum of intelligence smack of a coarseness verging on blatant vulgarity.

Florie would have been surprised to discover this attitude. She had been brought up to believe that her betters, whilst knowing how to frolic with style, were far cleverer than any ordinary person could ever hope to be. Else, why would God have put them in charge of things?

The Blakes, Stafford-Reids and Palfretts acknowledged this superiority as a fact, not a view, but that didn't mean one had to go around pondering the universe all day. What thought must necessarily be expended by a gentleman beyond crushing the bloody impudence of the lower classes, and instilling in their sons the virtue of doggedly sowing their wild oats before ardently beseeching the hand in marriage of a woman of beauty, breeding and fortune? The desire for one's girls to make spectacular, or at the very least creditable marriages, perhaps burned more fiercely in the maternal than the paternal bosom.

The Stodmarshes had husbanded their wealth well and, lacking charm or wit had, as already observed, done nothing to bring dishonour on their name. Yet no Blake or Stafford-Reid parent had ever encouraged, let alone endeavoured to coerce, an offspring into marriage with a Stodmarsh. The very idea was unthinkable ... intolerable. Every celebration, every funeral henceforth ruined! One could laugh if the prospect were not so wretched.

Tales of forbidden love would have been right up Florie's alley. Growing up, she had thrilled to her mother's stories about her own days in service, before she had been married, with a titled family named Tamersham in Northumbria. Their illustrious ancestral home had possessed a moat, turrets and battlements, a portcullis and, casting an even more alluring spell, an old man with long, matted hair and beard dressed in a rough-spun robe dwelling in a cave in a wooded embankment. He was not there by happenstance – Sir Peregrine Tamersham had adhered to a tradition of employing ornamental hermits – although Florie's mother mistakenly believed this to be a fascinating eccentricity peculiar only to that family.

This whimsical folly dated back to the eighteenth century, when some of the upper-crust believed no self-indulgence could be too ridiculous, in keeping up with the Jones-Joneses. Advertisements appeared for male persons willing to serve in such a capacity. Essential requirements for an ornamental hermit included never cutting his hair, beard or nails, and upon leaving his shelter he meandered with his head bowed above an open Bible. The very air around him was steeped in saintly melancholy. It was a delightful fillip for house guests to espy him amidst the groves or by a woodland stream, as it was incumbent on him to ensure they did. He was not hard done by. Nature provided water, and food was brought to him from the house, but he was strictly forbidden from exchanging a single word with the servants.

As a child, Florie had loved listening to her mother's stories, and had particularly thrilled to the image of the pious ancient drawn so vividly by her mother. Oh, to work in such a place! She could not expect Mullings to possess this rare entrancement, but she had hoped for others. Perhaps a private cemetery where wisps of something more than mist drifted up from the graves at dusk, gathering shape and purpose as they slipped across the grounds to seep through walls and windows, back to where they rightfully belonged. Who would not wish to cling, however vaporously, to a world forever glittering with merriment or plunging into thrilling turmoil, where the days swirled from one to the next in a dazzle of privilege? Of course, Florie didn't put it that way to herself as a little girl. But many years later, as housekeeper of Mullings, she would spread it out as such in a letter to her cousin Hattie Fly in London.

The fourteen-year-old Florie who had arrived at the servants' entrance to Mullings, tremulous with anticipation, had looked as much a ghost as any she had hoped to glimpse in a richly appointed corridor or on a dark turn of the stairs. The mature Florie was wont to smile, albeit ruefully, at such starry-eyed simplicity.

Mrs Longbrow, the housekeeper in 1900 when Florie arrived, having reduced Florie to a squeak and nod of the head, continued making it clearer than glass for the next five minutes that the Stodmarshes were the worthiest of county families. They did not indulge in escapades or tantrums.

'So there'll be no point in attempting to listen at keyholes.'

'No, Mrs Longbrow.' A dipped curtsy.

'Not that you'll have reason to leave the kitchen, except to go outside to the privy, until bedtime.'

'Yes, Mrs Longbrow.' Another dip. Within another half hour Florie had learned that the lord's Christian name was Edward and Lady Stodmarsh's was Lillian. They had two sons – Lionel, aged fifteen, and William, only eleven months younger.

'Both bode well to follow solidly in their father's footsteps. Never a scrap of trouble from either of them since the cradle.'

The consolation for this depressing information was being told to sit down before being handed a cup of the best tea Florie had ever tasted. At home in the cramped house twelve miles away, the amount of leaves that went into the pot could have been counted out, and when the situation demanded they were re-brewed until there was little or no colour or flavour left.

In the course of that first day at Mullings, Florie's hope that the stories she would one day be able to tell of her years in service began to dim around the edges. The spurt of interest aroused on hearing that Lord Stodmarsh had possessed a youthful enthusiasm for putting on theatricals in the gallery was quickly doused.

'He long ago abandoned such ideas, which did rather worry his father, to concentrate devotedly on overseeing the estate, which includes Farn Deane, the home farm. Lord and Lady Stodmarsh used to attend the occasional play in London, but she's no longer fit for the journey.'

'I'm sorry to hear it, Mrs Longbrow.'

'No life's without its sorrows, as the vicar enjoys reminding us from the pulpit. Well, Florie, standing here feeling sorry for our good lady won't bring her improvement. There's the larder shelves still to be done and the vegetables peeled

15

for Mrs McDonald.' Mrs McDonald, the cook, had never been married; the *Mrs* was a courtesy befitting her position in the household. Though immensely proud of her Scottish heritage, she'd not once been further north than Yorkshire.

'I've already seen to both, Mrs Longbrow.'

'Then you can help get the soup on.' This said, the housekeeper swept away to have a word with the head housemaid about turning the library carpet, something that was done every three months to even the wear.

The poor health that often kept Lady Stodmarsh confined to her bedroom turned out to be nothing more interesting than rheumatism – not a chronic violent hysteria that would have required her door being locked from the outside. The sons were red-haired, fair-skinned and blue-eyed. Boys of that description could, unfairly or not, never grow up to be unflinchingly heroic or fascinatingly ignoble. Red hair might even mean ginger. Undoubtedly there would be freckles. The death knell to dreams indeed!

And yet, for a girl prepared to make the best of things, there were indications of compensations at Mullings. Mrs Longbrow, though strict sounding, did not seem unkind; the butler looked a little like Florie's father. Mrs McDonald was red-faced without looking scarily fierce, and the lesser members of the staff (though all far above herself on the importance ladder) seemed willing to welcome Florie into their midst. During the evening meal, a feast of sausages, pork pie, bubble and squeak, and apple Charlotte, Lady Stodmarsh's lady's maid smiled at her. The bootboy winked.

By the end of the week Florie was included, somewhat hoveringly, in the other girls' giggling chatter in those rare free moments between scrubbing, polishing, sweeping, fetching and carrying. She missed her parents and younger brother and sister, but wasn't homesick. A fortnight later the bootboy had asked if she would go with him to the Dovecote Hatch Summer Fair. She wasn't put off by his impishly cocksure manner; she rather liked him for it, but she wasn't ready for holding hands, let alone kissing, so she encouraged him to take the other kitchen maid instead. She was sure it was Betty he really fancied, but was afraid she'd toss her head and tell him he had a nerve to think she'd be seen out with him. Betty was pretty enough to be pert. Florie wasn't, not even in her best dress with the collar daintily stitched from two lace-edged handkerchiefs given to her mother as a wedding present by the titled lady in Northumbria.

The looking glass didn't tell fibs. She was overly tall and reed-thin, with a pale, narrow face and hair that, though thick, could not have been described as anything other than mousy. And there was something else to cause diffidence. Her passionate love of reading made her different from many other young people of her class. A vivid imagination stirred by her mother's storytelling led to her grasping for any book she could lay her hands on, from penny dreadfuls to Jane Austen, Thackeray, the Brontës, and Dickens; and then there was poetry, especially Keats and Shelley. The elderly book-seller three streets away from her home had at first sold her badly worn copies for a penny and then begun giving them to her because he said her smiles brightened his week. Not something to be talked about if you didn't want to be thought above yourself. She had learned to guard against using big words or allowing her grammar to veer into something better than that spoken around her. She must be even more careful at Mullings. A kitchen maid seeming to give herself airs would have laid herself open to ridicule anywhere, devastatingly so in the world below stairs. Far better to be viewed as awkwardly shy.

Fortunately she was kept too busy scurrying to complete two or three tasks at once to worry about much else. By the time she crawled into bed in the box-like room she shared with Betty she was tired out, but never unhappy. She knew she was giving satisfaction, especially to Mrs McDonald, whom she'd once overheard saying to Mrs Longbrow, 'That Florie has a quick mind in addition to getting more out of five minutes than Betty ever could in an hour.'

Florie did not catch a glimpse of Lord Stodmarsh until a month after her arrival when she was about to leave by the woodland path at the rear of the house for her first day off. He was crossing a stretch of lawn with a golden Labrador at his side. She had learned that he was in his late thirties, but his burly build, grizzled hair, side whiskers and drooping moustache made him look almost elderly to her youthful eye.

Seeing her, he raised his hat and inclined his head in her direction. It was a courtly gesture at odds with the less than patrician appearance. She was so surprised she almost tripped over her feet in fumbling a curtsy. This was something – small but still exciting – to tell her mother on reaching home.

In the coming years her opinion of Lord Stodmarsh as a kind and considerate man was confirmed, as was the case with Lady Stodmarsh in her gentle way. When Florie's father died unexpectedly, Mrs Longbrow told her that the master and mistress wished to see her in the drawing room to express their sympathy. She returned to the kitchen additionally heartened by permission to go home for a week without loss of wages. On every Christmas Day each member of the staff was presented with a gift, handkerchiefs or gloves, and on New Year's Eve the entire staff was invited into the hall for a celebratory cup of punch.

By the age of twenty-four Florie was head housemaid and had gained sufficient assurance of being liked and respected at Mullings to no longer feel the need to conceal the fact that much of her free time was spent reading. Indeed, on encountering Lord Stodmarsh outside Craddock's Antiquarian Bookshop one Saturday afternoon, she unhesitatingly responded to his enquiry as to what she had purchased by showing him the volume – a copy of *The Tempest*.

'Ah, yes!' his eyes revealed a wistful gleam. 'When I was a very young man we performed that play at the house. I played Prospero. Wonder where my costume for that part and others went! I expect up to some trunk in the attics. We Stodmarshes have always been loath to throw away anything that might one day be put back to use, even a hundred years hence! Good day to you, Florie. I trust you find your mother well if you are about to go and visit her.' How could some members of the gentry regard him as a buffoon? He hesitated before adding, 'I hear you and the younger Norris boy are courting. I consider you both fortunate.'

Florie knew herself to be so. The Norrises were the tenants of Farn Deane, the home farm. She had become acquainted with Mrs Norris, conversing pleasantly in the village street, before being invited to tea on a day off when she wasn't going home because her mother had gone to nurse a cousin who was ill. It was on that occasion that she met Robert, the older son – his brother Tom was off at market – and was immediately drawn to him. She liked his warm respect for his parents; saw he had a sense of humor that had at its core a keen intelligence. And there was something else. A fluttering of attraction that had her fearing she would flush when he looked at her. He wasn't handsome – his build was too lanky, his face long and bony – but she felt that he was a man she'd never tire of seeing come through the door.

Florie and Robert married within the year and such was her happiness that she felt little sadness at leaving Mullings. Besides, she could frequently walk over for a visit with the staff or have them over to visit. Tom was yet unmarried and shortly after Florie's settling in at Farn Deane her mother-in-law suffered a heart attack, which left her permanently fatigued and often breathless. It was a relief to her and her husband that Florie could take over the running of the house. As the years passed without her conceiving, Florie tried not to give up hope that she and Robert would be surprised, like other couples, by the eventual arrival of a baby. Otherwise their marriage had in every way fulfilled the promise of their courtship.

Then came the declaration of war against Germany in 1914. A dark cloud swamped the village at the thought of its young – and not so young – men donning uniforms and marching off to who knew what fate. The former bootboy at Mullings, now a tanner's assistant, was amongst the first group to go. Florie shared the general anguish, but had little dread for Robert or his brother Tom: surely farmers were too much needed at home to be called upon. She should have known her husband would writhe against what he perceived as an avoidance of duty. One sunny morning – she was always to remember the incongruity of the cloudless sky – he told her the decision he had reached. Tom could manage well enough without him and their father, although in his sixties, still relished getting up at five and going down to the barns and dairy before heading for the fields. There was no argument she could bring to this, and the depth of her love for him and her respect for his viewpoint made selfish pleas unthinkable.

She knew with a numbed certainty the day she

saw him off in 1915 that she would never see him in this life again. She read the same anguished awareness in his mother's eyes and they clung together before reminding them- selves it was wash day and humble duties must go on. A telegram brought the news of Robert's death three months later. Florie was yet another war widow; more fortunate than many in that she didn't have to worry about keeping a roof over her head or putting food into hungry little mouths. And yet she chafed to leave Farn Deane, to escape the aching emptiness of rooms he would never again enter. Unfortunately she was more needed than ever, especially when her mother-in-law died in 1919. Everything changed the following year, when Tom married Gracie, a farmer's daughter from Kingsbury Knox, who was more than capable taking over the house- hold reins.

Florie was considering her future with an optimism she had not felt for a long time, when Mrs Longbrow, the housekeeper under whom she had worked at Mullings and who was now well into her seventies, came to see her. This was not an unusual occurrence – she quite often stop- ped by for a cup of tea and a chat – and Florie had retained her fond interest in life at Mullings. She had gone to the church to see Lionel marry and had grieved when he and his wife were killed in a motoring accident, the fault of the other driver, on returning home from a weekend in London. They left behind them a two-year-old son named Edward after his grandfather but called Ned. His presence, Mrs Longbrow had assured Florie on several occasions, had done a world of good in bringing solace to Lord Stodmarsh and his good lady. Mr William had also married. When those who had not seen his bride asked for a description of her, the most frequent response was, a fine figure of a woman – so often the more tactful way of saying *stout*. On the occasion of her latest visit to Farn Deane, Mrs Longbrow brought news on her own account.

'It'll be a sad wrench, Florie, but the time has come for me to take life easier. I'm going to live with my widowed sister in Weymouth, and what I'm here to suggest is you take over from me at Mullings. You're the right age, close enough to what I was when I was taken on as housekeeper.'

Florie's teacup rattled as she set it down in its saucer. 'It's very good of you to think of me.'

'I did think of you,' the old lady's face crinkled into a smile, 'but it was His Lordship that suggested it. He's always thought very highly of you. So don't go disappointing him or Lady Stodmarsh, who's none too well, as you'll have heard – crippled now with the rheumatism and so tired much of the time.'

'Thank you, Mrs Longbrow – there's nothing I'd like better.'

'Well, that's a relief! I'm sure it won't make difficulties that Mr Grumidge the butler and some other members of the staff are new since your day. You've got what it takes to get along without giving in, which, when it comes down to it, is what this job entails.'

And so Florie returned to Mullings at the age

23

of thirty-five. In doing so, she felt that she had left Robert's grief-imprinted image behind at Farn Deane, allowing her to remember only the happiness. She received an especially warm and respectful welcome from Mrs McDonald the cook, who looked very little different from the old days, and was just as nimble on her feet despite her fifteen stone.

'Nice, hard-working little Florie is how I thought of you when you first come here, Mrs Norris, if you'll forgive the remembering.'

Almost imperceptibly over the years she had become 'Florence' to her family, with the exception of her cousin Hattie Fly in London, whom she did not see as often as she would have liked, but was in regular correspondence. In the eyes of the others, she had gone too far up in the world from her beginnings for 'Florie' to be right or proper. She wished it weren't that way, but nothing she lovingly said or did had any effect, except to bring awkwardness to the situation. Even her mother rarely slipped back to the shortened version. Other than Hattie, there was only one person who still addressed her as Florie.

This was little Ned Stodmarsh. Now seven years old, he was a remarkably articulate child who quickly captivated her heart with his pluck and mischief, which Mrs Longbrow was complacently certain he'd outgrow. Equally endearing to Florence were his ginger hair and freckles. He rarely mentioned his parents, but Florence was sure that he had not forgotten them completely even though he had been several months short of his third birthday when the accident

24

occurred. She discovered shortly after her return to Mullings that his learning of the accident and the consequence that his mother and father weren't ever coming home to him again had imprinted itself starkly on his little mind.

Shortly after midnight one evening, a tap came at her bedroom door. It was Ned's nanny, dressing gown sagging off one shoulder and cord untied. The ring of housekeeping keys lay on the dressing table, but Florence, having just finished writing a lengthy letter to Hattie, was still in her navy-blue dress with the round, silver-plated brooch Robert had given her on their wedding day at its throat. Surprise escalated into concern as she faced the woman – saw her lean into the wall, hand pressed against it as if to maintain her balance.

So far Florence had had few encounters with her. From these she had gained only an impression of sombre bustle and a disinclination to continue a conversation, let alone start one. She appeared to be in her late fifties, a shortish woman of medium build with coarse, greying hair. Anything more meaningful had been learned from other members of the staff, not Ned. She was a Miss Hilda Stark, previously employed by a family named Rutledge in the northern part of the county. Understandably, she was now bleary-eyed and frowsy-haired, as anyone would be after being roused from a night's slumber – or, possibly, from being drunk. Florence caught the fumes of whisky from her breath. Saw her stagger when her hand slipped off the wall. Belligerence, rather than distress, contorted her

25

features.

'What's wrong, Nanny? Is Master Ned ill?' The enquiry was unusually sharp for Florence.

'Not the fever sort of ill.' She noted the thickened, slurred voice. 'Just his nibs having a screaming fit; woke from a nightmare, he said; but if you ask me it was sheer naughtiness. Claimed he'd go on bellowing the house down if I didn't fetch you.'

'Had he calmed down when you left?'

The mouth worked itself into a grimace. 'I told him I wouldn't take a step if he didn't. What I should've done was tape his wretched mouth shut.'

'Not so easy to do for someone lacking control of her limbs.' This was a Florence even Robert wouldn't have recognized. She'd never at Mullings had to deal with such an ugly situation, but now she had to get to Ned.

'And why wouldn't I be all of a shake, roused out of a deep sleep by that ear-piercing racket he made? You saying anything different will be a wicked lie that'll you pay dear for!'

The woman's face, contorted by spite, verged on the grotesque, with its florid complexion and slack lips, spittle dribbling down her chin. Did she see no reason to rein herself in, or was she too sozzled to know half of what she was saying?

'Go down to the kitchen and get yourself a cup of hot milk,' Florence ordered, and brushed past her to head down the corridor. She had been sorely tempted to add, 'and not a buttered rum', but to have aggravated the situation would have

26

been foolhardy. The respectable front that Nanny would seem to have created for herself, at least to pass muster in daylight hours, had abandoned her – or she it. She hurled her response at Florence's retreating back. That the words were slurred did not lessen their force.

'Hot milk, my foot! That slop's for the likes of the mistress. It's a wonder nobody's dosed her nightly cup with more than the bicarb she takes in it! Talk about enjoying ill health to the hilt! You'd think her husband for one would've had enough of it by now. The man might as well be wed to his grandma for all the good that limp lily will do him under the sheets! Or would it be more respectful to say Lillian, you posh-voiced stuck-up piece?'

Florence pivoted. 'Either go downstairs without another word or I'll rouse Mr Grumidge, who I'm sure will be in agreement that you should be removed from this house within the hour.' She waited for the woman to go before continuing along the corridor and taking the short flight of steps to the night nursery. First things first. She needed urgently to make sure that Ned was all right; then she would decide whether or not to wait till morning to report the situation to the butler.

Even in the short, narrow bed, Ned looked pathetically small when Florence went in to him. The room was dimly lit, accentuating his pallor amidst the freckles. She loved those freckles, loved everything about him, even at his naughtiest times.

She sat down on the coverlet beside him, her

27

heart aching, brimming with the need to reassure him of the wakeful world's safety.

'Tell me, dear.' She gently cupped his hand in hers, as if cradling a wounded bird.

'It was a bad, bad dream,' Ned whimpered, all his customary bravado gone. 'It was the one I often have – about Mummy and Daddy. They hated having to go and live in the cemetery. They kept trying to tell people before they got buried that they were scared of going down into the dark and the cold. They didn't want to leave me or Mullings.'

'No, of course they didn't; but when they got to heaven they'll have stopped being sad; knowing they'd always be with you – in a different, but very special way.'

'I want to believe that ... I do most of the time.' Ned relaxed against her shoulder. 'You won't ever leave me; will you, Florie? Not ever in a hundred years, even when I'm older than Grandpa? Promise me you'll stay!' The green, amber-flecked eyes held hers in desperate appeal. 'Promise, honour of a Stodmarsh. You're the nearest possible to one, aren't you?'

'Well, it's very kind of you to think so. Your family has been a big part of my life for a long time now.' How should she continue? Florence had always thought it terribly wrong to lie to a child. She knew as well as anyone that in life there is no certainty; something can always happen beyond our control or deepest wishes that alters everything. Tomorrow, next week, next year, any time during his growing-up years, the ground could shift beneath her feet and his. But

28

she couldn't bring herself to look into those stricken eyes and slide behind the use of unsatisfying soothing noises – saying she would do her level best; that he mustn't worry about it. She drew him to her and stroked the spiky ginger hair back from his damp brow.

'I promise, Ned.' He had insisted sternly on her third day as housekeeper that she not address him as Master Ned. 'But what's most important is that you'll grow up here with your grandparents; they love you enormously. And they're such wonderful people.'

'Not more special than you.' The mulish note, which had undoubtedly irritated, if not infuriated, Nanny, entered his voice. 'Grandfather is marvellous, of course, and I do love Grandmother, but being unwell all the time she can't ever play games or even read to me very long without getting tired. I know she can't help it, but anyway ... I wish a blackbird would come down and peck off Nanny's nose for saying it's all put on.'

Florence answered carefully. 'People can be mistaken in their views at times, as is the case with Nanny about this. Lady Stodmarsh most certainly does not wish to be ill.'

'I know.' He patted her hand, becoming the soother. 'Nanny tells fibs. Big ones. The vicar could put her in hell for it.'

'Try not to think about her right now.' Hopefully the woman had made it down to the kitchen and had not yet returned to her bedroom, which had access to the night nursery through the communicating door. But Florence had heard no

29

sound from behind it.

'I hate Nanny! I know we're not right to hate anyone, but I do her! She told me I've a bad streak in me that I got from my mother ... that she was wilful, too, and that she and Daddy probably had a row in the car that night that made the accident happen, and most likely it wasn't the other driver's fault at all.'

Florence, the even-tempered, was seized by an almost overpowering urge to haul Nanny out of the house by her hair. Mrs Longbrow had described Jane Tressler during her engagement to Lionel Stodmarsh as a spirited girl but sweet-natured with it. 'No doubt sparks will fly between them, and so much the better for both!' Nothing Florence had heard afterwards suggested the couple were not ideally suited.

'Ned, have you told your grandparents about this?'

'No.' He stirred nervously within the circle of her arm. 'She said if I told she'd say I was lying or imagining it – which would be worse, because...' his voice cracked and his small hand tightened on hers '...because mad people make up things and we all know what happens to them. They get locked away.'

A physical pain stabbed through Florence's outrage. 'You're a perfectly normal, healthy little boy. No one, especially Lord and Lady Stodmarsh, could think there's anything wrong with your mind.'

'But they might start to wonder, not wanting to, but unable to help it because of my other grandmother. She had to be sent away for a while after Mummy was born because she started thinking all her teeth were rotting and about to fall out. And that her dog, a nice old spaniel that she loved, had got possessed by a devil and was going to tear her to pieces.'

'Oh, Ned! The poor lady!'

'She got better and came home.'

'It happens to women sometimes after childbirth.'

'Does it? Then maybe I needn't worry, because men don't have babies.' Ned shifted closer. 'That's a good thing ... although it seems unfair that it's always left to the mother and isn't turn and turn about with the father.'

'There's something to that,' agreed Florence gravely, 'but I think a lot of women like being the ones to have babies.'

'Perhaps.' Ned stiffened. 'But after the accident it happened again, and that time Grandmother Tressler was away longer. At a place called Meadow Vale.'

'Again, Nanny could be mistaken.' Or might there be truth to this particular revelation? Ned hadn't accused Nanny of lying about this – and would the woman have bothered inventing the name of the facility?

Ned shook his head. 'I overheard Uncle William and Aunt Gertrude talking about it before Grandma Tressler came to stay here for a fortnight last year. Uncle William got very loud. "For God's sake, old girl, don't go upsetting the woman and send her off the deep end again!"' The mimicry of the man's deep voice by a child was uncanny. '"We've never in the history of

Mullings had to lock up a mad woman, and I'd just as soon not bloody well start now!"'

'I'm sorry you had to hear that.' Florence fought down fruitless anger.

'Then Aunt Gertrude said, "No one can disagree that she's mental, William, but I'm not sure that's quite the same as mad."' Ned did almost as good a job with his aunt's stolid voice as with his uncle's bellicose one.

'Did you say anything to your grandparents about this?'

'Of course not.' Ned's chin went up. 'That would have been dishonourable. Ungentlemanly. I shouldn't be telling you now, but...'

Florence reassured him, 'It's helping fill in the picture about Nanny.'

'You can guess what Uncle William roared back at Aunt Gertrude?'

'My mind doesn't work as quickly as it should at night.'

'"Balderdash!"'

Florence smiled, but she was remembering when she'd thought the notion of a mad woman being confined to a secret room was the height of enthralling mystery. She knew very little about Mrs Tressler, other than that her Christian name was Eugenie and that she had been widowed a year or so before her daughter and only child married Lionel Stodmarsh. And then, a few years later, she had lost that child in an accident. What woman might not have fallen apart – especially if she was at that time going through the change? There had been a woman two doors down from the house where Florence

32

had grown up, who'd been 'taken bad' after childbirth and then again in middle life. On the latter occasion she had not recovered, as it would seem Mrs Tressler had done.

'It's Uncle William that makes scenes, not Aunt Gertrude. Anyway,' the bravado was creeping back, 'who cares what they think?'

Florence stroked his arm. It was not permissible for her to comment on his relations' attitudes or behaviour, but what he said of his uncle and aunt was true. Loyalty did not prevent an inward denial of fact. William Stodmarsh was a blusterer and his wife a mild woman – outwardly, at least. Florence had wondered at times if her emotions were not as well corseted as her stout figure.

Ned yawned and after a moment turned on his side. 'I think I can nod off now, Florie.'

'Good.'

'Stay a little while, please.'

In a couple of minutes he was asleep, but she waited another ten or so before getting off the bed and tapping on the communicating door. On opening it she saw, as expected from there having been no sound from that quarter, that Nanny had not returned. The bed did not look as though it had been slept in earlier. A bottle along with a glass containing an inch or two of whisky stood on a table next to an easy chair. Where was Nanny – passed out in the kitchen? Florence was halfway down the corridor when she heard heavy, laborious footsteps on the back stairs. A moment later, four persons came into view at the top – two of the maids holding Nanny up under the armpits and another propelling her from the rear. She went instantly to their assistance and with their combined efforts got Nanny into bed. The room was immediately filled with raucous snores.

Annie Long, a timid and extremely nervous kitchen maid, liable to collapse into hysterics if she heard the word mouse, let alone saw one, now burst into tears, and Florence hurried her and the other two girls out of the room.

'It was Annie what found her lying on the kitchen floor,' explained the sturdily built, rosy-cheeked girl who had been doing the propelling. 'She'd gone down because she kept waking up, worrying she hadn't put the scrubbing brush in the right bucket and there she was,' cocking an eye to the closed door, 'lying on the floor.'

Annie had wiped away her tears but continued to snuffle. 'It give me such a turn, Mrs Norris. I come over right queer. I thought she was dead. Then I heard the snoring and I run up to fetch Molly and Violet. We was struggling to get her upright when Mr Grumidge come in.' Annie's voice trailed off. Florence thought vaguely that there wouldn't be much work got out of her that day. Molly, who had spoken previously, picked up the thread.

'He'd heard the running up and down stairs and wanted to see what was going on. He picked her up, talked soft but firm till he got her moving – like sleepwalking, it was – told us to get her into bed and then wake you and ask if you'd go down to him.'

Molly was a girl destined to become head

housemaid. The silent Violet struggled to suppress a yawn and Annie hiccupped. Florence thanked them, asked them not to talk about any of this to other members of the staff and sent them back to their beds.

She found Mr Grumidge, dressed and alert as if the working day were well begun – in the kitchen, where she had expected him to be. At this hour propriety forbade a conference in either the butler's or housekeeper's room. He was a neatly built man, probably a few years older than herself, with a grave manner suited to his position but none of the pomposity prevalent in his species. His pale hair and complexion served to heighten the keenness of his eyes. Florence both respected and liked him, and believed he felt the same about her; making for a harmonious relationship.

'I apologize for asking you to come down, Mrs Norris, but I thought it right to inform you immediately of this regrettable incident.' His composure was as it would have been on learning of any other household infraction.

'That's perfectly all right, Mr Grumidge.' The kitchen, with its scrubbed stone sinks, old cupboards and vast deal table, gave off a peaceful sense of having seen and heard anything and everything many times over, and had survived to witness modern cook stoves. Florence relaxed for the first time in over an hour. 'I had been sitting with Master Ned.'

She followed quickly with her account of events, including ordering Nanny to go to the kitchen and heat herself a milky drink. 'I'm sorry to say she was very belligerent. Fortunately, Master Ned seemed not to have noticed the state she was in – having wakened terrified from a bad dream.'

'Poor child.'

'He did say that Nanny has been treating him unkindly – increasingly so, it sounded – of late.' Florence did not elaborate; doing so would have violated what Ned had said to her in confidence. Mr Grumidge did not press her; there was a heightening of that keenness in his eyes.

'A possible contribution to his nightmare. He cannot have informed Lord or Lady Stodmarsh of her treatment or she would have been dismissed. Our English code of not carrying tales may be good for the character, Mrs Norris, but it does not always serve the practicalities well.'

'I could not agree more.' Florence clasped her hands, recalling the feel of Ned's small one. 'I'm sure that but for his distressed state Master Ned would have thought it unmanly to tell me what had been happening. If only suspicions that she was inclined to the bottle had been aroused! But I never heard a whisper.'

'Nor I, Mrs Norris.'

'I'd prefer to believe this a one-time lapse, but sadly – for Nanny's own sake as well as the family's – I can't. Master Ned's account of her behaviour suggests that she has been increasingly unable to control her emotions.'

Mr Grumidge nodded. 'There is, however, no point in blaming ourselves or other members of the staff for failing to recognize there was a problem. Perhaps we might have done had she been with Master Ned during the mornings. But with his spending the hours between nine and twelve-thirty taking lessons from the retired schoolmistress, she will have been free to return to her bed after seeing him up, dressed and breakfasted. Also, secret drinkers must of necessity become adept at allaying suspicions. I have sometimes thought that women may be more prone to secrecy because society allows men so much more latitude when it comes to libation.'

'She may have started slowly, Mr Grumidge. Indeed, I have to believe that she wasn't anywhere close to getting out of her depth when she came here, or the family that recommended her to Lady Stodmarsh would not have done so.'

'One would think not, but the Rutledges had a large number of children very close in age, making, I've gleaned, for a cheerful if somewhat chaotic household. This may have inclined them to be grateful to any nanny who had been willing to stay.'

'What now, Mr Grumidge?'

'I doubt she took a hard fall, more likely crumbled to the floor, but I believe telephoning the doctor is in order. An examination will prove me right or wrong on that and should also provide confirmation of her inebriated state. Such an action on my part will necessitate rousing the master, but hopefully the mistress will not need to be disturbed.'

'A wise course of action. I think I should go back to the night nursery so Master Ned has someone with him should he be awakened by footsteps or voices from the adjoining bedroom.'

'Excellent.' Those keen eyes appraised hers. 'You must, however, be exhausted at this hour.'

Florence assured him she was not tired, but within moments of sitting down in the armchair across from Ned's bed, where he was sleeping peacefully, she felt herself beginning to doze. She must have dropped off for almost an hour, although it seemed only moments before she heard a tap at the door to the corridor. There stood a stocky, grizzled man, black bag in hand.

'No head injury, Mrs Norris,' said Doctor Chester in his comfortable manner. 'I'm on my way down to talk with His Lordship, which means that you can go to your bed, my dear, reassured that all will be dealt with as it should be. We both know he won't send her off without something to live on. I hope Miss Stark will agree to let me help her, but I doubt she will; they rarely do.'

Florence went gratefully to her bed. She woke at seven, an hour later than usual, feeling well rested. At ten Mr Grumidge informed her that Lord and Lady Stodmarsh requested her presence in the elegant but restful drawing room. They greeted her warmly and invited her to sit down on one of the cream- and gold-striped Regency sofas. After thanking her for all she had done on the previous night, they spoke of the future. Nanny had declined a pension in favour of a settlement and would not be replaced. Ned would be moved from the nursery down to his father's old room, where his daily needs could be handled by one of the maids. Florence suggested Molly – the sensible, sturdy girl who had propelled the barely awake woman up the stairs. Earlier that morning His Lordship had placed a telephone call to a Mr Shepherd, headmaster of Westerbey Junior Boys' School, halfway between Dovecote Hatch and Large Middlington, and had arranged for Ned to start there in a couple of weeks instead of at the start of the new term, as had previously been intended.

'It sounds ideal.' Florence's smile lit up her face. 'It will be good for Master Ned to be with other boys, and I'm sure he'll take to Molly – she's a very cheerful girl. Do please let me know if there is any way in which I can be of help.' She started to rise.

'Oh, do stay a few moments longer if you can spare the time,' said Lady Stodmarsh in her light, musical voice. 'My husband and I want you to know how important it is to us that you continue the close relationship you have begun to establish with Ned. He told us earlier this morning how he had confided in you in the small hours about what Nanny had told him regarding his other grandmother – so unkind. Certainly she had a couple of distressing episodes, but is now recovered. It says so much that he unburdened himself to you after keeping silent for too long.'

'It had frightened him.'

'Of course it did.' Lord Stodmarsh shook his head. 'How could he not worry at the idea he might inherit a mental weakness? Your reassurances appear to have helped a good deal, Flor— Mrs Norris. That he trusts you completely, as we all do, is apparent. He is always at the heart of our thoughts and we greatly enjoy spending time with him, but...'

His wife gave him her sweet smile. 'You, my dear, are as active as you ever were and can completely fulfill your role with him. Regrettably, I am unable to provide all that I would wish by way of activities to make for a happy childhood, and an orphaned boy needs a woman's daily touch to help soften the rough edges of life for him, if he is not to grow up with an empty place in his heart. Our daughter-in-law is kind, but admits neither she nor our son has a way with children. So, to come to the point!' Lady Stodmarsh looked hopefully at Florence. 'In addition to your other qualities, you have the benefit of being of his mother's generation. We do hope our asking you to help nurture him is not an imposition?'

'Of course not.' Florence had not felt such deep happiness since Robert's death. 'Would it be all right if I took him with me to Farn Deane, when I go to see Tom and Gracie? It has been agreed that I shall have midday dinner with them one Sunday a month and remain through afternoon tea.'

A short, cheerful conversation followed. Knowing that this was His Lordship's day for going through the estate's accounts, Florence got to her feet and was about to excuse herself when Lady Stodmarsh spoke ruefully.

'I should not allow a dark thought to intrude, but I suspect that we have made a lasting enemy in Nanny.'

'An ill-wisher perhaps,' responded her husband with tender affection in his eyes, 'but what possible harm can she do us?'

'None, I suppose, unless her bitterness should one day align itself with some unforeseen circumstance.' Lady Stodmarsh shivered, and then smiled. 'I cannot lay claim to being fey, as I understand Mrs McDonald does, and it is well documented that in all these hundreds of years nothing in the way of melodrama has ever touched Mullings. So silly, that feeling that a goose has just walked over my grave.'

TWO

To the majority of those living in Dovecote Hatch, the lack of a colourful tapestry woven into the lives of the Stodmarshes throughout the centuries was not held to be a disadvantage. But it did come as something of a let-down to George Bird when he took over the Dog and Whistle in January of 1929. He was at that time a widower, approaching fifty, childless but with a godson living in Bexleyheath, where he had himself been born and bred. The boy's name was Jim. Much to his parents' pride, he had passed the scholarship to Dartford Grammar School when he was eleven and was now at university reading art history. No surprise there. Even as a tot he could draw a treat, George remembered.

41

He wrote to Jim regularly and met up with him as often as possible, knowing the lad to be genuinely fond of him. At his last pub George had taken some good-natured ribbing from old buffers who claimed to be able to recite Jim's letters by heart and said they couldn't understand why the lad wasn't up on a column along with Lord Nelson in Trafalgar Square.

Bexleyheath had been good to George but the decision to move to Dovecote Hatch following Mabel's death had been a wise one. A change of scenery meant meeting new people; it took him out of himself – exactly what his late better half would have urged with a playful poke in the ribs. George didn't let the grieving widower show at the Dog and Whistle. He was a balding, ruddy-faced man of vast height, with a personality as expansive as his stomach, which portion of his anatomy spoke volumes for his belief in good, honest English grub.

He also thoroughly enjoyed a good yarn spun for his benefit and believed he in turn owed a contribution of the same sort to strangers coming to the Dog and Whistle. It was his belief, as it had been that of the young Florie Wilks, that the gentry inhabited a world that was more fiction than reality and thus infinitely more fascinating than the one reserved for the Joneses, Smiths and Browns. On first standing at the gates of Mullings and looking down the sweep of elm-lined drive to what could be made out of the house's serene splendour, he let out a whistle. Talk about fit for a lord! He could almost feel Mabel's clutch on his arm and hear her: 'Whooh!

Me and my party frock! Wouldn't you love to hear that house gab, George?'

Unfortunately, he discovered as Florie had done that the place offered up no worthy anecdotes to be handed out with a pint of bitter or a glass of Mother's Ruin. No whispers of a long-ago lord being switched at birth with a washerwoman's baby, no recently discovered priest's hole with a skeleton inside, no spending of the night by a male member of the royal family – spotted come morning creeping out of the mistress's bedchamber.

Alf Thatcher, postman for thirty-odd years, put it this way to George one evening while lighting his decrepit old pipe. It was early enough that only a few of the regulars had filtered in. 'The other upper-crust families hereabouts made up their minds nigh on two hundred years ago that the Stodmarshes are country bumpkins not worth the knowing, and it'd be like breaking a blood oath to change their minds.' Alf reached for his pint of bitter. 'Now, I'll admit the present lord's father did drone on about his prize-winning pigs over at Farn Deane, the home farm, but we've all got our ways. Our Lord Stodmarsh is as pleasant spoke and open-handed a gentleman as you could wish to meet. Never fails to ask how life's ticking along when he sees me.'

'Is that right?'

'Shame his son, Mr William Stodmarsh, don't take after him sufficient.'

George stood idle a moment, waiting in hopes of hearing that said personage had run off to South America with a chorus girl, or in some other way drastically blotted his copybook.

'No disrespect intended, but Mr William Stodmarsh is summat of a curmudgeon, like his grandfather was afore him.'

'Ah.' George polished a glass.

'Her Ladyship's a kind, gentle soul – sadly frail and fair crippled with rheumatism, so not seen out and about much, save for opening the Christmas bazaar and such. But you'll meet His Lordship soon enough, Mr Bird. He comes in here every fortnight or so and makes sure to have a chat with one and all. Often as not he brings along the vicar. And that's a kindness above and beyond. Feels sorry for him, is what I think. An odd duck, if ever there was one, is the Reverend Pimcrisp. Got one of those narrow faces and the long nose and hooded eyes of a medieval geezer in a stained-glass window. His tipple's fizzy lemonade that he sips like it's something nasty the apothecary ordered.'

George pulled a pint of mild for a tottery old gent in a mustard-coloured cardigan with a cap the wrong way round on his head, and watched till he made it safely back to his seat. He then asked wistfully if there had ever been a minor scandal at Mullings since it had been built.

Alf twinkled back at him. 'Not one blinking, common or garden murder. No ghosts to lend that right touch of swank. Florence Norris, housekeeper at Mullings, told me that when she started work there at fourteen she was really hoping to be half frightened to death by seeing a shadowy presence standing by her bed at night.' Alf looked thoughtfully at George. 'I've a feel-

44

ing you and Florence would take to each other. Lovely woman, she is, and on her own like yourself. Widowed in the war. A good bloke, was Robert Norris. His brother Tom will be along here one of these nights. The Norris family has worked Farn Deane for the Stodmarshes since no one remembers when. Shame is, Tom and Gracie don't have any children to carry on after their day.'

George said he'd met Tom Norris one night when he was out taking a walk.

Alf returned to his former topic. 'Of course, there's some as thinks there's a reason Mullings isn't haunted.' His expression soured. 'I've heard tell the Blakes over at The Manor at Large Middlington have their little joke that none of the Stodmarsh forebears would have the spirit,' leaning in with a tightening of the mouth, 'to come back and haunt the place. And I suppose there's a few in the village as agrees it's a proper waste of the old ancestral, as they call it. Make that next one a pint instead of a half, Mr Bird. What I call lack of spirit is bunking off for safer pastures when diphtheria's going round, or developing flat feet and weak eyesight when a war's on. And different from some – like the Blakes and such – you won't get that from the Stodmarshes. They prefer the quiet life to stirring the daily pot is all. They've had their sorrows, same as ordinary folks like me and you. There was the deaths of the older son Lionel and his wife – pretty, spirited young lady. They was killed in a motor car crash, leaving a little son, named Edward for his grandpa, but called Ned.

He's sixteen now, and it has to be him that's helped his grandparents come to terms with their loss. That lad always kept everyone a-hopping.' Alf chuckled. 'A mind of his own, has young Ned; seems one day he decided he didn't want Hilda Stark to be his Nanny no more, said he wanted his Florie to take care of him. You should see the look on Hilda's face when Florence Norris or the Stodmarshes are mentioned.'

Hilda Stark was a regular at the Dog and Whistle, but not present that evening. 'Can't be easy getting the push.' George was ever a fair man.

'Right enough, but could be there was more to it than got out. Whatever the case, I sometimes think the only reason she's stayed on here in Dovecote Hatch is the hope of one day seeing them burned in oil. Make that another, Birdie.'

George had quickly become 'Birdie' amongst his regulars. The Dog and Whistle, originally a seventeenth-century coaching inn, looked, save for the glossy, brass-trimmed Victorian bar, much as it would have done back then. The tap-room had not been walled in half in order to offer a saloon and public bar. There was no need for such separation. The roughest bloke would-n't have belched without apology, let alone spat on the floor. They were a mingling lot here-abouts. Mr Shepherd, headmaster of Westerbey – which Ned Stodmarsh had attended until going to boarding school – was as like to be seen chatting with a farmhand or bricklayer as with Mr Craddock, the owner of the once general, now antiquarian bookstore. George, not being a boastful man, was unaware it was his hail-fellow-well-met personality that had quickly allowed the residents to forgive his being a foreigner to these parts.

'Go on, pour one for yourself, lad,' Alf proclaimed largely one evening within the first couple of weeks. 'Can't have you fading away before our eyes to below sixteen stone!'

That brought surrounding chuckles. George enjoyed receiving his full measure of communal jests at his expense. These included winks and elbow jabbing whenever Hilda Stark settled at a table with her Guinness and every two minutes or so slid glances towards the bar – ones that in a woman not wearing a battered felt hat and fingerless gloves might have been considered coquettish. Before long bets were being made during Hilda's rare absences that she'd get George to the altar afore Christmas. He was mischievously informed that several old blighters had only escaped her clutches by kicking the bucket in the nick of time.

'Here's to you, Birdie!' Alf chortled. 'Best ask Gracie Norris at Farn Deane to make the cake. She's a dab hand at marzipan, is Gracie, as her Tom'll tell you any day of the week and twice on Tuesdays.'

Tactless, perhaps, given George's recently widowed status, but he wasn't one to easily take offence. As so often happened, he could hear Mabel's voice in his ear. 'Oh, let the old girl find something to perk herself up, keep her from dwelling on what she sees as past wrongs.' So he joined in the jest. Yes, the patrons of the Dog and

47

Whistle were a good lot. Life in Dovecote Hatch grew better all the time.

His meeting Lord Stodmarsh was delayed because, on the day after his arrival, His Lordship had stepped off the footpath wending its way through his woods on to uneven ground which fell away into a ravine, and had sprained his ankle. The doctor was known to visit Mullings frequently to attend Lady Stodmarsh, so it had been a week or so before this news got out.

'There's a sign posting a warning if it's the place I'm thinking of, but it seems it was a misty night. And mayhap the dog bounded off.' Alf Thatcher shook his head sadly when putting George in the know. The path was strictly speaking a private one, but the Stodmarshes had a relaxed attitude about this, especially in spring at bluebell time. And Alf had been given permission to use it when making his newspaper deliveries to Mullings. 'Another pint, Birdie, to toast the good man's swift recovery. No doubt Vicar will be asking for prayers at Sunday service.'

George was not a religious man, but he quite liked the hymn singing and was interested in getting a look at the Reverend Pimcrisp after hearing the description of him, so he decided to go to church that Sunday. On coming out afterwards he was introduced to Florence Norris by Mr Shepherd. Within a few minutes he understood why Alf and others thought so highly of her. She was, he thought, a restful sort of woman, pleasantly interested in what he had to say without being nosy.

On Wednesday of the following week he met her coming out of Craddock's Antiquarian Bookshop and decided during that conversation that she had a sense of humour, revealed by her admission to having hoped on first coming to Mullings that it had seen more than its fair share of the macabre. This made him feel less foolish about his own feelings in this regard and he enjoyed telling her so. It felt good to have a meeting of the minds with a woman for the first time since Mabel died. That she happened to be good-looking in a ladylike sort of way was unimportant, or so he told himself on returning to the Dog and Whistle. He'd never had what you'd call a friendship with a woman, one without any strings attached, for he and Mabel had married early. Now he found himself thinking it would be pleasant to get to know Florence Norris better, and perhaps take the occasional outing together.

This train of thought might have been nipped in the bud if he'd heard what Mrs McDonald, the cook at Mullings (who claimed to have second sight), had to say on the subject. After seeing him talking with Florence outside the church, she had predicted, in the hearing of several members of the household staff, that she'd instantly been swept into a vision of a future romance. Then again, had George been aware that Mrs McDonald was no fey slip of a girl with a faraway look in her eyes, but a fifteen-stone woman who had as yet never foreseen anything with reliable accuracy other than that dinner guests would rave over her queen of puddings, he might have laughed.

On an evening six weeks after taking over the Dog and Whistle, George stood behind the bar, unnecessarily shining up glasses with a white cloth and letting the conversation around him become a distant buzz. He'd received a letter by afternoon post from his godson which had contained surprising news. Jim had decided not to take the job he'd been offered on leaving university the previous month as a junior museum guide, but was instead taking one as a waiter at a restaurant near Kings Cross, so as to give himself the chance to discover if his dream of eventually earning his living as an artist could be realized. His parents were understandably very upset. George could well believe it. To Sally and Arthur's notions of respectability, artists were a slice of shiftless society without morals, filled with naked women and all of them drinking and smoking more than they should. They were, like many kindly people, very keen on the penalties of hellfire and brimstone for wickedness.

He picked up another glass to needlessly polish. Here he was with enough money saved up through the years to have helped the lad out financially, but that possibility was out. It would have been going over Sally and Arthur's heads; and even if that wasn't an issue, Jim would want to do this on his own. Independent from a little tyke, he was. 'Soon as I learn to ride a big-boy bike, Uncle George, I'm going to get a paper route!' He'd been three at the time, bless him. Perhaps it was because Jim had pictured him feeling helpless on reading the letter that he'd included the last paragraph. No, he'd have put it in anyway, thought George. That was Jim all over, wanting to help out where he could. He'd heard that his former grammar school maths teacher, who'd been pathetically inept at maintaining discipline, had finally been dismissed. A bundle of nerves from the sound of it, poor man. It was Jim's belief that, after being mocked by the boys every day, he'd gone home to be nagged by his widowed mother, who had a mind to a champagne lifestyle on a beer income.

'Here's the interesting thing, George,' Jim had written. 'Word has it he's applied for a job in at Westerbey, a junior boys' school near your Dovecote Hatch. His name's Cyril Fritch, and if he's successful I'd appreciate your taking him under your kindly wing.'

Now there was a coincidence for you. On the previous evening Mr Shepherd had been in the Dog and Whistle not looking at all himself. He'd confided to George over a rare whisky and soda (usually it was cider) that he'd had to turn down a Mr Fritch for the vacancy in the second form. Within five minutes of talking with him it had become clear that teaching was the last thing the poor chap was cut out to do. The seven-year-olds would have him for beans on toast before morning break. He'd had a better tale to tell this evening. A half-hour ago Mr Shepherd had smiled across the bar at George. He'd encountered Mr Fritch in the street moments before and learned that, following the unfortunate interview, he'd walked the three miles from where the school was situated between Large Middlington and Dovecote Hatch and gone into Craddock's Antiquarian Bookshop. His hope had been to find a volume to lift his spirits, and after getting into conversation with its owner he had been offered the job of bookkeeper. He'd only be required to help serve the customers when necessary but, admitting now to being painfully shy, that hadn't come as a disappointment. Now the only thing worrying the chap was breaking the news to his widowed mother that he was taking what she would consider a big step down in employment.

Well, she'd just have to lump it, thought George now – as would Sally and Arthur when it came to their son's choice of doing what he wanted for a living. Tomorrow he'd write back to Jim offering wholehearted encouragement, and also give him the good news about Mr Fritch. George wasn't much of a reader when it came to books. It was a different matter with the newspaper – that he wouldn't skip morning or evening if his life depended on it. But he'd go into Craddock's as soon as word went round that Mr Fritch had started working there and make his acquaintance. It didn't seem likely that the man would frequent the Dog and Whistle – not an overly sociable sort, from the sound of it, and it was unlikely his ma would allow it. You had to wonder why people who enjoyed themselves making life a misery for their nearest and dearest didn't get bumped off more often.

George shook his head. Maybe he'd pick up a detective story at Craddock's as a way to meet Mr Fritch. He'd never been all that keen on scaring himself half to death, but like Mabel used to say, the stuff that went in the papers could give you a heart attack any day of the week. George's hands stilled. Why was he thinking like this? Did it come from a deep-down fear that Jim might end up living in a rough part of London, with nasty types lurking around corners ready to pick the nearest pocket, if not worse? Bosh! he told himself roundly. Jim was no namby-pamby and could look after himself.

Setting aside the polishing cloth, he pulled his thoughts back to the present to focus on Alf's grumbling that his lumbago was back something wicked and the wife had gone on at such a pitch about it being a put-on job, so's he could loll around all day, that he'd been fair driven to crawl out of the house for fear of coming down deaf as well. He'd just shifted to the additional grievance that poultices and heat rubs did bugger-all when the outer door opened and Lord Stodmarsh walked in.

The men not already standing got to their feet to the accompaniment of a chorus of male and female voices greeting his arrival as if it made for a red-letter day. This might have been due to expectation of a round of free drinks, but George didn't believe that was the case. There was an almost palpable feeling of affection flowing from all parts of the room that said otherwise. Even without the attention paid to this elderly man in country tweeds, George would have been in no doubt of his identity from His Lordship's resemblance to the son.

George had spotted Mr William Stodmarsh on

a couple of occasions coming off the Mullings footpath into Sixpenny Lane, where the Dog and Whistle stood on the corner facing the village green. On each of these occasions Mr Stodmarsh had been bareheaded, but his gruffly mumbled, barely pausing, acknowledgement of George's presence on the pavement, suggested he might not have exerted himself to raise his hat had he worn one. As Lord Stodmarsh now stood chatting in a pleasantly modulated voice with those closest to the door, the mark of the true gentleman was apparent in his lack of pretension and kindly, attentive interest. He could be described as bulky in build rather than decidedly stout, as was the case with Mr William. Both men had a walrus moustache and gray eyes under bushy brows. Had the son inherited the curmudgeonly personality of his paternal grandfather, as described by Alf Thatcher? In George's book that didn't make for much of an excuse, but it could be that he'd judged the younger man too hastily. Mabel always used to tick him off when she thought him too quick to write someone off as not his cup of tea.

Well, there was no chance of George not taking to William Stodmarsh's father now they were about to meet. After working his way up to the bar, His Lordship introduced himself, extended his hand in a firm shake and apologized for not having been in sooner to offer his welcome to the village.

'Settling well, I hope?'

'Very nicely, sir. It's a big change moving to the country from the outskirts of London, but

I'm glad I made the leap.' George felt himself relax under that kindly gaze. 'The folks I've met have been more than decent.'

'So I've always thought, but good to hear.' His Lordship's smile had the effect of a fire in the hearth. 'I feel blessed to have been born and bred here, but I suppose most people think that way about their home turf. I've heard you come from Bexleyheath – wasn't that Dick Turpin territory? As a boy I loved reading about the famous highwayman and his devotion to Black Bess.'

George's joviality expanded along with the rest of his mammoth self. 'You've got it, sir! Shooters Hill coming into Welling – that's the town before Bexleyheath – is named for Turpin, so I've heard. It's funny some of the people we take pride in.'

'I imagine it's because most of us have more in common with the sinners than the saints.' The walrus moustache quivered with rueful amusement.

George beamed back. 'That has to be it.' He inquired about the injured ankle and was assured that it had been more a nuisance than painful. 'Now, what can I do you for, Lord Stodmarsh? Whatever it is comes on the house.'

'If I may I'll accept your kind offer another time, Mr Bird. Tonight I'm buying, whatever you like for yourself and a round for the house. I'll take a small brandy and soda.'

While George was pouring the requested tipple into a gratifyingly sparkling glass, His Lordship mentioned that a cousin of his wife would be coming to Mullings the following week for an extended visit. 'We're both very fond of her. Indeed, we both hope she will make her home with us henceforth.'

Two anticipated newcomers to Dovecote Hatch, the lady guest and Cyril Fritch – talk about making George feel like an old timer! 'Well, Mabel,' he said to the empty pillow beside his after getting into bed, 'I've no doubt in my mind you'd have spotted Lord Stodmarsh for a good sort, just like I did. And another thing before I nod off, old girl, one day Arthur and Sally will admit to being wrong about it being a bad idea for Jim to set up as an artist. Mark my words, the lad will make a name for himself and I'll be reading about him in the papers.'

A few weeks after meeting Lord Stodmarsh for the first time, George found himself speaking up on behalf of the newly resident cousin. He did so in response to a heated whisper from Hilda Stark. As usual, she was wearing her battered hat, fingerless gloves and a pinny under her ancient dark coat.

'Have I got a juicy tidbit for you, Mr Bird?' There was an unpleasant gleam in her beady black eyes as she stretched her neck across the bar; even more unsettling was the malice bubbling up in spittle around her mouth. 'At long last,' she clawed for his hand, 'there's a story worth telling about them up at Mullings. A little bird's tweeted in my ear that the woman they've got staying at Mullings, a Miss Madge Bradley, was left standing at the altar when the bridegroom didn't show up. Talk about being made a laughing stock! You'd have thought she'd have done herself in if she had an ounce of pride. Wouldn't have taken me three minutes to climb the church tower and jump. Instead this one crawls to Dovecote Hatch to wallow in her shame at Mullings!'

'It's the man that should be dying of it.' Such was George's surge of dislike for Hilda Stark that he barely managed to keep his voice level. He didn't often lose his temper, but when he did – look out!

'He could've had his reasons...' The smirk showed yellowed teeth.

George stared at her coldly. To his mind there was a big difference between passing on a tale about people long dead and buried and gossiping about living ones. He withdrew his plate-sized hand out of reach of hers. 'You should be ashamed of yourself, Miss Stark, for not letting that piece of tattletale die in your throat.' He'd almost inserted the word craggy – in fact, he wished he had.

'And who're you to talk to me like that? You great pile of suet!' Her face contorted under the brim of her battered hat. 'Not in this place five minutes and thinking yourself Lord God Almighty!'

George was still breathing heavily as she stumped off, muttering venomously. Mr Shepherd was shaking his head, as was Stan the baker, and Miss Teaneck, the local seamstress, usually a meek little soul, was looking quite fierce. The street door slammed shut behind the dark-coated figure.

'Take it easy, Birdie.' Alf Thatcher was suddenly at the bar, leaning forward, gnome-faced. He dropped his voice. 'The old girl's always had a tongue on her. Several round here, me included, always thought there was more to Hilda being let go as nanny to Master Ned than was given out. Doesn't overdo the booze in here, as I think you'll agree, but her landlady let on to my missus that she's no doubt from the state of her come morning that she's at it all night long. But then, mayhap there's some excuse for what blew out of Hilda's gob just now. Could be she got wind about the others and me teasing you a while back about her having designs on dragging you to the altar, Birdie. It's easy to call the kettle black but...'

'It's not the same at all,' George protested. Even so, Alf's viewpoint did give him pause when he remembered how he'd joined in the chuckles. Mabel would have said a joke's never funny if the butt of it's not laughing as hard as the rest.

'I'm not saying Hilda in't a spiteful old cow,' conceded Alf. 'One thing I do know for sure is she didn't hear that story about Miss Bradley from any of the staff at Mullings. Florence Norris knows what she's about with the maids – kind but firm – and Mr Grumidge the butler also knows his stuff. So my guess is it came from the Stafford-Reids or the Blakes. Move in a very small world, them sort of people do. And nasty oft times with it.'

'I suppose so.' George was working his way back to a better frame of mind.

'Chin up, Birdie. This Miss Bradley couldn't have come to a better place to make herself a new start, and having her cousin at Mullings may perk up Her Ladyship no end. So focus on the good, why don't we?'

'Right you are, Alf.'

The next day George couldn't quite rid himself of the feeling that something had changed, either in his perception of Dovecote Hatch or the place itself, but this passed. Unpleasant people like Hilda Stark were to be met everywhere. She stopped coming to the Dog and Whistle. Alf invited him to come and meet the wife, and his friendship with Florence Norris grew as they took occasional, companionable outings together. It was a good life, for all he continued to miss his Mabel. But years afterwards he was to wonder, while struggling with guilt, fear and sorrow, if his arrival in the village had not been the first tossed pebble stirring up ripples, resulting in a series of sea changes destined to thrust the Stodmarsh family out of centuries of tranquil shallows into uncharted and dangerous waters.

THREE

Florence would always have remembered that Sunday in early September of 1929, even had it not merged into a Monday made sorrowful at the time and dire in retrospect. It was also the day she went with George Bird to her childhood home so he could meet her mother for the first time.

Since meeting George in late February she had increasingly come to value the hours she was free to spend time with him. Her first impression of George, on being introduced to him outside the church, had been of a warm-hearted man going out of his way to put a smile on the day. On further acquaintance she was drawn to his sense of humour, admired his kindness and enjoyed his interest in what was going on in the world, gleaned from conversations or newspapers. George read the daily and evening editions without fail, which she did not – sometimes not looking once at a paper during the week. That he rarely picked up anything in book form wasn't a drawback for Florence. He'd mentioned early on that he relished a good story, real or imagined, and was soon encouraging her to tell him about the novel she was currently reading. Not only did he enjoy listening, but

afterwards they would get into stimulating dis-
cussions about the plot and characters, and he'd
instantly grasped what she'd meant when talking
about style.

'Two people can come up the bar and tell you
the very same yarn and somehow it comes out
different.'

There was also George's devotion to his
godson, which Florence fully appreciated, given
how dear Ned Stodmarsh was to her heart. Not
that she could talk of him as freely as George did
of Jim – the different nature of the relationships
prevented it. Then, most important of all in
forging a bond between them, was their having
both been blessed with such happy marriages.
Florence had discovered she could talk more
about Robert with George than anyone else. He
was as interested in hearing about her late
husband and their life as he was in talking about
his Mabel. There was comfort and enjoyment in
that sharing. Florence had found that, within a
year or so after her widowhood, most people,
including Robert's brother Tom, tended to shy
away from mentioning his name.

It was the ordinary that remained so dear,
bringing out such confidences as: 'Robert was
always losing his pipe. Those were the only
times he'd stand looking helpless. I used to say
he must think I'd started smoking it on the sly,
before pointing to it sticking out of his pocket!'

'I know just what you mean!' George's smile
would take over his whole face. 'When Mabel
couldn't find her best white tablecloth she'd give
me that accusing look, like I'd hung it out the

61

window as a peace sign, in case the Russian army should come riding up.'

By mid-August Florence had accompanied George on several occasions for a midday Sunday meal at the home of Alf Thatcher and his wife. Doris Thatcher was a mettlesome little woman who seemed to get great pleasure out of ordering her husband around. If he was seated he had to get up and fetch something; if he was on his two feet he was looming. A considerable feat for a man of five foot three, Florence would think with amusement. It was clear to her that Doris's bossing was done for show and that it tickled Alf to pretend that he was henpecked.

'Gives me a right sounding excuse for spending evenings at the Dog and Whistle,' he murmured to Florence. 'The other one is the woman next door, always popping in for a natter, and there's no shoving her off afore ten. Too soft-hearted, is Doris, though she tries not to show it, and I'm blowed if at my time of life I'll take up crocheting so's not to feel left out while the two of them click away.'

At first, Doris had been a little intimidated at having the housekeeper of Mullings in her home, but she soon got over that when Florence admired her skill with the crochet needle and asked if she would teach her. It was clear that the Thatchers were very fond of George.

'A real lamb of a man for all he's so big,' said Doris on the Sunday before the start of September. Florence was wrapped in a borrowed pinny while Doris washed up and she dried. 'Thought about taking him to see your mum and the rest of the family?'

'I have, but...'

'You're bothered they'll get the wrong idea – that there's more between you than just being good friends? Which it's plain to me isn't in neither of your heads.' Doris did not pause for a response. At times her conversations sped along like a train intent on not running out of steam before reaching the station. 'And very sensible too, if you asks me.' She handed Florence a washed plate. 'I've a sister what was widowed and couldn't smile at the bus conductor when paying her fare, let alone help a blind man across the street, without someone thinking she's on the lookout. She got so fed up with that nonsense she married to put an end to it.'

'How did it work out?'

'Biggest mistake of her life. Miserable old bugger from the start, he was, and now she's pushing him up and down the high street in a bath chair with never a kind word. Not that you'd have any fear of that sort of life with George, well or poorly.' Doris wiped off the sink and draining board. 'But it wouldn't do, would it? Not with both your hearts having long ago been given away for keeps.'

'I'm so pleased you understand.' Florence sur- prised herself by kissing Doris Thatcher on the cheek. 'And you're right; I am concerned about my family, especially my mother, leaping to the wrong conclusion. She's still a romantic. Even in older age she's a romantic. It comes from her getting a glimpse of life's brightness when she was in service before her marriage. Holding on to that memory got her through all the drabness and hardship that comes with bringing up a family on very little money in a house desperately in need of repair, with the landlord refusing to do anything about it. Then my father died, shortly after I started at Mullings. Years later, Robert wanted my mother to come and live with us when we got married – it was a case of the more the merrier at Farn Deane – but she wouldn't. By then my sister Ada and her husband had two babies and my brother Fred's wife was expecting.'

'No need to tell me you've done all you can to help out.' Doris set the saucepans on the cooker to air out.

'Ada and Fred look out for her on a daily basis – they both live just around the corner from her – and that's worth more than money. I'm glad we've had this talk, Doris. Tom's wife Gracie and I get on very well, but I've gathered from things she's said in the past that she doesn't believe a man and a woman can be friends without hoping for more. You've made me realize that I've been unfair not to take George to see my mother, which I know he'd gladly do. If it makes her happy to think there's something in the works, he won't mind, and I shouldn't either.' Florence smiled. 'I could take along one of Mrs McDonald's steak and kidney pies.'

'What just happen, if memory serves me right, to be a favourite with George,' said Doris, looking around the orderly kitchen with satisfaction, 'but if I was you I'd let your mum have a chance to fuss over the two of you, even if she has to buy one at the corner shop. Let her feel she's still up to putting on a little show now and then.'

'I think you're right,' said Florence.

She broached the subject of the outing to George after they'd left the Thatchers, and he was obviously pleased. She already knew that he regretted having few family members of his own, especially since losing Mabel, and Florence didn't need to be told that what mattered to her had come to mean a lot to him.

A couple of Sundays later, George met her early in the afternoon at the village end of the Mullings woodland path, then they drove the twelve miles to her mother's home in George's elderly car. They had decided on going early in the afternoon and staying for tea, rather than putting her mother to the business of preparing a cooked midday meal.

Florence found herself surprisingly glad to be heading further away from Mullings. George's substantial bulk gave her a feeling of security that had nothing to do with anticipation of her mother's reception of him. They had reached that stage of their relationship where they could sit in companionable silence, and she was grateful that they did so now after conversing for the first few minutes. She had been unusually on edge for the past few days, for some nebulous reason that she couldn't put her finger on.

The tenor of life at Mullings during the week had been different from usual, in two ways that were apparent to all. One was the introduction to the household of a four-month-old puppy. His Lordship's beloved old Labrador had died in the

65

spring and he'd stated at the time that it would be a long time, if ever, before he could give his heart to another. Lady Stodmarsh had told Florence she was biding her time until the moment felt right to contact the breeder and ask him to select and deliver the perfect little successor. When the surprise was revealed, Lord Stodmarsh had been delighted as much with his wife's thoughtfulness as with the adorable, but rambunctious bundle of fur. By the second day the newcomer was making his presence felt by bouncing out of nowhere and everywhere at the sound of approach, or padding up silently. Either way he quickly mastered the trick of getting under as many feet at one time as possible. On the Wednesday afternoon Mr Grumidge had been forced to sidestep the puppy to avoid tripping over it; even so, he'd almost dropped the tea tray that he was bearing down the hall to the drawing room. Florence had been in the hall to witness the incident having just come downstairs after taking a reel of navy-blue thread up to Miss Bradley's room. Seeing that Mr Grumidge had not entirely regained his balance, she had opened the drawing-room door for him so he wouldn't have to pause to set the tray down on the side table before doing so himself. They had laughed about it afterwards.

'One more wobble on my part, Mrs Norris, might well have meant disaster. That china is irreplaceable!'

The second difference from life as usual was that Ned's maternal grandmother, Eugenie Tressler, had come to stay for the week; something she customarily did twice annually. Ned called her 'Granny', to distinguish her from Lady Stodmarsh, who was 'Grandmother'. Never in the years since first meeting Mrs Tressler had Florence seen any indication that here was a woman who had on two occasions suffered a mental breakdown and might at any point, as Nanny Stark had so brutally suggested to Ned, need to be permanently confined. If anything, Mrs Tressler had the look of a capable schoolmistress. Any slight abstraction on this visit was understandable, given that she had made an appointment with her dentist on the day following her return home.

'Granny's pretty sure at least one tooth has to come out.' Ned had grimaced on passing this information on to Florence. 'She admits to not being all that keen on facing up to the pliers, and yet she intends to show up like a soldier and do her bit for the Empire.' He'd added: 'I know I don't always treat her as well as I should, Florie. I could be less stingy about going to stay with her in the summer hols, but I do see she's really quite a brick.'

Admittedly, Florence's encounters with his maternal grandmother were usually brief, but they always included a pleasant greeting or enquiry from Mrs Tressler, and either at the start or end of each visit she expressed appreciation for Florence's kindness to her grandson. Ned had the Stodmarsh colouring, but it was from Mrs Tressler he had inherited his thin face and angular features, which somehow served them both well. 'What's the use of a face that's beautiful or handsome, if it doesn't have a stamp on it?' Florence couldn't remember if she'd read that, or thought it.

She now became vaguely aware of the road slipping past the car windows in blurred glimpses that faded, half-formed. It was the same sort of feeling that had accompanied her attempts at figuring out the cause of her edginess. Surely it stretched things to call it unease. She had taken into account that neither the puppy's arrival, nor Mrs Tressler's visit, could be expected to occur, especially in conjunction, without a ripple.

Lord and Lady Stodmarsh always welcomed Mrs Tressler with great warmth, but Florence had picked up that William Stodmarsh and his wife did not put on any marked show of enthusiasm. Though it was never mentioned, the entire Mullings staff would have needed to be deaf not to know that Mr William had a roaring temper and never exerted himself to be pleasant to anyone. A frequently overheard bellow was, 'I want peace at any price!' That the walls were left vibrating must not have struck him as an incongruity. The irritation of being forced to rise from his seat more often than usual in acknowledgement of an extra woman's entrances and exits would this week have been exacerbated by the puppy's exuberance.

Mrs William Stodmarsh's Christian name was Gertrude. She was a stout woman of the well-corseted type who, it would seem, had come to terms with her husband's truculence, or was perennially oblivious. Florence was never sure from the stolidity of her manner which alternative was

68

more likely. Either way, she did not perceive Mrs William Stodmarsh doing more than was obligatory on Mrs Tressler's behalf. Her one weekly outing, other than church, was to get her graying hair finger-waved. Her main daily task was arranging the household flowers – an activity for which she had an admirably artistic flair. Otherwise she did little to occupy her time.

Then there was Miss Madge Bradley. Since coming to Mullings in the early part of the year, this cousin of Lady Stodmarsh – one of the second or once removed sort – had noticeably exerted herself to be congenial and helpful. In no way could it be said that she had projected an aura of gloom by dwelling on the distressing, pitifully humiliating, experience of being left standing at the altar, waiting for a bridegroom who never showed up. But what seemed to Florence so commendable about Miss Bradley's subsequent attitude had been viewed with less enthusiasm by Ned.

'I know you'll think it beastly of me, Florie, but sometimes I'd like to tell her to put a sock in it – all that falling over backwards to please, I mean; it gets on a fellow's nerves. So unnecessary! Admittedly Uncle William and Aunt Gertrude haven't done their stuff, but it stands out a mile that's just the way they are. She has to realize there's no chance the grandparents will one day decide to toss her out in the cold after inviting her to stay here for as long as she chooses. Even though she's not his relation, Grandfather has made it clear he has no objection to having her – offering to teach her to play chess and even sometimes inviting her to accompany him on his walks. If she's a hair of sense she has to see that's pretty big. Everyone knows he's always preferred to go on his own with his dog.'

Florence hadn't pointed out that Ned had missed an important point. Of late there hadn't been a dog. A hint of mischief had suddenly gleamed in his expressive eyes.

'You don't suppose, do you, that old Pimcrisp might take a fancy to her and take her off our hands? She is a vicar's daughter, after all.'

In Florence's view, this must have made what had happened to her all the more painful. All those dutiful appearances at parishioners' weddings, all those coy remarks by the insensitively well-meaning, that one day it would be her turn, that there was always a Mr Right around the corner and she mustn't give up hope ... The comments would be bothersome if she wasn't hoping, or make it harder to keep a smile on her face if she was. And then that day that was to be hers ... it didn't bear thinking about.

There was another thing Ned was missing. Miss Bradley had previously only met Lord and Lady Stodmarsh at occasional large family gatherings. The letter inviting her to make her home at Mullings must have come out of the blue, and she might well have feared it a whimsical impulse liable to be regretted at any moment. What she needed was time to gather her confidence, to begin to acquaint herself with people from Dovecote Hatch of her own generation. Her difficulty was having been left in straitened circumstances on her parents' deaths. There were, however, positives. She was a perfectly presentable woman, educated at an excellent school, and with only a little effort could be quite attractive in a rounded, wholesome sort of way, with that curly dark brown hair and eyes almost of the same colour. Perhaps given time she would begin to dress in clothes that flattered her, a more interesting choice of colours than navy or gray. Currently everything she wore she had made herself, and unfortunately she wasn't a particularly skilled needlewoman or knitter. Nor was she blessed with any creativity to compensate.

Ned had told Florence on the Friday before his maternal grandmother's visit that he fully expected Miss Bradley to make a complete pest of herself by fussing over Mrs Tressler to the point of not allowing her to pick up her own teacup, and insisting on taking the puppy outside every five minutes to do 'its little jobs'. But he had to admit she seemed to have gained some sense at last, if only for that week, and had instead been 'sufferable', neither underdoing nor overdoing things.

Florence had taken that to mean Miss Bradley had been jolly decent. So where did that bring things in her search for a source of what had been niggling away at her? Nowhere, except for convincing her there hadn't been any disturbing event. George roused her back into focus.

'Is your mother's road down this way?'

'Yes, the next left after that garage.'

The town of Westbridge had grown even more

71

smoke-grimed and crowded over the years, but Mrs Wilks' house, jammed in between its neighbours, had been given a sketchy new coat of paint by the current landlord, son of the old one. In return for this largesse, he'd upped the rent five bob a month. 'Bloody thievery,' Florence's brother Fred had called it, but Mrs Wilks had taken it in her stride.

Florence had hoped that the money she and Robert, then she on her own, had sent every month would be spent on comforts for her mother, such as a new carpet, furniture and wallpaper, but the interior was still the same, threadbare and down-at-the-heel. She supposed without being told that what was left of the money, after providing for absolute necessities, went to help out with her two siblings and the grandchildren. And she couldn't begrudge this if it made her mother happy.

Mrs Wilks opened the door to them and ushered them inside with a crease of a smile that preventing her lack of teeth from showing. Never having been a demonstrative woman, she did not kiss Florence but extended her hand to George, saying it was nice to meet him. His warm response helped overcome the dingy and disheartening appearance of the dark, narrow hall, but inside his head he could hear Mabel's opinion: 'It's a house to feel sorry for, like it's been left to its lonesome long ago – that staircase don't look like it's got the energy to go up or down one more blinking time.'

What Florence was noticing with a pang was her mother's yellowed white hair and wrinkles.

Had she looked so old a few weeks before? She was only sixty-three. Could it be that the lank navy dress and cardigan were the cause, or had she just woken from a nap? She'd been such a pretty girl once – prettier than Florence had ever hoped to be; photographs provided the proof. The curly, dark hair and deep blue eyes suggested some Irish in her background.

With little further said, Mrs Wilks led the way into the only downstairs room except for the kitchen. Here there was wallpaper that had to be sixty years old, with only one enlarged photograph hung from the picture rail, a sepia-tinted view of a grandiose house, at least three times the size of Mullings. A scarred dining room table and chairs occupied one corner. There was no couch; instead a scattering of mismatched, misnamed easy chairs huddled up to the unlit gas fire. Despite there not having been a hint of a chill to the day, its glow would have been welcome, if only to add a little colour.

Though he was rarely self-conscious, George wondered if the maroon tie he was wearing with his one and only suit might be a little too bright, and if he should have put on the black one he'd worn to Mabel's funeral. Then he realized from Florence's expression that things weren't going quite as well as she'd hoped and he beamed as if he felt right at home. When invited to sit down in the chair between Mrs Wilks and Florence, he did so to a cantankerous creaking of springs – not surprising, given his weight, although a fly landing on the seat would have brought the same result.

'It's kind of you, Mrs Wilks, to let me come along with Florence.'

'That's all right. She's told me a bit about you, of course. It's nice to know she has a new friend; so many of the old ones die off, even at her age.'

'Well, so long as there's still some of us left kicking,' George managed jovially.

'My other daughter, Ada, and her husband should've been here by now. Fred's got a cold or something.'

Florence wasn't entirely sorry that her brother wasn't coming; he'd grown sour since his wife had left him for a man who showed up at the door selling bibles. 'She must have read that passage about "whither thou goest",' Hattie Fly had said when hearing about it. But Florence didn't remember that now; her focus was on her mother. When had her voice become so flat? Where had the remembered magic flown?

'How are you, Mother?' she asked.

'Not so bad.'

Had she always sounded like this when she was not talking about what really interested her? Surely not. Or, a thought nudged unwillingly, had she always talked and not listened?

'You look a little tired.'

'No more than usual. You mustn't have Mr Bird taking me for an invalid, like your poor mistress at Mullings.'

'A lovely woman, as more than Florence would tell you,' enthused George, wondering if he should offer to go and make the tea. There were no cups or saucers, let alone anything else set out to suggest it was forthcoming. It couldn't

74

be expected, of course, the poor old lady didn't look or sound as though there was much spark left in her. Then, suddenly, it was there in her face and voice, a glimpse of how she must have looked when young and wholly alive.

'Lady Tamersham was always the picture of bloom and health.' Her eyes went to the photograph on the wall. 'That's Cragstone, the Tamershams' estate in Northumbria, where I was in service as a girl. I still believe there isn't another place to equal it. A dozen chandeliers in the drawing room, and the library designed by Sir Christopher Wren, and oh, the thrilling history of all the people who lived there before! Such personalities they all had! I suppose Florie's told you how she loved to hear me tell about the ornamental hermit?'

Until Mrs Wilks had got going on the topic of Cragstone and the Tamershams, George had thought her unlikely to put more than four or five words together at one time. Now he finally found himself relaxing, thoughts of a cup of tea forgotten, as she explained that what he'd taken to be a garden ornament was something – someone – much more interesting. She had many more stories to tell about Cragstone, of the very sort he'd hoped would be connected with Mullings. So absorbed did he become that he failed to notice that Florence sat silent.

For a few moments she too was captivated. This was the woman who had brought enchantment into her childhood, fuelling her imagination and stirring up a thirst for all the stories to be found in books. These were wonderful gifts

75

for which she would be forever grateful, but there crept upon her a discomfort that shifted painfully into a revelation – one so clear she was startled she had not seen it before. It had to be sensing George's reaction that had brought enlightenment. Her mother had in a sense stopped living after leaving Cragstone. Any real enjoyment she experienced came from memories of that brief, gilded period of her youth. As a result, her own husband and children had always had limited reality for her – except as listening ears – and Florence had been the best listener. Other than that, she and the rest of her family had been pasted over by far more interesting images. One painful thought followed another. Florence could no longer believe her mother had refused her and Robert's invitation to come and live at Farn Deane because she had too many family ties in Westbridge. How much more likely that she'd been glad to have the house to herself at last – empty of human distractions, as it was of any comforts that might take her prisoner to the present. All she needed, all she wanted, was somewhere to sit and wait for time to dissolve into a mist, through which she could step at will to find Cragstone and the Tamersham family unchanged.

Florence wondered if she was exaggerating, as her mother's voice flowed on past George's occasional, interested questions. After all, her mother had been very interested in hearing about Mullings when Florence had first gone there, and still sometimes asked her to describe it and the Stodmarshes. But then she realized that was because her mother could make comparisons, as she had just now when saying how much the larger Cragstone was of the two houses, and bringing up the superiority of Lady Tamersham's health to that of Lady Stodmarsh, ignoring the fact that the mistress of Cragstone was a younger woman at the time.

Florence felt wicked for allowing such thoughts; but she couldn't will away the realization now it had forced its way in, after perhaps subconsciously poking at her for years. She would love her mother none the less for it, but with the knowledge that no deep feeling was returned.

'I'll go and make a pot of tea,' she said, getting to her feet. 'No,' seeing a large figure start to rise from the inadequate chair, 'you stay put, George, it's been good listening to you and Mother chatting away, and perhaps you can tell her some stories about the Dog and Whistle.'

'Yes, that would be nice.' Mrs Wilks' voice floated after Florence as she went out into the hall. 'There was a Tudor inn not a mile from Cragstone, and the story goes that in the early eighteenth century the Tamersham heir set up a row of tankards on a shelf for target shooting and ever after claimed he'd proved himself a crack shot by getting the innkeeper square in the eye.'

'Well, that's one to tell my regulars,' said George.

Florence couldn't tell from his voice whether this tidbit had gone down well or not. She was by now longing for the afternoon to be over, and the small, deplorably dilapidated kitchen only increased her desire to get away. There was no clutter, no things left about to liven the place up – no kettle on the coke stove and no sign of a cake or biscuits. The familiar brown teapot was in the cupboard with the cups and saucers. Its top was furred with dust. Pity took over. No one, especially her own mother, should have to live like this. Florence tried unsuccessfully to block the thought that it was unnecessary and therefore had to be a choice. Her sister Ada would have done all she could on a regular basis if she'd been allowed to help. Florence had heard her explain more than once to their mother that with her two children now grown she had time aplenty on her hands and would be glad to get out of her own house before she forgot the way to the front gate. Her husband had chimed in each time, saying he'd much sooner have his Ada down at her mother's than at the pub, or off to the dogs. But Mrs Wilks' response had always been firmly discouraging. If she didn't mind things the way they were, why should anyone else bother? She'd never liked cooking, that wasn't something new, and it wasn't as though she was letting herself go hungry. A piece of salt beef could be stretched to do the week, and there you were.

As for today, Florence knew Ada would have turned up an hour or so ago with the cake and got everything ready for tea if she hadn't been told not to come till later. Even their brother Fred would have done his bit if he'd felt wanted at this or any other time. It was best not to think

78

about any of it any more right now, since doing so would impede her objective that George should have as enjoyable an afternoon as possible.

A search of the larder produced a saucepan, a tin of tea leaves, a third of a bottle of milk and a few digestive biscuits in a bag. No sign of sugar. George liked two teaspoons in his tea. Whilst waiting for the water to boil in the saucepan Florence heard footsteps, more than one pair of them, out in the hall. No need to take a look. That would be Ada and Bill, having let themselves in. Voices reached her from the sitting room. She took the teapot she'd washed over to the cooker and a couple of minutes later was carrying what she had assembled on a black enameled tray through the hall. Mrs Longbrow had long ago instilled in her the importance of a servant acquiring the habit of moving as soundlessly as possible, especially when above stairs. Habit carried over with Florence even when she was not at Mullings. The others could not have heard her; the sitting room door was open, but no one glanced her way as she was about to go in. The four of them were seated. George, Ada and Bill were talking cheerfully, but her mother sat silent, hands folded in her navy-blue lap. Something shifted in the recesses of Florence's mind. She was seeing something for the second time that week. She did not know what it was, just that it had some connection to the source of her unease. Never before had she been this tantalizingly close to knowing what it was. This time it did not slide away. It was snuffed out, as if by a firm hand. She had no opportunity to puzzle over the difference. There was movement in the room and Bill said to George: 'I'll take the tray off Florence. Ada's always on at me about being a gent.'

'Oh, go on with you! Anyone would think you was henpecked!' Ada roared a laugh.

She was a cheerfully fat woman with a mounded stack of hair and protruding eyes. In contrast, Bill was bald, short and skinny, with a habitually meek expression. Florence was fully aware that the timidity was cultivated for his and Ada's amusement. It was obvious from the gleam in George's eyes that he saw right through the charade and had taken to her sister and brother-in-law in a big way – they were his kind of people. She felt a pang of regret that she had not been as close to them over the years as she should have been. Fred had got in a dig at her more than once, saying she'd gone from a girl with a head stuffed with nonsense, to a buttoned-down woman who gave him a pain in the neck. She'd always dismissed this as completely unfair, but now she wondered, listening to George's laugh rise above Ada's, if Fred were right about her. She was rather relieved he wasn't here. He had soured considerably after his wife left him, and it wasn't only Florence he liked to criticize to the point of ridicule. Ada and Bill came in for their share, too. She'd heard him tell them they were the spitting image of the stout wife and petrified little husband in a comic seaside postcard. But was he right about her?

Ada and Bill had brought with them not only a

cut-and-come-again cake but a plate of sand-wiches – two kinds, fish paste and cheese and tomato. When everyone was seated, Florence was pleased to see her mother eat well and drink two cups of tea. Perhaps she'd been making mountains out of molehills, not just today, but for the better part of a week. It was so easy to let her imagination run away with her, especially as she had once had a tendency to be fanciful. 'Backsliding' would have been Mrs Longbrow's word for it. 'Form a bad habit and it'll always have a hold on you.' Florence smiled, remem-bering other strictures from the former house-keeper.

She and George stayed on for a very pleasant couple of hours. Both Ada and Bill looked sorry to see them go, but her mother was beginning to doze.

'I like your family,' said George as they drove away. 'Your sister and her husband remind me of Alf and Doris, down-to-earth sorts with hearts of gold. And your mother and I had that nice chat when we arrived.'

Florence looked at him. 'Did she strike you as a little odd?'

'Well,' he answered comfortably, 'we all have bees in our bonnets about something or other, and hers is about that family she worked for years ago. And older people do tend to live in the past.'

'Yes, but she was always that way. It struck me today, and I don't know why it took so long, that she never really left the Tamershams' estate in Northumbria.' Florence paused. 'I do hope I won't end up that way when the time comes for me to retire – that I'll be able to put some emotional distance between me and Mullings.'

'You'll do just fine, Florence. I've never heard you say anything as made me think you hankered after the place when you was at Farn Deane. If the old housekeeper hadn't asked you to go back I doubt you'd have thought of it.'

'You're probably right. What I'd been thinking about just before that conversation with Mrs Longbrow was to see if I could get a job at Craddock's.'

'That would've suited you a treat, books counting such a lot with you. That last one you told me about kept me up at night, thinking.'

'It was the same with me.' They turned on to the main road and Florence shifted the conversation to George's godson. 'How's Jim doing?'

'He wrote to say he'd met himself a nice girl.'

'That sounds promising.'

George chuckled. 'From the letter I just got from Sally and Arthur, I picture them down on their knees praying it isn't. Proper fusspots, the pair of them! They said she went by one of those silly, affected names that hoity-toity misses go in for these days, said they couldn't even be bothered to remember exactly what it was, but something like Fudge or...' George concentrated on turning a corner.

'Nougat?' Florence suggested, laughing.

'Possibly. And that wasn't the worst of her. She had a platinum streak in the front of her hair, claimed it was natural and came from being delivered by forceps, but Sally and Arthur didn't buy that for a minute. They're good-natured people as a rule, none better, but when it comes to what they think best for their one and only they can go all unreasonable.'

'What has Jim told you about her?'

'Not all that much, what funnily enough tends to make me think he is serious. Remember when I fell for Mabel, wanted to keep her to m'self, so to speak.'

'I know that feeling.'

'He did say as he got to know her because she'd sometimes come into the restaurant where he works, that she's an orphan and works in a bookshop in the same area so you and she might get on. What worries me is if Sally and Arthur keep going up against the girl, it'll cause a real rift with Jim.'

'Yes, that would be a dreadful pity.'

'I've just never understood people getting their knife into somebody for no good reason – not seeing the terrible harm it does to themselves as well. And another thing, I don't like being put in the middle. Sally and Arthur both know I never care to hear against people I know, let alone Jim.'

Florence couldn't remember George previously sounding off on something so material to him. What also struck her was that he could have been speaking for her. She felt a shift forward in their relationship, something beyond the affection she felt for him. It couldn't be love, of course. She'd known instantly on meeting Robert the true nature of her feelings for him, and anyway, this was quite different, but whatever it was brought a lovely sense of peace. All unease faded away.

'You're a good man, George. No wonder Ada and Bill took to you like a long-lost relative.'

'The feeling was mutual, like I said.' He eyed her hopefully. 'They did mention how they hoped next time we'd come to their house.'

She smiled back. 'We could pick Mother up and take her with us, if you'd be all right with that.'

''Course I would. Make it a little outing for her.'

'We'll have to be persistent. It's hard to get her to budge from her own four walls, but I think with your help it can be done.'

'That's the spirit!' The look on his large, kind face warmed her all the way through.

They continued to speak of various things and then sat contentedly quiet until they reached Dovecote Village. When they arrived at the foot-path into the Mullings woods, George said he was sorry to have the afternoon end. Despite the early part of the visit, Florence agreed whole-heartedly. He did not offer to take her up to the door; they had agreed at the start that this method was better. Neither minded everyone knowing about their friendship, but for Florence it was important to keep her private life separate from her job. Lord and Lady Stodmarsh would have been pleased for George to pick her up on the premises. What was avoided was unnecessary scrutiny from any member of staff who happened to be looking out of the window, when she was getting into or out of the car.

They parted on an agreement to plan another outing over the telephone. It took fifteen to twenty minutes for Florence to reach the back lawn of Mullings, but it was a pleasant walk. The leaves on the trees were not so much beginning to turn as to be thinking about it. No suggestion yet of copper, amber or flame, but a general dimming of the summer green, as if it had been worn too long and washed too often. And there was in the air that hint of smokiness, the tang of the earth that Florence always associated with autumn.

On entering the house and having removed her outer clothing, she went to the butler's pantry and found Mr Grumidge, occupied on routine tasks. He informed her how the day had gone. It had been uneventful. She then went into the kitchen to have a word with Mrs McDonald about purchase requirements for the coming week, but found the place empty. This was not unusual for six o'clock on a Sunday evening. Since the staff deserved a break from their usual working habits on the Sabbath, it was customary for the family to have their main meal at midday and partake of a cold collation at eight. Afternoon tea had already been served, and it was too early to start the minimal tasks needed to assemble the food that would be taken up and placed on the sideboard. Mrs McDonald didn't often abandon her kitchen to put her feet up elsewhere – she liked having it to herself with everyone else cleared out – but she had admitted to having a bit of a cold that morning.

Florence was about to head for the housekeeper's room to work on her accounts when Ned wandered into the kitchen. As always, her heart melted a little at the sight of him. No unbiased person would view him as a particularly good-looking sixteen-year-old, with that thin face, freckled skin, and red hair which tended to spike up rather than submit to convention and lie flat. Nor did he show promise of reaching anything above medium height. But Florence could not believe that anyone would fail to be charmed by the wiry build that exuded energy or the expressive mouth and green eyes.

'Hello Florie,' he chanted breezily. 'I come in search of Mrs McDonald's incomparable rock buns. How was your outing with Birdie? To tell the truth, I got to wondering, as the hours ticked by, if you'd be back.'

'Why on earth wouldn't I?'

The green eyes darkened. 'Your maidenly capitulation to an imposingly large man's sudden urging that you elope with him to Gretna Green.'

'Really, Master Ned,' she only called him this on the rare occasions he made her cross, 'what could possibly put such a foolish notion into your head?' She had located the necessary tin and handed him a rock bun.

He took it with the look of one not ready to be bought off that easily. 'Well, you can't pretend you haven't become quite pally with him recently, and from that it's not much of a leap to falling in love.'

'It would be for me,' she answered, 'and even if I had ideas in that direction...'

86

Ned waved a dismissive hand. 'You may sound convincing, Florie, but there's something in your face that isn't.' He took a large bite out of the rock bun. He'd loved them from child-hood on, much to Mrs McDonald's glowing pride, but he wasn't a little boy any longer, and that being the case, should not be allowed to get away with being provoking for his own amuse-ment.

'As I was saying, Master Ned, even if I had ideas in Mr Bird's direction, he has only recently become a widower. He's still mourning the death of his much beloved wife.'

Ned held out his hand. 'May I please have another rock bun, and do stop calling me that silly name. You have a bad habit, dear Florie, of trying to get at a fellow for no valid reason.'

'Dear me, I must mend my ways.' It was impossible not to smile.

Towards the end of demolishing the second rock bun he mumbled, 'I've nothing against Birdie. Everyone likes him. I like him. We have the jolliest chats when we meet in the village. More often than not he'll dodge back to the Dog and Whistle to fetch me a ginger beer, free of charge, that I can drink on the way home. It's just that being the self-centred beast I am, I'd just as soon you didn't marry him or anyone until I'm at least thirty. You did promise when I was little that you'd stay at Mullings as long as I needed you. And the thing is,' his fair skin flush-ed, 'I do still need you here, Florie.'

'Then we're each getting what we want, Ned. So let's hear no more about romantic escapades

87

unsuited to a woman of my years.'

'Quite right! I keep forgetting you're approaching eighty, like poor Miss Johnson.'

Agnes Johnson was the lady's maid who had been with her mistress since Lady Stodmarsh's marriage. Sadly she had now grown very frail. Florence had never forgotten how kind Miss Johnson had been to her when she first came to Mullings and now did all she could in response to Lady Stodmarsh's request that these days go as easily as possible for the faithful old lady. At that moment Mrs McDonald came in, looking a little bleary-eyed from her nap but intent upon getting back into action.

She shook her head. 'After my rock buns again, young sir? Very flattering, I'm sure, but your place is above stairs, as you should know well enough, seeing as I've drummed it into your ears since you was level with my garters.'

Ned grinned. 'Such talk, Mrs McDonald, to an impressionable youth! I wonder what the Reverend Pimcrisp would say if I were to discuss the issue with him?'

'Start stacking up brimstone. That's his job and he doesn't shirk it; no one can take that away from him.' Mrs McDonald shooed Ned out of the kitchen. Florence took the list of the upcoming week's provisions from her and settled down to her accounts in the housekeeper's room. The following hours passed peacefully without any distracting thoughts intruding. On Sunday evenings, like the family, the servants helped themselves to a cold meal. Theirs was set out on the kitchen's lengthy table, and they came and went as suited them best. At nine thirty the two kitchen maids and one scullery maid, assisted by the junior footman, restored order to the kitchen for the morning. Florence did not take long over her repast. Whilst she was entirely competent with figures, dealing with them always required a degree of concentration which did not allow her to be as quick as she would have wished. As ten o'clock approached, she was close to finishing and looking forward to joining Mrs Mc-Donald in the kitchen for a cup of tea and listening to that good woman's cheerful mulling over of the shocking way the world was going these days. High on her list, way above the wicked price of tea, was the difficulty of getting gentlemen's hair cream out of pillowcases. That neither Lord Stodmarsh nor Master Ned used one of the products did not alter her contention that they were a bane on society and that the Prime Minister should speak out against them. A moment later there was a knock on the door and Mr Grumidge entered.

'I'm sorry to interrupt, Mrs Norris, but His Lordship has just informed me that Lady Stodmarsh has a matter she wishes to discuss with you and would appreciate your attending her in her bedroom within the next half hour if possible.'

'Of course.' As Florence started to rise she heard what might have been described as a squeal or yelp from the kitchen region. It wouldn't have been audible had not Mr Grumidge left the door open. 'My guess is that was Annie Long,' she said. Poor Annie, still a kitchen maid when she should have moved up long ago, still liable to be startled into panic by a dropped tea-spoon, but a good, willing worker for all that.

'I imagine so.' Mr Grumidge had a soft spot for all timid creatures. 'There's no need for you to go up to Lady Stodmarsh before closing up your records for the night. It was made clear to me that you were not to hurry unnecessarily.'

'Then I will make use of the next fifteen minutes.'

It was a quarter past ten when Florence headed up the back stairs. Although it was unusual, she wasn't disquietened by this late-night summons. She suspected that it must have something to do with Mrs Tressler's intention of leaving first thing in the morning. Lady Stodmarsh did not rise early due to a propensity to sleepless nights, and she probably had some special requests. Florence received no response to her knock on the bedroom door, at least none she could hear, so she turned the knob and went in. Like the rest of the family's living spaces, it was an elegant but essentially comfortable room, with handome furniture and soft surrounding colours and fabrics. The bed was a graceful four-poster and in the subdued light from the rose-shaded lamps she could just make out Lady Stodmarsh's face on the lace-edged pillow and her outline beneath the silk counterpane.

Florence went to the bedside and looked down. On the table beside it was an empty cup – Lady Stodmarsh's late-night cup of hot milk, with bicarbonate of soda to aid digestion, was Doctor Chester's directive to help relax her for sleep.

Tonight it must have taken effect sooner than expected; Lady Stodmarsh's eyes were closed. Florence was moving to the door when Lady Stodmarsh's drowsy voice made her turn around.

'Please don't go, Florie!' The old name. It sounded affectionate and, somehow, trusted.

'I'm right here.'

Lady Stodmarsh reached out a hand to take Florence's and clung to it. 'You were the one person I knew I could confide in. You've always been so kind, so competent and practical. I've never before felt the need to,' her voice was fading, 'keep something from Edward.'

'Is it about your health, madam?'

Lady Stodmarsh's eyes had been open, but now her lids were drifting shut. 'No, not that. Something else. Don't want to frighten Edward when ... I could be ... wrong, but,' a word, a name that Florence couldn't catch, 'didn't think so. Seen it too often ... looking glass ... other faces when...'

'Seen what, Lady Stodmarsh?' Florence leaned forward. The clasp on her hand had slackened and now left it free. It took several moments for a response to come and the eyes remained closed.

'Sorry ... must be the milk. Doesn't usually send me off so quickly. Always ... wish it would. A little more bicarb ... than usual. It was seeing ... looking ... at the dog ... that made me realize ... hadn't been mistaken.'

'About what?'

No answer.

91

Florence knew it was no use attempting to rouse Lady Stodmarsh. She was asleep; from her breathing, already deeply so. Florence picked up the empty cup. There was a white residue which suggested there had been a lot of bicarb. She wondered on leaving the bedroom if she should inquire if His Lordship would see her, but instantly abandoned this idea. Lady Stodmarsh had stressed that she did not want her husband to know what was worrying her. Florence consoled herself that if whatever it was still lingered in Lady Stodmarsh's mind in the morning and she felt a continued need to talk to her, she would arrange to do so. There was an added feeling of reassurance in knowing that His Lordship always looked in on his wife before retiring to his own bedroom, which it was his custom to do at eleven.

Despite this sensible way of viewing the matter, Florence went down to the kitchen to have her nightly cup of tea with Mrs McDonald in an unsettled frame of mind. That good lady had the kettle boiling as she entered.

'Well, there you are, Mrs Norris, and ready for a sit-down without having to do your sums,' she said. 'I hope you wasn't startled when Annie let out that squeal.'

'I heard it. What was that about?'

'Hard to make head nor tail of it, the state she was in. I'd been having a chat with Molly in the china closet and didn't charge off straight away to find out what was going on.' Mrs McDonald warmed the pot, then spooned in tea leaves and filled it from the steaming kettle. 'Has it ever run through your mind, Mrs Norris, that there might be a little something between Molly and Mr Grumidge?'

'No, I can't say it has.' Molly was the sensible, robust girl Florence had suggested to the Stodmarshes as the ideal person to be Ned's maid, amongst her other duties, when Nanny Stark left. She was now chief housemaid.

'Well, I have to admit I've got it into my wee noggin that there's a fondness on both sides – nothing improper, of course – but I was rather hoping Molly would confide in me this evening. Maybe she would've done if Annie hadn't let out that squeal. I suppose it took five minutes to find out what it was this time.'

'And?' Florence took the teapot, now dressed in its knitted cozy, and set it on the stand on the table.

'Like I said, I couldn't get a tenth of it with all that blubbering and my ears being a bit blocked from this little cold I've got. It was utter gibberish mostly. The gist of it seemed to be that while she was heating the milk to take up to Lady Stodmarsh she saw a mouse. Well, at any rate, something about a mouse. If it had been Jeanie I'd've told her to stop her bellyaching and pull herself together. Of course, that one's tough as nails. Wouldn't turn a hair if a lion marched in and demanded his dinner – meaning her. Our Annie's always been a different story.'

'Poor girl! She truly does have a terror of mice.' Florence sympathized, not liking them herself. This likely explained Lady Stodmarsh's mentioning that there had been a little too much bicarbonate of soda in the milk. Annie's hand would have been shaking uncontrollably when spooning it in. 'But she must be given credit, Mrs McDonald, for taking the milk up anyway.'

'She said something about that, too, that I didn't bother to unravel. I sent her straight off to bed, without saying what I thought – that it should be a pleasure for her, or for Jeanie, taking on this little extra job now that poor Miss Johnson isn't up to it.'

Jeanie was the other kitchen maid. Though she was not by any means a nervous Nellie, Florence had a higher opinion of Annie. Both were diligent workers, but if ever Jeanie had a mishap she was always filled with excuses to the point of lying. If she dropped a plate it was because someone had nudged her, if the soup tureen was in the wrong place it was because Annie had told her to put it there. Florence's mind returned to what bothered her more – the brief conversation with Lady Stodmarsh. Brief, but disturbing. She was relieved that after finishing only one cup of tea, Mrs McDonald looked more than ready for bed. They parted in the corridor of the female staff's sleeping quarters and Florence went into her room, expecting to lie wide awake for hours.

After taking her evening wash and brushing out her hair she got into bed and almost instantly fell asleep. Her slumber was, however, restless and she bolted upright, startled awake, when it was still dark. The end of a dream, fading with each second, had dislodged the reason for her unease that week and it slotted neatly, with only a couple of loose threads, into what Lady Stodmarsh had struggled to tell her last night. Shivering, she was about to lie down and pull the bedclothes close, when the door opened. The ceiling light switched on and Molly, the ever solid head housemaid, came into the room. Florence's heart hammered. It was obvious from the look on that usually rosy face that something was terribly wrong.

FOUR

That Monday morning, Alf Thatcher delivered the sad news from Mullings to a good many residents of Dovecote Hatch along with the early morning post. The shock of it had nearly caused him to tumble off his bike on the Mullings woodland path, near where Lord Stodmarsh had wrenched his ankle not so long ago. One of his early stops was at Farn Deane.

'Say that again,' Gracie Norris, every inch the popular concept of a farmer's wife with her florid face, wiry hair and rotund build, stared back at Alf from the open farmhouse doorway.

'Lady Stodmarsh is gone.' Alf's lined face worked. 'Slipped away in the middle of the night, quiet as a mouse. Nobody heard a peep.'

Gracie admitted to her husband Tom later that she'd gone soft in the head for a moment picturing a knotted sheet rope being tossed out

95

of a bedroom window followed by a night-gowned leg coming over the sill. Then of course the penny dropped. 'You mean she's died, Alf?' Even as she said this she clutched at straws. Could he be talking about Mrs William Stodmarsh? A nice enough woman, no doubt, but not the sort to inspire village loyalty, and with all that weight on her maybe a stroke had been just a matter of time.

'Afraid so. His Lordship woke around four-thirty and went to look in on her, like he often does during the night.'

Not Mrs William, then. It had been foolish to hope.

'Doctor said she'd been gone hours before he found her.' Alf sank down on the step. 'Pegs are still unsteady under me. Heartbreaking, in't it?'

'Best come in, lad, for a cup of tea,' said Gracie kindly. 'Get something inside you before you get back on your bike. I suppose it shouldn't come as a shock, what with her having been poorly all these years, but it fair knocks you back, it being so sudden, don't it?'

She led Alf into the friendly-looking kitchen hung about with cooking utensils and other housewifely paraphernalia. Her mind was filled with what would be going on this minute up at Mullings. Oh, poor Lord Stodmarsh ... she winced away from the image conjured. Then there was Florence. Gracie still considered her a sister-in-law, though Robert had been gone these many years. It couldn't be said that her and Florence had become close friends; since marrying Tom, Gracie's life had been wrapped around him

96

and the farm. And, Florence was reserved, but –
like Tom said – you couldn't know her without
feeling the world wasn't such a bad old place
after all.

'Heart attack, was it?' Sighing, Gracie drew
out a kitchen chair for Alf.

He sat down gratefully. 'Seems that's what
Doc Chester thinks – that her ticker just gave
out. Said all those tablets and whatnot she had to
take for the pain gets to be hard on the system.
But there was no way round it with her rheu-
matics being so bad. He'd just left when I got to
Mullings.'

'Who told you what'd happened?'

'Jeanie Barnes as works in the kitchen. I
always take the post round the back and hand it
in. The other one, Annie Long, was all of a heap.
Quaking sort of lass at the best of times.'

Gracie set the kettle on the stove. 'My heart
bleeds, it does, for His Lordship.' Her voice
cracked and tears glistened in her eyes. 'That
good man won't know what's hit him.'

'That's what keeps going round in my head.'
Alf nodded bleakly. 'Your Florence come into
the kitchen just as I was leaving. Looked and
sounded calm enough, like you'd expect of her,
but she has to have taken it bad, her having bin
with the family on and off since she wasn't much
more than a child, and always so devoted to the
family. The ground may've shifted under Mullings, but she'll hold things steady.'

Gracie nodded. 'Fourteen, she was, when she
first started out there. Two years younger than
what Master Ned is now, and him still but a lad.

Florence started bringing him for tea here one Sunday a month when he was around six or seven and now he's over here every chance he gets, eager to learn all Tom can teach him about farming. Right fond he is – was – of his grandma, though it's clear Florence is more of what you'd call a mother figure to him, her having done most of the rearing of him since she went back to Mullings. I've heard him say, time out of mind, he wouldn't know what he'd do if she ever left.'

'I can see why, though it in't what you could call realistic not to figure that one day she mightn't want a personal life again.'

'Lads Master Ned's age don't tend to be realistic.' Gracie filled the glazed brown teapot. 'I've nephews of similar years that's making their mums and dads tear their hair out.'

'I suppose it's bin that way since Adam and Eve annoyed God; either visit people with floods or plagues of young 'uns.' It settled Alf's mind a little to shift his thoughts sideward. 'You'll know Florence has been seeing something of Birdie these past months. Me an' Doris have had them over for Sunday dinner a few times and yesterday she took him to meet her fam'ly. Oh, they both say it's naught but a friendship, but I can't keep from hoping that it'll come to something more. Though don't go telling Doris I said so, Gracie, if you meet up. She'd have my innards for garters.'

'My lips are sealed, Alf.'

His face turned bleak again. 'Shouldn't be getting off the subject of Lady Stodmarsh – it

98

isn't decent.'

'Rubbish!' Gracie placed a cup of strong tea in front of him. 'Thinking hopefully is what gets us through the rough spots in life. Tom and I've been thinking along those same lines about Florence and George Bird. We don't see it would be any disrespect to Robert's memory if she was to marry again. It'd be what he'd want. Lord and Lady Stodmarsh gave them the loveliest dinner service ever. Real china. It's still here, seeing as Florence took nothing much when they wed but her clothes and a framed photograph of Robert when she went back to Mullings, and I'll be more than happy to pack it up for her if she has a home of her own to take it.'

'Of course,' Alf shook his head, 'like we just bin reminded – there's no telling what lies round the next corner.'

'Now, don't go all morbid, saying each and every one of us could pop our clogs tomorrow. God doesn't get his fun that way. Let's think positive about Florence and George.' Gracie poured him more tea, set a plate of hot buttered toast in front of him and sat down at the table with her own cup. 'It's a good thing you're doing, Alf, spreading the word about Lady Stodmarsh being called above. It's best to let the village know as soon as possible, so people can comfort each other.' She blew on her tea to cool it.

'You're a good 'un, Gracie.'

'Feeling more yourself, are you, lad? Whatever will my Tom say when he comes in from milking? I'll wait here to give him the bad news, and then get over to see Florence. Or maybe, come to think of it, I'd do better giving you a note to take to her. Things are bound to be at sixes and seven today. Would I be sending you much out of your way, Alf?'

'It wouldn't matter if it did, but I'll tell you what – I always finish up at the Dog and Whistle, so's to have a chat with George. He's going to be upset when I break the news to him, especially for Florence. I'm sure he'd want to telephone her right away, but knowing what things will be like today at Mullings, I'd think he'll also decide on sending something written for the time being, so as soon as I leave him I'll take the woodland path back to Mullings.'

'Thanks, Alf. I'll ask Florence what'd be a good time for me to come and see her, or if she'd rather Tom picked her up and brought her here. What a sorrowful day this'll be for everyone hereabouts.'

Alf managed to finish off a piece of toast. 'Them I've already told took it bad, and it'll be the same all over Dovecote Hatch. Lady Stodmarsh mayn't have got out and about much in recent years, but a sweeter lady there never was.'

Let him talk himself through the shock of it, before getting back on his bike, thought Gracie. She had her own memories to share. 'They had me and Tom over for tea in the drawing room, she and His Lordship did, when we was about to be wed. Treated us like they was grateful we'd bothered to come, and gave us a very nice wedding present, just like they did Florence and Robert. Ours was enough linen sheets and pillowcases to last us out and our children too, if we'd had any. Along with that was a beautiful bedspread and eiderdown.

'The only person with anything bad to say about Lord and Lady Stodmarsh was Hilda Stark, that got turned out after being Master Ned's nanny, despite them treating her fairer than she deserved when it came to a pension or whatever. And what she put around about Master Ned's other granny being poorly a time or two don't bear repeating. Wicked, is what she is!' Gracie's eyes sparked. 'As Tom and I well remember, Florence was on her enemy list, too, for having supposedly got her the shove. There's always one of Hilda Stark's sort, more's the pity. You'll find them in a convent of nuns bobbing up and down in prayer, no doubt! Reckon she only decided to shut her mouth when she realized she was doing herself more harm than good with the villagers.'

'You're right for the most part about that,' Alf agreed, polishing off his second slice of toast, 'although she did have a dig at Miss Bradley after that lady come to live at Mullings. One time when Hilda was at the Dog and Whistle, she dredged up about Miss Bradley being stood up at the church; said as how the man could've had good reason for ducking out. Birdie laid into her good and proper.'

'Rightly so,' said Gracie staunchly, 'though I have to admit thinking to myself that there can be two sides to one story. On the face of it the bridegroom sounds a wretched excuse for a man, but what if something happened at the last minute? Perhaps he saw her do something nasty and realized he couldn't abide living with her till one of them kicked the bucket.'

'It won't do, Gracie.' Alf shook his head. 'He should've told her he was ducking out ahead of time, not left her to face the organ music, waiting on him like a figure of fun.'

'You're right, there's no getting round that. Probably I wouldn't be thinking that way if Master Ned had taken to her, but I know from talking to him that he hasn't. But, like we said, lads his age can take it into their heads to be awkward just for the sake of it.'

Alf looked thoughtful. 'It's understandable, I suppose, for him to be leery of any newcomer as might want to keep in with his uncle and aunt, as well as his grandparents. The lad makes no secret of not being over fond of Mr and Mrs William. An' why should he be? They don't never seem to have put themselves out none to help make up, by way of affection, for his parents being dead.'

'That's just what Tom and I think; though it can't be said Master Ned moans on about them. He makes more of a joke of it – says he'd sooner the vicar took him under his wing than they did. You get the point, Alf, seeing as Mr Pimcrisp only warms up when he's talking about fire and brimstone.'

'It comes from Mr William always being jealous of his brother, I've always thought, and with a temper like he's got, it don't seem likely his wife'd stand up to him by making a fuss of Master Ned. Still,' Alf always tried to be fair, 'it can't be easy being the younger son of one of the big families, knowing from early on your brother's going to inherit the old ancestral. Then when Mr Lionel and his wife got killed, he must've thought how he'd've bin in clover if it wasn't for the little tyke left behind. Put a grudge under his other armpit to match the first, that would.'

'I hadn't thought along those lines,' conceded Gracie. 'I tend to think of men that bluster and bully as not having all that much going on in their heads. But would Mrs William hold the same grudge against Master Ned?'

'She's a deep one, is what Doris thinks. She comes from a little place named Warley in Essex, and we knows a couple that's lived there forever. Well, they say that Gertrude Miller, as she was then, was an only child brung up by a widowed older mother as should have stayed an old maid. The sort that warns a daughter the night before her wedding that she'll have disgustin' stuff to put up with in the bedroom and to hang on to her prayer book till it's over. That sort of thing can warp a woman's mind when it comes to the male o' the species – even a boy as young as Master Ned was when he was orphaned.' Alf became aware that if he'd been more himself this wasn't a conversation he would be having with any woman but Doris. He cleared his throat. 'I hope you won't take what I've said as too off colour, Gracie.'

'Go on with you, Alf! I was a farmer's daughter before I married Tom. You can't grow up on the land, especially around horses, without knowing what's what. That said, even my

103

mother – sensible woman that she was – warned me that the best of husbands was given to making excessive demands.' Gracie laughed. 'From the looks of Mrs William, she probably wouldn't have known what she was born for when she married, and would've taken that to mean being forced to play bridge, whether she wanted to or not. Then again, appearances can be deceiving, and she could be the sort that would have given anything for a handsome lad to come riding up on a white horse.'

'Somehow I doubt that,' said Alf. 'From what our friends from Warley say, she didn't come from a lot of money and was verging on thirty when she was introduced by mutual acquaintances to Mr William.'

'Well,' said Gracie flatly, 'that surly disposition of his was likely to have sent other ladies running.' She brought the conversation back to the immediate situation at Mullings. 'I wonder how the two of them are taking Lady Stodmarsh's death? Even an old grouse like Mr William must've been fond of his own mother, but I wonder if Mrs William won't find comfort in the idea of becoming lady of the house until Master Ned marries, and that'll be way in the future. However it goes, I can't see neither of them being much comfort to His Lordship.' Gracie's kind eyes blurred with tears. 'He'll never get over losing his wife, he won't. I wouldn't be surprised if he doesn't outlive her by long; it happens that way often enough with devoted older couples.'

'It goes without saying,' Alf sighed. 'Love of

his life, she was, and well deserved. It puts me to shame when I think o' the times I goes on about my lumbago, and that dear lady so uncomplaining, crippled up like she were, God rest her soul.'

Gracie echoed this appeal to the Almighty. 'It's a good thing Master Ned's other granny is in the house for him. She won't be leaving now till after the funeral, and probably some time beyond. An interesting thing I've found with women that has done battle with their nerves in the past, they can be the ones that come through in a crisis. You stay put, Alf, while I go and write that note for Florence.'

By mid-morning Dovecote Hatch was in formal mourning. Curtains were drawn, black ties and armbands were spotted up and down the high street, and Craddock's Antiquarian Bookshop was one of several establishments to hang 'Closed' signs behind the glass in their doors.

George Bird, as both Alf and Gracie had known would be the case, had been stunned and deeply grieved. He immediately felt an urge to telephone Florence and tell her how sorry he was, but he was fully aware of how occupied she would be with all that must be going on at Mullings, and he wasn't about to add the interruption of being called to the telephone, when he could do as Alf suggested and write his condolences, asking her to get in touch when she had the time and felt up to it. After Alf left, he went behind the bar – not to pour himself a drink, but to wipe its spotless surface – back and

105

forth, forth and back. It had come to him that what he really wanted was to be with Florence right this minute, and wrap his arms around her.

Something had changed for him on that drive home from visiting her family yesterday. He hadn't thought right then that it was love; but last night, on getting ready for bed, he'd heard Mabel's voice clear – and pleased – in his head. 'Go on, my old dear, own up! It's going that way and you and me both know it. Truth is, I'm tickled pink. Do you think I want you mooning over me forever? I haven't liked to rub it in, but I'm having a rare old time up here. Like you've found out moving to Dovecote Hatch, give a new place a chance and you can be walking on clouds. In your case, love, that's in a manner of speaking, but you get the idea – what's good for the goose is good for the gander.' He'd smiled before drifting off to sleep. That there could be no smiles this morning didn't alter a thing. If he'd had his wish he'd have been with Florence right now, trying to comfort her as best he could.

It had flashed through Florence's mind on being told by Molly of Lady Stodmarsh's death several hours previously that she'd have welcomed the warmth of his arms around her. She had turned cold when Molly had entered her bedroom well before daybreak. It was impossible not to know instantly that Lady Stodmarsh was dead. That in itself was devastating, but the realization that had tugged at Florence on wakening – that her uneasiness of the past week and her beloved employer's agitated distress were linked – made

106

her feel she would never be warm again. The belief, amounting to certainty, that Lady Stodmarsh had not died from heart failure but had been murdered, held her in its frigid grip. What had come together out of her subconscious was the merging of two incidents – one relating to visiting her mother, the other involving the puppy.

The memory of being in the hall at Mullings to witness Grumidge bearing the tea tray towards the drawing room and becoming entangled with the puppy had always been clear, as had her reason for being there. Miss Bradley had asked earlier if she could save her a trip to the village shop by providing her with a reel of navy cotton, in order to finish the dress she was making. Florence had come downstairs after taking the required item up to Miss Bradley's room in time to provide assistance to Grumidge, by way of opening the drawing room door for him. It was what had followed that had finally resurfaced.

Standing in that opening, Florence had caught a brief view of the entire family seated within. Something glimpsed in the eyes of one of the assembled people must have tugged at her mind for a fraction of a moment. It was gone too quickly for her to keep a grasp on it – driven back into hiding, perhaps, by the entrance of Grumidge. Or, wondered Florence now, had she blocked it from her conscious mind because it was too chilling to be accepted? What she had been left with in the following days was that sense of something just out of reach that warned of trouble. It wasn't until yesterday, when she had stood with the tea tray in her hands at the open door of her mother's sitting room door and observed her sitting utterly still, with those unnaturally blank eyes, that Florence had felt the beginning of reclaiming what had frustrated her by its elusiveness. Now it was as though what had been a blurred image had developed into a photograph.

What Florence had seen in the eyes of one of those seated at Mullings had also been unnatural – with a difference. There had been nothing suggestive of a seriously disturbed mind where her mother was concerned. Those other eyes had glinted, however briefly, a malevolent, vicious hatred directed at Lady Stodmarsh as she sat with her husband while the puppy frisked around their feet. Last night Lady Stodmarsh had talked of the dog, making little sense at the time. In piecing scraps of phrases together and remembering those that had puzzled her most – such as the mention of the *looking glass*, Florence felt sure that someone with Lady Stodmarsh's welfare in mind had warned her to take steps to protect herself from possible harm. That this had happened yesterday seemed more than likely to have precipitated Lady Stodmarsh sending for her last night. Prior to being warned, had Lady Stodmarsh sensed that she had an enemy, someone without reason or restraint? And this someone was dear to her!

It didn't bear thinking about, but there was no escape from doing so. Florence knew that she must at some point decide what she could or should do. The thought of taking this matter to

His Lordship in his grief-stricken state was insupportable. She would feel less caught in a trap if someone else voiced suspicions of their own regarding the death. She was concerned that even the person who had sought to put Lady Stodmarsh on her guard might well keep silent for solid reasons, including self-preservation. Should there be a police investigation and no confession forthcoming, every member of the household, from family to staff, would be scrutinized as to opportunity and motive. That was Florence's deepest fear – that the wrong person would be seen to fit both categories. People had been and would continue to be wrongfully convicted. It was this that might – against conscience – keep her silent.

She hoped to avoid coming upon the killer in the near future, but on such a day it would seem unavoidable that everyone under the Mullings roof would be passed or glimpsed at some stage. Ned was the first of the family to seek her out. He was waiting outside her bedroom when she emerged within moments of Molly's departure. Outwardly as calm as always – smoothly dressed, every hair in place – Florence was the picture of a housekeeper who never allowed emotion to deflect her from her duty. To Ned she was someone more. She was his Florie. His eyes dazed, he reached for her hand and clung to it as he had done years before after waking from his nightmare.

'I never thought about Grandmother not being here one day. I know she hasn't been well for what seems like forever, but rheumatism isn't something like cancer that's almost certain to kill you, is it?'

Florence's voice cracked. 'There, my love, hold on tight as you like. Have you spoken with the doctor?' Why hadn't she thought of doing so herself later in the day? A tremor passed through him to her.

'I was with Grandfather when he talked to him, and he said her heart must have given out, even though she'd refused to take anything really strong for the pain. He'd reordered her prescription on Friday, and just to make perfectly sure of being on the solidest ground possible when signing the death certificate, he'd checked the bottle to make sure she hadn't taken more than she should by mistake, but the number of tablets gone was correct. Though if she had taken a few extra it wouldn't have mattered. The one good piece of news,' Ned's mouth twisted as he finally released her hand, 'is that there won't have to be a post-mortem.'

'Yes, I've heard that unpleasantness can usually be avoided, if a doctor's attended the patient recently.' So Lady Stodmarsh's own tablets were not the culprits, but there could be any number of bottles of drugs about the house prescribed at different times to different people. Florence thrust back the thought and forced a wavering smile for Ned. 'How about coming down to the kitchen so Mrs McDonald can make you a cup of tea and maybe you could even manage some scrambled eggs and toast? Even if the usual breakfast hour is moved up today, you need something to sustain you until then.'

'I don't know that I could get my mouth around anything for a week,' his green eyes were the darkest Florence had ever seen them, 'although I suppose I should try. I won't be much use to Grandfather if I pass out from not eating.' As they were heading for the back staircase, Ned continued, 'Another small comfort, Florie, is that I went up and talked to Grandmother last night after she'd gone to bed. I've always been closer with her than I have been with Granny.'

'Tressler,' Florence inserted as a gentle prod when he paused.

'Yes, but I know Grandmother had to be aware I enjoyed being with Grandfather more than I did with her.'

'She'll have understood that you could engage with him in activities that were inacccesible to her. Also, don't discount those afternoons when you were a day pupil at Westerbey and would come home and read Jane Austen or Dickens to her. I was there, don't forget, sitting with both of you in the drawing room, and I saw the happiness in her face. Those were treasured hours you gave her.'

'All well and good, Florie,' Ned halted in the corridor, 'but that stopped when I went to boarding school and I never got back to reading to her. Oh, sometimes I'd go and chat with her and get her laughing at some story about one of the beastly prefects snitching to the housemaster about some boy they'd caught smoking, or I'd accuse her of cheating at patience. But the truth is, those times weren't often or long enough. I wouldn't have gone up to her bedroom last evening if it hadn't been that I'd gone into the kitchen to wangle another rock bun out of Mrs McDonald. When I walked in that nervous girl Annie was all in a panic – gibbering and shaking. It was obvious she was in no state to take up Grandmother's hot milk, even after Mrs McDonald told her to get a hold of herself; so rather than wait for the other one, Jeanie, to be fetched, I said I'd do it.'

Florence's throat tightened. She was a couple of steps ahead of him down the staircase and had difficulty remaining standing; somehow she found the strength to look around at him. 'You ... you took the milk up to your grandmother?' If it were found, despite Doctor Chester's assurances, to have been tampered with, the police would have their suspect.

The barest suggestion of a grin touched his mouth. 'Why not? I'm not entirely the helpless young princeling.'

'That's not it at all, Ned,' said Florence huskily, 'I was just ... just wondering how Lady Stodmarsh looked and sounded to you. It must have been shortly afterwards that I went up to her bedroom. Mr Grumidge had passed along the message that she wanted to talk to me. I assumed it would have to do with Mrs Tressler's planned departure for this morning, but that wasn't mentioned; by the time I got there Lady Stodmarsh was very nearly asleep.'

'I wonder if it was about Granny that she sent for you,' Ned eyed Florence uncertainly, 'or if Grandmother had some sort of inkling that she'd die in the night.'

'Did she look ... sound ... different in any way?'

'More ill than usual, you mean? Not to me, but I'm not the most noticing person, am I?'

'Ned, dear! Don't do this to yourself.'

His mouth twisted and in the shadowy corridor his angular features had never seemed more sharply etched. 'I'm not sure Grandfather would agree with you, Florie. I remember his telling me that learning to be honest with oneself takes some doing, but you can't hope to live a clean life till you master it. As for Grandmother, she was fully alert during the ten minutes or so I stayed with her. It's what she said to me that has me wondering if she...'

'What, Ned?'

'Thought we wouldn't see each other again.'

'Do you mind telling me what she talked to you about?'

'When haven't I told you pretty much everything, Florence? It was about my not wanting to go up to University when I'm done with school. I'd broken the news to her and Grandfather earlier in the week, and they both suggested I take my time thinking such a big decision through, but I think they both knew I wasn't likely to budge. What I want, what I've wanted ever since I started going over to Farn Deane with Grandfather, and those Sunday afternoons with you, is to farm. If Tom and Gracie had a son it might be different – I wouldn't have wanted to shove him aside – but the way things are, after they're gone, some outsider will take over. I don't want that, and the thought of it makes

113

them sad.' Ned drew a breath. 'What Grand-mother said to me was that she and Grandfather had decided I should follow my heart and that if I wish to do so I can leave school at the end of the summer term next year if that's what I would prefer to going on to the sixth form.'

'Is that what you would like?'

'Oh, yes! As Grandmother pointed out, I also have to learn how to manage the estate, and perhaps the sooner Grandfather starts instructing me on finances and responsibilities to our tenants the better. Unfortunately, my weak spot is mathematics, but I promised Grandmother I'll sit doing pages of sums until kingdom come if necessary. She smiled and said not to wear my fingers to nubs along with the pencils. Florence, do you think from all this ... that Grandmother was giving me her blessing by way of goodbye?'

'I wouldn't be at all surprised.' It was an honest reply, but it occurred to her that Lady Stodmarsh might have struggled to talk posi-tively so as not to allow Ned to see that she was deeply troubled.

Mrs McDonald was alone in the kitchen, kneading dough on a carelessly floured surface, when they entered. She looked around at them; her eyes were red-rimmed and her nose swollen to twice its usual size. 'Oh, Master Ned, I'm that sorry for your loss. Once again, no time for you to prepare. Oh, I shouldn't have gone and said that – I should have my tongue cut out.' *It's not fair*, thought Florence, *that a woman of fifteen stone never gets to look fragile and in need of coddling.* But she was wrong about that this time. Ned went over and put his arms around Mrs McDonald, getting flour on himself in the process, which brought on a sneeze. He kissed her cheek before stepping back. 'Oh, just look at the sight of you!' She vigorously dusted him off. 'And all because I showed you a long face, instead of pulling m'self together for your sake.'

Ned produced what looked like a real grin. 'You could hardly be standing there laughing, could you?' He sobered instantly. 'I know how you felt about Grandmother, Mrs Mac. If you hadn't been so fond of her and Grandfather you'd never have stood for me being underfoot, helping myself to whatever had just come out of the oven every chance I got from the time I could climb on a stool.'

'Now, don't you go stretching the truth, Master Ned.' Mrs McDonald had herself back together as far as she was able. 'You know full well I'd've said plenty if you hadn't waited for me to hand you a jam tart or whatever it was you was after.' Looking rather like a polar bear with her fine coating of flour, she propelled him towards a chair at the table as she spoke. 'You sit yourself with Mrs Norris while I make you some of my scrambled eggs you're so fond of with the cream and chives and serve it up with toast, along with a pot of good strong tea.'

'Florie's a mind reader.' Ned's voice was overly bright, suggesting misery was returning full force. 'She said scrambled eggs.'

'Should keep you going till you and the family sit down to a proper breakfast, though likely the most anyone'll do is peck.' Mrs McDonald got bustling. 'Where's my head, I ask you? That bread dough has to go into a bowl and set in the warming oven to proof! What I'm hoping hard as I can is that Lady Stodmarsh's last day and evening was happy, Master Ned.'

'She wanted to go to church in the morning. She'd managed last week. It's nothing to get there in the car, of course, but yesterday she said at the last minute that sitting in the pew for an hour was beyond her, so Granny offered to stay behind too, while the rest of us went.'

'Very kind of Mrs Tressler.'

'Yes, it was. She enjoys going enormously and doesn't mind in the least that Mr Pimcrisp goes prosing on for what seems like forever. Grandmother assured her there was no need to forego attending the service, but she insisted.'

'Did you think Lady Stodmarsh might've liked some time alone for a bit of quiet, Master Ned?' Mrs McDonald eyed him as she reached for her whisk.

'I can't say I did at the time. I'd come downstairs in a tearing rush, without my gloves, and had to go back for them. Grandfather rarely gets huffy about anything, but making the family late for church just isn't on. If he'd thought Grandmother wanted to be left to rest, I'm sure he'd have insisted on being the one to remain behind. Still, you could be right ... I do recall she looked unusually drained when we got back.'

'I hope you're not fretting, Master Ned, that you missed that for a sign.' Mrs McDonald was pouring the beaten eggs into a saucepan that for all its polished gleam had hung from the same

116

hook for fifty years or more. 'Even me that sometimes has the sight didn't see this coming, not even after the butcher's boy told me Friday how he'd heard a dog howl three times on his way over here.'

Florence gathered her thoughts. She couldn't ask Ned directly if he'd gained any information on what the two ladies had talked about; not so much because it would have been inappropriate, especially in front of Mrs McDonald, but because her anxiety was so close to the surface she was afraid it would come through and set him to wondering just what was behind the question. 'Did Mrs Tressler seem worried about Lady Stodmarsh?'

Ned's brow furrowed. 'Come to remember, she looked a little wiped out herself. I'm wondering now if they'd been talking about my mother and father and their deaths. But I don't know ... it would've been a rare thing for them to do. Stiff upper lip and all that. Shouldn't go dwelling on the sorrow; best to reflect only on the happy stuff. They are,' he snagged on the word but did not correct himself, 'both tough in their different ways.'

'Even so,' Mrs McDonald spooned scrambled eggs on to two warmed plates and brought them to the table, 'there'd bound to be those moments between two bereaved mothers when there's no holding back their shared terrible sense of loss. Could be Lady Stodmarsh felt better afterwards, making for a blessing on her last day on this earth.'

'Hope so.' Ned reached absently for the toast

117

rack.

Florence knew she should make an effort to eat for his sake, but the thought of swallowing anything was inconceivable. 'Yes, that may well be right. How did Lady Stodmarsh look during the afternoon?' she asked.

'I wasn't there. I'd gone over to Farn Deane. Tom wanted me to take a look at the new calf. The evening, however, was wretched and must have been particularly so for Grandmother and Grandfather. It can't be easy watching your remaining son displaying himself at his worst. From the moment we all gathered in the drawing room before dinner Uncle William was in a foul mood, so much so that Aunt Gertrude, who wouldn't normally notice if a portion of the ceiling dropped in her lap, looked stretched tight as a drum. Halfway though downing his first whisky and soda, he started in on the new puppy, saying it was a damned nuisance. The little chap wasn't even in the room. Uncle William has always despised dogs, but last evening he went beyond the pale, saying he'd danced a jig when the last one kicked it.'

'Oh, surely not!' Mrs McDonald replenished the teapot. 'No disrespect intended, Master Ned, but I wouldn't have thought Mr William had the figure for it.'

Ned laughed. Was he thinking, wondered Florence, that Mrs McDonald, despite her own hefty build, was wont to dance like a fairy at the staff Christmas ball? His mirth subsided instantly. 'That wasn't enough for Uncle; he said for two pins he'd drive this latest poor excuse for fur a

118

sufficient distance out into the country that he'd never find his way back.'

Mrs McDonald, rarely bereft of words, was too shocked to respond. Florence's thought was how well it must have suited a person intent on murdering Lady Stodmarsh that Mr William had presented himself as a potential suspect, to at least one other already neatly in mind, should her death not have been accepted as occurring from natural causes. If only she might be wrong in her appalling suspicions and would come to realize once she had time alone to reflect that she had pieced them together out of the thinnest of cloth. And yet, even setting aside what she had remembered on waking, there remained Lady Stodmarsh's distressed, frightened state of mind last night.

'Florie, drink your tea.' Ned studied her anxiously. 'You don't look at all the thing.'

'I'm fine. How did your grandfather react to what your uncle said about the puppy?'

'Grandfather looked annoyed, but he changed the subject by asking Uncle William if he'd care to go with him to the lodge tomorrow – today – to bid goodbye to old Jeffers and his wife and thank them for their many years of faithful service before they set off on their retirement. They'll be living with their daughter and son-in-law in Somerset.'

'So we've all been aware for some weeks past,' said Mrs McDonald, 'and a right pity it'll be to see them go. Silas Jeffers' family has been lodge keepers at Mullings since no one remembers when.'

'That's what Grandfather pointed out to Uncle William, who flared back that it counted for naught with him if Jeffers and his wife had arrived in the ark, or what he and his wife aimed to do in the future. He didn't stop there – adding that since the end of the carriage days they'd been more ornament than use and he'd be blowed if he shifted an inch on their behalf. What was more, he ranted on about hoping Stodmarsh money wasn't going to be thrown away on a replacement. Cousin Madge kept her eyes fixed on her knitting, as she always does at awkward moments, and Granny began riffling through her handbag, which for some reason she always keeps to hand.'

Mrs McDonald, belatedly remembering her place, said, 'Perhaps other ears than ours would be better suited to these confidences.'

Florence remained silent, motivated by the wish to learn as much as possible about what had transpired within the family circle on the previous evening. Also she was keenly aware that Ned needed a brief diversion from dwelling on his grandmother's body awaiting removal by the undertaker.

'Fudge!' he retorted. 'As if I haven't sat in this kitchen a thousand times enlightening you and Florie on Uncle William's bursts of ill temper. This time,' the green eyes hardened, 'he might have done himself some real damage – had Grandmother not died and swept all else from Grandfather's mind. Uncle William kept digging himself in further, rumbling away about it being ludicrous to pander to the feelings of lesser

120

persons, or – and there he looked directly at Cousin Madge – to feel under an obligation to any not of the immediate family.'

'Dearie me!' Mrs McDonald gave no further thought to being mindful of her place. Hurt feelings were the same above and below stairs. 'That had to've cut the poor lady to the bone.'

'Beastly,' agreed Ned. 'My gripe against Cousin Madge, as you know, Florie, is she tries so gratingly hard to please – as opposed to taking living here for granted. And it certainly wasn't a case of her having pressed for the invitation by pleading her piteous state after being left at the altar. The idea was Grandmother's, fully supported by Grandfather, and they both seem entirely comfortable with the idea of her remaining on here as long as she chooses.'

'How did Miss Bradley take your uncle's remark?' Mrs McDonald removed the need for Florence to ask this question.

'I couldn't decide if she's blessed with the thickest of skins or was brought wretchedly low, because she still didn't look up from her knitting. But, if it eases your kind heart, Florie, no tears dropped on the inevitable navy blue. It was Granny who stepped into the breach, temporarily taking some of the wind out of his sails. I told you she's game, Florie. Before Grandmother and Grandfather could utter their reproaches, which would only have fuelled his ire, she turned to face Uncle William, gave him the broadest smile, and asked whether he was hinting ever so gently that she, being no blood relation, was barred from the dinner table and should instead partake of her meal in her room? The ensuing protests from around the room, including one from Aunt Gertrude, successfully deflected unwanted attention from Cousin Madge.'

'Good for Mrs Tressler!' Mrs McDonald responded heartily. 'I've always thought her an example to one and all for how to conduct theirselves after being dealt more grief than anyone should have to contend with in this life, even though the vicar makes out suffering's a special treat God only hands out to the deserving.'

'Puts Uncle William on the primrose path, doesn't it? Unfortunately he didn't grab the chance to shut up. In punishment for her lack of support, he rounded on Aunt Gertrude, bellowing that she might as well be a piece of furniture – an unwanted one at that. Worse, he spouted off a list of what he claimed were her grievances against the family. I never felt sorrier for the old girl in my life. For a moment she just sat there, like an overstuffed bolster, then she looked him full in the face and told him everyone had heard enough out of him for one evening. It's hard to credit, given her usual capacity to absorb his tirades unmoved, but the hatred in her eyes spoke volumes. I wouldn't have been surprised if she'd surged off her chair and throttled him.'

'Dearie me!' Mrs McDonald had noticed that the dawn light was seeping through the oblong windows and the work day beckoned, but she wasn't about to shoo the young master out of her kitchen on this worst of mornings, particularly when what he had to say held her in thrall. Besides, she thought virtuously, it was helping take their minds off the tragedy, and it wasn't like Mrs Norris wasn't listening just as intently. It was she who asked what happened next.

'Grandfather went over and placed a hand on Aunt Gertrude's shoulder, saying very kindly that her happiness and William's too mattered a great deal to him and Grandmother and, if she wished to be a mistress of her own home, arrangements could be made for the two of them to set up residence elsewhere, with no resultant hard feelings. That well and truly rocked Uncle William on his high horse. He was blustering about being taken all wrong, and if he'd sounded out of sorts it was because he'd mislaid his favourite pipe, when Grumidge came in to announce dinner was served.'

'That being the end of the matter, I hope.' Mrs McDonald wasn't often given to untruths, but she managed this one with the aplomb of a woman who could organize a seven-course meal and have sent it up for a duke and duchess to dine upon (not that such had recently graced Mullings).

'Pretty much,' Ned gave up on a half-eaten slice of toast. 'Conversation shifted into the normal between the time we sat down at the dining table and the soup was served. And very good it was too, Mrs McDonald. Cousin Madge was particularly complimentary as to the taste and texture, at unnecessary length, if you won't mind my saying so, then veering into her passion for soups in general – apart from turtle, which she regretted to say she had always despised.'

'That soup *was* turtle!' Few things fired Mrs McDonald up more rapidly than insults to her cooking. Her face appeared ready to come to the boil along with the kettle she had set back on the cooker.

'I know,' Ned soothed, 'but she didn't. Cousin Madge can be very trying, but she's not malicious.'

Florence wondered about that in the midst of her other thoughts. Miss Bradley had certainly been provoked that night, and setting William Stodmarsh off again, to his detriment, might have seemed a sweet revenge. If so, it seemed she had failed.

'Uncle William said only that he was particularly fond of turtle soup, although he didn't mind brown Windsor, which Cousin Madge thought it was. All in all he conducted himself better than usual and the atmosphere continued to lighten, but Aunt Gertrude didn't get back to her usual placid self – she kept plucking at the arm of her chair after we'd returned to the drawing room. Within five minutes, Grandmother announced she didn't wish for coffee and would retire for the night – nothing unusual in that. It was Aunt Gertrude who provided the surprise, by saying there was something she would like to talk to Grandmother about, so would it be alright if she went up with her.'

'And did she?' Florence was careful to make the enquiry casual.

'Oh, yes.' Resentment flowed from Ned. 'It isn't ... wasn't,' choked breath, 'in Grandmother to refuse; even though it should have been apparent to the man in the moon she was done up. Whatever Aunt Gertrude had to say to her – whether an apology for Uncle William's intolerable behaviour or a denial of what he'd said about her grievances – could have waited till today.' He drew a shaky breath. 'It wasn't as if she could have guessed that for Grandmother there would be no tomorrow.'

Silence hung for a long moment, to be broken by Mrs McDonald. 'Even me, with my second sight, never felt a shiver of warning. I suppose when it's a case of too close to home, the mind blocks out the messaging.'

Ned, who was not the only one to have never put any credence in her psychic abilities, did not have to repress a twinkle. 'No one on God's earth could have foreseen...'

Oh, my dearest boy, thought Florence drearily, *someone did know. Either that or I'm losing my grip on reality.*

Ned shifted restlessly in his chair before getting up, thanking Mrs McDonald for the breakfast and saying he must not delay longer in joining his grandfather. He turned on the point of leaving. 'Do something for me, Florie – be sure the news is broken gently to Johnson. She's spent most of her adult life as Grandmother's lady's maid, absolutely devoted, and she's bound to be devastated. They were friends.'

'I know. I'll send Molly up to sit with her till she wakes, which probably won't be for a while as she is grown so frail, and then have Molly fetch me to her.'

'Whatever would I do without you?' With that Ned was gone.

Florence had a flash of memory, of Agnes Johnson's kindness to her as a fourteen-year-old arriving at Mullings. Hard on its heels was the thought that a year ago, Miss Johnson would have prepared and taken in Lady Stodmarsh's night-time hot milk. Instead it had been Ned, and if something had been added to it, beyond the bicarbonate of soda, and an investigation was instigated, he could find himself in a hazardous situation. If not the milk in the cup, how else had the drug been administered? Florence had never before desired to be a fool; now she desperately wished to discover she was one. What a relief it would be to accept that the melodramatic fantasies of her girlhood had returned with a vengeance, leaving her gratefully laughing at her folly.

FIVE

The kitchen which Florence had long ago come to regard as a familiar friend closed in on her like an alien forest, blocking out strength of mind or direction of purpose. Even the pale sunlight creeping in through the window could not pinpoint a pathway upon which to venture back to normality. Mrs McDonald's voice might as well have been coming from the wireless reporting on some event occurring in darkest Africa.

'Of course, Master Ned was right in saying he's always chatted when he comes in here looking for something tasty to eat, but he's never confided in me the way he does with you, Mrs Norris. So to hear him tell about Mrs William and last evening's carry-on shook me up good and proper. I'd go so far as to say you could've knocked me down with a feather,' she paused, 'if I wasn't the weight I am, that is.'

'It is very troubling.' This was undeniable, but what, if any, bearing did his behaviour have on Lady Stodmarsh not living to see another morning? With so much that needed to be done, Florence still sat as if welded to her chair.

Mrs McDonald's dutiful attempts in the past to believe that Mr William wasn't all that bad compared, say, to men like Henry VIII – who mar-

127

ried women just so's they could chop their heads off – had received a major setback in the last half hour. She heaved a deep sigh. 'We all forget ourselves at times, Mrs Norris, and get a bit snappish, but there are limits.'

'I agree.' It was rehashing to no purpose. Unfortunately, Mrs McDonald couldn't be turned off with a button to allow for the possibility of restorative silence. It was unkind to wish to do so when the good woman meant so well and could have no suspicion that the words *Lady Stodmarsh murdered ... I'm not wrong about that ...* pulsed relentlessly through Florence's head.

'Such language! All that swearing, in front of his own mother! It's bad enough that his wife and the others had to get an earful.'

'Yes, very distressing.' *The motive, springing from a deranged mind ... because only such a mentality could embrace the delusion that Lady Stodmarsh's death would bring about the desired result...*

'That sweet, gentlest of ladies, God rest her soul.' Sorrow mingled with outrage. 'Not to mention his father! Only think how His Lordship must have felt trying to get matters back on an even keel short of grabbing Mr William by the scruff of the neck and shaking him till he rattled, which you know as well as I do, Mrs Norris, His Lordship would not do in a million years – him being cut from such different cloth. Never a finer man anywhere.' The commentary flowed on, while Florence continued to sit immobile.

Having cleared the table, Mrs McDonald bustled about the room, occupying herself with tasks necessary or not; her very thoughts seeming to clink louder than the shifting of saucepans and crockery. It was unlike her to ramble on without noticing a lack of responsiveness, beyond that of vaguely voiced agreement. How would she react if Florence were to confide in her about where her own thoughts were stuck? Would she think her the one with a deranged mind? Doing so was of course out of the question; the only possible disclosure at Mullings could be to His Lordship, but just supposing? Would Mrs McDonald be swayed on hearing of Lady Stodmarsh's dis-tressed state last night? Florence's head cleared a little. Far more crucial was the question that only now presented itself. How would George respond to such a revelation and the resultant dilemmas facing her?

'Of course, we had to know, while keeping our mouths shut, that Mr William's never been the easiest of gentlemen, but that nastiness to his wife, and her looking at him with hatred! I'd've said Mrs William wasn't the sort to be happy or unhappy to any marked degree. But like they say, "still waters run deep".' Mrs McDonald shut the oven door on the loaves of bread she'd put in to bake. Flour from her apron and hands puffed into the air. 'Still, that's beside the way. If he was my husband – presumption be blowed – I'd have given him one with the rolling pin. A good conk now and then could do most men a power of good...' Cupboard doors opened and closed.

George's response would be kindly. He'd be more than willing to listen – to hear Florence through as she explained why she couldn't

129

accept that Lady Stodmarsh had died of natural causes. He wouldn't instantly latch on to disbelief. He would mull the matter over carefully, ask sensible questions, make pertinent observations.

'If my hair wasn't white already,' Mrs McDonald's voice again broke through like that of a broadcaster interrupting the programme in progress to make an important announcement, 'it would've turned so on the spot listening to Master Ned confiding in us like he did. That one's a good lad, no doubt of that. Though I have to say, I don't think he's quite fair when it comes to being down on Miss Bradley for trying overly hard to please. Shows a grateful nature, is how I'd see it. It's a credit to her, not wilting away, after what she's been through so recently. Of course, youngsters tend to pick holes about silly things, even when they're fond of someone.'

'He is at that age.'

Mrs McDonald sighed. 'He'll grow up fast enough now, having to be His Lordship's support.'

'Yes, he will.'

'Which isn't to say he'll be ready to leave hold of your apron strings any time soon, Mrs Norris. You came along to save him, as he'll see it, when he was just a nipper being looked after by dreadful Nanny Stark. What with you being so kind and good with him ever since, it's no wonder he thinks the world of you.'

Florence did not hear more than two words of this. Despite still being seated at the table, she was back in the car with George yesterday, hear-

130

ing him say what he thought about people who stuck their knife into others for no reason other than choosing to do so. Would he think she had fastened on a suspect particularly vulnerable to injustice? What evidence could she provide? None, beyond claiming to have seen a look in a pair of eyes that she had subsequently forgotten (until conveniently remembered) and that Lady Stodmarsh had been worried, frightened even, last night. But there came the sticking point. She had not talked of someone being out to kill her, let alone named the source of her anxieties. Also it could justifiably be concluded that her disjointed ramblings came from the confusion common to many when on the brink of sleep. Additionally Doctor Chester had voiced no concern as to the cause of death. Given all that, wasn't it still worth the risk of confiding in George? Wrong question. The one that counted was – did she have the right to do so? This was not the time to think of herself, but if she decided she must carry this burden alone until the truth was discovered, if ever, how adversely would that affect their possibly blossoming relationship? Keeping something so important secret from him would not only be overwhelmingly difficult but would make a mockery of closeness.

'I know you won't take it wrong, Mrs Norris, that I defended Miss Bradley about Master Ned finding her irritating. And after what she's been through so recently, it's not surprising if her confidence is all shook up. Of course, Mr William being at his worst last night could've left her feeling glad as goblins she left that church without a ring on her finger and more than content to live out her days as a spinster. But, like I've been thinking about Mrs William, we can read people wrong as often as not, especially if their hearts are padlocked for one reason or another. Could be we're all dark horses in our way. I don't suppose any would think to look at me now that I was a real flibbertigibbet as a girl.' Mrs McDonald reached for a frying pan. 'Dearie me! This isn't getting the day going, is it?'

Florence agreed they must strive to see that everything went even more smoothly than usual in the hours ahead. 'Time for me to get moving,' she said. 'I've been disgracefully laggardly.' It finally occurred to her that Mrs McDonald's talk had not been of the oblivious sort, but an intentional endeavour to provide her with some respite before taking up her obligations.

Rising to her feet, Florence also realized there was something she could do to discover exactly how it happened that Ned had taken up Lady Stodmarsh's hot milk last night. As soon as there was a free moment, she would speak to Annie Long. Anything not to feel entirely helpless. Also she must lose little time in writing down as exactly as possible what Lady Stodmarsh had said to her, along with what could be gleaned from Annie.

Mrs Tressler had come into the kitchen. To Florence's eye she remained the image of the competent schoolmistress. At this moment she might have been surveying her form room intent on calming a disturbance. Florence wondered if she was about to ask to speak to her alone, to discuss with her how Ned must be feeling and what would best help him through the coming days.

Florence was wrong. Mrs Tressler addressed both her and Mrs McDonald. 'I do hope I'm not interrupting,' she began briskly, 'but I wanted to ask, knowing you will both have your hands full today, if there is any way I can be of assistance? I shall of course not be returning home today, but will remain till after the funeral and will be grateful for the opportunity to keep busy.'

'That's very kind, Mrs Tressler,' said Florence.

'Very kind,' echoed Mrs McDonald, although it did take some restraint on her part not to look at the clock, which even death could not stop. She'd just have to hurry the girls along at twice their usual speed, although what use Annie would be at her dithering worst, God himself couldn't guess.

A smile touched Mrs Tressler's mouth. 'I'm sure you both wonder what possible use I can be to you.'

'Not at all,' Florence responded.

'As it happens, I've always been of a domestic nature. My late husband was astonished when I once told him that my ideal of contentment would be living in a cottage and doing my housekeeping; he blanched and said he hoped if he was included in this arrangement we would at least have a woman come in and do the rough a couple of times a week.'

'Well fancy that!' Mrs McDonald chuckled. Was she assuming, wondered Florence, this was a joke, aimed at lifting the pall of grief?

Mrs Tressler's smile lingered. 'My husband proclaimed not to be amused. The rascal took to his bed for two days. In his defence he had simultaneously come down with a cold and had several novels by one of his favourite authors to hand. That being as it may, what I'm offering is to pitch in, hopefully without getting underfoot. For instance, I could assist the maids in preparing rooms for overnight guests attending the funeral.'

Florence considered this offer before expressing appreciation, adding that she would get back to Mrs Tressler when more was known as to the numbers that would need to be accommodated.

Mrs Tressler nodded. 'Lord and Lady Stodmarsh both being only children with no living aunts or uncles or many other relatives, it seems unlikely there will be an influx of overnighters, but one never knows. When it comes to funerals, people one never thought one knew can descend out of nowhere – morbid curiosity, however unexceptional the death may be.'

Was there something behind this observation? A subtle probing for a visible reaction? Florence hoped it wasn't apparent she'd stiffened. 'You're entirely right, Mrs Tressler,' she said, 'it is always advisable to prepare for any unexpected eventuality.'

'Meanwhile, let us start with today, which is of paramount importance. What can I do, however small?'

'There's the menus for luncheon and dinner to

134

be decided,' put forth Mrs McDonald, tears beading her eyes as the full impact of Mullings without its mistress overwhelmed her anew. 'Lady Stodmarsh always discussed with me on a Monday morning what she'd like served for the week, though most often she'd take up my suggestions, with only a special request here and there. So easy she was, bless her soul! I'd be more than grateful, Mrs Tressler, if you'd be so good as to have a talk with Mrs William Stodmarsh about her wishes, so's I won't have to trouble her. One of the maids can bring me down her instructions.'

'Gertrude has returned to bed with a bad headache,' said Mrs Tressler. 'So very understandable. It seemed to me inevitable someone would. I don't think she will object to my advising that you proceed on your own, keeping meals as simple as possible and allowing for flexibility on when they are served. I've frequently observed that in times of trouble people either can't face eating at all, or feel the need to do so at irregular times.'

Mrs Tressler broke off as Miss Bradley entered the kitchen with the little golden Labrador in tow on a lead. He was unusually subdued. Did he sense something seriously amiss, or had he decided to mend his ways? Something in the atmosphere had changed in an instant. In response, Florence experienced a numbing calm that would remain with her most of the day. These two women, she thought – much as if observing people standing at a bus stop – were not comfortable with each other. Their eyes barely met and no other exchange was made before Mrs Tressler excused herself on the grounds that what she had come for had been accomplished, and left the kitchen.

'Oh, dear,' Miss Bradley's face puckered, 'I hope she didn't rush away on my account, for fear of breaking down again if I mentioned dear Lillian's name, I mean.'

She had, thought Florence, a pleasant, melodious voice. Men, with the exception of Ned, might find it particularly attractive. With her dark hair and eyes, coupled with a fine complexion, she could have made so much more of herself. Did Ned believe she'd determinedly played the dowd at Mullings, the better to ingratiate herself? Was that at the root of his dislike? Ned's image brought on an icy trickle of fear. His having taken up Lady Stodmarsh's milk was bound to put him at the top of the suspect list in some minds if she were to talk of murder. Florence, who enjoyed detective novels along with her other reading, could hear an official voice stating:

'About that conversation you had with young Mr Stodmarsh on returning from your outing – you acknowledge that he wasn't his usual chipper self and that he expressed concern about your friendship with the pub keeper. Not happy about the idea of it leading to marriage, thus causing you to leave Mullings, was he? We've heard from the cook and others how devoted he's been to you – to the point of dependency, it could be said – but were his grandmother to die suddenly you'd have found it hard to leave him;

136

especially if he played his cards right, and lads at that age have all kinds of them up their sleeves. You do see where this is leading us, Mrs Norris? The opportunity arises and he jumps at it...'

Florence could not have missed much of what had been said between Miss Bradley and Mrs McDonald whilst her mind was elsewhere. The topic remained the same. Not surprisingly so, if Ned had not exaggerated Miss Bradley's long-windedness.

'Now don't you keep worrying about inter-rupting,' Mrs McDonald remained in full bol-stering mode. 'I'm not stretching a ha'pence of truth about Mrs Tressler being on the instant of leaving when you came in.'

'I can't help wondering how she'll hold up. She's not a young woman and she may have been bravely holding it in all week that she has the toothache. I've thought so a couple of times, just a little giveaway now and then – you know how nagging pain can alter one's features, and there's that appointment with her dentist for today that she'll now have to cancel. The strain has already taken its toll on Mrs William, pros-trated with a migraine. I do hope she has some-thing stronger than aspirin to take for it. If not, I have some tablets that might help, a calmative prescribed for me when I had my ... upset. I think I may once have mentioned having them to her when she looked at the end of her tether for one reason or another.' As a euphemism for *Mr William* this did well enough, but Florence sensed Mrs McDonald, however supportive of

Miss Bradley she might be, was beginning to wish on her a sudden attack of laryngitis if she didn't at long last state why she had come to the kitchen.

'Oh, dearie me, Miss Bradley!' the cook burst out.

'What is it we can do for you?' Florence added in her most encouraging manner.

'Oh, yes! That! I have been going on, haven't I? A fault of mine, I know. And this morning there's the shock.'

'Of course.'

Miss Bradley looked down. 'It's about the puppy. Will you kindly find something for him to eat?'

Grumidge's bracing voice, along with burbled responses from the recipients of his instructions, could now be heard from the passageway that housed the butler's pantry at one end and the scullery at the other. Time became increasingly of the essence.

'Why didn't I realize straight off that's what brought you here?' Mrs McDonald shook her head at her own dimwittedness. Just then the bundle of golden Lab began to sniff around the floor in a distinctly obvious way. 'Of course I'll fill up a bowl for him; there's some nice cold lamb I could chop up and mix with gravy, but, not to be impertinent, I hope, first things first. If you'll give me his lead, Miss Bradley, I'll get him outside before he has an accident.'

'Thank you. I do hate being a nuisance.'

There had been movement in the passageway which ceased when Miss Bradley spoke. Flor-

138

ence would have preferred to have taken the dog out herself, to have drawn in the outdoor air, but Mrs McDonald was also in need of its reviving benefits. Once back it wouldn't take her a moment to provide the puppy with a meal and water.

'I truly try never to overstep, Mrs Norris,' said Miss Bradley when she and Florence were alone. 'The difficulty is the thin line between that and helping. Or don't you agree?'

'Of course I do.' Florence gave no sign of feeling rushed, despite knowing Grumidge would wish to discuss how they should best manage the situation, and other members of the staff were being kept waiting. Mrs Longbrow had drilled into her that futile impatience was not only a waste of time but often prolonged delay. It had also seeped in on Florence that allowing her thoughts to wander would do her no good, particularly at a moment such as this. In detective novels, the sleuth, professional or amateur, mentally zeroed in on even the most trivial of comments. There was always the possibility of a slip of the tongue by the killer, or of a telling incongruency brought to light by someone else. Even bystanders on the periphery of the murder could be invaluable. Again she thought of Annie Long.

'Lord Stodmarsh has seen to all the little fellow's needs since he came,' said Miss Bradley, startling Florence from her reverie, 'but at such a time as this he might forget, along with a good many other daily doings, as is also likely of his grandson, so I thought I could take this small

139

thing on; it would at least be something.'

'I think that very kind.'

'I do appreciate that coming from you, Mrs Norris.' The fine dark eyes brightened. 'Lady Stodmarsh often mentioned how thoughtful you are. Looking after the puppy for as long as needed will be as much for her as for Lord Stodmarsh. As you know, she gave it to him. The final gift between husband and wife. Oh, dear! I mustn't start weeping.'

'There has been a good deal of that and will be more,' said Florence gently.

'So far I've held off, other than some private tears. The last thing needed by those closer to her than I is for me to be in floods.'

'That takes admirable restraint.' It did indeed.

'She was so good to me in my time of need and beyond, as has been Lord Stodmarsh – undeservedly so, because I was never the best correspondent.' A spill of tears threatened. 'I remember there was a year when I forgot to send them a Christmas card. As a vicar's daughter I was brought up never to neglect the smallest gesture of goodwill. Others might rightfully have taken umbrage. Dearest Lillian! It's so desperately hard not to speak of her every other minute. I do know it doesn't help.'

'But so understandable,' said Florence.

'One of my failings is a tendency to prattle on, even when all is well.' She then proceeded to do so. 'If she had not stepped in when she did, after of course talking the matter over with Lord Stodmarsh and his generously agreeing to open their home to me, I don't know what would have become of me. You may well have heard, Mrs Norris, that I was left in very straitened circumstances. My dear father had no private means, nor did my late mother, and although we lived circumspectly on his remuneration there was little to put by...'

'I'm sorry.'

Molly had come into the kitchen and was clearly anxious for a word. Behind her came Mrs McDonald and the puppy, enabling Florence to excuse herself to Miss Bradley and go with Molly into the passageway.

'You said to let you know, Mrs Norris, as soon as Miss Johnson woke up, and she just opened her eyes. I plumped up her pillows and told her I'd fetch her up a cup of tea.'

'Thank you, Molly, please make it strong with lots of sugar. And bring a hot water bottle.' Florence glanced towards Grumidge, who was standing in the doorway of the butler's pantry where she imagined he had the rest of the indoor staff congregated. He came towards her, sombre but composed as always.

'Breaking the news to Miss Johnson will be difficult for you and deeply painful for her to hear, so do not feel rushed, Mrs Norris. If His Lordship requests an interview with us whilst you are with her, I will send word to you.'

Florence nodded. 'Miss Bradley came for the puppy to be fed and Mrs McDonald will be seeing to that now.'

On her way up the stairs she heard Grumidge speaking with encouraging warmth to Molly. Florence was ashamed of having set Miss Johnson aside in her mind during the last half hour or so, but even so, her mind darted back to Mrs Tressler and Miss Bradley. They had both had solid reasons for coming into the kitchen, but had there been alternative motives in play? The desire to confide, or size up the moods of herself and Mrs McDonald?

The old lady's bedroom was midway along the hallway, two down from Lady Stodmarsh's room, beyond which was the one occupied by His Lordship. Florence opened Miss Johnson's door to see her lying listlessly under the bedclothes, only the meagre iron-gray hair providing any suggestion of colour to her pallid countenance. The ensuing conversation was every bit as distressing as Florence had feared. Miss Johnson did not break down, she was far too weak for that, but her face contorted and she started to shiver and then tremble. Florence sat on the edge of the bed, placed a hand on the two twitching ones, and continued to speak soothingly until Molly appeared with tea and the hot water bottle.

'Would you mind staying on with her for a while?' she whispered to the girl. 'I'm going to telephone Doctor Chester. Perhaps he'll give her something.'

Molly nodded.

On her return to the back stairs, Florence halted on hearing Mr William's voice coming from his wife's bedroom. Compared to his frequent roar, it was not much above a growl, but was so charged with rage as to make it audible to someone with less keen hearing than Florence.

She knew she should have crept on, but she couldn't ... didn't. The words were too startling.

'So are you happy at last, having killed my mother?'

'We'll talk about it later, when I don't have a headache.' That was Mrs William, whose deep voice possessed carrying power without needing to be raised. No hint of outrage, merely a matter-of-fact statement.

'Headache! I wish to hell I'd given it to you!'

'You did, dear.'

'I meant with a sledge hammer, you blasted fool! I knew what you were about the moment you followed her upstairs.'

'You're right, William. And please don't work yourself up further when I say it makes a change. I did want a confidential chat with your mother. I thought the moment right for it, but I was wrong. She was clearly preoccupied. Therefore, all I did was apologize for the evening having gone so badly, then left.'

'So you say! I still have it you killed her!'

'As you wish, dear. I don't understand, not having much of a brain – as you've told me often enough – why you should object if I did. You were never particularly fond of her. I've some-times thought the only tears you would shed if not only she but your father and Ned were put underground would be crocodile ones.'

'That's outrageous!' Mr William was heard to splutter.

His wife's response came soothingly. 'Had you been born the older son you might have been quite good-tempered.'

'Don't pretend with only me here, Gertrude, you've always wanted to be mistress of this house.'

'Only since Madge Bradley has been here. She annoys me, as she does Ned, with her endless desire to please. Or, as I see it, her usurping ways. Had I any say she'd have been gone.'

'Hang it, I should have left *you* at the altar!'

'Yes, William. We have never been happy, but now I must continue to resign myself.'

Florence dragged herself away from the bedroom door. She wondered about that *now* as she sped silently forward. Had Gertrude Stodmarsh used it in relation to her mother-in-law's death? If so, why had that in any way altered matters? As she headed down the back stairs, Mr William's accusation still rang in Florence's ears. Surely he hadn't meant it literally about her killing his mother; it had to be that the shock of some ... revelation, perhaps, had done so. Or was that wishful thinking, because it did not fit with the mosaic Florence had pieced together?

The following hour passed rapidly with not a moment to spare for introspection. She told Grumidge how she had found Miss Johnson. He agreed with her that the doctor should be fetched and saw no reason to bother His Lordship, or any other member of the family, by consulting with him beforehand, as Master Ned had instructed that seeing to her wellbeing was important to him. Doctor Chester arrived five minutes before Lord Stodmarsh requested Florence and Grumidge join him in his book-lined study.

'My wife held you both in the highest estimation.' His eyes lingered fractionally on Florence's face.

'We, along with all the other members of the staff, could not have hoped for a finer mistress.' It was Grumidge's voice that cracked. Florence wanted to say, 'I loved her.' Bereft of other words, she nodded.

'Thank you.' His Lordship's purpose in summoning them was to iterate that he relied with the utmost confidence on their keeping the house running as smoothly as possible. He would inform them of any alterations in the daily routine and their involvement in the funeral arrangements. Florence was just mentioning that Doctor Chester was with Miss Johnson in hope of easing her through the shock, when Ned entered the study.

'Jolly good, Florie.' He aimed an approving look at her. 'I told you, didn't I, Grandfather, she would see to Johnson's care.'

'So you did and it's much appreciated, Mrs Norris. Please let me know what Chester has to say.'

'Of course.'

'My wife and she were devoted to each other.' His Lordship attempted a smile. 'Lady Stodmarsh frequently said Johnson would have slain dragons for her.'

Alas, thought Florence, she hadn't been around, not actively so, when protection was most necessary. Would it have made a difference? Would she have perceived the need to do battle in time?

145

It was back to their responsibilities for her and Grumidge. They encountered Doctor Chester in the hall on his way out of the house.

'Good to catch the two of you,' he spoke with his customary good-tempered briskness, 'although I left word with Mrs McDonald that I'd given the old lady a sedative, which can be repeated every eight hours. She should sleep much of the time, but I do advise someone remaining with her. She's a sensible girl, that Molly, but another would do. I don't wish to bother Lord Stodmarsh further. Such a great loss – they were a devoted couple. Good day, if it can be called that.' With that he headed out through the front door.

'I think,' Florence said to Grumidge as they headed back to the staff quarters, 'that it would be best to let Molly return to her regular duties and for Annie Long to sit with Miss Johnson. Given that she's such a nervy type in general, and as Mrs McDonald doesn't think there'll be much work out of her today, I believe that would be putting Annie to the best use.'

'It's your decision, of course, Mrs Norris, but what if she panics at some outcry from Miss Johnson, for instance, and upsets her still further?'

'There is that possibility,' Florence returned Grumidge's keen-eyed look, 'but I'll check to make sure that Doctor Chester's sedative appears to be working, and Miss Johnson is sleeping peacefully, when I take Annie up there. I'll tell her that as soon as she sees a hint of waking she is to leave the room immediately and fetch

146

me. She has her weakness, but she is an obedient girl. I'm prepared to count on her not letting us down.'

'Then you have my support, not that you need it, on this. And as you say, Molly will be very much needed elsewhere.'

It crossed Florence's mind, even with everything else she had on it, that Mrs McDonald might not have been imagining things when she'd said there seemed to be a growing fondness between the butler and the head housemaid. She then thought about her other reason for wanting a private conversation with Annie Long.

When the staff sat down to their breakfast, after the meal above stairs had been served, Florence as usual sat in the chair at the opposite end of the table from the one normally occupied by Grumidge. Today he had chosen to settle for tea and toast in his office. Mrs McDonald took his place, saying, 'I'll be more than glad of the extra roominess provided by having no one to right or left. Though if I haven't lost a stone and a half within the last few hours it's a wonder!' Her sigh was followed by an inspection of the row of faces on either side of the table, which included, in addition to the maids, the young footman named Len, the chauffeur, and one of the under gardeners. 'But there's not a whit of good in fading away, is there, Mrs Norris?'

'No,' agreed Florence, noting that Annie was quivering, 'we each need every ounce of strength we can muster.'

Platters of sausages, bacon, fried bread and grilled tomatoes were being passed around.

Despite the savoury wisps of steam, the only two to fill their plates were Len, who though a bean-pole of six foot always tucked in well, and Jeanie, the other kitchen maid, who was not usually a big eater. Pretty and pert, she tended to enjoy bringing eyes her way, especially Len's and those of the good-looking under gardener. 'I know it's terribly sad and all that about the mistress,' she said, 'but it's not like any of us has lost our mum, is it? Yes, she was nice, but when it comes down to it, we work for the family; they're not our nearest and dearest. Suit your-selves; I'm not walking around all bloomin' day with a long face.' To prove the point, Jeanie pinched a slice of fried bread from Len's plate and followed this up with a wink.

Molly shook her head.

'That's enough, Jeanie,' said Florence mildly.

'Not to be rude, Mrs Norris, but I don't see why. In this day and age we've all the right to our opinions.'

'Not in my kitchen, you don't, Miss Cheeky!' Mrs McDonald shot back.

Emboldened by a grin from the under garden-er, Jeanie tossed her head. 'What us girls in service need to bring us out of the Dark Ages is unions looking out for us. Still, it won't bother me none getting the sack; though it'd be cutting off noses before the funeral.'

Florence chose to ignore her, rather than em-bolden her further. It would be better to take her aside later for an instructive chat. No point in wasting breath when Jeanie had the impetus of playing to an audience. Also, she might not be as

148

callous as she sounded. People reacted differently to death, and putting on a mask of bravado would be typical of Jeanie, who hated being thought of as soft. What she always had in her favour was that, like Annie, she was a hard worker. Florence was pretty sure on looking down the table that Mrs McDonald had worked her thoughts round in the same direction as her own.

It was Annie who spoke now, barely above a whisper. 'Lady Stodmarsh wasn't really old. My great-gran lived to be ninety-three.'

'Boastful, aren't we?' Jeanie giggled maliciously.

'Just talking kindly, which doesn't come easy for some,' returned Molly.

Jeanie looked expectantly at Len. 'It would only be boastful,' he said with blatantly assumed meekness, 'if Annie was to say that her great-gran reached her *grand* old age without an ache or pain in her life, and if she hadn't copped it when cycling up a mountain racing for England she'd still be with us.'

'Oh, let's not get silly! At least give her corns,' Jeanie chirped back.

Annie's eyes blurred and her voice cracked. 'She did have 'em. She suffered something cruel with her feet.'

'Just goes to show, death can strike from head to toe.' Before the under gardener had finished smirking, Florence rose from her chair and walked around the table to help Annie out of hers.

'Would you like me to lead the rest in prayer

149

while you're gone?' Mrs McDonald asked solemnly. ''Cos I daren't think what the vicar would be thinking if he was here to hear such catty talk. Though I'm sure we can count on him arriving to comfort the bereaved before the day's out.'

This was one thing of which Florence had no doubts. The Reverend Pimcrisp, an occasional guest at Mullings, had always appeared to hold Lord and Lady Stodmarsh in less dubious regard than he did his other parishioners. She did not think this was accounted for by their position in Dovecote Hatch. Even so, given his lugubrious view that ninety-nine out of a hundred were destined for the pit because of some slip-up noted and underlined by a heavenly scribe, Mr Pimcrisp would inevitably sprinkle some pessimism as to Lady Stodmarsh's chances along with his crumbs of solace.

In the housekeeper's room, Florence drew out a chair for Annie and settled her in it before turning the one at the desk around to face her and sitting down herself. From her pocket she produced an unused handkerchief. 'Wipe your eyes, dear, and take some slow, deep breaths.'

Annie did as bidden. She made a pathetic picture with her anaemic face blotched and her lank hair escaping from its pins, but the quivering lessened after a couple of minutes and the sobs reduced to the occasional sniff. Florence felt fairly secure in proceeding.

'It's perfectly understandable you should break down, Annie, what with the bad news and Jeanie being so unkind just now. I promise to

150

deal with her.'

'Oh, please don't go after her, Mrs Norris.' Annie clutched the damp hanky in her lap with thin, reddened hands. 'She didn't mean no harm, 'tis just her way, and I wouldn't want no falling out. Sometimes I wish I'd a bit of her spunk. Can't blame her and the others – 'cept Molly, she's different – for thinking me weak as water. 'Tis me own fault. 'Tisn't like I'm the only one got a shock this morning.'

'One of the things I've always admired about you,' said Florence bracingly, 'is that attitude.' Annie sat up a little straighter. 'But in this case your situation was different from the rest of us and that's because of the bad fright you had last night while preparing Lady Stodmarsh's hot milk. Something about a mouse, Mrs McDonald told me, though she couldn't get all you were saying because her ears weren't feeling right.'

'It weren't her fault. It were me. I'd bin struck of a heap, being terrified of them like I am, and couldn't put two words together that wasn't all of a jumble.'

'Did you see a mouse?'

'No, but when someone comes in and says ... but again, I don't want to make no excuses...'

'Especially if that someone was a member of the family.'

'I didn't mean to let that slip to Mrs Mc-Donald.' Annie twisted the hanky.

'Of course not. What was your immediate reaction on hearing the word mouse?'

'I screamed.'

'And then?'

151

'I turned to look.'

'As anyone would have done. I think the best way to put the incident behind you is to tell me the whole story.'

'But I don't want to sound like it was done intentional to scare me.'

'No one would think that.' Florence flinched inwardly at being deceitful. She also wondered if Annie's concern on this point suggested the unwelcome thought that she had been scared on purpose. That she suffered from her nerves did not make her incapable of thought or observation.

At the end of half an hour Florence had not only the name she had expected, but enough other information to make sense of what Mrs McDonald had gleaned, or misunderstood, from what Annie had managed to get out last night. After explaining about Miss Johnson, she took the considerably calmer girl up to sit with her, on the promise she would be relieved from this duty for her midday meal, and for briefer breaks when requested.

Later that morning, Florence managed to snare fifteen minutes to go up to her bedroom and write down, as precisely as she could remember, what Lady Stodmarsh had said to her last night. She then hid the folded sheet of paper in her handkerchief sachet.

The Dog and Whistle was packed that evening with villagers, desirous of a congregating point to talk about Lady Stodmarsh's death. The mood was one of sadness and shock. Far more was voiced than drunk, so George was not kept all that busy. He wasn't surprised at not hearing back from Florence. It couldn't be expected, run off her feet as she'd have been. He'd hear from her in good time. No bother there. What did bother him was that he hadn't been able to give her his support. She was a strong woman, no question, but that didn't mean she couldn't do with an arm round her at such a time. What he needed was the sight of her dear face, but it didn't do to hope for that before the funeral. Still, it helped to see Alf and Doris, who had joined her husband at the pub that evening. It was good to be with friends who were fond of Florence.

For all the talk about Lady Stodmarsh's death coming as such a bolt out of the blue, it never crossed the minds of any present that murder had struck Dovecote Hatch for the first time in living memory. Not even those of the two maiden ladies residing at Green Gates who checked under their beds every night with pokers in hand to make sure a man with evil intent wasn't hiding there.

Hilda Stark was the only person aside from Florence who thought that Lady Stodmarsh had been murdered. But, whereas Florence had reasons, Hilda fastened on the notion for no reason other than the malicious glee of the notion. What a comeuppance it would be for them at Mullings, all these years after she'd been turfed out on her ear, if it could've been that way. And why not? There was always murders happening in the better families ... too much time on their hands. Hilda had not darkened the doors of the Dog and

Whistle since the set-to with George over Madge Bradley. Sitting in her grubby bedsitter, she gave a cackle, then burped. Her drinking had only increased since being caught on the hop when she'd been nanny to that wretched child. She poured herself another gin. Who should she choose to have done it?

All that gabble she'd heard today about poor Lord Stodmarsh and how he was bound to be broke to pieces, brought on another cackle. From what she'd seen, those as seemed to take the death of a spouse worst recovered quickest. Especially when there was a hopeful party standing by, hand stuck out for a wedding ring! Over the past few months, Hilda had worked her way round to blaming Madge Bradley for George Bird having eyed her like she was muck just for saying how sad it must've been for the woman getting ditched at the altar, and she had come to positively ferment with hate for a woman she didn't know.

Another gin went down smooth as silk at the idea of Miss Bradley laying her plan to snatch at the chance for second time lucky by grabbing Lord Stodmarsh on the rebound – no matter that he must be all of thirty years her senior. Hilda was now well on her way to half believing Lady Stodmarsh had been bumped off. How wickedly lovely. 'Hee, hee!' She burped again as she pictured a ring-less hand stirring something that wasn't sugar into Lady Stodmarsh's bedtime cocoa ... no, remember, it was hot milk with bicarb. It didn't have to be Madge Bradley, though that was preferable. It would be almost as good if it were His Lordship himself, or, even sweeter, the mad grandmother who'd so handily come on a visit. That'd knock wretched Master Ned down a ladder of pegs. Better yet if he'd done it; less fun if it was Mr or Mrs William, but any of them would do. Her thoughts hiccupped towards Florence. What would it do to that tattle-telling witch if the police should start asking awkward questions? Here, Hilda had her best cackle of the night. She hated Florence Norris even more than she did Madge Bradley.

A week passed, during which Florence wrote to Gracie Norris and George. Gracie came over from Farn Deane, as invited, and spent an hour with her on the Thursday, but Florence did not suggest a meeting with George. Beyond expressing her appreciation for his concern, she focused on the possibility of overnight guests in the days ahead. As it happened, there were none beyond Mrs Tressler, who had been a mine of helpfulness not only making telephone calls and setting menus, but also in taking over the care of Miss Johnson. The old lady was not doing at all well. After one of his visits to her, Doctor Chester told Florence he did not expect her to linger long. If either Mrs William or Miss Bradley evinced resentment of Mrs Tressler asserting herself, nothing was heard of it below stairs. As for Mr William, Ned informed Florence he had been almost scarily subdued. Ned seemed to have garnered strength from being alert to his grandfather's every mood.

Lillian Stodmarsh's funeral took place on the

following Monday. The turnout would have surprised her modest sense of self. Even those from Dovecote Hatch who were barely ambulatory gathered to a tolling of bells in the rain-dripping churchyard with its ancient yews to witness the mistress of Mullings' coffin being lowered into the ground. Also present making an outing of it, thought Alf Thatcher sourly, there being some very pretty country thereabouts, were members of the Stafford-Reid and Blake families.

Sir Winthrop and Lady Blake were accompanied by their son, a young man who would have looked damply limp had the sky been bright blue and the sun beaming down. Their fourteen-year-old daughter Lamorna had remained at home with her governess. Not only was she deemed too young to witness life's grim culmination, it was unthinkable that she miss her lesson in deportment, a subject at which she excelled. Her ability to balance a book on her head whilst jumping a fence on her horse entirely negated the likelihood that she would ever learn to balance a check book. Where would be the need when she married into the nobility – an inevitability given her promise of astonishing beauty?

Enveloped in a happy daydream, Lady Blake barely glanced at His Lordship as Reverend Pimcrisp, in an irritatingly high-pitched voice, intoned that business of ashes to ashes, dust to dust and so on and so forth. Her husband was occupied smothering a yawn. Young Mr Gideon Blake was deep in contemplation of his next haircut ... a little longer in front would perhaps be desirable. Then again, did he wish it to drape over his right eyebrow, thus lessening the ability to raise it to amusing effect? Or were witty eyebrows not really the thing these days?

To most others, including George Bird in the suit he'd worn to his Mabel's funeral, Lord Stodmarsh appeared every one of his seventy-odd years. He stood flanked by his son, daughter-in-law, young grandson and Madge Bradley. The staff, outfitted in black, stood to their rear. Grumidge's keen eyes noted they all behaved with propriety. Any weeping, even that from Annie Long, was restrained. Florence was proud of them. On the return to the house, ahead of the family, it must be all speed ahead in making ready refreshments for the bereaved and the condolers.

Florence clasped her black-gloved hands tighter when she noticed George eyeing her with concern. She was both comforted and further saddened, having made the decision not to seek the benefit of his kindness and steady common sense. She had become surer by the day that it would be wrong to burden him with her suspicions. Strangely enough, it hadn't once occurred to her, even in her most stressed moments, to wonder what Robert would have advised. The memory of his funeral, however, came piercingly back to her now. The same churchyard, of course, and a similar rainy day. She had withstood his death and gone on, albeit with a heavy heart; as she must do now.

There had been times over the past week when she had allowed herself to wonder if Lady

Stodmarsh, driven by anxiety, might not have intentionally taken an overdose. Doctor Chester had checked her supply of tablets and found none unaccounted for, but that did not discount the possibility that she'd been able to lay her hands on others. Lady Stodmarsh had been a religious woman and as such would have believed taking her own life was a grievous sin, for which there could be no repentance. But, might not even the strongest of us reach a breaking point after years of physical suffering? And Lady Stodmarsh had been so very troubled that night – the hours when problems so often loom their largest.

Standing under a dripping elm, Florence looked from under her hat at a face that was probably as well concealed as her own, if only by the veil of rain. Then she looked at George, for what seemed like forever, although it was really just a sideways glance. She felt a distance opening up between them, and said a mental goodbye. Now that she had decided that it would be unfair to share her burden of suspicion with him, there could be no future for them – either of friendship or building towards a life together. In becoming surer than ever that the death of the woman she had liked and deeply admired wasn't from either natural causes or suicide, she had locked herself into a loneliness she never could have imagined in the depths of her grief for Robert.

Two days after the funeral she received the anonymous letter.

SIX

Florence happened to be in the kitchen when Alf Thatcher handed in the early morning post. 'One for you,' he said.

'Thanks, Alf,' she said, taking the batch.

'Looks like it come from a child. No return address; little 'uns always forget that. Anyways, right there on top.'

Florence automatically looked down. The cautiously printed pencil lettering on the envelope did not suggest a child's writing to her. She instantly guessed, with sickening trepidation, what was contained within.

'You all right?' Alf asked. 'Me and Doris has been worried about you. As for Birdie, he can't stay still five minutes, always shifting bottles around or buffing up glasses that's already got a shine on them you can see yourself in.'

'I'm doing very well, just extremely busy.'

'You must be, but any time you fancy a break, you and Birdie come round for a meal.' When she didn't respond immediately, he turned a little uncomfortable. 'Think about it anyways.'

'I will.'

'Best be off then.'

'Say hello to Doris for me.'

'Will do.' He hesitated, as if about to say

159

something else, before making for the door.

Florence was dimly aware that he was hurt, but her focus was elsewhere. She handed all but the letter addressed to her to Grumidge when she came across him in the passageway, and then sped into the housekeeper's room. On ripping open the envelope, she discovered she was right. On the coarse piece of lined notepaper, ripped unevenly from a pad, written with the same exaggerated care, were the words: 'WHICH ONE OF YOU DID IT?'

Unsigned, of course. Sinking down into her desk chair, she waited for her heartbeat to slow and her breathing to even out. To her mind there was no question who had sent it. Hilda Stark. She didn't think about being fair or the wrongness of prejudging the woman. Lady Stodmarsh had said long ago when Hilda was dismissed as Ned's nanny that the family had made an enemy for life. Who else in Dovecote Hatch bore a grudge against the family, sufficient to stoop this low? When occasionally passing Hilda on the village street in the years since she'd departed Mullings, Florence had felt an emanation of hatred, reaffirming her view that Lady Stodmarsh had hit the nail on the head. The opportunity for revenge might have taken a long time coming, but bitterness, when constantly stirred in the pot, made for the nastiest of brews.

Florence did not think Hilda Stark had been spurred to write those words because she really believed Lady Stodmarsh had been murdered. A polluted mind will wend itself down the darkest of roads without resorting to fact. It seemed far likelier Hilda had acted out of sheer malice upon the impetus of Lady Stodmarsh's sudden death. That, however, was really neither here nor there when it came to Florence's deciding what she should do, if anything, about the letter – if it could be called such.

Had it been delivered before the funeral, she was pretty sure she'd have felt compelled to take it to the police, which in Dovecote Hatch was Constable Trout, who currently spent much of his time helping old ladies across the road whether they wanted to go or not. The letter's impact was diabolically increased by the timing of its arrival. Florence felt sick picturing Hilda snickering to herself about this piece of cleverness. Turning the letter over to the authorities now could lead to an order to exhume the body. Regardless of whether or not anything substantive was found during the post-mortem, this would be an unspeakable ordeal for Lord Stodmarsh and Ned, as well as seriously unpleasant for all innocent parties concerned. There would be the initial scandal, followed inevitably in some quarters by murmurings of no smoke without fire. Evil, even from a twisted mind, can be exceedingly clever. It was not the first time in the last week and a half that Florence had faced that fact.

Hilda's malignant cunning was also apparent in the choice of wording. *WHICH ONE OF YOU DID IT?* could be construed to refer to any number of things other than murder, such as tossing a stone against her window to scare her. Was it Hilda's hope that panicked outrage at receiving such a message in clearly disguised handwriting would send Florence scurrying down to the police station, or that she would be left stewing? If the outcome were the former, and suspicion as to the sender was voiced, Hilda could deny the accusation, which was hard to prove, or admit to it on a trumped-up reason for doing so. Either way, from her sense of persecution she would surely spew forth her reasons for having been glad to see the back of Mullings ... one of which was that Florence was a lying backstabber deserving her comeuppance. If Mrs Norris had found the letter sinister, that was her choice.

Florence could picture Hilda looking Constable Trout squarely in the eyes, hear her hissing, *'I might be a drinker but I'm not the villain Mrs Norris was bent on making out. If there was some nasty business afoot, best to look no further than Mullings – where there was more than one sly customer that wasn't all they put out to be by half. And well that housekeeper of theirs knew it! Why all this muttering in the village that Lady Stodmarsh died awfully sudden if there weren't others that were thinking something wasn't right? And let's not forget Doctor Chester being on friendly terms with the family. Think he'd risk landing any of them within bells of the gallows by refusing to sign the death certificate? My Aunt Fanny, he would...'*

She tried to imagine Constable Trout's reaction to these insinuations. Would he send Hilda off with a flea in her ear? Or decide he wasn't worth his bicycle if he didn't press for more infor-

162

mation? Florence went down the list of people whom Hilda would name, in order to get it through Constable Trout's helmet there were motives aplenty for Lady Stodmarsh to have been murdered.

Miss Bradley had determined to escape the shame of being brutally jilted by getting His Lordship for a husband over his wife's dead body.

Mrs Tressler had suffered bouts of insanity, during one of which she'd believed her teeth were rotting in her head and her dog would attack and kill her. Word had gone round she had an appointment with her dentist and there was a new dog at Mullings.

Mr William Stodmarsh not only had an uncontrollable temper, as was generally known, but also hated his mother (and father) for having favoured their older son, the late Lionel Stodmarsh.

Mrs William Gertrude Stodmarsh was of an unnaturally repressed nature and was bound to fester with resentment at being treated like an unnecessary piece of furniture by the family. Also, a mother should know her son. Lady Stodmarsh had failed in her duty to have warned her against marrying William and ruining her life.

Florence's breath caught, causing her to sit like a block of unfinished sculpture, being chipped at unsparingly by a chisel. She could imagine Hilda's voice more clearly than ever: *'Lord Stodmarsh has, it's true, the reputation of being one of the finest men going, but who could say for sure that he'd not grown bone-weary of being*

163

tied to an invalid, when along came Miss Bradley? Her with all the advantage of being many years younger, and healthy to boot. Or perhaps he'd always had a fancy for Mrs Norris, who – you have to give it to her – pulled herself up from nothing with all that book reading.'

Florence continued to stand immobile. Yes, Hilda would leave no leaf unturned, before getting to Ned. *'Again, don't be taken in by what you think you see, Constable Trout. He never seemed to me what you could call normal. Don't forget I was nanny to him from when he was a baby till he was six. I've always thought the reason I was sent packing was because I'd got it figured out he wasn't right in the head. He was always flying into rages, like I heard his mother did in her time – and of course there's her mother – Mrs Tressler. You don't get put in insane asylums unless you're a danger to yourself or others. Go round the bend once or in her case twice, and it's not like it won't happen again. I suppose we should feel sorry for the boy – can't help what nature hands on, can we? His being so dependent on Mrs Norris strikes a number of people as very odd – still clinging to her apron strings like he's still six. Goodness knows what could've got into him if he got the idea she was about to up and leave Mullings, and there's been quite some talk about her and George Bird getting all lovey-dovey.'*

Florence kept coming back to Ned, and his taking up Lady Stodmarsh's hot milk that night. The police were bound to focus on motive and opportunity ... not necessarily in that order. Ned

164

had to be protected at all costs; he had suffered enough in his young life to be put through the wringer again. It would be different if there was one chance in a thousand he'd killed his grandmother – that she'd been mistaken about what she'd glimpsed in another pair of eyes; but she wasn't ... couldn't have been. But who would listen to her on this? Possibly Constable Trout, but not his superiors. Of course she'd assert roundly that Ned would never hurt a fly. The trouble was that people always said that about those they loved. Even when presented with the most damning evidence, loyalty had the ability to triumph over reason. And yet ... what about duty to society? What about allowing the wheels of justice to turn as they should?

Florence sat for a full five minutes before going up to her bedroom and hiding the letter in her handkerchief sachet, which already held the one George had written her and the notes she'd made of what Lady Stodmarsh had said – seemingly eons ago. It was silly to feel that Hilda Stark's spite was physically contaminating, but she couldn't help it.

It would be a mistake, she decided, to secrete the sachet away. Leaving it in the usual place should draw less attention to it than if it was concealed, should her room be searched, which she didn't think sufficiently likely to be much of a concern. It was impossible to know for sure, but she didn't think she'd given herself away, so as to pose a threat in the mind of the guilty party. Murder had to require some arrogance, and she hoped that, in this case, it would lead to complacency.

The remainder of the day passed slowly, despite all that had to be done. She should have been relieved that Annie was much restored emotionally, Jeanie was behaving herself and Mrs Tressler had let her know that Miss Johnson was no worse than she'd been yesterday; but she could not get the words *WHICH ONE OF YOU DID IT?* out of her head for more than a few minutes at a time. Grumidge asked her twice if she was feeling all right, and Mrs McDonald had her say when they sat down with their cups of tea before retiring for the night: 'You look wash-ed out, Mrs Norris. It's you Doctor Chester should be taking a look at when he next comes by. What you need is a tonic and a week's rest. Why don't you go and stay with that cousin of yours in London for a bit? The one you're so fond of, that takes in lodgers. Let her spoil you, like you deserve. She sounds just the sort for the job.'

'Hattie is a born caregiver – she took devoted care of her elderly parents until they died – but I don't think I could visit her right now, thanks all the same for the suggestion.' Florence stretched a smile. 'You're a kind woman, Mrs McDonald.'

Why hadn't she reached out to Hattie? she thought. The answer was both simple and fool-ish. The wish to unburden herself to George and trust her hands and heart to him had blocked out any thought of turning elsewhere for advice.

Nothing could quickly assuage the pain Florence felt at having put a distance between her and

George. She did this outside church after Sunday morning service. That this was where they had first met – just beyond the stone steps – was not lost on her; but continuing to deflect his attempts to get together without explanation would be cowardly and cruel. Three weeks had passed since the funeral, during which there had been no time for more than the briefest exchange. An explanation of her discourtesy since was well overdue. His sad-eyed but kindly acceptance of the one she produced only deepened her regret and remorse. Having too much on her plate at Mullings, along with involving herself more fully in her mother's life, to allow for much else, might sound reasonable in the short term, but was unconvincing as permanence. She'd walked back to Mullings wrapped in shame, her thoughts rarely straying from what he was doing and thinking.

An unsurprising result of her talk with George was the reproach she saw on Alf Thatcher's face during the coming week. Thereafter, whilst being as polite as ever, he made no attempt to have a chat if she were in the kitchen when he brought in the post. That his wife, Doris, equally resented Florence's treatment of their friend Birdie was apparent by her always being in a hurry if the two women crossed in the village street. At times Florence feared that the resilience life had instilled in her would fail her at this juncture, but mercifully it did not. She hoped and prayed the same would be true for George.

That her inward and outer composure did not

167

mesh quite so well as before was inevitable, since life at Mullings was irrevocably altered and remained suspect. She kept alert, as Hattie had suggested when she'd eventually been in touch with her, to what was going on within the family that might offer further enlightenment regarding Lady Stodmarsh's death. Nothing had been achieved there beyond the attempt. Life must and did move on. There was consolation gained by spending much of her off time visiting her mother. She was warmed by her sister Ada's open appreciation and grateful to her for not pressing, or allowing her husband and brother to do so, about what had really happened between Florence and George. That there was more to it than that both decided to pull back must have been clear.

'Well, he is so recently widowed,' said Ada after a moment's thought. 'Don't worry about the men – they know not to yap when I tell them to shut their traps. Me and you haven't been as close as we should've been over the years – I don't suppose either of us rightly knows why – but the time's come when I want to be there for you if needed.' She followed this with a sisterly hug that meant the world to Florence.

Miss Johnson, as predicted by Doctor Chester, had not outlived Lady Stodmarsh by many weeks, but he continued to visit Mullings frequently to keep his eye on Lord Stodmarsh. In July, at the doctor's suggestion, Ned – who had by then left school – urged his grandfather to get someone in to assist on a part-time basis with the estate records, at least until he himself could get a better hang of things. Receiving no protest, Ned telephoned Mr Shepherd, who'd been his headmaster at Westerbey prep school.

'I'd try Cyril Fritch,' was Mr Shepherd's response. 'Used to be a maths teacher, but unfortunately wasn't cut out for keeping control of a classroom, Mr Stodmarsh.'

'Ned, please; I only pretend to be old enough for long trousers.'

Mr Shepherd laughed. 'You may know of him. He works at Craddock's Antiquarian Bookshop – some selling but mostly bookkeeping. I know Craddock thinks highly of Fritch and my guess is he'd be glad of the added income. He lives with his widowed mother, who's said to go through money like water.'

'Thanks, Mr Shepherd. I'll give it a go.' Ned had encountered Cyril Fritch and had immediately sized him up as a twitching rabbit in rimless specs, but what did that matter if he could get his sums right every time – something that Ned himself failed to do more often than not?

'Talk to George Bird about him if you like – his godson attended Dartford Grammar, where Fritch taught.'

Ned decided against this part of Mr Shepherd's advice. He had lingering guilt over the part he might have played in Florence's severing her friendship with the pub keeper. She had assured him when he'd brought this up that nothing he'd said had led to her decision, but for once in his life he hadn't believed her.

In short course Cyril Fritch began working

three evenings a week in the capacity offered him. Ned acknowledged to Florence that for once he felt gratitude towards Madge Bradley for making it part of her zealous helpfulness to take the man under her wing – by frequently checking to see if there was anything he needed in the room set aside for him.

Lord Stodmarsh warmly assured both Ned and Cyril Fritch how much he appreciated the new assistance, but it became increasingly noted within and without Mullings that he walked more slowly and seemed to have shrunk in height as well as build. These days he rarely entered the Dog and Whistle. George, who, whilst putting a good face on it, had indeed been knocked sideways by the break between him and Florence, was deeply saddened by the change in His Lordship. Lord Stodmarsh's kindly smile was still there, he chatted attentively as always with those present, but the zest was gone.

Word went round Dovecote Hatch that Doctor Chester had ordered a tonic and a change of scene. Some good that'd do, was the general opinion. Pining, plain and simple, was what ailed His Lordship. This sentiment amused Hilda Stark, who cackled as she sat drinking by herself. 'Not a man alive couldn't play the role of broken-hearted widower, especially if he'd taken part in theatricals at Mullings when he was a youngster. But don't be so sure you'll be the one to get him, Miss Bradley.' Her merriment sent gin dribbling from her mouth. 'I still say you've got competition from Florence Norris. And if she winds up with a ring on her finger

170

you can bet your knickers there'll be another letter written all neat and tidy and put in the post.'

To anyone else in Dovecote Hatch, the possibility of Lord Stodmarsh ever again tying the knot with any woman on earth would have been more unthinkable than the man in the moon coming down a ladder into an allotment patch, or someone in their midst walking round free as air after committing a murder under their noses. It was enough of a surprise when a year to the month after his wife's death His Lordship finally gave into Doctor Chester's exhortations that he take a holiday.

'I'm delighted, of course,' Ned perched himself on the edge of Florence's desk, 'though I wish he'd let me go with him.'

'It's understandable he should wish for some time alone,' she answered.

'I know, but he's not at all himself, Florie. Something could happen without anyone there to look out for him.'

'Or he could come back looking and feeling much improved.' Florence smiled, though she had her own misgivings. This thinking, however, turned to optimism when what was intended as a fortnight in Weymouth stretched into a month. The reason, when it was revealed, would rock Mullings, above and below stairs, like a gale-force wind. Mrs McDonald would have to renounce all claims to have been gifted with second sight, because lie she couldn't, that she'd seen this coming.

On the evening of his return to Mullings, Lord

Stodmarsh did not immediately announce his news, since he knew it would likely destroy his family's appetite for dinner. In preparing for the announcement, his primary concern was for Ned. The dear boy would brace up, but the thought of causing him pain deeply troubled Lord Stodmarsh. William, he knew, would be sufficiently furious to burst a blood vessel. Gertrude would do her utmost to calm him and be congratulatory, whilst leaving to conjecture what lay beneath her controlled expression. Madge would be in the uncomfortable situation of knowing her response was immaterial to any but himself.

Nine o'clock. They were all now gathered in the drawing room, seated around one of two elegant fireplaces – unlighted due to the warmth of the early October evening. For all its splendid size and classic architecture, it was (as Florence had always thought) an essentially liveable room, divided front from rear by a wide archway, hung with the same ivory and green damask silk as both sets of curtains. Upholstery fabrics, Persian carpets and the patterned silk wall covering had all muted through the years to restful hues. A room that had aged as gracefully as a woman with the right bone structure and a serene disposition. Lillian ... she and the room had epitomized each other. Tonight he might have been in an unknown setting.

Lord Stodmarsh looked at the expectant faces turned towards him and made his announcement: he had become engaged. The woman in question, called Regina Stapleton, had been

172

staying at the same hotel as him. The other occupants of the room, seated in sofas and arm-chairs, shifted position and exchanged looks as if poked at by unravelled springs. The golden Labrador, Rouser, stirred from his nap and abandoned his basket to trot hesitantly here and there, as if wondering what contribution he could make to the conversation. Madge was the first to offer congratulations in her melodious voice. If she were stunned it did not show through her warm smile. She gave no hint that she might be wondering what this might mean to her future at Mullings. Ned gripped the arms of his chair and squeezed out something incomprehensible. Another attempt faired little better. His Lordship wordlessly conveyed his understanding.

There followed a long and intensely awkward silence – finally broken by William. His face blew out like a red balloon, clashing with hair faded over time from rust to yellow. His barrel chest heaved. 'Blast it all, Father,' he ejaculated, 'you've gone and lost your bloody marbles!'

His wife, every finger-waved gray hair in place, intervened stoically. 'It is a blessing, William, that Father is still able to get out of bed in the mornings after the year he's had; I see no call to be peevish that he wishes to get...'

She was rewarded with a snarl. 'Spare us your indelicacies, Gertrude!'

Her voice raised not a notch in response. 'I was going to say get on with his life, nothing outré in that, my dear.'

'He's not supposed to have one without Mother! The very idea is sacrilegious!' The outraged roar should have sent every ornament and candlestick in the room flying.

'But William,' Madge attempted bravely, 'surely dear Lillian would not have wished Cousin Edward to mourn forever?' She was silenced by an upflung hand.

'No one needs your opinion! If this is your idea of a joke, Father, I'm not chortling!' His mouth contorted like a gasping fish. 'Where's that fool Grumidge with the brandy?'

Ned strove to control his features. It would be too infantile, at seventeen and a half, to race off like a little kid in search of Florie. She would be there when this part was over. She was always there. He drew a shaky breath. There was no flinching from what she would tell him – that he should manfully support his grandfather's opportunity for renewed happiness. That for many being widowed was an incredibly lonely business. Just the imagined sound of her voice helped to steady Ned. Grandfather wasn't doing anything wrong. And it wasn't as if Grand-mother had died last week.

'I wish you both happiness, sir.' He sounded very nearly cheerful, and the shine in his green eyes could have been taken for happiness.

'Thank you, my boy.' Lord Stodmarsh looked at him with deep affection coupled with concern. His eyes then went to the chair that had been Lillian's; its short seat and straight back had made it easier for her to rise from. Had he not gone to Weymouth, he might now be conversing with her in his mind and heart, letting other conversations flow over him; but what was done

174

was done.

'Smarmy pipsqueak!' William tore at his moustache as if wishful of throwing it at Ned. 'Confound it all, Father! You must know that this winter romance of yours has come down like an avalanche.'

'Let's say a surprise, dear.' Gertrude did not flinch under yet another glare. It had been apparent to all but her husband that since her mother-in-law's death, any fear of him was gone. Beneath what she saw as socially required behaviour, her indifference was complete. 'If I have failed to congratulate you, Father, I do so now.'

'Thank you, my dear.'

The door opened and Grumidge entered with a decanter and glasses on a silver tray, which he deposited on a table between a pair of facing sofas. Upon his departure Lord Stodmarsh picked up the discourse. 'I understand this decision of mine will take a good deal of adjustment. My intended wife is a longtime widow, of similar age to myself. Her family, the Tamershams, have a place in Northumbria, to which she returned after her husband's death. Be assured that my feelings for her do not detract in any way from the love I bore my beloved lifetime companion.'

William snorted.

Lord Stodmarsh continued evenly, 'It is, however, my hope that Regina will be welcomed warmly into this household. The wedding will take place one month from now at her home church in the village of Larchmont Field, with only closest family members invited. My wish is

175

for the four of you to be present, but should any, or all, decide not to attend I will understand.'

'Blast it all, I'll have to think that over.' Despite his still-fiery face, William seemed to have calmed sufficiently to consider the pros and cons of what he was up against. He shot a demanding glance from under his bushy eyebrows at his wife.

She drew upon what she considered her one wifely requirement, which was to make them less odious as a couple. 'Of course William and I will be there, Father. This has to be about you and your wife-to-be. We wish you both many years of contentment. Don't we, my dear?'

William poured himself a sizeable brandy before muttering agreement. Then his temper again got the better of him. 'Regina! What a confounded silly name! Why not call her Queen Victoria and be done with it! I'll have you know, Father, this woman of yours had better not come queening it here if she knows what's good for her! Let her once tell me to rein in my temper and she'll regret it.'

'Now why would she do that, dear?' Gertrude inquired.

Ned addressed Lord Stodmarsh. 'I'll admit it took me a moment, Grandfather, but I'm all for it. Truly I am. Any chance of my being best man?'

Lord Stodmarsh's eyes moistened. 'Thank you, my boy, but that has to depend on whether William wishes...'

William's face flamed up again. 'By all means let him do the honors. I always knew where I

176

stood with Mother and you, Father. Bottom step of the ladder.'

'I'm very sorry you feel that way. It's untrue.'

William plowed a secondary path. 'Beats me why you should feel the need for female companionship when you've got Madge here, always ready and eager to play chess with you of an evening, or discuss some dull old book, without all the other rigmarole involved.'

Ned, seeing Madge's colour rise, gave her a sympathetic look and his uncle a withering one. She picked up her knitting, the back of a navy-blue cardigan, which she'd placed on a table next to her chair on coming into the drawing room, and eyed it carefully as if for a faulty stitch. Ned felt even more uncomfortable. 'How about a toast for the bride and groom?' he suggested and was relieved when she looked up and marshalled a smile.

Half an hour later the family dispersed for bed, leaving His Lordship uncertain whether or not the evening had gone as well as could be expected. He slept to dream neither of his late wife nor his bride-to-be, but of an ancient male personage with long, unkempt locks and beard, in a coarse robe and clutching a Bible in hands with nails grown into talons as he meandered through the woodlands at Mullings.

Florence had experienced such dreams in the past, but would never have thought anyone else in the household would have cause for such images to invade their sleeping state. She, Grumidge and Mrs McDonald had sensed strongly upon his return that something of a

177

changing sort had happened to His Lordship whilst he was in Weymouth, but were utterly in the dark as to what it might be. Even before Ned had left the drawing room, he had mastered his instinctive need to pour out his heart to his Florie. It was his grandfather's right to inform her and the rest of the staff that he was soon to remarry. To precede him would be betrayal. The dear old chap deserved better. Ned had gone upstairs feeling the mantle of adulthood settle around his shoulders. Oh, he'd cast it off frequently in the future – he'd be bound to. He had sufficient self-awareness to know he could be wilful and selfish at the drop of a hat, and there was little chance of that changing completely, but at least he had himself in check for now.

At seven the following morning His Lordship left the house by way of his study door for his customary early amble. He was grateful to have Rouser – Lillian's precious last gift – at his side as he stepped down from the terrace. The air was crisp under a pearl-gray sky, but he did not feel its invigorating benefit. To his right the end of the front drive merged into a flagged courtyard between the house and the former stables, converted some twenty years earlier into a garage. To his left lay the wood with its path providing access to and from the village. The unsettling dream still lingered.

Within a few yards of the terrace were twin sunken rose gardens with central fountains and statuary. Beyond these the expanse of velvet lawn was graced by several groupings of majestic oaks. With Rouser at his heels, Lord Stodmarsh made his way towards the summer house. Built of locally quarried stone, with an abundance of windows and French doors, it stood twenty yards from the ornamental lake now mirroring the pearl of the sky and the reflected tresses of weeping willows. To Lord Stodmarsh, there had always seemed to be a piercing poignancy to their leaning – as if what they sought to perceive, moment by moment, day after day, was some remnant of youthful freshness not ravaged by time and its inevitable sorrows. On the other side of the lake was a deep stretch of thicket, above which could be seen the top of a wall of the same faded rose brick as the house.

He stood, hesitating, at the entrance to the summer house. This had been Lillian's favourite retreat on summer days, from her arrival at Mullings as a bride until the walk down to it had become too laborious. Many a time he had joined her while she read or embroidered, seating himself across from her, the better to absorb her serenity, the lovely stillness that sometimes had made him wish he were a poet. Now his hand reached for the doorknob, but he couldn't bring himself to turn it. Instead he seated himself on a stone bench facing the lake. Rouser lay at his feet. How much closer the distant past seemed than his stay in Weymouth.

On the evening of his arrival at the hotel he had noticed an elegant, silver-haired woman in wine-coloured silk and pearls seated at a table across from him in the dining room. She too was alone, and had also chosen the turtle soup, followed by lamb cutlets. Her aura was one of indifference to her surroundings; dining alone had to be more awkward for women than men. She had his sympathy. Already he was regretting acceding to Doctor Chester's urging that he take a holiday.

The woman did not join the majority of the other guests – including himself – in the sitting room where coffee and liqueurs were served afterwards, nor did she appear at breakfast the next morning. She had not, however, departed the hotel. Upon returning from a walk that very much lacked Rouser, he went into the conservatory to find her seated with an unopened book on her lap. There being no one else present, he felt it encumbent upon him to ask if he might take the chair angled towards hers. In repose her narrow face with the aquiline nose looked stern – even hard, but she acquiesced with a softening of the eyes and mouth. Within moments of introducing themselves they were conversing.

'I noticed you in the dining room last night,' said Regina Stapleton forthrightly, 'and I thought, there is a man who rarely takes a walk without a dog at his heels.'

'Did you, indeed?'

'A retriever, or...' her dark brown eyes looked into his '...probably more a Labrador.'

He was intrigued. 'You are clearly gifted with omniscience. I have always had labs; my present one is a fine fellow named Rouser.'

The book she had with her was Shakespeare

180

and they agreed in preferring the comedies. His Lordship mentioned that he had played Prospero in a production of *The Tempest* he'd put on for the entertainment of family and friends at his home when a young man.

'Very amateurish,' he confessed.

'But what fun!' Hers was a richly deep voice. 'Do you attend the theatre much?'

'Haven't done in years. My wife's severe rheumatism made travelling difficult for her, and since her death a year ago I haven't had the inclination.'

Regina not only commiserated, but encouraged him to speak of his loss, expressing understanding, having been widowed herself.

'That, however, was a great many years ago. The grief never goes away, but one adjusts ... eventually. For you the pain must still be a constant ache.' Her voice soothed, invited, while her hands lay restfully on her lap.

It was so much easier to talk about it with a stranger. He hadn't realized how much he had needed to talk about Lillian without burdening those who also mourned her loss. Prior to parting they were on Christian name terms.

'At our ages there is no reason to be formal,' Regina said, her eyebrow arched.

'I agree.' He smiled.

From that day on Lord Stodmarsh had spent much of his time in Weymouth with Regina, sharing a table during meals and doing some leisurely sightseeing. She was not a strong walker, and without his cane, neither was he these days. The hotel recommended a man willing to drive them where they wished to go. On Regina's discovering that a local theatre was performing *As You Like It*, they attended a matinee performance and then decided on a day trip to London to see Bernard Shaw's *Pygmalion*.

It wasn't until the second week of their acquaintance that Regina Stapleton gave him an account of her personal history. She had previously told him only that she had returned to Cragstone, her family's ancestral home in Northumbria, following her widowhood. He had wondered at what had seemed a studied reticence, but that was now explained. They were again seated in the conservatory; none of the other chairs was occupied. Her story unfolded in her forthright way once started. Having been left virtually penniless by a profligate husband – dead at thirty from influenza – and with a baby daughter to support, she had been grateful for her brother and sister-in-law's generosity in offering to house them both.

Regina fingered the long strand of perfectly matched pearls. Their dainty size had the *jeune fille* look of having been given to her as a young girl. 'Unfortunately, Rupert, his wife and later their son, never let a chance slip of making us feel like a pair of burdensome dependents, whilst giving the impression to outsiders that we were one united family.'

'That must have been highly distressing to endure.' What a contrast, Lord Stodmarsh reflected, such behaviour was to Lillian's in warmly inviting and welcoming Madge Bradley,

182

who had been at a low point in life, to Mullings.

'It was harder on my daughter, Sylvia, than me. She was always a spirited girl and as the years passed she became rebellious as a result of being constantly criticized by her aunt.' Regina Stapleton's clasped hands tightened. 'At seventeen she ran off with the groom. All my efforts to trace them failed. Several months later she wrote to say she was pregnant and begged to be allowed to return to Cragstone. My brother, at his wife's urging, refused. I begged, to no avail. I sent money, but they had moved to other lodgings and the envelope was returned with its contents intact. The next news came from the former groom. She had died in childbirth, and the baby with her. It was, understandably, an embittered letter.'

Being a sensitive man, Lord Stodmarsh had to clear his throat before answering. 'I am most heartily sorry.'

'It was nearly twenty-five years ago.' Regina's eyes met his steadily. 'I have an annuity, sufficient to indulge myself in this holiday and other jollifications, but not nearly enough to enable me to set up my own household. His son, who inherited the estate, wishes me gone, but shrinks from the talk that would be occasioned by tossing me out on the world.' She drew in a breath. 'Forgive me, Edward, I must sound a querulous and exceedingly tiresome old woman.'

'Not a bit of it, I appreciate your confiding in me.' It was time for luncheon and he escorted her inside to what had become their table. The Dover sole was probably delicious, but His

183

Lordship was unaware of what he ate. His ready compassion was deeply stirred by the story of Regina's daughter, and her possibly avoidable death. His imagination presented him with a hovel and a half-witted old crone presiding over the birth. There was also Regina's present situation to be deplored. It distressed him profoundly that she must return to a life of dependency at Cragstone. A sigh escaped him. There was not a thing he could do to help, except by endeavouring to make her time in Weymouth as enjoyable as possible. He would extend his own stay, until her return to Northumbria.

'Are you missing your beloved Labrador, Edward?' The inquiry was a little wistful.

'No, my grandson Ned writes that they are providing each other with plenty of exercise. Why do you ask?' He was touched by her sensitivity.

'That sigh, just now.'

'I was thinking how quickly a holiday passes when in enjoyable company, and that I would like to stay on longer here,' he hesitated, 'if I would not be making a nuisance of myself.'

'Are you sure it might not be the other way round?' The look in the dark brown eyes was intent.

'My dear,' he replied earnestly, 'meeting you has brightened my life more than you can know.'

It did not cross his mind that he might have implied more than an appreciation of her company, that she might misconstrue that statement as a declaration of deeper feelings, leading up to a proposal of marriage. He was not a worldly

184

man; indeed, he was very much an innocent abroad in his present situation. Thoughts of anything more than friendship never entered his head. He liked Regina Stapleton, found time passed quickly in her company, and realized that what he'd initially taken for a hard edge to her expression was the determined compression of painful thoughts.

The subject changed, as they sipped their post-luncheon coffee, to the pleasure of listening to plays on the wireless on wintry evenings. It failed to occur to him that Regina might assume he was painting a permanently companionable portrait of the two of them ensconced in wing chairs, savouring a hearty blaze in the fireplace. His mind was otherwise occupied, considering various expeditions that might appeal to Regina during the remainder of their stay, including another London play or perhaps a concert.

It wasn't until the evening prior to each returning to their homes that he realized he had un-wittingly misled her. It was still light and they were seated in their usual places in the con-servatory. The sliver of moon was barely visible in the pale sky. Nearby branches rustled gently, and the air was permeated with the scent of woodsmoke and damp earthiness that always seemed to signal autumn. Edward was feeling the awkwardness preceding their adieux, sharp-ened by the possibility – indeed, the likelihood, of their not meeting again. He was now eager to be home, which brought a pang, verging on guilt, that she could not be feeling the same pleasurable anticipation.

'I shall miss you,' he said. Then, impulsively, 'It is my great wish that you should come to Mullings...' Before he could add, *on a visit so I can show you our countryside, which is regarded by many as delightful,* she forestalled him. Her look was both direct and steady, accompanied by her rather thin lips curving into a mischievous smile. He dared not allow himself to think of Lillian.

'I shall not flutter my hands and say, *this is so sudden,* because you must know I have been pleasurably anticipating you asking me to marry you, my very dear Edward; and, yes, I will be honoured to be your wife.'

His Lordship was staggered. It took a long moment for him to realize that this wasn't an unreasonable assumption on her part. The past month unfolded in his mind like a map, revealing all the little byways to this destination. He had unintentionally raised hopes that were now impossible for a gentleman to dash. Only a cad would do so. This being the case, was it such a bad outcome? Regina would be removed from a life of being housed under sufferance, and there could be benefits for members of his own family. He sometimes worried that Madge felt obliged to provide him with company to the extent of curtailing her own inclinations for relaxation. She was still a relatively young woman. She should be going on outings with people of a similar age to herself and enjoying the opportunity to pursue interests beyond discussing books and playing chess with him. His Lordship was very fond of Madge – considerably more so, regrettably, than he was of his daughter-in-law, Gertrude, admirable though he thought her in many ways, particularly in her sufferance of William's boorishness, for want of a better word. There was no condemnation sufficient, in His Lordship's view, for the man who had brutally abandoned Madge at the altar. It was unconscionable, as would be his subjecting Regina to humiliating rejection.

'Edward,' her deep voice sounded unaccustomedly hesitant, 'have I been precipitate? Have I made a pathetic fool of myself?'

'Absolutely not,' he responded resolutely, 'I have grown very fond of you during these past weeks and we have much in common.'

'Then I could not be happier at this moment.'

'That being the case, we must begin planning our future together.' He placed his hand on hers, its thinness and raised blue veins offset by the manicured nails. With that simple gesture the irrevocable commitment was made, as bindingly in his view as if accompanied by the wedding vows. He wondered if an observer would see their smiles as one. He hoped so; because from this time forward her happiness and peace of mind must be his primary concern. Not easy in a second marriage with a family to consider, but so it was written. With sensitivity and co-operative goodwill, a unity of thought and purpose could be achieved.

'Your going suddenly quiet just now worried me, my dear. Foolish, I know, but I am afraid my self-esteem has taken something of a battering over the years, causing me to doubt my personal value, especially to a man of your calibre.'

He stood and kissed her on the forehead before returning to his chair.'You have been surrounded by people unworthy of you, but this is a new start for both of us.' The attempt not to think of Lillian failed. Her face was there vividly behind his eyes and her beloved voice spoke to his heart from out of the past: 'We are so often frustrated in our desire to make the world a better place for the many who suffer, but we can make a difference for the better in the lives of some we are destined to meet.' That memory brought him a measure of peace. As if Regina read his mind, her eyes met his eyes squarely.

'There is something I have to say, Edward, which I hope will bring you ease of mind. That your feelings for me will never come near to equalling your love for your late wife is as it should be. It not only causes me no distress, but indeed heightens my estimation of you. My aspiration is that our union will be built on a different foundation, one of companionship, affection and shared interests. As for,' she paused, 'physical intimacy, I think it unnecessary at our time of life. Your not wishing for it, either from disinclination, or because it would cause you to feel like an adulterer, suits me very well. Even as a young woman, perhaps because of my husband's insensitivities in that direction, I never had much interest in that side of marriage. If I am wrong regarding your wishes, I do hope you will tell me so.'

It would not have done for His Lordship to respond that Regina had greatly relieved his

188

mind on this score, and that to have lain in the biblical sense with any woman other than Lillian would have seemed tantamount to adultery; he again reached for her hand, his expression warmly appreciative.

'I am very grateful for you being forthright and frank with me, Regina, and I am in full agreement that we have much beyond what would have been considered important in our youth to build upon.'

She sat looking thoughtful for several moments.

Concern showed on his face. 'Now you are the one to turn quiet. Is there something else you feel needs to be discussed?'

'Nothing monumental, but there is something else I would like to broach. It concerns a tradition that has existed in our family and a favour I hesitate to ask of you, yet I feel an obligation to do so.'

Lord Stodmarsh listened attentively and having heard her out agreed to the request. He did so out of an understanding of her feelings, which he thought admirably compassionate. And yet, he had recoiled from the image evoked – the one that had triggered his disturbing dream on the night of his return to Mullings. Now, on the following morning, he returned to the present to discover that he had grown physically chilled sitting on the stone bench by the summer house, and that his heart was still troubled.

With Rouser trotting at his heels, His Lordship returned to the house and partook of a solitary breakfast, the other family members not yet having risen. He then requested that Grumidge attend him in his study. After informing the butler of his impending marriage, he requested the news be disseminated to the rest of the staff. He sat alone for a half-hour in the leather chair behind his desk, the portrait of Lillian painted in the first year of their marriage facing him above the fireplace. Eventually, he pulled the bell rope to summon the housemaid. At her prompt appearance, he asked her to request Mrs Norris to come to the study to join him at her convenience.

Florence arrived within minutes. He rose and invited her to take the chair across from his before reseating himself. Looking at her, he found himself remembering the reed-thin girl she had been when she had first come to Mullings. There were now some threads of gray in her abundantly coiled hair, but to him she would always be in part the eagerly wistful Florie Wilks. A snippet of memory had come to him on his return journey to Dovecote Hatch. Sometime during her many years at Mullings she had mentioned her mother having been in service with a family in Northumbria which had continued an eccentric tradition, long after it had passed out of vogue. As with many attentive listeners, he had excellent retention of minute detail, and in this case it was the name of that family – Tamersham.

He invited Florence to sit down. 'Grumidge has given you the news, Mrs Norris?'

'Yes, Lord Stodmarsh.' She expressed her best wishes for his future happiness with no visible sign of the concern that made her glad to be sitting down.

Some of the foreboding Lord Stodmarsh had experienced since wakening ebbed away as he thanked her. They talked for several minutes about the obvious – that change was always unsettling initially, but he had every confidence she and Grumidge would ease the understandable anxieties of the staff, and, he concluded, 'ensure that my wife will be given a reception deserving of,' here he paused, due to a catch in his throat, 'of the new mistress of Mullings.'

'Have no worry, sir. Lady Stodmarsh will be accorded the warmest and most respectful of welcomes, and any alterations to the running of the house that she requests will be immediately instigated and adhered to without question.' Florence felt a twist of pain as she spoke. Added to the trepidation already assailing her, she had a strong sense that something had propelled him into this marriage that had little, if anything, to do with love.

'As I told Grumidge, no one amongst the staff need fear dismissal in a clean sweep.'

'That will relieve minds, sir.' Hands folded on her lap, Florence waited for His Lordship to continue. She could see he was bracing himself to tell her something he had not imparted to Grumidge. Discomfort was visible in his eyes. The urge to ease the words from him, as she would have done with Ned, must necessarily be stifled; doing so caused her insides to tighten.

Lord Stodmarsh reached for his pipe and studied it, as if hoping it might prove helpful, then laid it back down. Rarely, if ever, did he actually smoke it, but Florence thought it probable he was sorely tempted to do so at this moment. When he finally spoke he did so with awkward abruptness. 'Mrs Stapleton's maiden name was Tamersham.' His gaze met hers expectantly.

'I see.' This was indeed information to be assimilated. 'My mother's employers were Sir Peregrine and Lady Tamersham.'

'Mrs Stapleton's parents.'

Florence felt the finger of fate moving down her spine. 'Grumidge said your future wife was from a Northumberland family, but I didn't consider the possibility of it being the one my mother worked for. There are other, notable titled members of society in that part of the country – the Reverend Pimcrisp's cousin, Lord Asprey, for instance. The Tamershams – especially Her Ladyship – were very kind to my mother.'

'Yes, I remember your telling me so. I have very much enjoyed our conversations, unrelated to household affairs, over the years, Mrs Norris. And I know how much my wife valued your ones with her.' His Lordship shifted the inkwell on his desk. His discomfort appeared to increase sharply on drawing out his next utterance. 'I found your mother's tale of the family's idiosyncratic tradition intriguing and thought-provoking. Mrs Stapleton's brother, and only sibling, Sir Rupert Stapleton, recently informed her of changes he wishes to make to the estate, one of which distressed her deeply. It was in regard to ridding the property of the ornamental hermit. Never a practice she had favoured, but the idea of turning the old man out upon the world after being so long withdrawn would, she believed, be devastating for him.'

'Yes, it would seem very likely he'd have difficulty readapting.' Florence could not be unaware of what was coming. Everything within His Lordship's make-up must recoil from the demeaning, even sacrilegious usage of one's fellow man, by arrogant members of the upper class for the titillation of inane vanity. The result in this case bringing matters to a sorry pass for the equivalent of a cast-off trinket. 'Could Sir Rupert not have waited until...?'

Lord Stodmarsh answered her uncompleted thought. 'Mrs Stapleton begged her brother to allow the man to live out his days on the estate, but he refused, saying he was doing more than sufficient in providing him with a small pension.'

'May I assume, sir, he is to come here?'

'Mrs Stapleton felt impelled to make the request and I could not refuse.'

'Of course not,' Florence smiled in hope of cheering him, 'you are far too compassionate to deny the poor man the chance to continue living as he has done. His arrival will cause a stir in the village, but hopefully it will be of the nine days' wonder sort.'

Lord Stodmarsh nodded. 'I have utmost trust in the profound good nature of the locals, Mrs Norris, but word will inevitably spread well beyond Dovecote Hatch. How can such a personage inhabiting our grounds fail to attract attention from the curious and voyeuristic?'

'I agree, Lord Stodmarsh.' In Florence's view, some shopkeepers wouldn't mind at all, and it would also be good for business at the Dog and Whistle, but in the main locals would object, albeit silently, to the invasion, and she was sure George would be with them – hang the benefits.

'It seems to me, Mrs Norris, that a "No Trespassing" sign posted where the woodland pathway enters the village would not deter the determinedly curious, making it necessary to encircle that area with a wall. That does not sit well with me. It has always been accepted that we not only permit but encourage those living in Dovecote Hatch to take walks in the woods whenever they so desire. And then there is Alf Thatcher, who uses the pathway as a short cut when delivering the post.'

The sigh that escaped His Lordship wrung Florence's heart. 'What about a gate, sir, which could be unlocked with keys given to those of your – and the future Lady Stodmarsh's – choosing?'

'Thank you, Mrs Norris. An idea well worth considering.' He rallied determinedly. 'As to housing for the poor fellow, there is that hut used for storing fishing tackle close to where the stream broadens at the base of the big waterfall, and within a few yards of those two entwined trees that all the children – including Lionel and William, then Ned, and doubtless generations before them – have loved to climb. I will have the hut reconstructed and furnished to make as comfortable a dwelling for him as possible, with plenty of warm blankets and a stove for heat. Which of the maids to send out with his meal will, of course, be your decision. It should always be the same one, to provide constancy, especially important in this new environment.'

'I'll make sure to select the right girl.'

'May the newcomer find contentment here, Florie.' The old name slipped out unaware. 'Will you please convey to Grumidge what is to occur? I wanted to talk with you first because of your understanding of the nature of ornamental hermits and how they wend into the Tamersham heritage.' His Lordship rose from his chair. 'Thank you, Mrs Norris, for listening patiently.'

After leaving the study, Florence did not immediately seek out Grumidge but went into the housekeeper's room, closed the door softly behind her and sat down. She needed time alone. It had been obvious that Lord Stodmarsh was not happy about his forthcoming marriage, which strongly suggested he'd been manipulated into it, something that could only have been accomplished by a very wily woman – but if there had to be a new Lady Stodmarsh, wasn't it better that she should be one with all her wits about her? Florence stared unseeingly at her hands resting on the accounts book. Over the past few months she had begun to think she might have added two and two together and made six in regard to Lillian Stodmarsh's death, and sacrificed George in vain. She now prayed fervently that either this was the case, or that murder wouldn't strike at Mullings again.

SEVEN

At the Dog and Whistle that evening the regulars could talk of nothing other than Lord Stodmarsh returning from Weymouth as a newly engaged man. Once past the initial shock, George Bird's thoughts concentrated on Florence, as conversations buzzed around him. What would she make of His Lordship marrying again? Was she worrying that the new Lady Stodmarsh would insist on changes that would turn Mullings inside out?

Despite the passage of time since Florence had severed ties between them, a day rarely went by when George didn't think of her and hope she was getting along all right. He still had his little chats with his departed wife Mabel, but these didn't bring the comfort they once had; instead they brought home to him the depth of his loneliness. Far from a conceited man, he'd believed Florence had grown fond of him. So what had happened? Her explanation hadn't rung true. He could still picture her face; it had been etched with anxiety.

Had she guessed on the drive back from her mother's home that he'd come to love her and, not being able to reciprocate, decided the kindest thing possible was cutting off any hope of a

shared future? If it wasn't that, was there something else wrong in her life, some trouble at
Mullings that she felt obliged to keep strictly to
herself, but feared might leak out if they continued seeing each other? Or had one of the
Stodmarshes been headed for a breakdown, or
someone turned nasty after Lady Stodmarsh's
death because they didn't think they were
getting their due from the will? It could be any
of a dozen things. It didn't do to keep dwelling
on questions without answers. By the end of the
first week after he'd received the blow, he'd
given himself a stern talking-to. A man of his
height and girth standing around looking pitiful
would make a joke of himself, and that would
wear thin fast with the customers. He'd straightened his back and shined up his smile. It wasn't
like he was the only one with heartache these
days.

His godson, Jim, had broken things off with
his young lady after facing up to the fact that it
could be years before he earned enough from his
paintings to provide for her in marriage. It
wasn't right to keep her dangling, missing out on
meeting a man who had no reason to delay proposing to her. His parents, Sally and Arthur,
made the big mistake of telling him they were
over the moon that he'd come to his senses. A
girl of that sort – with a silly name and a platinum streak in her hair – wasn't the daughter-in-
law for them. That she was the one for Jim didn't
come into it. He admitted in a letter to George
that he'd slammed out of their house and didn't
know when he'd want to see them again, if ever

– harsh words that told George the lad must be head-over-heels in love with the girl and heart-broken at feeling morally compelled to give her up.

Alf Thatcher's voice broke through the burble of overlapping conversations that evening at the Dog and Whistle. 'Well, Birdie,' he said, having elbowed his way up to the bar, 'if this isn't a right turn-up for the book, His Lordship marrying again, I don't know what is. Nobody's business but his own, of course.'

'Doesn't sound that way from in here.' George refilled Alf's glass with another half-pint. 'Can't expect anything else, of course, human nature being what it is, but what I say is – no good speculating on the whys and wherefores; best just to wish him and his intended well and leave it at that.'

Alf eyed him sharply. 'It doesn't go down well, does it, all this stuff about getting himself caught on the rebound?'

'You're right about that,' George's return look was appreciative, 'becoming a widower doesn't mean a man's senses have got to fall out of his ears, or that there's always a desperate woman out to bag him.'

'I know, I know, Birdie, never thought that about you an' Florence; all I said was I didn't like the way it turned out for you.' He lowered his voice. 'What bothers me with His Lordship is his health going downhill this past year. When you don't feel fit, it's not so easy to think clear, is it now?'

George had to give him that. 'That doesn't

mean his intended isn't a wonderful woman.'

'That's what me and Doris had been telling ourselves, till the vicar's housekeeper said something puzzling to her when they ran into each other doing the shopping this afternoon. She said Mr Pimcrisp turned white as a sheet when she broke the news to him at around eleven this morning. She'd taken him in a cup of tea as she always does at that time and his hand shook so bad he knocked the cup off his desk.'

George smiled. 'I don't see much odd in that. It's typical of the narrow-minded old geezer, I'd say, to think anyone marrying at over seventy should be ashamed of themselves – another sign of unclean living taking over mankind worse than ever.'

'That's what Doris thought, till the house-keeper said it was when she told the vicar the name of the wife-to-be and that she comes from Northumberland that he turned from disapproving to queer. She couldn't figure out why at first, then it dawned on her. Mr Pimcrisp's second or third cousin – whatever it is – Lord Asprey, also lives in Northumberland, and the two of them keep in touch by writing to each other once a month. The vicar's one worldly vanity, she told Doris, is being on fairly close terms with His Lordship. Not that we don't know that already from him dropping the name like pennies in the poorbox when he's bin in here with Lord Stod-marsh. It could be, she thought, that the two families – Lord Asprey's and the lady's in ques-tion – live quite close to each other and he'd heard something against her that he passed on to the vicar in one of his letters.' Alf stopped talking when other customers shifted up alongside him wanting refills. George saw to these, either briskly or leisurely depending on whether the customer wanted to chat or not. Then he waited for the tide to draw them back into the sea of general conversation, before picking up the threads of what the vicar's housekeeper had said to Alf's Doris.

George shook his balding head. 'A fat lot that means! According to Pimcrisp's strict bookkeeping, not getting out of bed till noon would be the deadly sin of sloth. And not going to church regular would be as bad as burning down every cathedral in England.'

'I know, I know, as do Doris, but she said that didn't stop a shiver go down her spine for fear His Lordship could be making a terrible mistake. When a man's good through and through, like he is, he don't always see what others do in a person.'

'Now then, Alf,' chided George, 'I know how well thought of Lady Stodmarsh was, and more than well deserved, but we've all got to give the new one a fair chance. Happen to know her name?' It was just something to say to weave his friend away from gloomy thoughts.

'Not her married one, her being a widow. It didn't stick with Doris if the housekeeper mentioned it, but the maiden one did, 'cos it put her in mind of them hats Scotchmen wear. You'll know the ones...'

'Tam-o'-shanters?'

'That's them! Give me a mo ... ah, got it!

Tamersham was the lady's maiden name.' Alf misread George's expression. 'I shouldn't have said anything even to you, Birdie. I know how you feel about people passing round rumours and the harm it causes nine times out o' ten. Haven't forgotten how you went at Hilda Stark that time she talked spiteful about Miss Bradley.'

'This isn't the same,' George reassured him, 'you've got His Lordship's interest at heart. She hates the lot of them up at Mullings and would gladly see them all hung, drawn and quartered. It was that name that surprised me. Florence's mother was in service in Northumbria with a family whose name was Tamersham before she wed.'

It was the first time in a long while that he'd brought up Florence's name when speaking to Alf, let alone anyone else. Alf was hailed away by the postmistress, leaving George to his own thoughts. Coincidences happened all the time and this one didn't seem sufficient to explain the prickle of superstitious discomfort he was feeling. Unless it came from remembering Florence's mother's fixed stare while talking about that strange business of the Tamershams' ornamental hermit. Each to his own, of course, and it didn't mean for a minute that His Lordship's future wife was cut from the same cloth as her arrogant forebears. Still, he wished her maiden name was anything but Tamersham.

At around the same time at Mullings, Mrs McDonald was renouncing all claims to be gifted

201

with second sight. 'I'm not saying I didn't have it once upon a time, Mrs Norris. Must have fallen out of my shopping bag somewhere along the road, though, because I certainly didn't see this coming.' Privacy was ensured by their being in the housekeeper's room; even so, Florence kept her voice low.

'No one could have, but that's neither here nor there. What's required of us and the rest of the staff is to be pleased for His Lordship and ready ourselves to smooth the household path for the new Lady Stodmarsh.'

'How do you think Master Ned's handling the surprise of it all?'

Florence smiled. 'Gallantly.'

Mrs McDonald's thoughts shifted to the vicar. 'I wonder if Mr Pimcrisp's nose will be put out of joint that it won't be him performing the ceremony?'

'I wouldn't think so; it's always the bride's privilege to be married from her own church.'

''Course it is, but like we all know, vicar's an odd duck, especially where women is concerned. Thinks their wants should be strictly rationed.' Mrs McDonald hesitated before going on. 'Speaking of him, and feel free to call me a gossip...'

'What about?'

'Something Jeanie told me. As you know, her aunt's housekeeper at the vicarage and the two of them met up for a chat in the village this afternoon, it being Jeanie's half-day off. Well, we all know the girl can't hold water. When she got back she told me something curious.' Mrs

McDonald proceeded to recount the story that had also been relayed to Doris Thatcher and passed on from Alf to George. 'Strange, him reacting that way to the mention of Mrs Stapleton's maiden name, don't you think, Mrs Norris?'

'As you just said, he's an odd duck,' replied Florence. Her thoughts were, however, not as vague as her voice. Mr Pimcrisp's cousinship to Lord Asprey had already figured in them. Wasn't it quite likely the vicar had mentioned in a letter that His Lordship would be taking a holiday for his health's sake in Weymouth and even mentioned dates he would be there and the name of the hotel? Here she drew in the reins. It was wrong, very wrong, to take this a step further and fabricate the possibility that Mrs Stapleton had got wind of His Lordship's plans and decided he might be a man worth pursuing with an aim to matrimony. That she might have manipulated the situation after meeting him by chance was one thing, but this other ... Florence closed the door firmly on such dark thinking. Her concentration must be on the hope that His Lordship would find contentment with his second wife, who'd turn out to be a lovely woman, eager to make Mullings a happier place. If only she need not bring with her the distraction of the ornamental hermit ... Florence could not believe His Lordship would ever fully adjust to the idea of a solitary man being out there in the woods.

The days passed and it seemed no time at all

before Lord Stodmarsh left with his family for Northumbria and returned after less than a week with his wife at his side. The ornamental hermit arrived some hours later, accompanied by Lady Stodmarsh's lady's maid in a car driven by the chauffeur. He was conducted by Lord Stodmarsh to the shed that was to be his new home near the great tree that Stodmarsh boys had climbed for at least a century. Regina Stodmarsh did not accompany them, saying she was too fatigued by the journey to do so. Florence, whilst thinking this a thin excuse, composedly took her up to the bedroom formerly belonging to Lillian Stodmarsh and expressed the wish to be entirely at her service.

'I hope we'll be able to deal together, Mrs Norris.' The black eyes took in every inch of Florence from top to toe. 'It will be preferable if things can go on as before, but I will not tolerate any member of the staff showing me the smallest lack of respect.'

'Quite rightly, madam.'

'I understand from Lord Stodmarsh that your mother was once in service to my family.'

'Yes, madam.'

'And you heard from her about our tradition of ornamental hermits. Do you have any views on the subject? Does it strike you as unpalatable?'

'If I did,' replied Florence, 'I would not allow it to permeate the attitudes of other members of the staff.'

'Have you selected someone to take him his meals?' Lady Stodmarsh fingered her long string of dainty pearls.

'Yes, Jeanie, one of the kitchen maids. The other one, Annie, is far too timid to venture anywhere near the edge of the woods, but has many excellent qualities.'

'I'll make my own assessments, Mrs Norris, but I appreciate your efforts on my behalf.' Regina Stodmarsh's mouth thinned into a smile. 'The flowers in here are very welcome.'

'Thank you, madam. Mrs William usually does the cutting and arranging, but with her away, Molly, the head housemaid, saw to them.'

'And very prettily – maybe she should take on that task in future.'

'If you'll forgive my saying so, Mrs William enjoys doing them.'

'We'll see. That's all for the moment, Mrs Norris.'

Florence headed downstairs with the thought tugging at her mind that Regina Stodmarsh was exactly the sort of woman to be murdered in books by one of half a dozen people with adequate motives. But that didn't mean another murder was destined under this roof. It would be too risky, she reminded herself, for a healthy-looking woman – and Lady Stodmarsh was that – to die shortly after arriving at Mullings. Her family might insist on a post-mortem. And Hilda Stark was bound to send another anonymous letter, possibly to the police this time. Not that the killer knew about the first one, but even so, wouldn't a sense of self-preservation come into play? She could only pray so.

To Florence's immense relief, the advent of the ornamental hermit turned out, as she had predicted, to be no more than a nine days' wonder for Dovecote Hatch, and Regina Stodmarsh did nothing immediately to disrupt life at Mullings. The only employee dismissed was the lady's maid she had brought with her; this because Her Ladyship had returned sooner than expected from a drive in the country and on going up to her bedroom caught the girl parading in front of the full-length mirror in her fur coat. A replacement was found and nothing said below stairs. Nor did Lady Stodmarsh attempt any lavish entertaining. Mr Pimcrisp was invited to dinner a couple of times and on both occasions declined with an acceptable excuse. Ned confided in Florence that whilst he had loathed the woman on sight, and received the distinct impression her relations were not overly fond of her, he had to admit she appeared the devoted wife, intent on putting her husband's needs above her own.

Madge, said Ned, was keeping a low profile, frequently leaving the drawing room after evening coffee to go and talk with Cyril Fritch in the room he occupied doing the bookkeeping. She meticulously left the door open when doing so and sometimes in walking past it Ned heard laughter from within – hers rather more often than Fritch's, but then he doubted the man had ever got in the habit of cheeriness, given the life he'd led with his carping, spendthrift mother. As for Uncle William, he seemed, according to Ned, to be holding his fire better than usual. Nothing, he added, was to be gained from trying to assess Aunt Gertrude's feelings towards her new mother-in-law. But he did think her recent announcement that she had attended a meeting of the Ladies' Church Guild and agreed to head the Altar Flowers Committee, suggested a need to escape Mullings for several hours at a time each week. No opinion of Lady Stodmarsh was voiced below stairs, even between Florence and Mrs McDonald; it was as though a seal had been placed on all lips, not by Grumidge, but by a warning hand. It was a telling silence.

Death did come to Mullings the following spring, but it was not Regina Stodmarsh it came to claim by fair means or foul. It arrived for His Lordship. There was no question of any but natural causes this time. Doctor Chester had suspected leukemia before the trip to Weymouth. Increasingly His Lordship's walking stick had become a necessity instead of an accoutrement, and he had come to spend much of his time in bed. Mullings was plunged once more into mourning.

When it came to the reading of the will, the prevailing atmosphere of grief and sorrow did not prevent fireworks from Mr William. The family had assembled to hear its contents from His Lordship's long-time solicitor, Mr Seymour Cleerly. Ned, when a child, had never heard the name without grinning. The widow responded sanguinely to Mr Cleerly's dry recitation of the terms. As well she might! William seethed, foam appearing at the corners of his mouth. Regina Stodmarsh was granted all control of interest from the estate until Ned reached the age of twenty-seven and the capital passed to him, at which time all other legatees would receive their individual bequests. However, if Regina pre-deceased Ned reaching his twenty-seventh birthday, then their inheritances would be released after her death.

'Monstrous! Talk about a slap in the face for me, his only living son!' Mr William bellowed. 'I'm to become this woman's pensioner? Damned if I don't take this to court! Knew my father had gone round the bloody bend when he married her! My sainted mother will be turning in her grave!'

'I do hope not, dear. So bad for the digestion, one would think,' responded his wife, 'and no bicarbonate of soda within reach.'

'Fool!'

Madge Bradley blenched at the roar; her face had paled in the last few minutes. 'It's understandable she was dismayed,' Ned said to Florence later. 'It can't be pleasant knowing she'll have to kowtow to Step-grandmother for as long as she's allowed to remain here. She could be booted out tomorrow. She'll get a nice sum when the time comes, but it wouldn't have occurred to Grandfather that she might not be welcome after his death.'

Mr Cleerly departed as soon as possible, stopping at the Dog and Whistle for a stiff brandy before catching a train back to London.

Within a couple of months Regina Stodmarsh had made arrangements to have the old horse paddock converted to a tennis court. This start made, she proceeded to put Mullings on the county's social map, with weekend parties that included the Blakes, Stafford-Reids and Pal-fretts. Far from shunning such invitations, they fell over themselves to attend. Ned raged inwardly at such inclusions. Hadn't all of them spurned the Stodmarshes for centuries? That, however, was before he, against conscience, fell breathlessly, blindly, as only the very young can, in love with the incredibly beautiful Lamorna Blake.

EIGHT

The prospect of a wedding is not invariably greeted with foreboding. A year and a half later, shortly after New Year in 1932, Dovecote Hatch was taken mildly by surprise, although generally pleasantly so, when Miss Madge Bradley's engagement to Cyril Fritch was announced in both *The Times* and the county newspaper. It might have been seen as an unlikely coupling in some circles, given the difference in their social positions: she a gentlewoman residing in spacious comfort at Mullings; he responsible for the bookkeeping at Craddock's Antiquarian Bookshop as well as the Stodmarsh estate a few evenings a week. Regina Stodmarsh had not countenanced Ned's request that he be employed full time. Mr Fritch lived with his widowed mother in a modest house in Tweed Lane around the corner from the Dog and Whistle, and although not creating much notice previously, he had been viewed sympathetically because of her dominating ways.

George Bird could have done with two extra pairs of hands at the Dog and Whistle on the evening after word spread. The regulars were more than ready for any good news from Mullings. The taproom, though packed to the elbows, was less smoky than usual because few were inclined to stop talking or listening long enough to fish in their pockets for pipes or cigarettes. There was much back and forthing over the odds of Lady Stodmarsh allowing Fritch to move in after the wedding.

Pulling yet another pint, George counted his blessings. It being winter when visitors were rare, he didn't have to waste time fobbing off questions from strangers about the ornamental hermit. George was pleased for Fritch. Who would have thought events would turn out so well for such a timid bloke? Things hadn't started well for him here – applying for a teaching job he didn't get and having to make do with one at Craddock's, which couldn't pay half as much.

George thought back to the letter Jim had written about his former grammar school teacher moving to the area and asking him to do what he could to befriend Fritch. He hadn't been successful in doing so – the man's painful shyness had prevented that – but all's well that ends well. It was nice for him and Miss Bradley, who deserved a second chance at love after going

through the pain and humiliation she had suffered. George's mind lingered on Jim between
every drink served and the accompanying chats.
The lad still hadn't achieved the degree of success he'd hoped for with his paintings, but his
financial situation had recently been relieved
somewhat. He'd been offered bed and board by
an elderly lady he'd got to know from her
coming into the restaurant where he worked. It
was no surprise that she'd taken to Jim in a big
way, him being such a kindly, pleasant lad. He'd
refused the offer at first – didn't like the idea of
scrounging off anyone, did Jim – but she'd
persuaded him she wanted the security of having
a man living in the house. This he could see,
especially when she mentioned having a nephew
always turning up and scrounging for money.
This was very different from Jim, who'd never
once hinted to George he could do with a spot of
cash or accepted help from his parents. It was a
right shame their attitude towards their son had
remained frosty since the tiff about the girl he'd
been seeing, when they'd branded her an arty,
immoral piece, without even having met her.
That was the trouble with people making their
offspring their entire world as Sally and Arthur
had done – they felt they were owed equal turn-
about down the road.

As still happened with George, Florence
slipped into mind. He remembered telling her
about Jim's romance, then in its early stage, on
the drive back from her mother's. This led him
to wondering if Miss Bradley's engagement to
Cyril Fritch had been a day brightener for her at

Mullings, which from many accounts was now a stressful place to work with Regina Stodmarsh ruling the roost.

Alf appeared at the bar. 'Give a ten-bob note I would, Birdie, to know how Hilda Stark's swallowing news of the engagement, her having had it in for Miss Bradley for no reason but kicking someone who's already down.'

'The woman could've turned a new leaf; she hasn't been around here in years,' said George. 'It doesn't do to hold grudges.'

Alf chuckled. 'Know what your trouble is, Birdie? You can't think ill of anyone for above five minutes. You need to take something for it.' He raised his glass. 'Here's to the engaged couple.'

'Happiest news coming out of Mullings in a long while,' agreed George wholeheartedly.

'I bet Fritch can breathe better after being strangled all his life by his mother's steel apron strings. My Doris sat next to the woman on the bus once and said she'd rather have been at the dentist's; nothing but bragging about the holidays she takes and the necessity of buying new clothes for every one of them. Then clapping on about having to live on a small income because of her son's lack of ambition.'

'Some mothers! Selfish, greedy old goat, that one,' struck in Tom Norris, now standing beside Alf, empty beer glass in hand. 'I don't see how she can afford all that gallivanting. Fritch couldn't have been making much a week when he was only working at the bookshop, and like as not it's been a case of catching up since he started doing

212

the bookkeeping for the estate.'

George refilled his glass. 'Could be his mother has means of her own, Tom. You never know what people have socked away.' He was back to thinking about Jim. He'd written that the elderly lady, who'd kindly taken him in, had told him that, though no one would have guessed it from her shabby old house in a run-down road, she was very comfortably off. She'd gladly have helped out her nephew if she hadn't sized him up way back as having a shifty, possibly criminal bent.

'Whatever happens to his money, it doesn't seem like he spends it on himself.' Tom spoke through a foam moustache. 'Never seen him in anything but that suit he wore when he first got here.'

'Abstemious fellow,' interposed Derwent Shepherd, who'd regretfully been unable to offer Cyril Fritch the teaching post at Westerbey for which he'd interviewed him. His long face, flattened hair and dedication to gray cardigans instantly brought blackboard chalk and desk inkwells to mind. 'Couldn't be happier for him and Miss Bradley.'

'Pity, though – her getting stuck with Mrs Fritch for a mother-in-law.' Alf was on his second half-pint.

'Can't see her going down well at Mullings. She'll only have to walk in decked out like mutton dressed up as lamb,' Tom shook his head as if dodging the image, 'then start in about her gadding off on one holiday after the next and Lady Stodmarsh'll make mincemeat of her.'

213

'I'm itching to know how she's taking the engagement,' said Alf.

'Who, Lady Stodmarsh?' asked Derwent Shepherd.

'Well, her too, but I meant Mrs Fritch. Will she be gnashing her teeth, even after taking them out at night, now that her son's finally flown the coop, or will she be tickled pink at the leg-up in society?'

'You have to be fair,' said George. 'It could be said he should have more backbone instead of letting her get away with keeping him under her thumb so long.'

'Easily said, if you haven't had your confidence stepped on a dozen times a day from childhood on,' answered Derwent Shepherd with his ready sympathy for the strugglers of this world.

George had to inwardly agree. If Cyril Fritch couldn't stand up to a classroom of schoolboys it was hardly likely he'd be a match for a ruthlessly controlling woman. 'Well,' he raised his own glass, 'let's drink to a happier future for the fellow. Anything going around as to when the wedding'll be?'

Tom offered what he knew. 'Got it from Master Ned – he won't have me call him Mr Stodmarsh – that it looks like to be a longish engagement, seeing his step-grandmother's made it clear she won't be offering him a roof over his head along with Miss Bradley when they marry.'

A Miss Milligan, with a face remarkably similar to those of the boxer dogs she bred and showed, paused in passing to interject her barking voice. 'Heard Fritch couldn't afford to buy her a ring, gave her the one that'd belonged to one of his grandmothers. It only has a diddly stone, but it's the thought that counts, isn't it?' Alf almost got jabbed in the eyes by the cigar Miss Milligan was brandishing. 'I've got wind of something else that could put a crimp in things. Old Craddock is thinking of selling the bookshop – he's still on the fence about it, but if he does and the new owner decides not to keep on the old staff, Fritch will be out of that job. Whoops! He told me that in confidence.'

Alf cupped an ear. 'Can't never hear a word when it's noisy in here.'

A mirthful woof came from Miss Milligan before she disappeared out of sight.

'There have to be changes,' said Tom, 'but nothing's been near the same since His Lordship died.'

Alf stared into the beer he'd forgotten he was holding. 'At least he's where he wanted to be, reunited with his lifetime love. Dear lady that she was. And he was ready, no doubt of that.' He cleared his throat. 'You could tell at a glance he knew he'd gone and made the mistake of his life marrying again. Enough said.'

A silence followed, to be broken by Derwent Shepherd. 'I hear young Ned is still taking a keen interest in Farn Deane?' This was received with a big smile from Tom.

'He tells me I couldn't keep him away with a pickaxe! You'd think farming was in his blood – that he was born to work the soil, mend fences, milk cows and shear sheep.'

'Is he interested in the business side?'

Tom nodded. 'Like you wouldn't believe, apart from the bookkeeping. I tell you, it's a big relief to me and Gracie. With us not having children we'd worried what would happen to Farn Deane when we're gone. Oh, it wouldn't be hard for the Stodmarshes to find another tenant farmer, but who'd ever love the old place like we've done, the Norrises' roots being so deep after all the generations living and working there? But now there's Master Ned.' He paused. 'Of course, as Gracie keeps reminding me, it could be partly him wanting to get away from Mullings every chance he gets, what with all the lunches, bridge parties, dinners and overnight guests going on there these days.'

'Wasn't never the Stodmarshes' way.' Alf shook his head glumly.

'Master Ned has to still be grieving his grandparents.' George wiped up a beer splatter. 'Bad enough being an orphan without losing them too.'

'Too much for any young 'un to have to handle.'

'He seems to be dealing with it, Alf,' replied Tom.

'I wasn't surprised when he decided against going up to university,' said Derwent. 'It's good to know he's found his niche. And maths never being his strong point, he made a wise decision in hiring Fritch to handle the records.'

Miss Milligan was heading towards the bar again with that glint in her eye that warned she

216

was about to enthuse about one of her boxer bitches being due to whelp and how thrilling it always was, unless something went wrong. She would list all the possibilities in minute, gory detail.

'Time to scarper!' Alf set down his glass. 'See you, Birdie!' Tom and Derwent Shepherd followed him out into the cold night.

Five minutes later the door opened and in came Ned Stodmarsh, stamping his feet, either to get the circulation going or to be rid of the dirt. The room had been thinning out for the past half hour, providing a straight line to the bar. He didn't drop by the Dog and Whistle often, but the regulars always hailed him with enthusiasm, to which he never failed to respond cheerfully.

'Join you in a moment,' he called over to the remaining cluster of villagers before greeting George. 'Busy night, Birdie?'

'Couldn't but be, sir, what with news of the engagement up at Mullings.'

'Suppose not,' Ned grinned. 'It's not the romance of the century, but we have to be glad for Madge. She has to have been living on tenterhooks since Grandfather died, afraid that Regina will send her packing if she opens her mouth the wrong way. Not that I think she would – she gets too much fun out of playing cat and mouse. It's her favourite occupation, with the rest of us too. She can't toss us out, but if there's a way to make Uncle William, Aunt Gertrude and myself chew nails she'll find it.'

'Is that so? What'll you be having, sir?'

'Half of cider. I tried beer, wanting to prove

myself the manly sort, but I don't much care for it.' Ned stood musing as George drew up a glass and shifted it towards him. 'I'm betting she'll live to a hundred for the sheer spite of it. She's already stopped Aunt Gertrude doing the flowers, knowing how much she enjoyed that one responsibility.' Another grin. 'I shouldn't be talking out of school. Florie wouldn't approve.'

'Is that so?' said George again.

'Florie's the one person I don't like to let down these days, but she's always known I'm no saint and she could only do so much to prepare me to follow in Grandfather's footsteps.'

'Done a fine job of it too, sir.'

'Her level best, certainly.'

'How is Mrs Norris?' George could not resist asking.

Ned eyed him awkwardly. 'As ever, the complete brick. If she and Grumidge didn't keep the house running on oiled wheels they'd have been gone, along with the half-dozen of lady's maids Regina's had during her reign at Mullings.' He stood musing. 'I think Florie was the only one who saw this engagement between Madge and Fritch coming. I like the chap, but couldn't have imagined him getting up the courage to pop the question. Have to believe it was the other way round and Madge did him the honour.'

'Nothing wrong with that, sir.'

'I do wish you'd stop sirring me.' Ned's fair, freckled skin flushed. 'I'd much prefer "Ned".' He hurried on before George could answer. 'Look, there's something I've been wanting to say for a long time – to offer an apology.'

'Whatever for?' George caught himself before adding the 'sir'.

'Making Florence feel she should, for my whiny sake, end her friendship with you. I'd got the idea, you see, that you'd want to marry her.'

George smoothed a hand over his bald spot. 'It takes two in agreement for a walk down the aisle.'

'Well, if you couldn't see how fond of you she'd grown, I could, and I didn't like the possibility of her leaving Mullings one bit. I let her know it when she got back from that outing you both took to her mother's, reminded her how she'd promised when I was little to remain as long as I needed her.' Ned looked a good way upward from his five-foot-seven to meet George's eyes squarely. 'It was a beastly trick to pull, but Florie had always been my backbone and I wasn't ready to grow one of my own.'

'It's good of you to tell me.' This would take some digesting. Was it enough to answer the question he'd asked himself so often? George wasn't so sure.

Ned thought he'd better change the subject. 'How's your godson getting along?'

George told him that a recent customer at the restaurant where Jim was a waiter had been impressed by a couple of framed watercolours on its dining room wall. He'd asked Jim for the artist's name, and on being told they were his work, had offered to show them to an acquaintance, who in turn agreed to host an exhibition if Jim could come up with a collection of equal merit within the next nine months.

'Good for him! You both must be chuffed.'

'Hopeful, but can't lose sight of disappointments in the past.'

'Forget them.' Before Ned could add anything to this, Miss Milligan surged up on him, cigar in hand. 'Good to see you, young man. What's this I've been hearing about you and the Blake girl getting cozy?'

Ned scowled, as he frequently did when embarrassed. 'We've been playing some tennis together, that's all. She's frightfully good and I've been keen since boarding school.' That being so, he'd still been furious on principle when his step-grandmother had the court built. He knew she had done so in an attempt – beyond the ornamental hermit, whose presence he found distasteful – to lure visitors of the sort she wished to entertain, none of whom had been interested in hobnobbing at Mullings in the past. He'd been determined to loathe all who showed up, but that had been impossible when it came to Lamorna Blake. After an initial coldness he was lost. How could any red-blooded male not feel his soul soar in her presence? The agony was the unlikelihood of her preferring him over his rivals – including the Palfrett and Stafford-Reid lads, who were forever cluttering up Mullings when she was there.

'Nothing more to it?' Miss Milligan woofed at him. 'Wonderful little pedigree! Best in the show, in these parts. Hook a lead on to her while you can, is my advice, young man.'

'Thank you,' Ned returned coldly. He decided

not to stay on for a chat with the regulars; they'd understand his need to escape the woman.

Florence hadn't needed to be told that Ned had succumbed to the heaven and hell of first love. It was written all over him from the first time Lamorna Blake had put in an appearance at Mullings, along with several other young people from society families. All of them, along with their parents, had never been within a mile of the place before, but Regina Stodmarsh had determined to put Mullings prominently on the map. Ned's casual mention that he was thinking about taking up riding had confirmed Florence's opinion that it was a serious case with him. He'd never before shown any interest in the sport, whilst Miss Blake was known as an excellent horsewoman, in addition to her enthusiasm for tennis, which Ned already shared. Florence wasn't sure whether to smile or worry. She thought the age of twenty was much too young for him to form a lasting relationship; but such bedazzlements so often blew over.

As for Miss Bradley's engagement to Mr Fritch, her thoughts were jumbled. Recognizing that it was going to happen had startled her. She couldn't believe it a love match, though on reflection it made sense as a convenient move for both of them. From what she saw of him, Mr Fritch seemed a decent man, but given his extreme shyness, none could have appeared more the confirmed bachelor. She hoped he would not come to rue his walk along the bridal path. Mrs McDonald had told her rumour had it his mother was going about telling anyone she could trap into listening how she'd never got over his abandoning her without a word of forewarning. Whether or not this was her entire thinking, Florence thought questionable. Being able to boast of her connection to Mullings should have some appeal for a woman who liked to crow. One thing was certain: she would never be given anything but the most sneering reception at Mullings by Lady Stodmarsh. Florence caught herself as she often did when thinking negatively about the lady of the house. What mattered above all was that no attempt on her life had been made, and it had come to seem increasingly unlikely given the passage of time. Florence's thoughts echoed with what Ned had said to her, as well as to George at the Dog and Whistle – Regina Stodmarsh seemed destined to live to be a hundred.

Mrs Fritch did indeed have mixed feelings about her son's engagement. It was shocking to have behaved in such a sneaky way, letting his own mother be caught on the hop along with all her acquaintances. So undutiful not to have asked her permission before broaching the subject to Miss Bradley – just what she could have expected from his father! The muddle-headedness of this did not occur to her. But following much righteous fuming, she began to see the advantages. Financially the union would be a godsend. From now on it would be Italy or the South of France for her holidays, instead of the British Isles. Whether Miss Bradley had funds of her own didn't matter overly. It was all around her at Mullings. Surely if Cyril had, since the move to Dovecote Hatch, managed at times to pull money out of thin air to do right by his mother, he should easily be able to persuade a wife into wangling sufficient out of her family for such a worthy end. The only rub for Mrs Fritch in the gratifying picture of herself as a guest at Mullings was her always liking to consider herself as the most cultivated person at any gathering.

She was seated on a bus one day when a frowsy elderly woman in an old black coat and battered hat sat down beside her, then turned for a stare.

'Aren't you Mrs Fritch, mother of him that's got himself caught up with that Miss Bradley?' It was asked in the despising tone of voice that appealed to Mrs Fritch's mood of resenting Cyril's defection, regardless of benefits.

'Yes,' she said with what she hoped was the right amount of frigidity. The woman's statement would be unpardonable if it were not so interesting.

'Asking for trouble, he is, and I'd watch my back too if I were you.'

Mrs Fritch feigned suitable alarm. 'What do you know against her?'

'Nothing for gospel,' the woman lowered her voice enticingly, 'but she struck me from the start as a dark horse. Lots of them in the village feel sorry for her because of getting left standing at the altar before coming here, but none of them questioned why the man got cold feet all of a sudden.'

Mrs Fritch pressed a hand to her forehead. 'I hadn't thought he could have his own side of the story.'

'Just like everyone else – just took it as fact he was a cad and her a true Christian martyr. As for the Stodmarshes...'

'Yes?' This was getting better.

'They're not the pillars of salt they make out to be,' the woman lowered her voice further to raspy whisper, 'and I should know, having been nanny to the boy till he was around seven. I could tell from the start he wasn't right in the head, I could. It comes down from his maternal grandmother, who's been in and out of the loony bin. As for the rest, I wouldn't trust a one of them farther than you can kick a piano. Stab you in the back soon as look at you.'

'Oh, my poor Cyril!' Mrs Fritch pressed her fingers to her forehead. 'He's been doing the bookkeeping at Mullings for insultingly low wages, so perhaps I shouldn't be all that surprised by what you're saying...'

'Here's my stop coming up. Best keep all this to your chest, particularly with your son, unless you have sufficient influence to persuade him to break the engagement – not all mothers do.' The woman got up and started towards the front of the bus. Mrs Fritch heard a chuckle but did not connect it with her recent companion.

She wouldn't give one word of warning to Cyril. Wanted to make his own decisions, did he? Well, he'd just have to live with the results, however badly they turned out. The woman had looked a drinker. So what! That didn't make her blind and deaf. What mattered was that Mrs Fritch would have it up her sleeve, and it would enable her to look down her nose on the Stodmarshes if they tried coming all superior over her. Never had she enjoyed a short bus ride more.

Winter merged into spring. One fine Tuesday in early May, George left the Dog and Whistle at around nine in the morning to walk along to the newsagent's three doors down to buy a paper. The weather being fine, he took it over to a bench on the green and sat down to enjoy a leisurely read. Miss Milligan, coming from the opposite side of the green with two of her dogs walking to heel, saw him crumple over.

'What to make of that, chaps?' she asked the boxers. 'Odd time of day for a nap!' On nearing the bench she bayed: 'Rousie! Rousie!' Taking this as an order, Hercules and Harold shifted sideways and plunged forward on their leads. 'Sit!' she bellowed, to instant effect, and to the consternation of Constable Trout pedaling down the road. Attempting to look as though he was intentionally getting off his bike instead of being bumped from it, he came over to investigate.

'What's to do?' he inquired portentiously.

'George Bird.'

'Can see that for meself without need for spectacles, Miss Milligan. No mistaking a man of his size for anyone else, even with his head down. I expect he's fainted, is all.'

'That's your sex for you! Don't need the excuse of wearing tight corsets! I expect he did the silly and skipped breakfast.'

Constable Trout did not approve of the word 'sex' in any context. He got the party on the bench, as referred to afterwards in his daily notebook, sitting upright and held him in place. George stirred, but neither opened his eyes nor attempted to speak. Mr Smith, the newsagent, came out of his shop, crossed the road, and stepped on to the green.

'What's to do, Constable?' he called out.

'It's George Bird. Passed out, he has, but I think he's beginning to come round. Hope it isn't a heart attack.'

George was now mumbling about being all right and wanting to get back to the Dog and Whistle. Some colour had returned to his face. 'Where's my newspaper?' He fumbled a hand across the bench.

'In your lap, old boy,' said Miss Milligan.

Mr Smith handed it to her. 'We'll give it back to you, Birdie, when we get you home. First thing's to get you perpendicular.'

The two men heaved him up and each took hold of an arm in manoeuvring him back to the Dog and Whistle. Miss Milligan followed with the newspaper, which she handed over at the door, saying she wouldn't come in because of the dogs. George tried to dissuade Constable Trout and Mr Smith from doing so either.

'I'm feeling back to normal – no need to waste more of your time. Been feeling a little under the weather for the past couple of days, that's all.' It was no good. They insisted on at least see-ing him into a chair. Constable Trout was all for fetching Doctor Chester, but George was adamant that he didn't need him. Five minutes later they reluctantly departed, each having urged him to go back to bed. He had never before been so anxious to have the place to himself.

A couple of hours later, Sir Winthrop and Lady Blake were seated in their library at The Manor, Large Middlington, utterly unprepared for a conversation with their daughter Lamorna that would turn the bright spring morning into darkest winter night. The library, with its walls of unread leather volumes, deep leather chairs, and ponderous oils of hunting scenes, could have been switched with one from any comparable country house without anyone being the wiser. Even the liver-and-white spaniel positioned just so on the Turkish carpet would be interchangeable, having been chosen to blend in perfectly with carpet and fabrics.

Sir Winthrop was reading the newspaper, skipping the pages featuring political commentary in conflict with his own inclinations. As usual he muttered a running commentary, to which his wife, as usual, paid no heed.

'What's the world coming to with all the crime these days? Elderly woman stabbed to death whilst knitting near King's Cross. Thank God we don't go in for that sort of thing round here; it lets Britain down. Mark my words, Clarice, it could lead to our losing hold of the Empire. Never takes much for the French to gloat that we're no more civilized at heart than savages in the jungles. They're usually referring to our cooking. But damn it all, we don't have to hand them opportunities to have a go at us!'

Lady Blake was thinking about their son, Gideon, wondering why his focus had shifted from haircuts to growing a beard. This scene, which had replayed itself with minor variations for the past thirty years, was shattered to smithereens when their eighteen-year-old daughter, wearing the very latest vogue in tennis dresses, swept through the door and flung at them the defiant declaration that only the wickedest of the wicked would try to stopping her from marrying Ned Stodmarsh.

People who saw Lamorna Blake for the first time were prone to wonder if the wondrous blue of her eyes outshone the glory of her golden hair, or whether it was the other way round. Nor was hers a beauty that paled with familiarity. Even her parents were frequently struck anew by her loveliness, but this morning their focus was not on her looks but on her horrifying announcement.

She threw herself into a chair. 'Ninnies! Don't just sit there with your mouths open! You know I've been seeing a lot of Ned ever since I got released from finishing school. At first he didn't seem to admire me at all, which has never happened with a boy before, and it was terribly exciting, but then he turned out to be so sweet. Felicity Giles is beside herself over him.'

Sir Winthrop recovered the power of speech ahead of his wife. 'My dear child, you can't marry a man because another girl wants him!'

Lamorna closed her eyes, the exquisite little fans of dark lashes displayed to great advantage against her white-and-rose petal complexion. 'God wouldn't be so cruel as to let that happen. And it isn't just tennis. He's proved his devotion by taking up riding to please me. Who could deny that such dedication deserves the ultimate reward?'

'Are you saying he's proposed?'

'Don't be simple, Daddy. Of course he has, or we wouldn't be talking about it, would we?'

'When?'

'Yesterday afternoon at the Stafford-Reids' picnic.'

'And you said nothing last night?'

'How could I? You'd gone to dinner and bridge with the Belchleys when I got home and weren't back when I went to bed.'

Sir Winthrop gazed helplessly at his wife. 'Clarice?'

Her Ladyship kept a grip on her composure. 'He should not have dreamed of approaching you until he had spoken with your father.'

Lamorna raised her eyes to the ceiling. 'Don't be so frightfully old-fashioned, Mummy. It isn't Daddy he wants to marry.'

'I should hope not!' Sir Winthrop occasionally attempted a joking manner. Her Ladyship's look informed him she was in no mood for frivolity.

'Anyway, Ned just blurted it out. I nearly tripped on a loose stone on the path when we were walking around. He put his arms round me to prevent my scraping a knee or worse and then said the sweetest thing in the loveliest husky voice about wanting to keep holding me for the rest of our lives. And I asked him to tell me exactly what he meant, and he said...'

Lady Blake stopped listening. Such a frightfully awkward situation in which to be put! Just a few years ago a refusal to listen to such foolishness would have been automatic, an alliance with the Stodmarshes – that family of most frightful bores – unthinkable, to be avoided like the Great Plague and the Fire of London combined. But that was before Mullings had become a place to which people would kill to be invited. They were all desperate to have the chance to tramp through its woods, in hope of catching one teensy glimpse of a tangle-haired, long-bearded figure in sackcloth slipping to or from his grotto.

'We barely discussed the ring, if that makes you feel better about the proprieties, Mummy; only that I want it to be a sapphire to match my eyes, with a diamond on each side. There's so much less fun in getting engaged if ones friends aren't green with envy.'

'Better an emerald, then,' said her father.

Lamorna let this pass. 'Ned's fearfully sweet!'

'Is he?' Lady Blake feigned interest.

'And incredibly amusing.'

Her Ladyship wished her daughter back at finishing school. To forbid the marriage might sit so ill with that witch Regina Stodmarsh that all social intercourse between the two families would be severed. The prospect was too utterly humiliating! Anyone who was anyone was to be encountered at Mullings these days, on weekend or overnight visits. Initially, Regina had played the role of a woman not given to entertaining lavishly, claiming to have lived a quiet, almost reclusive life in Northumbria. That had all changed after Edward Stodmarsh was lowered into the ground.

Reaching for her bottle of smelling salts, Lady Blake begged her husband and daughter to give her a few moments. How to face the smirks of those toadies the Stafford-Reids and Palfretts with their insufferable delight in declaring themselves intimates of Regina Stodmarsh, if they, the Blakes, were ostracized by her! But for her prestige as a hostess, she was a ghastly creature – arrogant, needling, and so diabolically clever.

It had been a brilliant stroke on her part to reveal that story of her seventeen-year-old daughter running off with the groom years ago, denying anyone else the pleasure of doing so behind her back. Not a woman to willingly risk making one's enemy. Oh, that Edward Stodmarsh's lachrymose first wife had not petulantly succumbed to what with another woman might have been a trifling cold! Lady Blake was tempted to pass over the smelling salts and slap her daughter's face instead. Never had she more devoutly wished that Mullings was located two hundred rather than twelve miles from her gates. Why God could not think of the Blakes above all others she had always deemed the most mysterious of His ways. It was so very tiresome of Him, but that was the male species for you! Let Him not expect to see her in church on Sunday morning! Meanwhile, she must make an attempt at reasoning with Lamorna.

Her daughter's voice broke in on her thoughts. 'Have you died, Mother?'

Lady Blake was tempted to respond that she hadn't the emotional energy to do anything so taxing. She smiled. 'Darling, I'm sure Ned Stodmarsh is a fine young man, but at twenty, rather *too* young, one would think, to be contemplating matrimony.'

'That's silly, he's frightfully mature! You should just see him on the tennis court. Felicity Giles nearly swoons every time he serves.'

'The girl should see a doctor,' said Sir Winthrop.

Lamorna ignored this callousness. 'Ned never lets that rotten cheat Miles Palfrett get under his skin. Playing doubles with Ned for always and forever is my every dream come true. Last month I thought it would be scratching Elizabeth Palfrett's eyes out for having the nerve to wear the same gown that I wore at the hunt ball, along with the Palfrett diamonds to give her all the sparkle she doesn't have. But since then I've grown up and am quite content to go on despising her in a perfectly friendly way, just like every other girl in our crowd.'

'Admirable.' Sir Winthrop judiciously refrained from pointing out that Elizabeth Palfrett, despite the scorn heaped upon her by competing eligible females, had just become engaged to young Viscount Briarwood. 'But where would you be, Lamorna, if Ned Stodmarsh should injure his knees or otherwise be forced to stop playing tennis three days after the wedding? I can't see such a situation being grounds for an annulment.'

Lamorna pouted, fully aware that it made her look even more heartbreakingly beautiful. Rising from the sofa, she gracefully threw out her arms in despair. 'I suppose, Daddy, that what you and Mummy really want is to make me wait until I'm as ancient as his cousin Madge Bradley before getting engaged.'

'The woman's hardly old, can't be more than forty.' Sir Winthrop had a kindly streak, which he must have come upon accidentally, because it wasn't an inherited trait, and his nanny had instilled in him that soft-hearted little boys didn't grow up into manly men.

'She's had to settle for a bookkeeper, of all creepy things.'

Lady Blake agreed this was indeed scraping the bottom of the trough.

'Those ink-stained fingers!'

'Honest work,' said Sir Winthrop, 'unless there's some fiddling of accounts, of course. More of that sort of thing going on these days than when I was a boy.'

Every attempt must be made, decided Her Ladyship, to persuade their daughter to step back from the brink of incredible folly. 'I'll concede Ned Stodmarsh is not a bad-looking boy; but, oh, my dear, that ginger hair! Think of your children! Especially if it should show up in a daughter!' She hoped she had made this sound as ominous as an offspring encumbered with two heads. 'What is marginally acceptable in a man

233

is not so with females.'

'Queen Elizabeth had red hair and it did not keep her off the throne,' Sir Winthrop felt obliged to interpolate when Lamorna cast him a glance that threatened a torrent of tears.

'Indeed so,' his wife's tone made clear he would be well advised to remain seen but unheard. 'I've no doubt being called ginger-nob as a girl was what made her so irritable – cutting off people's heads all over the place. Such an unsanitary practice, I've always thought. Also,' Her Ladyship saw nothing amiss in turning the thumbscrew, 'let us not forget she died an old maid.'

A dreamy expression entered Lamorna's astonishingly lovely blue eyes, fringed by those incredible lashes. 'I wish someone would behead Regina Stodmarsh. As even you two innocents must have guessed, the wicked old thing is determined to ruin everything for Ned and me.'

Lady Blake assumed a sympathetic mien, contrary to the relief that flooded through her. Praise be to a forgiven Almighty! Here might be the way out of what had seemed for several shuddery minutes an insoluble dilemma. How utterly charming of Regina to accord herself the role of villainess! 'Tell Daddy and Mummy all about it, my dearest darling!'

Lamorna glided over to the French windows before returning to recline artistically on the sofa. 'The problem is with the Stodmarsh money. I know it's a horribly vulgar word, that you've taught me never to say out loud, but there's no bearing it! Regina has full control over it for years to come, because of that stupid thing old Lord Stodmarsh set up after he married her.'

'Called a trust,' answered her father knowledgeably.

'You're right, as always, Winthrop,' his wife congratulated him in her excess of revived good spirits.

'Is that what it is?' Lamorna converted a yawn into a sigh. 'Ned tried to explain the bitter facts to me, and what it comes down to, when you leave out all the fussy stuff, is that he has nothing but a quarterly allowance from the interest on the estate until he is twenty-seven, or she does the considerate thing and dies in the meantime. Ned, being so sweet, doesn't blame his grandfather for setting things up that way, but I think it was wicked of him. Anyway, Ned told me when I rang him up before coming in here that he'd spoken to her about us last night and she refused to withdraw a penny so we can buy a flat in London. Honestly, I could tear my hair out.' Untrue – Lamorna's golden tresses were one of her main reasons for climbing out of bed in the morning and staying up most of the night, but this declaration achieved the desired result.

'Oh, my dearest,' exclaimed her mother, 'never think such sacrilege! Take my smelling salts instead!'

Sir Winthrop nobly forewent glancing longingly at his newspaper. 'What's this about a flat?'

'We must have one.'

235

'Ah! Wouldn't have thought that something any Stodmarsh would be keen as mustard about. I've heard it said the family's secret for maintaining and, must be admiringly said, increasing its fortune is that traditionally the heirs have not come into their full inheritance until their twenty-seventh birthdays, an age when they should be less easy prey for sponging relations.' Sir Winthrop spoke with the aplomb of a man who never admitted even to himself that in his youth he had hounded every aunt, uncle and cousin after his parents had finally refused to honour his debts. That his own son was now blithely going through money like water, he laid down to these modern times. 'Any idea what Ned's relatives' current situations are, Lamorna?'

'You mean his aunt and uncle? They're in the same boat as Ned, having to make do with what's dolled out to them every quarter, so there's no hope of them coughing up any lolly.'

'My dear, such a turn of phrase,' rebuked Lady Blake.

Lamorna ignored this. 'My darling understands completely that we must have a flat in London as an escape from Mullings on weekends and,' she added fervently, 'almost every day in between, because I'd simply die if I had to live at Mullings with that horrible woman presiding over every inch of it.'

'Could he not ask his maternal grandmother for assistance?'

'He won't. He says it would be a wretched thing to do seeing he's never been as thoughtful of her as he ought to have been. I adore him for being noble, but it is rather a nuisance.' Lamorna raised beseeching eyes to her parents. 'So it's all up to you, my precious poppets – to help us out financially until we can swing things on our own. Ned didn't want me to ask, he said he'd think of something.'

'Clarice?' Sir Winthrop retreated crab-like further back in his leather chair.

Lady Blake chose to delay what was bound to be one of Lamorna's worst tantrums ever – and she certainly had a gift for them – by keeping the blame where it rightfully belonged. 'I do agree with you about Edward Stodmarsh mismanaging the whole business dreadfully. He was a foolish man and undoubtedly believed every word fed to him by Regina – about her having lived a life of miserable dependency on her brother and his family. Utter falsehoods from what I now hear from mutual acquaintances, but ones gaining her the ends she desired – that she not be put in a similar position at Mullings should he die before her.'

'I know, Mummy, but I can't tell Ned I despise his grandfather.' Lamorna drew her feet fastidiously away from the spaniel who had presumed to edge her way. 'He was dotty about the old man and says that it's absolutely understandable that Edward Stodmarsh acted to protect Regina's interests, especially knowing his scowly son William would have bunged her in the coal cellar, or something equally vengeful, given half a chance. Now, of course, the boot's on the other foot and she's the one having the merriest time watching everyone squirm. Yes, one day someone really should chop off her head and set it spinning like a top on the floor.'

Sir Winthrop found the blaze of ice-blue in his daughter's eyes so bone-chilling it shocked him into silence.

'Darling,' her mother replied, 'your being melodramatic will get us nowhere. Shall not Ned receive an inheritance from his late mother?' A depressing thought, which nevertheless had to be addressed in order to continue appearing sympathetic.

'Yes, but not until he's twenty-five. Her family, like the Stodmarshes, thought twenty-one too young. Horribly stuffy, but there you are! Ned definitely won't like the idea of you both having to buy us the flat in London...'

There could be no further delaying and Sir Winthrop was visibly incapable of doing his part in bringing down the axe. All this talk of beheading did intrude! Lady Blake squared her shoulders and braced herself against the avalanche of rage imminently hurtling her way. 'Regretfully, Lamorna, that is impossible. Your father and I may disagree with Regina's Stodmarsh's decision to withhold financial help, but it would be entirely wrong for us to intercede and thwart her obvious opposition to the marriage at this time.' She saw her daughter's mouth open in what seemed to be slow motion. 'Am I not right, Winthrop?'

'I'm afraid so; not at all the done thing.' He had no time to plug his ears before the scream erupted.

238

That piece of hysteria accomplished, Lamorna swept towards the library door, where she stood poised for a poignant moment, before issuing the ultimate threat. 'I shall never speak to either of you again as long as I live.'

'Think she means it, Clarice?' Sir Winthrop inquired after the reverberations from the slammed door had quivered away.

'At this moment I most devoutly hope so, Winthrop. You will accompany me to church on Sunday.'

Twenty minutes later Lamorna telephoned Ned at Mullings. He had been expecting the call, having spoken with her earlier, and when notified by Grumidge, he took it in the study. In his haste he left the door to the hall ajar. That he adored her was unquestionable, but a night's reflection had left him uncertain that he'd done right in asking her to marry him with circumstances being as they were. The thought nagged that his grandfather would have been disappointed in him on this account and that Florie would also think that he had been thoughtlessly immature, which was why he hadn't confided in her that morning.

'Lamorna?'

'Darling,' she spoke through a cascade of sobs, 'I was petrified you might be out, that you'd gone over to that farm.' Over the past weeks she had made it clear in the sweetest possible way that she did not understand his enthusiasm for working with Tom Norris at Farn Deane.

'Lamorna, I haven't left the house for a minute since we talked.'

'I wish you'd call me your treasure.'

Ned flushed at the deserved rebuke. 'You know that's what you are.'

'Then say it, darling.'

Despite reminding himself he was the luckiest man in the world to have her love, he went hot round the ears. He wasn't cut out for flowery language, had never seen the point of it. He'd have to start practising in his bedroom. 'My treasure.' There! Done! Next time maybe he wouldn't feel such a fool. 'What's wrong? Why are you crying?'

'You could have added – my sweet.'

'Look,' he said, frankness escaping, 'I'm worried about you and that means I can't waste time on sunshine and roses.'

'Oh!' Surprisingly, Lamorna sounded as though she savoured this display of masterfulness. No man had ever dared attempt such a thing with her before. 'Well, yes, I am horribly upset. Mummy and Daddy won't help with the flat either. They said they couldn't possibly go against Regina.'

Ned cringed. 'You weren't going to ask them. You promised you wouldn't.'

'So I did, but...'

'I told you I'd think of some other way.'

'So what have you come up with?'

'Well, I can talk to Seymour Cleerly, Grandfather's solicitor – mine now – and see if he can't find some loophole to free up the funds we'll need. He's a decent chap...' Ned's voice trailed away. He didn't think it at all likely anything would come of the attempt.

Lamorna seized on his hesitancy to begin weeping again. 'It's all too cruel! I was just saying to Mummy and Daddy that the only hope is for someone to murder that heartless witch!' Her voice rose. 'Are you listening to me, precious, or are you beginning to wish you hadn't proposed to me?'

It crept in upon Ned, that he was close to regretting his impulse of the previous evening; that what he'd really wanted was to remain forever in the dizzying delight of love's enthrallment, with his feet never touching the ground and every breath an intake of glorious anticipation of when he'd see her next. The guilt arising from such cowardly thinking caused him to respond forcefully to what she had said.

'Of course I don't wish I hadn't asked you to marry me. As for Regina, I'd gladly murder her; I just have to think how to do it without landing in the soup!' At that moment he saw movement through the gap in the doorway. Someone – or perhaps several people – was in the hall. No need to worry about Regina as she was gone for the day visiting the Stafford-Reids – unless she'd returned unexpectedly. And, anyway, neither she nor anyone else would take what they'd overheard seriously. The house was full of people bound to have wished Regina underground almost daily.

'Would you really – for me?' Lamorna had brightened.

Irritation surged as it might not have done if she had been in the room with all her physical enchantments. 'Just joking,' said Ned, 'as I

241

know you were too.'

'No, I wasn't,' came the petulant reply, 'although I'll admit it would be more convenient, as I told Mummy and Daddy, if she were hauled off to the Tower and had her head chopped off. I'm not usually bloodthirsty,' she added reassuringly, 'but that flat in London means everything to me – you do see that, don't you, darling?'

Ned winced. 'Yes, of course. Look, I have to go ... sweetheart. I'll phone Cleerly when I get back from taking Rouser for his walk. I have to see to him now.'

'If he's more important than I am!'

It was several prolonged moments before Ned could replace the receiver and go into the hall, now empty of any presence but his own, then head down to the lower regions, where Rouser was always to be found when not in his company. Although Mrs McDonald did not want the dog in the kitchen when meals were being prepared, she was always willing to supply him with a bone to take into the scullery. Ned was not sure that he was ready for a talk with Florie. There was so much to get sorted out in his head first, and even when that was done, wouldn't it be cowardly to cast himself upon her for moral support? But on entering the kitchen he found her engaged in conversation with Alf Thatcher and saw at once that she was distressed. She turned to him, hands clasped.

'Troubling news, Ned.' She never called him that in front of others. 'George Bird collapsed on the green early this morning and required help getting back to the Dog and Whistle.'

'I'm sorry.' Ned forgot his own worries – the feeling of being a rat caught in a trap. He pulled a chair out from the table for her to sit in. 'Any word on how he's doing?' He directed this to Alf.

'Popped in to see him half an hour gone, Mr Ned. He insisted he was fine, just a dizzy spell, and didn't want the doctor. Said he'd refuse to see him if he showed up. Irritable, he was. That's not like Birdie by a long chalk. I don't know that I did right coming to tell Mrs Norris, but I felt she'd want to know, seeing they was friends once upon a time.'

'I'm so grateful you did.' Florence sat down. 'I want to see him, but would he resent my showing up after putting him out of my life as I did? The last thing I should do is upset him.'

Alf rubbed his chin. 'Perhaps it'd be best to leave him be till it's clear he's on the mend. He could be annoyed that I told you. My Doris is forever telling me I stick my oar in where I shouldn't, but somehow I got to thinking a while back that whatever pulled you two apart, you was meant to be together.'

'I'm not as sure as I once was that my reasons had validity and now it has to be too late for me to step back into George's life and offer support if he's ill with something more than he claims.'

'Leave it to me,' said Ned. 'I'll go along and see him. It's about time I started thinking beyond myself, Florie.'

Something in his voice told her all was not well with him and that it probably had to do with

243

Lamorna Blake, but this was instantly over-shadowed by worry about George. Could it be heart trouble, or something equally serious? She had not cried in many years, but she did so on going up to her bedroom after Ned and Alf had left. Robert's death had been anguishing, but unaccompanied by regrets. She must not allow them to consume her now; but it would not be easy to hold them at bay if Ned did not bring back encouraging news from the Dog and Whistle.

NINE

On the day after George Bird's collapse on the village green and Ned Stodmarsh's unhappy realization that he wasn't as glowingly enthused about becoming engaged to Lamorna Blake as he should have been, Florence's cousin Hattie Fly rose, as she always did, at six in the morning. After attending to her ablutions, she descended the narrow staircase and crossed the dim strip of hall to the kitchen.

In appearance Hattie epitomized the drab old maid on the shady side of fifty with indeterminate features, salt-and-pepper hair scraped back into a small bun and steel-rimmed spectacles perched on her nose. There was, however, a lightness to her step and a sparkle to her eyes

– even when, as now, merely anticipating putting on the kettle for a cup of tea – which revealed that, far from believing herself short-changed by life, she was entirely contented with her lot. She was grateful to still be living in the house where she had been born. Hurst Row was a back alley off Kings Cross, and number twenty-nine was jammed midway in the sooty-bricked Victorian terrace. All the houses opened directly on to the street and had little in the way of back gardens, but the neighbours were in the main friendly, and just around the corner were several small shops that supplied household needs. Hattie considered herself supremely blessed that her home had an upstairs bathroom and lavatory, which many such dwellings lacked.

That the house did appear to have seen better days beyond the exterior grime was undeniable, but it was cheered inside by the smell of polish, shining brass, cozily hued curtains, and the comfortable three-piece suite in the front room, bought from a neighbouring family who were emigrating to Canada. Hattie had loved her parents dearly and, as their only child, begrudged not one moment of taking care of them in their infirm old age. Nor did she mind the necessity since their deaths of housing lodgers to supplement what she earned from taking in ironing. There had been a series of them, always two a time – though never a couple – occupying the pair of bedrooms at the top of the stairs, leaving for her use the tiny boxroom a half-flight up from them. Mr Page, a middle-aged shoe salesman, had now been with her for three years, and Miss Toffee Jones, aged twenty-five, for four months.

Mr Page was an ideal lodger, pleasant but unobtrusive. Hattie knew little more about him than she had done when he'd first arrived – that he was a bachelor and did not eat fish, except for kippers, which he liked to have for breakfast three times a week. Hattie, in addition to breakfast, provided an evening meal for her lodgers if they wished it. Mr Page more often than not ate at a restaurant on his way back from work. Toffee usually had dinner with Hattie and made a cheerful table companion. She always insisted on helping with the washing-up afterwards, which extended their conversations, often inconsequential, but occasionally otherwise. During one of their chats she'd mentioned having recently stopped seeing her young man.

'We found out we didn't suit,' she'd said lightly. 'No broken hearts.'

Hattie, who'd quickly become fond of Toffee, wasn't sure she believed this; the girl struck her as the sort to put a brave face on disappointments. Toffee was obviously not her real Christian name, but one that suited her perfectly. Her shiny bobbed hair and eyes were a warm brown, and the hair had a silver streak at the front. Hattie had assumed it was artificial, but Toffee had told her it resulted from being delivered by forceps and that her mother had died after giving birth to her.

Her father, a groom turned chauffeur, had passed away when she was ten. But she'd been fortunate in being from that time housed and educated at a private school by his employers until she was sixteen, at which time the son decided he was in love with her. Realistically, his parents' generosity had its limits. They had informed her kindly but firmly that it was time to make her own way in the world, with fifty pounds to support her until she found a job. According to Toffee, this had been not only reasonable but an exciting opportunity to spread her wings. Was this another case of her putting on a brave front? Being alone in the world at so young an age must surely have been somewhat scary. She had for several years now worked in a bookshop and said it was her dream to have one of her own. Like many young women, she was neither particularly pretty nor sadly plain, but there was a woodland nymph quality to her that had its own appeal, coupled with a vitality that was a breath of fresh air in the old house.

Hattie brewed her pot of tea and turned on the wireless before sitting down to enjoy it. There was the usual mention of what Parliament was doing, or rather not doing, before the announcer turned to the brutal stabbing on Monday evening of Ethel Joiner, aged sixty-nine, a long-time resident of three, Ockton Drive, Moorhead. A police search continued for the suspect, twenty-five-year-old Arthur James Leighton, who had fled the scene after being discovered standing over the body with a bloodstained knife in his right hand by a friend of Mrs Joiner, at present wishing to remain anonymous. Mrs Joiner's nephew, Mr Bernard Brook, had provided information to the effect that his aunt had recently taken Mr Leighton, a struggling artist, into her home because she believed in his work and wished to assist its continuation.

A terrible thing, and it had happened not more than a couple of miles from Hurst Row. It was typical of Hattie that, in addition to sorrow for the victim, she felt a pang for the perpetrator. Such a dreadful burden to have to live with, whether caught or not, because surely the wicked had some conscience left in them.

Hattie still felt guilty for having once passed a blind man in the street without putting anything in his mug. She had been worried about her cousin Florie, who was then struggling with a problem relating to a suspicious death in the house where she was housekeeper, but that was no excuse for Hattie not digging into her purse for a half-crown. That murderer, if there had been one – and Florie had seemed less sure of that recently – had not been discovered. She had never, of course, breathed a word of this to Toffee Jones, but had seen no harm in telling her about Lord Stodmarsh's subsequent remarriage to a woman named Regina Stapleton, who had brought an ornamental hermit with her to Mullings. She hadn't needed to explain to Toffee the nature of this oddity. She'd instantly said she'd read about them in an old book in the shop where she worked.

'How interesting that your cousin's mother had worked for the new Lady Stodmarsh's family, the Tamershams, you said, years before; but life is full of coincidences, isn't it?' Toffee had sat looking thoughtful. 'Makes you wonder if there's some unseen force moving us around like pieces on a chessboard, doesn't it?'

Hattie had agreed she'd sometimes felt that way. She now turned off the wireless before pottering into the front room to open its curtains and do a quick dusting. The vase on the window-sill contained a bunch of flowers Toffee had brought in on Monday evening. Decidedly she was a kind, thoughtful girl, always happy to handle some errand such as putting letters Hattie had written into the pillar box. Mr Page had left his copy of the *Evening News* on the brass tray-topped Indian table in front of the couch; she picked it up as she always did and took it back to the kitchen to read later before putting it in the dustbin. She was tempted to look through it at once to see what was written about the murder – there was nothing on the front page – but Mr Page would be down at seven for his breakfast and it was now twenty minutes to that hour. Hattie cut the rind off the streaky bacon, which he preferred to gammon, and put it into the frying pan. When he entered the kitchen pre-cisely on time, she set before him an oven-warmed plate with the bacon, fried tomatoes and fried bread.

'Very nice, Miss Fly,' he said with, as ever, an inclusive look at the filled toast rack, butter dish, jar of marmalade and brown glazed teapot. At twenty-five past seven he bade her good day, collected his hat and coat from the hall tree and left the house. There was something very soothing in Mr Page's unfaltering routine and yet Hattie had sometimes wondered if he didn't occasionally feel the urge to do something that would surprise her along with others – such as parting his hair to the side rather than in the middle, or having a lie-in at weekends once in a while.

Toffee Jones did not live life to a pattern; she was either in a rush to get to work on time or had so much extra she would take old Mr Turner's dog for a walk. She was the sort of girl who was unbothered by being caught in the rain without an umbrella, laddering her last pair of stockings, or a cat jumping in through an open window on to her lap. The pity was, she'd once told Hattie, that nothing in the way of grand adventure had yet presented itself to her since setting out on her own, but she lived in hope of it doing so one day. There was never any telling whether she would eat breakfast. When she did it was tea and toast.

Having cleared the table and washed up after Mr Page, Hattie sliced bread and put the kettle on a low flame; she then settled down with last night's newspaper. The murder was prominently featured on page two. The photo of Arthur James Leighton was, she thought, too grainy to be of much use in identifying him to the public. So engrossed did she become that she did not hear Toffee come down the stairs, the sound of which usually alerted her to turn on the grill for the toast if wanted and turn up the gas under the kettle, but it soon became clear that didn't matter. She entered the kitchen wearing a beige spring coat and a brown beret, tipped down over her forehead.

'Nothing to eat or drink this morning,' she

250

announced. 'I'm going away, probably for only a few days, but I've left the rent money paid up till the end of the month on the dressing table, just in case I'm delayed returning, Hattie.' Toffee had stopped addressing her as 'Miss Fly' shortly after moving in.

'Off on a little adventure?' Hattie asked, following her recent train of thought as she stood up. Being a romantic, she hoped it would be something as exciting as having received an invitation to visit a distant relation thinking of changing his or her will in Toffee's favour after quarreling with every other family member.

'Nothing in the fun line. I have to go and see someone who's going through a rough patch. I'm not sure if I can help or not, but I have to try, or I'll hate myself afterwards.'

'Yes, of course you would.' Hattie was not one to pry beyond what was offered, but even had she felt so inclined she could see Toffee was not going to tell her more. There had to be a good reason for this, because she wasn't usually secretive, or so Hattie had always thought.

Toffee didn't look or sound worried or distressed. 'I didn't make up my mind until I got into bed last night, so I'll have to stop by the shop and tell them before setting off. I don't suppose they'll be annoyed at the short notice, but if they give me the sack it'll be all right. I'll find another job.'

'Let's hope it doesn't come to that, but there are other bookshops, or maybe you could try for a job at the library.' Despite Toffee's poise, Hattie was gripped by the thought that something was wrong, very wrong. She hadn't seen Toffee last night because Hattie had gone to the pictures with her friend Vera from two doors down. The meal she'd left prepared hadn't been eaten; unusual, but not worrisome, until viewed at this moment. She laid a gentle hand on Toffee's arm.

'Don't worry about the rent. Take with you what you left on the dressing table.'

'Are you sure?'

'Certainly.'

'You are dear, Hattie.' Toffee glanced towards the newspaper on the table. 'Anything new on that murder?'

'No. And it's the same on the wireless – the police are still searching for the suspect.'

'I hope they get him soon, before he kills again.'

'That's the worry, if he's guilty of this one.'

Toffee looked at Hattie sharply. 'But he was caught by the friend of the old lady standing over the body with the knife in his hand and then took to his heels – surely not the act of an innocent man.'

'I'm not so sure I'd have stayed put with all that evidence stacked against me, and all I could say was I walked in and pulled the knife out of the deceased. Now I'm not saying I think that's likely, but it is possible, isn't it?'

'Oh, Hattie, you are such a softie.' Toffee leaned forward and kissed her cheek. 'Now I really must go; I'll get something to eat before catching my train. I'll be in touch within the week.'

'I'll miss you, my dear.'

After Toffee left, suitcase in hand, Hattie found herself unable to get on with her usual routine. Why did she believe it wrong to assume the young painter's guilt when she had been convinced on far less evidence that murder had been committed at Mullings? The answer followed instantly. We put our faith in those we know and trust – not blindly, but certainly with a bias towards their viewpoint. Other thoughts followed as if they had been waiting to have their say for the last couple of hours, as snippets from Florie's letters came back to her. These left her feeling shaken and in a quandary as to whether or not to write to her cousin. This uncertainty was capped by a disturbing question – how well did she really know Toffee Jones?

The young lady in question was at that moment standing at a bus stop outside the bookshop where she worked. The owners, a husband and wife, had been very understanding about her request for time off and even offered her an advance on a fortnight's wages, telling her that, if she liked, it could count for her Christmas bonus. Toffee had accepted with expressions of gratitude. She was even more grateful that neither had been in the shop yesterday afternoon, and that she'd had the place to herself when the man in the beige raincoat had entered, removed his trilby, and questioned her as to when she had last seen, or heard from, Arthur James Leighton. There had been no gauging from his impassive face if he'd believed what she told him. What she didn't doubt was that he, or one of his kind, would show up elsewhere, if

253

they had not done so already.

The bus she caught took her to Victoria. On alighting she walked for ten minutes before entering a hairdresser's, which she had telephoned the previous afternoon. The young lady assigned to her showed Toffee where to hang her coat and beret before taking her to a chair. Their eyes met in the mirror facing them.

'Are you sure about going platinum blonde?' the young lady, who'd identified herself as Ivy, asked doubtfully.

'Absolutely. Why not?'

'Well, if you won't be offended, you don't have the complexion for it. It could make you look a little hard.'

'Really?' Toffee smiled.

'The streak you have in front now is nice – eye-catching.'

'So I've been told.'

'Till you're sick of hearing it?'

'Not to be rude – yes.'

'How about a honey blonde?'

'Platinum.'

'Let's get going then.' Ivy's reflection added 'your funeral'.

'Afterwards I'd like it set in waves.'

'Righty-ho!'

It had been chilly under a colourless sky when Toffee had set off from Hurst Row. On leaving the hairdresser's, wearing a headscarf instead of the brown beret, she noted it was now grayer overhead than the pavement, and she felt the immediate effect of a nippy breeze poking and prodding, flapping her clothing and burrowing down her neck. Usually she didn't mind the cold, but now, foolishly, she wished she could be hugging a hot water bottle. The person she had seen in the mirror when Ivy had finished with her was a stranger, whom she had no desire to befriend. Reminding herself sternly that this had been the aim, and that improvements still had to be made, she entered a chemist's, where she bought a bright red lipstick, a black eyebrow pencil and a pair of tweezers. From there it was a matter of walking on until she came to the right sort of clothes shop – one offering cheap, flashy merchandize for the working girl with delusions of looking like a Hollywood film star. She found exactly the place halfway down a side street. A couple more stops completed her purchasing.

It was now past noon and a joy to be practically blown through the door of a café, find a table and set down the suitcase and packages and check in her handbag to see what money she had left. Enough for the train fare and some to spare. While eating egg and chips and drinking a cup of tea strong enough to supply a steel backbone, she considered her next move. Changing into her new clothes could be quickly done in a public lavatory and provided the advantage of her being virtually unnoticeable going in or coming out, but plucking her eyebrows would take time, and the last thing she needed was the attendant banging on the door to see if there was a problem. That might be remembered – unlikely, but any risk was one too many. She'd have to find a park bench and use her compact mirror. Given the weather, there shouldn't be too many people basking outdoors.

Was it ridiculous – this concern that the police might have posted a series of plain-clothes detectives to keep watch on 29 Hurst Street from the time she arrived back there last evening till this morning, with instructions to follow her when she stepped outside? There hadn't been anyone in the street except for old Mrs Wardle sweeping off her step, or any cars parked at the curb, which would have been significant seeing as nobody in Hurst Row owned a car, but this had not brought reassurance. Eyes could be on the alert from around corners or from behind shop windows. No, thought Toffee, her anxiety was not ridiculous. Thinking that the law wouldn't clutch at every available straw that might lead them to their quarry would be the mug's game. She preferred to arrive at her destination in the evening, and making this choice allowed her time to lead any pursuer on a wild bus chase. The trick would be to get on a bus at a stop where she was the only person waiting.

One of these took her to a secluded square off the King's Road where she sat shivering on a bench doing the beastly eyebrow tweezing. Never again, she thought, even if they grew back like caterpillars; this was followed, between 'ouches', by the reminder to herself that what she was enduring could be worse – other people had gone to the stake for their beliefs. The result revealed by the compact mirror was a thin line with some unevenness that could be smoothed out by the dark pencil. She still had the feeling that she was wearing someone else's face, but the discomfort she had felt on leaving the hair-dresser's was replaced by a flood of reassurance. If she had trouble recognizing herself at this stage, then even the trained eye might fail to do so once her disguise was complete. Added to which, she would arrive at her destination with her cover story in place. The only issue was her surname, but that could be handled.

Despite her lifted spirits, Toffee bore in mind that over-confidence could be her undoing. She changed trains needlessly before alighting at the railway station closest to her destination at half-past six in the evening; she then took a bus the rest of the way. A young man seated opposite stared at her with slack-faced admiration. The stare from the middle-aged woman beside him was fiercely disapproving. Toffee, unused to either reaction in her former existence, was satisfied with both. They informed her she'd converted herself into the sort of female who would be either ogled or deplored. When she got off the train, it was raining – not hard, but in a fretful drizzle. The pavement was as slick and black as her new patent leather court shoes. Their heels were higher than she was used to, causing her to tread cautiously whilst looking out for the sign above the premises she would enter. Ah, there it was! She drew a deep breath before opening the door with the hand not hold-ing the suitcase.

The Dog and Whistle wasn't packed that even-ing, but there were enough regulars present to keep George Bird sufficiently busy to hold anguish and dread at bay for several minutes at a time. The buzz of conversation flowed around him like lapping waves. At the moment the talk was about old Craddock's decision to sell his bookshop and retire to the West Country – would a new owner keep on the present staff, including Cyril Fritch, fiancé of Miss Madge Bradley? Or would he be offered the option of working full-instead of part-time on the bookkeeping at Mullings? This led to a mention that Fritch's mother, the gallivanting widow, had taken off on another of her holidays, on the grounds that she was in desperate need of restoring her nerves because the new owners of the house next door had dogs that barked day and night and Constable Trout refused to do anything about it.

George hoped he was doing an adequate job of appearing to be back to his old self since passing out on the green and that none beyond Alf Thatcher and probably his wife Doris had guessed what ailed him. Not that Alf had said peep; it was the sympathy in his eyes that had done the talking. No unbearable questions asked, no useless attempts at consolation, no irritating advice offered. The best of sorts, was Alf. If Alf had realized from the start what was up, he wouldn't have told Florence that he, George, had required physical support from the green back to the Dog and Whistle. The truth having dawned, Alf had apologized for telling her – saying he should have minded his own business. George had replied he'd have done the same in his place, and anyway someone or other was bound to tell her he'd been taken poorly.

If there was anyone in the world he wished he

could confide in it was Florence, but he wouldn't burden someone he held so dear with a secret that must be guarded against discovery, especially if doing so burdened the conscience. It had been painful to tell Ned Stodmarsh when he'd asked if George would be willing to see Florence that he'd just as soon not; that there was no picking up where they had left off. The real reason, of course, was that he couldn't risk a meeting. To deceive her with assurances that all was well with him was as undoable as saddling her with the truth. It was some small comfort to believe she would fully comprehend his state of turmoil – that if it were Ned in dire straits, she would have held to her faith in him. Not blindly, but out of what she knew of his character.

George turned from replacing a bottle of brandy on its appointed shelf to see a young woman with bleached blonde hair standing at the bar. Not the usual sort for the Dog and Whistle, as made evident by the eyes of all present being riveted on her. It wasn't just the hair; it was the pencilled eyebrows, flame-red lipstick, long jet earrings and cheaply smart get-up of feather toque and black coat pretending to be astrakhan. But George wasn't one for automatic negative judgments. *Got nice eyes*, was his thought.

'What'll it be, love?'

'Gin and orange.'

'Used to be my late wife's chosen. Nasty night – passing through in your car?'

'I'd be lucky! Train and bus.'

'Staying hereabouts overnight?'

'That's the plan.'

'Fixed up somewhere?' The Dog and Whistle did not offer overnight accommodation. George placed the gin and orange in front of her.

Toffee thought, *He's got nice eyes.* 'I'm not expected,' she shrugged, 'but I don't think I'll be marched out the door.' She dug into her handbag for her purse and handed him a folded ten-bob note, inside which was another sort of note. On it she had written: 'I'm Toffee. Have you seen or heard from him? Have the police tracked you down?' She watched him ring up the till and waited for him to make the discovery. Would he say anything? Or would he give her her change and leave it at that?

He looked down at her from his vast height, handed over the coins and shook his head. Toffee deflated like a pricked balloon. 'More looks than sense, some of you young people.'

'That's what the older generation always say,' another shrug.

'No umbrella in this weather, you need that pretty head examined.'

'Oh! Yes, I suppose so.'

'You get on with your drink and I'll fetch one from the passageway.'

'Thanks.'

Outside the rain was indeed coming down hard. From around the corner of the Dog and Whistle came a darkly clothed man pushing a bike with an unlit lamp. No one else was out and about in that vicinity, but had anyone observed him they might have detected something furtive in his movements. Behind him came a cacophony of barking dogs, and he moved faster towards the iron gate in the wall built to prevent trespassers entering the Mullings woods following the arrival of the ornamental hermit. The gate was, of course, meant to be locked at all times, with only family members and the postman Alf Thatcher having keys to it, but over the course of time a laxity had set in and more often than not the gate was left unsecured. The man tried the latch and a moment later was pedalling on the unlighted bike along the woodland path. He did so uncertainly because he'd never been much of a cyclist in broad daylight and perfect weather. Only the desperation of his situation propelled him forward in the near dark and rain. The bike suddenly slithered under him and his attempt to rebalance only served to increase the swerve and send him pitching down into the ravine, in a series of wild bumps before the thud that toppled him to the ground.

Back at the Dog and Whistle George had returned from the passageway with an umbrella. 'Took me a while to find one that didn't leak,' he told Toffee, who had finished her gin and orange unhindered by anyone joining her at the bar. What man wanted it reaching his wife or girl that he'd been spotted chatting up a tarty blonde over his pint of bitter? And none of the few women present looked like they'd budge an inch in her direction unless they were dragged. 'Some had more holes in them than a sieve,' George added for good value.

'I never had one that the material didn't perish in a week, that's why I've stopped bothering with them.' Toffee knew what had delayed him –

he'd been considering the question of whether or not to trust her.

'This one's a bit fiddly to put up; I'll come outside and see to it for you.'

'Aren't you the knight in shining armour?' On their way to the door Toffee winked at the scrutinizing faces. Better the brazen hussy than a girl afraid to be noticed. For good measure she wiggled her fingers and mouthed 'bye-bye'. Once outside, she and George moved several paces away from the entrance. The rain was still coming down, but in a half-hearted manner. The street was empty of all but a cat scurrying around into the shelter of a doorway.

'I don't know why in the world you should trust me,' Toffee said, looking up at him. 'I could be out for revenge because he broke things off between us.'

'Then you wouldn't be the girl he wrote to me about.'

'You look just the way I pictured you.'

'And you nothing like.' George flexed the umbrella.

'So why believe I am who I say I am?'

'If you was sent to fool me it wouldn't be with a whole head of platinum blond – just the one streak in front, like I knew about.'

'Unless the police are too clever by half – thinking it out from your perspective. Have they been here?'

'Yesterday evening.' George had the umbrella up. 'A man pretending to ask for directions. I don't think any of the customers twigged. I came outside with him like I've just done with you. He

262

seemed satisfied when I told him I hadn't seen nor heard from...'

'Our friend.'

'You got it.'

'And was that true?'

'It so happens it was.'

Toffee eyed him speculatively. 'I doubt you've ever told a proper lie in your life and are hoping against anything you won't have to do so, whilst still standing ready to help if he does show up.'

George pretended to adjust an umbrella spoke. 'I keep going round in my head about what would be best, but every time I think I should urge him to turn himself in, I think of how innocent men have been hung in the past. What has you thinking he'll come here?'

'Well, friendship can go by the wayside when it comes to the crunch, and he wouldn't go to his parents, would he?'

'No. His father telephoned to tell me the police had been round to see them and in the course of the conversation they'd told them about me and given my address. I'm not blaming them, you understand. If it hadn't come from them it would've come from someone else.'

'I've gone over and over things in my mind too. I'm sure the last thing he'll want to do is drag you into this horrible business, but if he runs out of money – and I can't think he'd have had much on him – then he may think you're his only means of escaping ... to France, say. There have to be boatmen who can be bribed, wouldn't you think? Or is that only in adventure stories?'

'I wouldn't know.' George felt the first twitch

of a smile in days. 'Until now I've lived a very dull life.'

'And so you shall again,' said Toffee firmly. 'This is all going to turn out all right. It has to, or there's no justice in the world – the real murderer will be discovered. We're not going to think that only happens in books. As for the money, I have a plan – it's connected to my cover story for coming to Dovecote Hatch.' She took the umbrella from him. 'I'd better get going.'

'Where?'

Toffee had already started walking away, but turned back to grin at him, 'You'll find out soon enough. Tongues will be wagging and you'll need to be as surprised as everyone else. I'll be in touch tomorrow.'

She'd received directions from the bus conductor and was prepared for a goodish walk, which wouldn't have been a problem but for the high heels. It was tempting to take them off and continue in her stockinged feet, but she soldiered on.

At that same time Ned, with Rouser the Labrador at his side, was returning to Mullings from Farn Deane, reluctantly so, because he relished his days there – working with Tom Norris and always learning something new about farming. Also, it weighed on him that he had still not told Florie about his engagement to Lamorna Blake. Initially this had been because he knew her thoughts were occupied with George Bird, but increasingly he found himself trying not to think about his imprudence unless driven to do so by telephone communications with Lamorna, which were ever more plaintive on her part. He couldn't blame her for that – poor darling, he would insert conscientiously at the end of each session, followed by a sigh – dutiful husbands were one thing but surely the term shouldn't apply to fiancés. He was a cad, as despicable a rat as the one who had ditched Madge Bradley at the altar; not that he would back out from his commitment to Lamorna, but the thought that he should never have asked her to marry him given his financial situation was treachery in itself.

As he had expected, Seymour Cleerly had informed him that funds could not be released to him without Regina's authorization. Lamorna had been less squealing than expected when he relayed this information, saying she really hadn't expected the old stick to come through, therefore he must stop thinking like a silly and twist his Grandmother Tressler around his finger. Ned had shuddered at the phrase; but did he owe it to Lamorna to set aside squeamishness on this point?

Indifferent to the rain, he approached Mullings by the rear grounds and saw Madge Bradley in mackintosh and Wellington boots come out of the summer house. Drawing level with her as she put up her umbrella, he asked with the requisite smile if she'd like to race him to the house. Rouser shook his coat in readiness for those thrilling words – ready, set, go. If a dog could smile, he did. Madge didn't smile, but it wasn't really to be expected that she would, seeing that she had next to no sense of humour. Despite his own burdensome thoughts, he saw she was looking grave. 'Anything wrong?'

'Not really. I'd arranged to meet Cyril inside.' She pointed to the summer house. 'He telephoned half an hour ago to say he really needed to talk to me in private, and you know how difficult that can be up at the house.'

'I certainly do,' Ned said, remembering his concern that he'd been overheard telling Lamorna on the phone that he would be willing to murder Regina, 'unless you're prepared to fly in the face of convention and take him up to your bedroom. No, no, forget that! It wouldn't do to give *la femme horrible* an excuse to give you your marching orders.'

'It's difficult; sometimes I think I should leave of my own accord, but where would I go? Cyril can't ask his mother to move out – it wouldn't be right – but she'd make both our lives miserable if he brought me there. I suppose that makes us cowards.' Madge sighed. 'And now he's worried about Mr Craddock selling the bookshop and what that will mean for his job there. That's what he telephoned me about; it's got him in a real quake.'

'It shouldn't,' said Ned, 'he can work more hours at Mullings. Regina doesn't have any say about business expenditures. I've suggested to him several times that he could come on board full-time, but he insisted he didn't think it right to leave Craddock because the old chap gave him a job when needed.'

'That's Cyril for you.' Madge nodded. 'Some-

266

thing's delayed him, so I think I'll start down the woodland path and hope to meet up along the way.'

'You could do with a torch.'

'I have one.' Madge patted a mackintosh pocket.

Ned looked towards the darkness of the trees. 'Would you like me to walk with you until you spot him?'

'Oh, no! I'll be fine. No need to fuss about me, Ned. You know how I hate to be a nuisance to anyone, it makes me feel so upsettingly beholden,' Madge flustered. 'Not that you have ever done anything to make me feel unwanted...'

Ned cut the burbling short. 'I understand how it is, old bean. Being cooped up all day with William and Gertrude, to say nothing of Regina on the prowl, maintaining sanity demands time alone. Just be sure and watch your step with the ground being slick, and if a spectre emerges from the gloom, remember it's only the hermit; so don't take a flying leap and break an ankle.'

'That poor creature! One does feel for him!'

'Yes, well, if he's any sense left in his head he'll be snugly in his hut with a fire going in the stove.' Ned was eager to be gone; not getting much shelter from Madge's umbrella, he was feeling like a damp parcel left on a step. And if parcels could feel irritable, this one did. As soon as she'd put a few yards between them he sprinted for the steps up to the terrace and entered the house by the study door. After a couple of turns around the room, Rouser settled in his basket by the desk, and Ned went up to his bedroom. There

267

was still more than an hour until dinner, allowing time for a leisurely bath.

He was descending the stairs with the intention of telephoning Lamorna from the study before joining the family in the drawing room when he saw Grumidge approach the front door. Presumably the bell had rung, meaning a visitor, who, if uninvited, had chosen an awkward time. It was a centuries-old tradition that dinner never be delayed except in cases of fire, flood or famine, and Regina, whatever other changes she had chosen to make, adhered rigidly to this rule. Staying where he was halfway down the staircase, Ned saw Grumidge open the door and heard the butler's enquiring voice and an answering female one. His hand grasped the banister rail and his heart thudded. It had to be Lamorna – come to have matters out in a scene out of a Victorian melodrama, and really he couldn't blame her. He'd left her adrift in a sea of doubtful hope, instead of acting like a man and telling her there could be no London flat until he came into his independence; that marrying now would mean living full-time at Mullings.

Grumidge was stepping back into the hall, making way for a platinum-haired female to enter. He deposited a suitcase he now had in hand on a nearby table before closing the door against the rain and gathering wind. Through a haze of relief, Ned saw that the young woman was dressed in a cheaply smart manner and was giving her surroundings a raking glance that took in his presence on the stairs. To his amazement she winked at him. No offence taken. At that moment Ned could have kissed her – whoever she was. He had yet to take in the import of the suitcase.

She returned her gaze to Grumidge's impassive face. 'Is it all right to leave the umbrella on the porch? I borrowed it from the pub and it's an awkward old thing that I couldn't get to come down.'

'Quite acceptable, miss.'

'Jones.'

Ned saw the smile that emerged. He was also aware that Grumidge, who, like all good butlers, had eyes in the sides of his head as well as the front and back, had seen him and was wishing he'd come to the rescue. Meaning that, for some reason, here was a tricky situation.

'I'll take your coat if I may and conduct you to a room where you can wait in comfort while I inform Lady Stodmarsh of your arrival.'

'Oh, no,' came the perky response, 'no need for that kind of silly fuss; I'll come in with you.'

Ned eyed Grumidge kindly; the poor fellow was struggling manfully not to demean himself by looking aghast.

'I think it would be preferable...'

In three leaps Ned bounded to within inches of them, clapped a hand on Grumidge's shoulder and announced grandly that the young lady could be left in his care.

'Indeed, sir.' The butler bowed himself off, leaving the platinum blonde to eye Ned with amusement.

'Very la-de-da, all this! Lovely wainscoting

269

and furniture, proper ancestral I call it. Wish I had a camera.'

'I'm sure one can be provided!' Ned responded in lordly fashion. He was completely at sea, but for some reason feeling quite jolly about it.

'Oops! Can it be I'm addressing the master of the house?'

'No,' Ned grinned back at her, 'I'm the boot-boy, up to my usual naughty tricks. Let's hear who you are, damsel washed in by the rain. Jones is a suspiciously common name; perhaps you should change it to Smith.'

'What are you getting at, Ginger?'

'I scent mischief afoot ... that feeling in the thumbs, or maybe it's the toes.'

'You're far too young to be so cynical.'

'At twenty a person can have been through a lot.'

'Now that sounds honest.' The brown eyes sparkled. 'I've four years on you, but I'm still a sweet young innocent under this brave exterior, desperately hoping to find acceptance after ruthlessly being cast aside to live as an orphan in the storm but for the charity of those disposed to offer it.' The blonde interrupted this burst of poesy to clutch at Ned's arm. 'Gosh, I could do with something to eat – a piece of bread and butter, anything. I shouldn't have had that gin and orange at the pub on an empty tummy. Nothing for breakfast; egg and chips for lunch, but that was eons ago.'

'Feeling faint?' Ned took her by the shoulders. 'Want to sit down?'

'I don't know, maybe. It wouldn't do to pass

out when bearding the dragon in her den, would it?'

'Meaning Regina Stodmarsh, otherwise unfortunately known as my step-grandmother?'

'No need to sound so sorry for yourself.' A wilting sigh. 'Put yourself in my place.'

'Which is?'

'I'm her granddaughter; Sylvia Jones.'

'But you can't be; you died at birth,' said Ned nonsensically. He almost added, 'Don't you remember?'

TEN

'Thank you for breaking it to me that I'm the late lamented,' said the proclaimed Sylvia Jones wryly. Her thoughts seemed to buzz around her head rather than inside it. It was crucial not to be caught out. She needed to blot the girl called 'Toffee' out of existence. The problem was the Jones part. If Hattie Fly should write to her cousin Florence and mention that her lodger, a young woman with the same surname, common though it was, had unexpectedly suddenly taken herself off for an indefinite period, suspicion might be aroused that she'd headed for Mullings. There hadn't, however, seemed any way round that problem. On the optimistic side, Hattie was a woman of routine who always took care of her correspondence on a Saturday, and hopefully by the time a letter arrived there would no longer be a Miss Jones staying at Mullings.

'Sorry. Didn't mean to be rude,' said Ned, still holding on to her in case she crumpled, 'but that's the story Regina has put about – that your mother died giving birth and you with her.'

'The part about my mother is true. Her Christian name was also Sylvia and my father chose to call me after her. Later he wasn't so sure that was a good thing – too painful. He died when I was ten. I haven't fared badly in the meantime. I say, do you think you could...'

'Get you something to eat? Of course. I'll take you to Florie; she'll fix you up and make you feel better. She always manages to turn mountains back into molehills.'

'Who's Florie?'

'Our housekeeper and my friend. Want me to carry you?'

'Don't be absurd.'

Ned eyed her reprovingly. 'No need to sound so crushing, it's bruising to a fellow's ego.' He led her into a sitting room across from the study where Grumidge would likely have taken her. It was sometimes occupied these days by Madge and Cyril Fritch in his non-working hours, but Ned doubted they would be using it this evening. If he guessed right, they would either spend their time together at the summer house or – if they had any sense – at his house, enjoying the absence of his mother. A pity she always returned from her jaunts. Make hay while the sun shone should be Cyril and Madge's motto; although it

272

did boggle the mind to imagine the two of them conducting their courtship in any but the most decorous manner.

'Comfortable?'

'Very,' said Toffee from the chintz-covered chair that matched the curtains. 'It's lovely and cozy with the rain coming down outside. I feel I should be embroidering a tray cloth.'

Ned rumpled his hair. 'And I feel I'm wandering in circles on a fog-shrouded moor. Have I introduced myself?'

'You claimed to be the bootboy.'

'So I did. A hankering for the good old days. We don't have one any more. I'm Ned Stodmarsh.'

'I suppose that almost makes us related.'

'Best not to think that way, silver top. I don't like most of my relations and, to be brutally frank, I loathe the woman you claim as your grandmother.'

'Again, you put things so delicately.'

'Back in two shakes then.' Ned nipped out, drawing the door to behind him, and went in search of Florence. He found her as anticipated at her desk in the housekeeper's room; her face in profile would have struck him as a little sad, had his mind not been elsewhere. He waved at her to remain seated.

'Are my cheeks bulging? I feel as if they are with the news I bring! Prepare to be startled, dearest Florie!'

She turned towards him, eyes gentle, a smile on her lips. 'You've asked Lamorna Blake to marry you.'

Ned blinked, realized he hadn't closed the door behind him and did so. 'Oh, that! Yes, I have, been feeling beastly for not telling you about it. The thing is, I leaped before I thought and now find myself in the devil of a fix. She's insisting on a flat in London for weekends at least, to which she's entitled, of course. One as lovely as she shouldn't be expected to spend all her days and nights in the company of what's left of the family. Though the women aren't so bad these days, what with Madge getting engaged to Fritch and Aunt Gertrude involving herself in church activities – altar flowers and whatnot.'

'She attended a meeting at the vicarage this evening,' said Florence. 'Mr Grumidge mentioned a few minutes ago that to his knowledge she had not returned and dinner is due to be served within the quarter hour.'

Ned waved a hand. 'No matter! She's been late back a few times recently and they've gone ahead without her. It's just another excuse for Regina to look down her nose and Uncle William to bluster. But forget Aunt Gertrude or Cousin Madge, who for that matter may still be out with Fritch; forget for the moment my engagement to Lamorna. Something momentous has occurred and there's about to be the ruckus of a lifetime. No, don't get up,' he said as Florence started to do so, 'you need to hear the latest sitting down.'

'Dear Ned, what are you on about?'

'I didn't think Grumidge would have said anything; he'd leave it to me.'

'Say anything about what?'

274

'Guess who's just shown up with a suitcase?'

'Your Grandmother Tressler? She's not due until tomorrow, but there's nothing to that. Her rooms are always kept ready for her.'

'Not Granny. I'd be pleased for her to come early of course, but...'

'Her arrival wouldn't put that look of unholy glee on your face.' Florence laughed, relieved at the interruption in worrying about George. 'Ned, what has you so amused? I've never been any good at guessing games.'

'Even if you were it wouldn't do you any good this time. It's too far-fetched! I'm not even sure she's telling the truth. She may be an imposter, although that would be equally interesting in itself. Anyway, I've left her in the small sitting room where Grandmother was fond of sitting in the morning. And I do think she's at least speaking the truth about being hungry, so if you can get Mrs McDonald to rustle something up it would be a worthy deed, whether or not she really is Regina's granddaughter.'

'*Granddaughter?*' Florence rewarded Ned with the right degree of astonishment. 'There was another child?'

'As opposed to the one that died at birth along with the mother?'

'Oh, Ned, do take that grin off your face,' exclaimed Florence in rare exasperation with him. 'Of course that's what I mean. A surviving twin, is that it?'

'Now that would have been a clever thought for her to come up with if she's laying a con game, and from the looks of her – a tarted-up

275

platinum blonde – she fits the bill all right. But no, she says she's the one that supposedly didn't make it. Her father died when she was ten, I think she said. So here we are with questions begging – was Regina misinformed, or has she been lying through her teeth all these years rather than acknowledge a child born to her daughter?'

Blocking any more fascinating conjecture, Florence stood up, looked at her watch and then squarely at Ned. 'Lord Stodmarsh, I require your instructions on the course of action to be taken forthwith.'

'Who ... what?' Ned gaped at her. 'Excuse me, Florie, while I reposition my jaw. It just dropped six inches.'

'It's time for you to think as the Master of Mullings. No matter that Lady Stodmarsh may control the purse strings; when it comes to capital this is your house.'

'It doesn't feel that way.'

'Perhaps now is the time to decide that it should, if you'll pardon me speaking out of place, sir?' She could not hold back a laugh at his expression. 'You're faced with a convergence of events. Mr Grumidge is due in less than five minutes to announce dinner is served. An immediate announcement of the young lady's presence will prevent her having a meal on her own before being thrust into what, as you predict, is bound to be an unpleasant scene. It is unlikely that the family, including Lady Stodmarsh, will be able to enjoy a morsel of what is placed before them. But delaying matters until the return to the drawing room for coffee is not a decision to be made by me or Mr Grumidge. It has to be yours – if indeed that is your wish.'

Ned drew himself up to his full five foot eight and a fraction. 'I know your methods of old, Florie. I've been feeling a complete worm over Lamorna and you're giving me this chance to square my shoulders and march forth filled with noble resolve to protect a girl who may be a rotten little widget – although I have to admit to taking to her – from being torn limb from limb when in a weakened state by THAT WOMAN! Gosh! What wouldn't I give to know how she managed to get Grandfather to marry her! Alas, she'll never tell, and gentleman that he was, he took that secret to the grave!'

'That's as maybe,' said Florence. She had long ago accurately worked out how that game had been played and won – gain the sympathy of an unhappy and unworldly man in failing health removed from his usual element, and manoeuvre him into believing he had implied more than intended and must choose between dashing hopes he had raised or marrying her. Lord Stodmarsh being who he was, the outcome could be serenely anticipated. 'As you've said, there's going to be a ruckus. Is it to be immediate, or briefly delayed?'

'Delayed. I'll bounce along and join the clan for dinner and you get a meal to our visitor. Then, after we re-gather in the drawing room, send Grumidge along to inform Regina that a young lady has arrived wishing to speak with her. She'll inquire as to identity and he'll tell her.

How's that?'

'Clear and concise.'

Ned saluted, then turned as he was halfway out the door. 'This could be hoots of fun, that beastly woman finally getting some kind of come-uppance, being the one to jig on red-hot coals instead of watching others do it for her amuse-ment. The trouble is the girl – there's something about Sylvia Jones that got to me.'

Florence understood what he meant when she entered the chintz-furbished sitting room fifteen minutes later. The scrimped artificial silk dress, patterned in black and gold, the cheap high heels and feather toque, looked best suited to a seedy restaurant in an unlighted alley; nothing appeal-ing there. But within a moment Florence was making a more thoughtful appraisal. The girl, seemingly oblivious to no longer being alone, was standing sideways staring out into the rain-shrouded grounds, her profile thoughtful; and when she looked round her eyes were sad. They were brown eyes – toffee coloured, thickly lash-ed, complimentary to her warm complexion and utterly incongruous. They belonged in the face of a young woman who wasn't overly bothered about how she looked. Of course there were answers to that incongruity: an impulse for a new look that would change all else, a desire to shock one's elders, or to please a young man who had his heart set on a blonde dressed in tawdry fashion.

Florence reminded herself as she set down the loaded tray that the situation was sufficiently intriguing without her crocheting trimmings for it. Before she could introduce herself as the housekeeper, the young woman spoke with a lightness that didn't ring true, understandably so in the circumstances. She could hardly be expecting a grandmother's delighted welcome to be shortly forthcoming.

'Those woods out there may be a picnicker's delight on a sunny day, but passing them along the way on such a dreary night they struck me as horribly forbidding.' Her hands clamping her arms, she shivered, somewhat theatrically, Florence thought. 'I heard there was a path through them, but you wouldn't catch me taking it on a bet, especially with that creepy old hermit straight out of the Middle Ages creeping amongst the trees, ready to pounce up from behind and cosh you over the head with a relic clawed out of the catacombs.'

'That's an understandable fear, but he's been here long enough to have proved harmless, poor soul. If you don't mind my asking, how did you know of him?'

The young woman removed the feather toque and tossed it on to the settle in front of the fireplace. It was a gesture in keeping with her appearance, as was the brittle edge in her voice when responding. 'Oh, I heard someone talking about the hermit on the bus I took from the train.' She moved casually over to the table where Florence had placed the tray and glanced at it. 'Good of you to bring this in. I suppose you're the housekeeper young Mr Ginger Nob mentioned as if God had blessed him with his personal archangel. No offence intended.'

279

Florence smiled. 'None taken.' It was evident the girl was, very sensibly, getting into the part of herself – or one created for taking on Regina Stodmarsh. A good-natured girl displaying a hint of diffidence would find herself dispatched into the night before getting out two sentences. 'I'm Florence Norris and I've been here long enough that nothing surprises me unduly, Miss Jones.'

'I wasn't going to explain myself to you.' A haughtily raised plucked eyebrow followed by a look of abject misery that could surely not have been improvised unless she was a professional actress. 'I'm sorry!'

'Don't be, my dear, I'm always far from my best when tired and hungry, to say nothing of being uncertain what the next hour or so holds in store.' Florence drew her towards the chair next to the table with the tray on it and watched her sit down. 'Lord Stodmarsh asked me to reassure you that you will have more than an hour to yourself as the family is presently at dinner. He thought you would be glad of the extra time to unwind after your journey.'

'You are one of the nicest people.' It was said sleepily, weariness having taken hold. 'I knew you would be, of course...' the brown eyes blinked open '...from how your devoted young gentleman spoke about you. He seems quite a love,' said in a return of the flippant tone.

'I've known him since he was a small boy, Miss Jones.'

'Apple of his parents' eyes?'

'Both killed in a motor accident when he was very young.'

'I can sympathize, knowing what it is to be orphaned.'

'I'm sorry. A loss unfathomable to most of us, and we often do not appreciate what we have. It helped with Ned ... Lord Stodmarsh, that he was brought up in the family home with grandparents who loved him dearly.'

'Lucky for him, but maybe,' an attempted laugh, 'I'm about to make up for what I missed out on since my dad died. Slim chance, wouldn't you say?'

'I'll pull this table in front of you.' Florence suited action to words. 'Those are roast beef sandwiches; there's horseradish and mustard in those little pots if you wish it, and a slice of veal and ham pie – Cook makes it herself – a Scotch egg and some cheese and biscuits.'

'Fit for a queen. You wouldn't tell me, would you, what's she like? If she's mellowed over the years? Your Lord Stodmarsh made it plain he loathes her, but he would, wouldn't he? It can't be easy seeing another woman in your grand-mother's place.'

'I'll be back in five minutes with a pot of tea.' Florence had no intention of saying any more, but found she didn't wish to leave it at that. Heretofore only Ned had profoundly tugged at her maternal heartstrings, but this stranger – this dubious girl – did so, to a lesser degree to be sure, but undeniably. 'What I am willing to state, Miss Jones, is that I'm of the opinion that you have it within you to stand up to a marching army if what is important to you depended on it.' She was out of the room – allowing no time for a response.

On passing the closed dining room door Florence wondered how well Ned was doing in restraining his anticipation, possibly taking the form of roguish amusement, of what was to come. At least it would keep his mind off his entanglement with Lamorna Blake. His announcement as to how things stood had come as no surprise. It had seemed inevitable to her for weeks that his infatuation would bring on a proposal. She had also expected from what she knew of Miss Blake that she would accept, not only because of Ned's undeniable charm, but for the pleasure of distressing her parents, who would abhor the connection, despite Lady Blake's desire to be included among those visiting an establishment boasting an ornamental hermit. And it was clear from Ned's alarm at Lamorna's demanding a London flat that he was already disenchanted. It was all a storm in a teacup, because with the money tied up as it was, the marriage couldn't possibly come off, unless his Grandmother Tressler offered to step in, which Florence thought highly unlikely. Ned would be remorseful, hiding his relief, and Miss Blake would be entitled to bring down the curtain after a display of hysterics that would do credit to Sarah Bernhard. Her thoughts returned to Sylvia Jones and how long she had been preparing for her appearance on stage at Mullings.

Florence's entrance into the kitchen went unnoticed by Mrs McDonald, who had Annie Long and Jeanie Barnes dodging in circles in response to a flood of instructions. 'Did either of

you think to give that hollandaise for the poached salmon another whisk? And what about the
lamb gravy? Don't tell me one of you's added
more salt? Oh, for heaven's sakes! If I could
grow another pair of arms, I'd tell the pair of you
to take off and join the circus.'

'Now that's an idea,' responded Jeanie cheek-
ily on her way to the stove, 'fancy myself on a
trapeze, I do!'

'Oh, not me.' Annie froze in her tracks. 'When
I hear the mattress springs going once in a while
in Mum and Dad's room and know they're
bouncing about like a couple of kids having a
pillow fight, I worry something awful that one of
them will fall off the bed and hurt themselves
bad.'

Mrs McDonald glared Jeanie into silence
before giving Annie the once-over. 'Remind me
how old you are?'

'Twenty-six.'

'Well, takes all kinds.' Mrs McDonald shook
her head and spotted Florence. 'Would you say
so, Mrs Norris?'

'Yes, and the better for it. Annie's a good girl
and we all know it.'

'And what am I? Day-old bread?' Jeanie jerk-
ed angrily.

'You're appreciated too,' said Florence, wishing despite the truth of this that the girl wasn't so
often on the defensive, not only because it
heightened stress, but because Regina Stodmarsh had her ear to the ground when it came to
the servants and she was a woman who blatantly
took pleasure in dismissing them given the least

provocation. Her reaction to her personal maid trying on one of her fur coats was typical. Lillian Stodmarsh would have been amused, touched. How long ago that era now seemed.

She had to remember what was sound and solid and remained, and this of course included Mrs McDonald, who told Annie and Jeanie to go into the passageway and await the descent of the two footmen with the dishes and cutlery from the soup course. Tonight it had been celery and apple, following on from tomato aspic; next to go up would be the poached salmon accompanied by the hollandaise sauce. As a fifteen-minute interlude was customary at this period of the meal, Mrs McDonald had time to draw breath and prod Florence for information about the mystery guest. She had little hope of having her curiosity satisfied. It wasn't in her nature, however, not to make the attempt. It went without saying that Mr Grumidge's lips had been and would remain sealed. But, like she'd always said, the blanker his expression – as had been the case when he returned after answering the front doorbell – the more you knew there was something on his mind.

It didn't work with Mrs Norris to try and get in by the side door. Best to come out with it straight and see what that gave. 'Come on, give us a hint who you took that tray of food up to. Not that I'd begrudge it to a beggar, but him or her would have come round the back, and if it was an acquaintance of the family they'd've been requested to return at a more convenient time, or invited in to dine.' Mrs McDonald paused to stare at Florence's back as she went about filling the kettle. 'Oh, my lord!' She clapped a hand to her massive chest. 'So that's it! I've seen this at the pictures! A woman stumbles in through a stranger's door at the height of a wicked storm, cries out that her child is coming and there's a rush round to boil water. Saucepan upon saucepan of it! I never knew what for, but then I've never given birth. Here, let me give you a hand.'

'To make a pot of tea for someone – I'll keep it at that – who as I was leaving was about to partake of the meal I just took up.'

'Drat!' Mrs McDonald pounded a weighty fist into an outsized palm. 'I'd forgotten about that. Again, I don't know for a fact, but I can't imagine a woman in the throes of labour thinking I must tuck into a little something before getting on with this business.'

'Never mind,' said Florence, spooning tea leaves into the pot, 'but what I will tell you is, this is the calm before the storm.' Inevitably her thoughts switched to Ned and whether he was relishing the prospect of Regina Stodmarsh being shown to have lied about her granddaughter's death or if he was caught up in anxiety for the one who was about to confront her.

The dining room at Mullings was furnished in accordance with the rest of house's timeless grace. Richly dark wood, serenely patterned wallpaper, carpet and curtains. All taken for granted and thus unnoted by Ned. At that moment he was reflecting with deplorable cheerfulness that he couldn't be faulted for failing to telephone Lamorna as intended. He'd heard its distant ring a couple of times in the past fifteen minutes, knew in his bones that it was her on the other end of the line and taken a last swallow from his glass of hock. Lamorna would survive a bout of petulance unaided, but Sylvia Jones might require picking up in pieces from the floor. His mind shifted with the fluidity of the young to the rest of the meal. He hoped for roast lamb. Mrs MacDonald, knowing his partiality for it, had coyly hinted that morning that it might be on the menu. For once it didn't irk him that Regina occupied what had been his grand-mother's chair at the dining room table. Tonight she was elegant in sapphire-blue, which comple-mented the silver hair, blue eyes, and patrician features, but did nothing to counteract the im-pression of chiselled marble. *Queen of Mullings! Enjoy it! The judgement seat is at hand!* So far she had contributed little to the conversation, other than to comment negatively on the soup and request William to apply his napkin to his moustache if she were not to be taken mortally ill by the disgusting sight of it.

'Wish that was all it'd take to put you in your coffin,' he'd groused into his soup bowl. Regina's response was the thinning of thin red lips into a disdainful smile. These little ex-changes were to her the champagne of life, the sparkling, bubbling lift that energized and kept her looking younger than her age.

Ned directed a thought his uncle's way. Poor blighter! He'd gone the way of all blown-up

286

balloons: the air had finally seeped out of him. His raucous outbursts had become less frequent over the past couple of years. One reason, perhaps, was that the victim of choice, his wife, was gone from the house a good deal these days – her pleasure in attending to the altar flowers having extended to other church matters. Also he'd gained a considerable amount of weight, limiting much of the huffing and puffing of yore to the business of catching his breath. An ageing, overly stout fellow reduced to an emotional shadow of his former self. It came to Ned at that moment, perhaps because the arrival of Sylvia Jones had subconsciously nudged at his own notions of family, that despite William's never having paid him much account and having a disagreeable impact on those around him, the man was his grandparents' son and his father's brother, and such ties mattered.

Watching Regina finger the pearls she always wore, Ned revelled in a vision of her choking herself with them on being presented with Sylvia Jones.

Madge's voice brought him back to the moment. It was typical of her to fill in silences, searching out any piece of verbal flotsam and poking it downstream in the hope of reeling in a response that would get everyone chatting, but this did not appear to be her present aim. She was clearly upset and Ned realized belatedly that she was addressing him. 'Poor Cyril. It really is too mean of whoever stole his bike.'

'It certainly is,' Ned replied.

'Of course it's not new, but that's not the point,

is it?'

'I should say not!'

'And coming on top of finding out Mr Craddock's intention to sell the bookshop, you'll understand how depressed he's feeling.'

Regina cut in, voice icy, eyes mirthful. 'I hope, Madge, this plaintive tale is not a hint that I buy him another.'

'Of course not.' Madge flushed, whether from anger or embarrassment, Ned could not gauge, but the impact of colour against her dark hair and eyes resulted in a prettiness that made it more understandable to him why Cyril Fritch wished to marry her. 'I have the money in my Post Office account.'

'For a bookshop?' Gertrude asked, out of what Ned assumed to be Christian politeness. She had little interest in Madge and none in Cyril.

'For a new bike, but Cyril is fond of the one he has!' A sob caught at the words. 'He dislikes change.'

'Then one can only assume,' Regina's voice had never been more sneering, 'that you held him at gunpoint until you got a marriage proposal out of him.'

'That's a filthy thing to say!' Ned shot up in his chair. Vile woman! He couldn't wait to feed her to Sylvia Jones.

'I'm merely supplying an answer to what has puzzled so many. Not Lady Blake, however – such a clear-sighted woman on occasion. She's in no doubt, Madge, that you did that sad little excuse for a man the honour of begging his hand in marriage. By the way, Ned, speaking of wedding bells, I've invited your betrothed along with her parents and brother to tea tomorrow. I trust you appreciate my thoughtfulness in making this gesture...' Her gaze shifted away from him as Madge, head ducked, fled the room. 'Oh, dear! Did I say something to wound her?'

'I don't think that question merits an answer,' said Gertrude in a voice as stout as her figure. Ned had risen to follow Madge, but the advisability of allowing her time alone struck him and he settled back into his chair to eye his aunt with respect. All this churchy business must be applauded for having supplied the old bean with sufficient backbone to have her casting off her corsets in the near future. Really, he was becoming quite fond of her.

William muttered something about damned, prattling women. Regina opened her gash of a mouth to respond, but closed it upon the entrance of the better looking of the two footmen with the fish course. Any continuation was thus forestalled until the door closed on his retreat, whereupon Ned beamed at Gertrude.

'Back to what you were saying, Aunt.'

'The usual meaningless drivel, but if you must encourage her,' Regina gave a dismissive smile, 'I shall not attend.'

Gertrude took her time swallowing a forkful of salmon coated in hollandaise and then dabbing at her mouth. 'I am happy to repeat that most of what you have to say is without merit. On the subject of snaring husbands, I believe you can speak from the wisdom of experience. One of course dislikes being judgmental, but...'

'Do let's,' Ned urged. 'It's such a pleasure to see you coming out of your shell, Aunt, after all these years.'

'Pink muck,' groused William, staring at his plate.

'Can't agree with you there, Uncle. In my opinion, both Keats and Shelley might have been inspired to write "Odes to A Salmon Mousse" had they tasted Mrs McDonald's.'

'She's been slipping lately, to the point where I've been enquiring into locating a replacement.' If Regina hoped a protest from Ned would end the rest of what Gertrude had to say she was mistaken.

'Miss Hendrick, the vicar's housekeeper, says if we don't encourage people to take a good peek into their weaknesses they'll never change for the better. It is true some may wonder how Madge and Cyril Fritch came to be engaged – the difference in their walks of life would assure that – but I cannot think there has been near as much speculation about them as there has been on how you manoeuvred my father-in-law into marrying you.'

Regina's expression did not alter by the flicker of an eyelash; she continued poking at her salmon mousse, yet the temperature seemed to drop – as if a window had been opened to introduce an icy draft.

'It has also been of interest, to myself amongst others, that the Reverend Pimcrisp has practically shunned this house since your arrival. Miss Hendrick is fond of him, and she and I have become good friends. We seem to fit together, like two pieces of a puzzle; it seemed a little strange at first ... and yet so nice to be regarded as a reliable confidante. I say this to explain that she isn't a gossip. Only our closeness allowed her to tell me this afternoon how upset she had been by Reverend Pimcrisp's distress, mounting to alarm, when Edward returned from his visit to Weymouth engaged to you.'

'Indeed?' Regina's tone expressed boredom.

'He blamed himself.'

'Why?' Ned leaned forward.

'For the sin of worldly vanity that had led him to include mention in correspondence with his cousin, Lord Asprey, of his friendship with a man of such stature as Edward Stodmarsh. In the pertinent letter he'd written of Edward's imminent visit to Weymouth, providing dates and the name of the hotel.'

'I see where you're leading,' said Ned, 'but how was that information relayed to...?'

'My charming self?' Regina's laugh was airy. Despite her comment that Mrs McDonald needed sacking, she had finished her salmon mousse and now sipped her wine.

Gertrude reached for the salt cellar. 'Lord Asprey lives in Northumbria and is friendly with your family, the Tamershams, and he acknowledged on inquiry from Mr Pimcrisp that he had passed along word to them of the holiday, along with the information that Edward was a grief-stricken widower in failing health. Was it a coincidence that you should visit Weymouth at the same time? The embarrassed Lord Asprey didn't think so, any more than the vicar had. In his letter of apology, he described you as a malevolent woman who had made her brother and sister-in-law's lives wretched for years and had driven her daughter to escape, by eloping with the Jones lad, then refused to aid the girl when pregnant and impoverished. When she begged you to send the jewellery given to her by her grandparents you laughed as you tore up the letter and refused to give her uncle or aunt her address.'

Ned sat rigid, picturing Sylvia Jones in the sitting room and hoping she was an imposter. Being related by blood to Regina should not be wished on anyone.

'And you heard this fairy tale from your Miss Hendrick?' Regina fingered her pearls.

'This afternoon, as I said.' Gertrude saw her husband remove his pipe from his pocket, shook her head and watched him return it, grumbling. 'It has played heavily upon her mind that Mr Pimcrisp continues to do penance by giving up crumpets with his afternoon tea. It was her hope that I could persuade you into a life of atonement, which if he were to know about it might ease his mind.'

'Atonement! For taking a trip to Weymouth, even if it were in pursuit of meeting an eligible man? I couldn't compel him to offer marriage!'

'Oh, but I think, as does the poor vicar, that you could and did. You certainly had no difficulty in believing Madge pulled the same rabbit out of the hat with Cyril Fritch.'

'None of this comes as a surprise.' Ned's eyes glittered like green glass. 'I was never angry with Grandfather for marrying you, or for the trust he set up afterwards, but there was a hurt – now it's all for him. You played your cards so splendidly, Regina, with your stories of being ill-treated by your family and your fear of finding yourself a dependent at Mullings after his death.'

'All that fascinates me about this conversation,' Regina waved a dismissive hand at him, 'is the glow your aunt radiates when she's talking about her Miss Hendrick – for all the world as if she's swept up in a schoolgirl crush on the games mistress. Can it be she's amongst those who never outgrow that stage?'

'What? What?' William roused himself to growl.

Gertrude placidly advised him not to excite himself. Ned could not guess at the true state of her feelings; she'd always had the ability to constrain her emotions. 'Regina is merely suggesting, my dear, that I'm a woman of unnatural inclinations.'

'Harrumph! Hate to agree with a word out of her mouth, but have to for once. All this prancing down to church! Not normal!' He ruminated for a moment or two. 'It could get around that you regret not taking the veil.'

Ned relaxed fractionally before Regina spoke again. 'What a fool you are! No wonder your parents had little time for you!'

'Damn you to hell, you vicious swine!' It was the old William Stodmarsh rearing up, face empurpled, eyes bulging, fist thumping the table.

'Have we not all heard,' Regina surveyed Ned

and Gertrude wonderingly, 'this man, using the term loosely, bleat ad nauseam about being the ignored, unloved younger son?' A hush, thick and impenetrable as smog, descended.

In light of all that had preceded, Ned should not perhaps have been as aghast as he was, and there was undeniable truth on Regina's side in this instant, but when he saw the look in his uncle's eyes – a mixture of hate and defeat – he knew that a mortal wound had been dealt. He would from now on be a walking corpse.

Ned saw, for the first time in his memory, Gertrude look at her husband with compassion bordering on tenderness. She went to his chair and helped him to his feet. Ned started to rise, but she shook her head. 'There, there, my dear, let me help you to your room and I'll read you a comforting piece from the Bible. You'll see,' she continued as she led him shambling from the room, 'that there are none forsaken, none left unloved by the one who counts above all.'

They had just passed into the hall when the footman came in. Expertly trained as he was, he showed no surprise at finding Regina and Ned alone at the table. Ordinarily Ned felt it appropriate to provide an explanation, but he was convinced that if he did so Regina would counter it with a blistering one of her own. It seemed to him that the meal would never end. The minutes ticked by in silence, save for the clinking of cutlery and the rain pattering forcefully against the windows. At last! Regina rose and he followed suit, but the sequence was not as he had imagined it. Instead of joining him for coffee in the drawing room where he had arranged for Grumidge to inform her of Sylvia Jones's arrival, she instead swept upstairs to her room.

Not an unfortunate turn of events, he decided. It was now appropriate to send Florie to relay the message, but this would need to occur quickly – before Regina could use the excuse of having retired to bed for refusing to see the girl. Ned hastened from the hall back into the dining room and asked the footman who was clearing the table if he knew where Mrs Norris was to be found.

'I saw her go into the sitting room across from the study a moment ago, sir.'

Ned thanked him and darted down the hall to slide to a standstill when Florence came out of the door to which he was headed.

'How is she?'

'Asleep. I'd taken her in another cup of tea but she was too worn out to take more than a couple of sips before her eyes closed. I put her feet on a hassock and here I am.'

'The timing couldn't be better.' Ned nodded at her approvingly. 'I need to go up to Regina's bedroom where she has withdrawn – I would like to think to lick her wounds, but more likely to rearm for tomorrow. Dinner was hellish, I'll tell you about that later – the point is that Grumidge won't do, so it has to be you who breaks it to her that she's a grandmother and the proof's here at Mullings. Poor Florie, I never stop putting you through it, do I?'

'I do my job, sir.'

'What nonsense!' Ned's mock frown was

295

followed by a hug and suddenly they were both laughing, albeit uneasily.

'Lady Stodmarsh may be taking a bath.'

'Haul her out!'

Florence saw him go into the sitting room as she went up the stairs. Regina Stodmarsh responded to her knock on the bedroom door with an order to enter. The interior was one of luxurious silk and satin, plush carpeting, marquetry, gilded mirrors and ornate molding. It had not been that way at the time of Edward Stodmarsh's death, but it had to be said that Regina had generally made few alterations, extravagant or otherwise, to the house. Wisely so, given its near perfection of good taste, as perhaps she was aware.

Regina was standing before her dressing table mirror, her back to the door and Florence; the light from the overhead chandelier brought out the sapphire fire of the pearls' clasp. In comparison the reflected eyes appeared drained of their usual blue – their shine was that of polished steel.

'Is the drawing room on fire, Mrs Norris?' she inquired, without turning her head.

'No, madam,' Florence answered without inflection. 'A young lady has arrived who wishes to speak with you.'

'At this hour?' Contempt tightened the reflected face.

'She arrived as dinner was about to be served and she agreed to wait until its conclusion so as not to cause a delay.'

'Agreed?' Regina Stodmarsh revolved in slow

296

motion. 'Pray tell me she is a duchess, Mrs Norris, otherwise, as so frequently occurs, you overstep your position in this household.'

Florence chose not to say that Ned had instructed her to relay the information. 'The young lady says she is a Miss Sylvia Jones and that she is your granddaughter, Lady Stodmarsh.'

'Nonsense. Impossible!' The words were fired like shots from a pistol, but it was Regina Stodmarsh who looked as if she had taken a bullet. Her eyes stared blankly; she swayed and in doing so backed into the dressing table, hands grabbing its edge for support. Florence experienced a flicker of sympathy. She was about to offer to help Lady Stodmarsh into a nearby chair, when the woman rallied sufficiently to speak in a trembling voice containing a multitude of emotions warring with each other. 'I have no granddaughter. This is trickery. I wouldn't be surprised if my step-grandson thought it up as a way of getting back at me for refusing to finance his marriage to the Blake girl.' She was regaining confidence with each hissing word.

'Do you wish her to be fetched, Lady Stodmarsh, so you can tell her so?' Florence replied at her most detached.

'Get out! Go downstairs and tell the butler and footmen that if they hope to be employed here five minutes from now they will get hold of her, by the hair if necessary, and throw her out of my house.'

'Not so,' came Ned's voice from the doorway. Florence turned to see him leaning against the jamb, hands in his pockets, feet crossed – a negligent stance that could have sprung from boyish confidence, or a man's steady determination. 'The decision as to who comes or goes at Mullings is mine by right of birth. Grandfather did not appoint you my legal guardian; what control you have is limited to what is tied up in the trust. You know that well enough, or you would – threats notwithstanding – have tossed Madge out of here an age ago.'

Regina Stodmarsh's hand curled. 'This is a matter pertinent only to myself.'

'I don't see it that way.' Ned's eyes lit with mockery. 'Call me nosy, but I'm very much interested in finding out how you explain a granddaughter who, according to your account, died at birth. Perky little thing for a corpse. Didn't know they could grow.' He turned, beckoned, and Sylvia Jones came in, platinum head held high.

'Hello, Granny, dear,' she said.

At a nod from Ned, Florence slipped from the room and made her way down to the housekeeper's room. Going to the kitchen was not an option, given that Mrs McDonald would be avid with curiosity, which it was not her place to satisfy. In the hallway she came upon Mr Grumidge. He gave her an appraising glance, but made no enquiry. She was about to pass silently into her room when she saw Molly come out of the kitchen and paused to bade her light a fire in what was known as the rosebud bedroom and put a warming pan in the bed.

'Yes, Mrs Norris.'

'It is possible we may have an overnight guest.'

Mr Grumidge's face remained impassive, but Florence was not misled. She was certain that he was preparing himself for a major eruption, and that he and Molly would be sure to talk between themselves, given the personal nature of their relationship. Discreet they might be, but the indications had been there for some time that they would marry. She sat at her desk, her thoughts contorted by anxiety amounting to dread. There was some indefinable connection with the sense of oppression that had haunted her off and on since the death of Lillian Stodmarsh. She felt that the pages in some black book were still to be turned, that something which had been resting was stirring, yawning itself awake...

'The first place I look I find you,' said Ned, closing the door behind him. His grin flashed before his eyes narrowed. 'That was some scene you missed. Talk about savage rage – a mauling by a tiger would have been sweet nothing compared to the way Regina lashed out at Miss Jones – but I have to say the girl held her own when she could get a word in. The outcome is, she's staying the night and we just have to hope she isn't murdered in her bed.'

'Oh, Ned!' Florence barely managed a smile as she stood up. 'Don't tempt fate, as Mrs McDonald is wont to say. Where is Miss Jones now?'

'I just returned her to the little sitting room. Will you escort her to her quarters while I put

299

Grumidge and Mrs McDonald in the picture?'

'Of course.'

'Thanks, Florie, dear!' Ned was about to open the door when he clapped a hand to his forehead. 'My godfathers! I forgot all about phoning Lamorna. Too late now, I'll just have to ring her first thing in the morning and then take Granny Tressler over to the Blakes after picking her up at the station. She won't fuss about coming here first; she's not that sort.'

'I understood that Sir Winthrop and Lady Blake are coming here for tea tomorrow.' Florence straightened her belt.

'That's off!' Ned's grin was back full force. 'Regina's final venting of spleen included telling me to have Grumidge uninvite them. Silly of her, because there'll be no keeping Miss Jones under wraps – it would have been much more sensible to feign delight at their discovering each other after all these lost years and thereby reduce the situation to a nine days' wonder.'

As Florence crossed the hall to the sitting room, she remembered encouraging the late Lord Stodmarsh to believe that such would be the case with the ornamental hermit. For a moment she pictured the bearded, hoary-locked, robed figure huddled in his hut while the rain hammered upon the roof and tree branches gyrated in the wind. She had never seen him close up in her walks through the wood, although she would have welcomed the chance to do so and ask him how he was faring.

Jeanie, who took him his midday and evening meals, might, human nature being what it was, have attempted to break the rule of not speaking to him; if so she had hugged failure or success to herself. She was a girl who liked to feel important, and the unusual element to these sorties elevated her, at least in her own eyes, to a position of mystery tinged with danger. Annie continued to say she would die before going anywhere near the hut and Florence suspected she was not alone in Dovecote Hatch in allotting him eerie powers drawn of superstition. Would Sylvia Jones be viewed as uncannily emerging from the grave by those prone to a shiver down the spine, or simply as a juicy piece of gossip by one and all?

She found Miss Jones seated on the edge of a chair, hands gripped, and face tightened by whatever she was feeling. 'If you'll please follow me,' she said, 'I'll take you to your room.' She led her upstairs to a bedroom papered with rosebuds on a silvery white background and furnished to the taste of a young girl, the firelight from the hearth reflected in flickers of apricot on the polished wood. On the bench under the window was the suitcase brought from London. Florence looked towards it. 'Would you like me to send one of the maids to unpack for you?' The answer was as expected.

'No,' said Miss Jones quickly, 'it will be such bliss to be alone. Oh,' she caught herself, 'that does sound rude and I don't want you to rush away; you've been so nice – just as I expected when you brought me supper. Ned, he told me to call him that, said you're one of the dearest people in the world.'

'He's a very caring young gentleman.'

Miss Jones nodded. 'It was awfully good of him to go to bat for me the way he did. At one point I thought that woman – my grandmother – would strike him. She's every bit as horrid as my father told me she was. He was a blunt man, rough around the edges, with little education apart from what he got from books.'

'That's not a bad way to learn.' Florence smiled.

Again Miss Jones nodded. 'He loved my mother and I don't think her feelings for him were a silly infatuation arising from a desperate need to escape. I feel I know her from what he told me about her. He was a great dad.' She broke off as if needing to do so, her eyes roving the room. 'This is all so pretty.'

'The furniture was in the first Lady Stodmarsh's bedroom when she was growing up and she brought it with her when she married. The wallpaper is a replica of what she'd had.'

'Perhaps she imagined having a daughter.'

'Very likely.' Florence was about to ask if there was anything else that could be provided for Miss Jones's comfort when the girl's voice exploded fiercely.

'Those pearls! Ned said she always wears them! They belonged to my mother, a gift from her grandparents on her seventeenth birthday – a few months before she ran off with my father. She meant to take them with her and sell them – they're worth a lot – but when it came to it they left in too much of a hurry. She later wrote and begged for them to be sent to her but that woman wrote back a blistering refusal.' She paused to draw breath. 'If you don't believe me, think about the sapphire clasp – it's in the shape of an S for Sylvia.'

'Of course I believe you,' said Florence, and meant it. 'Did you ask Lady Stodmarsh for them just now?'

Miss Jones laughed. It was a harsh, ugly sound. 'I think if I had she'd have flushed them down the nearest toilet. It was obvious that even her eagerness to be rid of me did not counter her spite. I was very much aware of that possibility when I decided to come...' Her voice trailed away.

'You need sleep,' said Florence gently.

Fifteen minutes later, having talked with an animated Mrs McDonald as briefly as possible, Florence went to her own bedroom, undressed and got into her nightgown. With everything replaying itself in her mind, she did not expect to fall asleep for some time after getting into bed. In fact, she soon dozed off, only to awaken a couple of hours later, at half an hour past midnight by her clock, and got up to fill a glass of water from the carafe on the chest of drawers by her bed. While drinking it she wandered over to the window and stared out into the night. The rain had ceased and the light from a near full moon separated the darkness into blurred but distinct shapes: the fountains in the sunken rose gardens, the garden seating, and the summer house etched against the shimmer of the lake. She caught her breath. Something moved. A figure detached itself from the water's edge and crossed the lawn to disappear into the woods. It took a moment for Florence's common sense to assert itself. Other members of the household had glimpsed the hermit gliding about at night. It had to be him. She finished the glass of water and went back to bed.

George Bird had also woken from a restless sleep to stand staring out of his bedroom window. Doing so relieved to a small degree the feeling of being boxed in, helplessly tied up in knots, at times seeming not to be able to get enough air in his lungs. If he only knew where Jim was, that he was safe for this one moment – that he was asleep, briefly forgetful that he was on the run, a hunted man. It comforted George a little that he wasn't the only one who believed Jim innocent of murdering that old lady. That girl Toffee had made it clear her faith hadn't wavered an eyelash and she'd do anything to help him; which couldn't be said of the lad's parents, Sally and Arthur. They were all over the place in their thinking. One minute he wouldn't hurt a fly, and the next, they'd always worried what getting in with a bunch of layabouts with loose morals would do to him. George was about to turn from the window when he saw someone – he was unable to tell if it was a man or a woman – open the gate leading to the footpath through the Mullings woods and instantly be absorbed into the trees. Could it be Jim? His heart thudded, then slowed as he remembered the detective who had visited him saying, meaningfully, that Constable Trout or another policeman would be patrolling the area at all hours in case the young man decided to try and hide out in Dovecote Hatch.

Florence started up in bed again at around two in the morning, for no accountable reason other than that she must have had a bad dream. She sank back again into sleep, but woke feeling unrested to start the day. Five minutes after she had entered the kitchen to have a cup of tea with Mrs McDonald, and had barely started on the subject of Sylvia Jones, Ned flung into the room, his hair spiking upwards as if he'd spent the night grabbing it by the roots, anxiety written all over his face.

'Have either of you seen Rouser?'

'No,' said both women. His panic spread to Florence.

'Wasn't he in the study when you came down?'

Ned shook his head vehemently. 'No. And he never strays from there until I fetch him in the morning a little after five. Grandfather trained him to stay, even if the door was left open, but last night I closed it. I remember distinctly. When it's raining I think it has to be cozier for him shut.'

'Well, then,' said Mrs McDonald comfortably, 'someone must have come along, Mr Ned, and opened it after you went to bed, maybe looking to see if you was still in there. How about this granddaughter of Lady Stodmarsh wanting a word of advice as to how to comport herself in a tricky situation?'

Ned took another grab at his hair. 'I'll ask her
305

and everyone else, of course, if they could accidentally have let him out, but there's still the question of why he's not in the house. I've searched every inch.'

'Including the cellars?' Florence asked.

'And the attics. They were my last hope, and when I went up there I did find the door ajar, but no sign of the old fellow.'

Florence wrapped her hands around her teacup, drawing upon its warmth. A goose was walking over her grave. 'Either the person who opened the study door, or somebody else, must afterwards have left the house for a while.'

'Why on earth?' Ned jeered. 'To take a pleasing stroll around the garden in the rain?'

'We all know, Mr Ned,' Mrs McDonald eyed him bracingly, 'that people, even the reasonable ones, take odd notions into their heads betimes. I suppose you've been out calling him? Well, of course you have, silly question!'

'I woke around midnight,' said Florence slowly, 'and from my window I saw a figure by the lake; it then crossed a stretch of lawn to the woods. I think it likely I would have noticed the additional shape of a dog, if there'd been one near it. I roused again a couple of hours later – I assumed from a dream, but maybe I'd heard something ... his bark. Ned, he has to be trapped, caught, somewhere.'

'We don't have snares in the woods. We've never had any trouble with poachers.'

'The hermit's hut!' exclaimed Mrs McDonald triumphantly.

'I thought of that straight off. With all the rain

and wind the door could have swung open. It wasn't when I checked, but I tapped, raised the latch and tiptoed in, not wanting to frighten the old geezer out of his wits, but there was only him huddled down under the blankets.'

'I won't tell you not to worry, Ned; I know how much that dog means to you.' Florence's throat tightened. 'I'll ask Mr Grumidge to set up a search party.'

'I'd rather take him out with me on our own, have him search one side of the wood and I the other. A well-meaning throng blundering about won't do us any good. Fortunately I have bags of time before setting out in the car to meet Granny Tressler at the railway station. Her train gets in at one.'

He went off in search of Grumidge, leaving Florence and Mrs McDonald looking at each other with troubled eyes.

'I don't like it,' said the cook, arms folded, face set. 'That dog always comes first thing when called by Mr Ned, just as he did for His Lordship. I particularly don't like it when two strange happenings come one on top of another – that girl arriving out of the blue last night and now this. Mark my words, Mrs Norris, my Scottish blood tells me that there'll be a third occurrence before the day's out, to set us wondering what dark forces have taken hold at Mullings.'

ELEVEN

'What did I tell Mrs Norris? And here we are! Disaster strikes again!' exclaimed Mrs Mc-Donald at ten o'clock that morning. Jeanie had just fallen down the back stairs after being sent up to fetch Lady Stodmarsh's breakfast tray, which Annie had taken up an hour earlier. Every piece of rare and valuable china, including the coffee pot, lay scattered on the passage floor. Whether that was worse or less significant than a quickly swelling twisted ankle was debatable in Mrs McDonald's mind. Her kind heart went out to the girl as she helped her on to a kitchen chair and removed her left shoe. They were painful things, sprains, but she'd be right as rain soon enough if she didn't act silly and try to stand on it too quickly. The big worry was the one Jeanie voiced herself.

'She'll have a right carry-on about the breakage. She's given others the sack for less, so what are my chances of holding on to my job? And it's not fair, it isn't!'

'Well,' Mrs McDonald mulled this over and took the optimistic view, 'it may be better on this day than many another. You know me, never wanting to speak ill of the woman, her being who she is, but my thinking is she'll be in such a vicious mood about that granddaughter of hers showing up to make a liar of her, she won't have it in her to go on much of a rampage about an accident of the sort that happens every day – although, thank the good Lord, not in this house!'

Jeanie winced as pain shot up her leg. 'But it wasn't! That's what's so unfair.'

'Wasn't what, my girl?'

'An accident.' Jeanie sucked in a breath. 'I was pushed. On purpose.'

'Go on with you!' Mrs McDonald experienced a qualm under her dismissive tone. 'Either you're imagining things, or you're making excuses like you're all too prone to do.'

'No, I'm not!' Jeanie blinked away a tear. 'All right, I tell fibs, Mum was always calling me a confounded little liar. Better that than the wallop of her hand! But I'm not making this up. Someone came up behind me at the top of the stairs and gave me a hard shove in the back.'

Florence, who had been in the study with Ned listening to his frustration and distress at still not having found Rouser, had been standing in the passage doorway for the last minute or so. A chill went through her, but the moment called for focus on Jeanie's injured ankle. After a brief conversation with Mrs McDonald, she decided upon not sending for Doctor Chester until Mr Grumidge had taken a look at the injury. He had performed first aid in the war and would know a sprain from a break.

Forty-five minutes later, after reassurances from Grumidge that a soothing poultice and an

309

elevation of the foot were all the treatment that was needed, Jeanie was in her bed being offered lemonade and sympathy by Molly.

'I don't know why I believe her about being pushed,' said Mrs McDonald. 'I shouldn't, with her not always knowing one end of the truth from the other, but somehow I do. Question is, why would anyone do such a thing? And if it was just a matter of bumping up against her on accident, why not go to help when she fell? There's always squabbles amongst the staff; wouldn't be natural if there weren't. Jeanie can be snippy, we've both had to take her to task for it, although I'd say she's been much better this past year – but spite to the point of injuring somebody, that's something different.'

'I agree,' Florence restrained herself from pacing. 'We may be alarming ourselves unduly, but I think we are right to worry to the point of being more on the watch than usual.'

'For what?'

'Anything, however small, that strikes a wrong chord.'

'There's something getting at you that you're not saying.' The eyes that met Florence's were shrewd under the heavy eyebrows. 'I know you well enough after all these years to be sure of that, Mrs Norris, and I'd say it's weighing on you like a boulder.'

Florence fought back the urge to confide, remembering another created diversion from years back. Someone coming into this kitchen and exclaiming the word *mouse,* scaring Annie into screaming hysterically – her attention removed from the hot milk she had been about to take up to Lillian Stodmarsh. Florence still did not believe she had died from natural causes that night. At times her conviction as to the identity of the murderer wavered, from a questioning of her own judgement, but never for long. What she had never doubted was that the killer remained at Mullings. It was something she had learned to live with to the point of numbness, allowing her to focus only on what needed to be addressed at a particular moment when coming into contact with that person. Her fervent hope was that the killer would decide it was too risky to strike again – would savour success, and not take out the noose a second time and try it on for size. Why decide now that it was time to raise the curtain on act two? A sickening possibility gripped Florence: could the entrance of a scapegoat be the trigger? When Mrs McDonald spoke, Florence feared she would faint – something she had never done, even when receiving word that Robert had been killed in battle. She dragged forward a chair and sat down.

'From what you say,' said Mrs McDonald, 'Miss Jones seems a nice enough girl, and one that's had as hard a time as shouldn't, but we don't know any more about her than what she has to say for herself. Could be she's every bit as nasty natured as her grandmother. Let's not forget how Regina Stapleton pulled the wool over His Lordship's eyes, turning him sweet, even managing to keep up the act – not showing her true colours till after his death, when much of the money was tied up in her favour. I know you've spent time with Miss Jones,' Mrs Mc-Donald acknowledged, 'but like they say, blood's thicker than water.'

Florence wasn't sure about the last bit, but it would have been counterproductive to raise the question that the girl might only be pretending to be Sylvia Jones, having heard the story of the girl who had eloped with the groom and the evil mother.

'Maybe,' Mrs McDonald persisted in response to her silence, 'she gets enjoyment out of such tricks – sneaking off in the middle of the night with a kind young man's dog or pushing people down staircases. People that have had things tough sometimes resent them that's had it easy. Or,' she amended, 'in Jeanie's case – easier.'

Florence stopped herself in time from saying that perhaps that was what someone wanted them to think. Now her head was no longer swimming, she got to her feet, smoothed out her skirt, and smiled wryly. 'I hope we're not drama-tizing the situation. There really isn't anything we can do except, as we said, be on the alert for further mischief.'

'Right you are!' Mrs McDonald heaved herself into action with an enormous mixing bowl and giant spoon, 'The good Lord knows I don't want to make judgements on anyone.'

'I wasn't being critical,' said Florence, 'but we can't stick our heads in the sands either. I'm going outside for some fresh air, to try and clear away the cobwebs.' Once outside she wandered into the kitchen garden and sat on a tree trunk against the drystone wall. The sky remained

312

shadowy with cloud and there was little sun. She realized she was being forced to think deeply for the first time in a long while about Lillian Stodmarsh's death and her own subsequent behaviour. Was the lack of tangible proof a good enough excuse for not taking her suspicions to the police? She could have given the *anonymous* note from Hilda Stark to Constable Trout and let the situation play out as it would. Hadn't she allowed her devotion to the Stodmarsh family, the desire to protect Ned from suspicion that could have ruined his life, to govern her conscience? Was devotion the right word, or was *obsession* a better fit? Was she as unbalanced in this regard as her mother was about the Tamershams and their ornamental hermit? She thought of George Bird and how she had allowed him go out of her life rather than trust him as a confidant. No wonder he no longer wished to have anything to do with her.

She pondered over the current situation in relation to the past. Was she so swept away by her powers of deduction that she saw menace without justification in happenings that were not unusual – a dog gone missing and a kitchen maid taking a tumble down a staircase? Someone had undoubtedly let Rouser out during the night, but why leap to the conclusion that it had been done on purpose out of spite, or for some other, as yet unfathomable, reason? Jeanie claimed she was pushed down the stairs, but she was not always truthful and this time her job was at stake. What benefit could these two incidents provide a possible instigator?

313

Florence sighed. She could worry away at coming up with an answer until her head spun and not get an inkling of an idea. A somewhat reassuring thought slid into her mind. Maybe the murderer had no desire to kill again, even having been presented with a potential scapegoat in Sylvia Jones. Hatred and resentment might have faded to be replaced by apathy – a sluggish need to leave well enough alone.

Florence heard voices as she stepped into the courtyard after leaving the kitchen garden, and she saw Ned and Sylvia Jones crossing the lawn towards her. Rouser was not with them.

'Is he back?' Ned called out as they drew near.

'Afraid not, unless he came round the front and was let in during the last ten minutes while I've been out here.'

'Even if he hasn't, you can't lose hope.' Miss Jones laid a hand on his arm, her platinum hair close in colour to the silvery clouds overhead. 'Call me foolish, but I truly believe we can will happy endings.'

'That's the spirit!' Ned's smile could not mask his quivering lips. He went over to Florence and put an arm round her. 'Don't look so sad, Florie, I'm supposed to be a grown-up capable of dealing with the knocks of life,' he murmured against her cheek. 'Sylvia,' he added in a louder voice, stepping away from her to look at the girl, 'was kind enough to walk over with me to Farn Deane so I could find out from Tom or Gracie if Rouser had been seen around there this morning. But no luck.' Again his mouth quivered but he forced himself on. 'They're great people, don't you think, Sylvia?'

'Yes, but there's no need for gratitude that I went with you. I was glad to get out of the house.' Her brown eyes brought Florence into what she was saying. 'Breakfast wasn't too bad. Mr William Stodmarsh didn't show any interest in me whatsoever. His wife asked why in the world I would want to get in touch with, let alone meet, my grandmother, and Miss Bradley merely said she hoped I liked the marmalade and that she always found spreading it on her toast soothing.'

'Needless to say,' interpolated Ned, 'Regina did not grace us with her presence.'

'And as I had no intention of bearding her again in her den, I was glad of the chance to get out of the house.' Miss Jones beamed at him as if she didn't have a care in the world. 'Especially as the three other family members disappeared after leaving the table. And there's me worrying about disrupting the entire household, because of Granny's,' her lips curled around the name, 'sins.'

'I'm glad your fears have been put at rest,' said Florence, 'and it's obvious Ned ... Lord Stodmarsh is glad to have you here. If you'll please both excuse me, I should get back to the house. It has to be close on time for luncheon to be served.'

'Lord, yes!' exclaimed Ned, looking at his watch. 'Almost noon! I want to stop in at the police station and report Rouser's disappearance to Constable Trout before meeting Grandma Tressler at the station. Makes for a rushed wash

315

and brush-up. Want to come in with me through the study door, Sylvia?'

'If you don't mind, I'd like to accompany Mrs Norris so she can introduce me to the cook, who so kindly sent up nourishment for me last night.' This sounded reasonable to Ned.

'Right-ho!' He made a dash for the veranda steps.

'That's true,' said Miss Jones as they crossed the courtyard to the servants' entrance, 'but I also feel the need for a chat with you, even if it's about this, that or nothing. You're one of the most restful people I've ever met. Do you ever lose your temper?'

They paused on flagstones facing the door leading to the realm below stairs. Florence considered the question. 'Rarely. Displays of anger are trained out of those in service. Control is the byword, but that doesn't mean I'm no longer capable of anger ... at least I hope not.'

'On your own behalf?' Miss Jones sounded as if she really wanted to know.

Florence hesitated. 'Sometimes ... not often ... perhaps not.' This sounded to her own ears like an admission of weakness. She saw that her world had narrowed through the years and there was no room in it for herself.

'I understand.' Sylvia Jones took hold of her hand. 'Look, the way I see it – to be angry on our own behalf we have to realize we're worth the fight. I've never had that sort of confidence – it's so much easier to go all out for someone else in need, to try and right wrongs done to others. That's partly ... mostly ... why I'm here, but I

316

also have to prove I'm not one to throw away a chance of happiness for myself, if it's there – if not, I'll have found the strength to carry on independently.'

Florence, usually undemonstrative, kissed her on the cheek. 'You've settled one thing for me, Miss Jones.'

'What's that?'

'That you haven't fabricated the story of being Regina Stodmarsh's granddaughter. I wasn't sure about that.'

They went though the passageway into the kitchen where they glimpsed the hovering footman. There was minimal hustle and bustle. A pan of sautéing sweetbreads was evident on the stove. Platters filled with tempting arrays of salads, lobster patties, and fruit were set out, waiting to be carried upstairs. As Mrs McDonald said often enough, 'If a mother with three or four young 'uns clinging to her legs can get a meal on the table the minute her man walks through the door, I have no reason on God's earth for huffing and puffing before dishing up for a small number of people, and some of them out half the time.' Not that she'd go so far as to say she got paid for sitting on her bottom, but no one would hear her moan she had it hard! On this occasion, her colour was up and her bosom heaved with emotion. The source, Florence saw immediately, was Annie Long, looking more whey-faced than ever as she cringed, twitched and wrung her hands while backing away as if from a persecutor.

'Please! Don't ask it of me no more,' she

gabbled. 'I can't do it; I'd be too afeared. What if he came at me with them long nails of his and clawed me to ribbons? What if he tried to interfere with me?'

'Spare me!' Mrs McDonald begged the ceiling. 'The poor man has to be eighty at least!'

Florence knew what was at issue, but waited to insert herself until appealed to by her friend and colleague. She saw that Sylvia Jones looked interested to the point of working up to a verbal contribution.

Annie carried on gabbling. 'My mum says no man's to be trusted when it comes to that until he's boxed up and nailed down, and even then he'll try wiggling it through a crack in the wood.'

Mrs McDonald threw up her hands. 'Tell me she hasn't taken leave of her senses, Mrs Norris? Could you have ever imagined such language coming out of our Annie's mouth? It's enough to make me become a Methodist!'

'I had to put it that way, Mrs Norris!' Annie was now sobbing brokenly. 'She wouldn't listen when I said he's not human flesh and blood. He's from the Devil – that's what the vicar told me Auntie Jess.'

There was no point in protesting this viewpoint. 'Very well, Annie, I'll have to send one of the other girls.' Florence waved her away. 'Calm yourself and find something else to do. And in future please don't refer to Mrs McDonald as *she*.'

'Oh, I won't!' Annie snuffled against the back of her wrist. 'Never again I won't! I'm that grateful, you don't know, madams!' Her knees buckled in what might have been a remorseful curtsy, or a sign that her legs were about to give out. She wove her way into the passageway.

Mrs McDonald shook her white woolly head. 'Ten minutes wasted. I should have known better, Mrs Norris, than thinking I could persuade her. And here's me,' looking apologetically at Miss Jones, 'ignoring this young lady who's a guest of the family. Leastways, I'm thinking you must be Lady Stodmarsh's granddaughter.'

'For better or worse, that's me.' Miss Jones showed an unexpected dimple when she smiled. 'Thank you, Mrs McDonald, for sending a meal up for me last night. It was the perfect one for someone coming in out of the rain. Breakfast was also very good.'

'Kind of you to say so, miss.'

'Miss Jones came in with me,' said Florence, 'especially to voice her appreciation.'

Mrs McDonald expanded from a very large woman into a tree bursting into blossom. Her face had gone from a flustered red to a pleased pink. 'What a very nice young lady you must be! I'd one of my feelings I'd take to you right off, and so I have. If there is the least thing I can do, I'm more than pleased to make your stay a happy one, you've only to ask.'

'That's so dear of you to say. One more person on my side.' Miss Jones's eyes shone with either pleasure or tears; Florence's opinion was a mixture of both. 'Lord Stodmarsh and Mrs Norris have already been so nice to me. What a wonderfully warm and welcoming kitchen this is;

319

but I mustn't distract you from your work.'

'There, miss, I wish I didn't have to get on with things, but needs must. Any other time ... and there'll be another one, of course. Who'd you like me to send out with the poor old blighter's meal, Mrs Norris?'

'Let me do it,' Miss Jones nipped in quickly with the offer. 'I'd be glad of the walk. I enjoyed the one to Farn Deane and I can never get enough of being outdoors, besides, if my grandmother should descend for lunch, I'd just as soon not be there. If she's come up with anything to communicate with me she can save it until we're on our own.'

'She's gone out, miss.' Mrs McDonald could have been letting her know that the weather prediction was for unclouded skies and brilliant sunshine. 'Mrs Palfrett from the Chimneys in Kingsbury Knox came in her car an hour ago and they went off to lunch with Mrs Stafford-Reid at her home – Hidden Meadows in Small Middlington. Lady Stodmarsh informed Mr Grumidge that the afternoon will almost certainly turn into an evening of bridge, meaning she would not return until late. Mr Grumidge, from past experience, assesses that to be ten or later.'

Florence looked at Miss Jones, questioningly.

'I'd still like to go. I noticed a ladder in a pair of stockings I brought and I could buy another in the village. I've got my purse with me,' she touched the side pocket in her dress, 'so after taking in the meal I'll continue on. All I need are directions to the hut.'

320

While Mrs McDonald assembled a tray of bacon sandwiches, cheese and an apple crumble, over which she spread a cloth, Florence explained the quickest route for Miss Jones to take. It was not by way of the woodland path, but through a cutting further down, close to the edge of the lake. 'If you go straight, you'll hear a waterfall and come to a clearing by a very large tree. You'll be able to see the hut a little way beyond.'

'I understand I'm not to talk to him.'

'Sounds inhuman, doesn't it?'

'That's how I see it,' said Florence, 'though after all these years in isolation, he might die of fright if he was startled out of decades of silence. Then again, maybe not. I wouldn't be surprised if Jeanie, who usually takes his meals out to him, has tried. He's been reduced to a myth – a fabrication of fear or fantasy according to temperament.'

Sylvia Jones took the tray from Mrs McDonald. Florence opened the outer door for her and then returned to the kitchen. Within the next few minutes luncheon was sent upstairs, and Mrs McDonald returned the conversation to Mullings' latest house guest.

'Well, I must say, Mrs Norris, if she's a wrong 'un you could fool me! That bleached hair could put off someone without sense enough to see beyond it, and I'll admit I've always been one for preferring the natural look, but that face and manner was what spoke volumes. Took her to my heart, I did, and I'm that sorry for the nasty thoughts I let take hold before setting eyes on

321

her. You could blow me down with a feather if it turns out she'd anything to do with Mr Ned's dog disappearing or Jeanie's accident.'

Florence leaned against the table. 'I like her, too, and no longer have any doubt that she's Lady Stodmarsh's granddaughter. I wonder what confidences, if any, are being laid before Mrs Palfrett and Mrs Stafford-Reid.'

'If she's any sense she'll keep her mouth shut.'

'I wonder. If you'd seen and heard her last night you might have wondered if she wasn't in imminent danger of disintegrating.'

'For fear of her world coming crashing down, you mean?'

Florence nodded. 'One good thing, breakfast seems to have gone off with barely a ripple of curiosity from Mr and Mrs William or Miss Bradley regarding Miss Jones's presence. Any idea how they are each spending their day?'

'No idea about Mr William; most likely he'll be around somewhere grunting to himself between puffing on his pipe. Mr Grumidge told me Mrs William will be gone this afternoon, at the church or vicarage, and, like Lady Stodmarsh, probably won't be back to dinner, and Molly says she barely got to make Miss Bradley's bed before being hurried away so's she could have a day at the sewing machine.'

'I'd like to think she's working on her trousseau, in the hope that her marriage to Mr Fritch won't be too long delayed.'

'Wouldn't that be nice?' Mrs McDonald's sentimental streak showed on her face. 'Though with this talk about Mr Craddock planning on selling the bookshop and perhaps Mr Fritch not getting to keep his job, the sound of wedding bells could be even longer in coming than already expected. Being the nervy little man he is, I'd think he'll be all of a twitch about getting the boot.'

'Hopefully he won't. Mr Ned says he's a wonder with figures, accurate down to the last farthing.' Florence looked up at the clock, thinking that the train with Mrs Tressler on board should be pulling into the station right now. Ned would be glad to see his grandmother; he had grown considerably more attached to her over the past few years. Would his pleasure, however, be dampened by the need to tell her he had proposed to Lamorna Blake?

As it happened, other than thinking Mrs Tressler looked well and as comfortably practical as always in her sensible coat and hat, Ned's thoughts were on Rouser's disappearance. It wasn't until they were in the car that Lamorna crossed his mind, and then only because he remembered that he'd considered himself duty-bound to drive his grandmother to The Manor at Large Middlington.

He'd finally got around to telephoning Lamorna that morning before setting off for the station, and for what seemed like five minutes had been prevented from getting two words in because Lamorna had run the gamut from shrieks to peevishness over his failure to return her call of last evening. But when she at last drew breath, providing the opportunity for him to speak, she cheered up instantly. Had he not been so down in the dumps about Rouser, he would have pitched into anxiety, knowing her aim would be to twist his grandmother around her finger and extract an offer to come up with the funds to purchase the London flat.

'It's so good to see you, Grandma,' he said as they drove from the station, past the church and vicarage, a string of cottages, and then turned on to the road to Large Middlington. 'I only wish I was in better spirits at this moment.'

'I could see you looked troubled when you crossed the pavement towards me. Do you want to talk about it? I know sometimes it helps and at others it's the last thing we want to do. I notice we're not heading towards Mullings.'

'Do you mind not going there straight away?'

'Of course not. Where's it to be?'

'The Blakes.'

'Very good.'

How easy she was, how unruffled. It said much for her strength of mind that it was hard to believe she'd ever suffered a couple of such severe breakdowns that she'd had to go to that nursing home, Meadowvale. Ned was seized by regret that he had failed over the years to value their relationship as he should. For him life had always been primarily about Mullings.

'I've been the most frightful ass, Granny.'

'Haven't we all at one time or another, especially when young?'

By the time they reached the broad lane leading to The Manor he'd poured out the folly of proposing to Lamorna Blake, including the

324

damning fact that he was presently far more distressed about Rouser being gone than he was about the sensibilities of the girl he was supposed to love.

'I'm sure she's going to plead with you to come up with the money for the flat. Am I being noble or wretched in asking you to refuse?'

'I shall offer,' responded Mrs Tressler, 'and you will decline my generosity, with the result that Miss Blake will dissolve into tears and say she'd never really wanted to marry you, all is off, and there are far better fish in the sea. You will accept her decision manfully and we will make our departure.'

'You really think that's how it will go?' Ned asked, sounding very much like a small boy.

'Not a doubt in the world.' They were on the elm-lined drive and the house was in view.

'You're a very special grandmother.' He felt the urge to kiss her cheek, instead he touched her shoulder. 'You shouldn't be dragged into my troubles.'

'I call it being useful, my dear.'

They had no sooner come to a halt outside The Manor than the door opened and Lamorna ran down the steps, a vision of golden-haired delight to stir a poet's heart, if no longer Ned's.

'My precious darling,' she cried when he got out of the car, 'you have brought her as you promised? Oh, yes,' peering through the front window, 'there she is! Do help her out quickly so we can talk. I know I can wheedle her round to our point of view. Jennie Stafford-Reid was just on the phone telling me about the sweetest little flat ... well, not all that little, it has a library as well as two other reception rooms! Angel, why are you looking at me like that?'

Fifteen minutes later Mrs Tressler and Ned were back on the road to Mullings. If not for Rouser, Ned would have been happier than he'd been in days. His grandmother had from the start wisely refrained from offering up useless consolation. He suddenly remembered he hadn't told her about Miss Jones and proceeded to do so to her obvious interest. As was to be expected, she said nothing pejorative about Lady Stodmarsh, simply commenting that she could understand his sympathy for the young woman.

They stopped at the police station, which was also Constable Trout's cottage. He wasn't there, but his wife, a pleasant, rosy-faced woman, said he'd telephoned Mullings before he'd left to say that so far there had been no sightings of the dog. They were both heartily sorry not to have better news for him. Such a lovely mellow animal, unlike them ones in the house round the side of the Dog and Whistle, bringing complaints from the neighbours about the constant barking. Swallowing his disappointment, Ned drove off. He was tempted to stop in at the pub to see how George was doing – he couldn't focus only on himself – but he had no idea whether his grandmother had ever been inside a public house or how she would feel about entering one. There was so much he didn't know about her.

Grumidge appeared the moment they drew up outside Mullings, welcomed Mrs Tressler with less than his usual impassivity, and instructed the hovering chauffeur to bring in her suitcases before parking the car. The interior appeared devoid of family members: not a soul in the drawing room, nor any sign from the windows of anyone out in the grounds. This was partially explained by Grumidge stating that Lady Stodmarsh and Mrs William were out for the day. Ned wasn't surprised that his uncle wasn't around, as he had taken to holing up much of the time in what was known as the gun room, although only empty racks were in evidence.

'Any idea where Miss Bradley is, Grumidge?'

'I understand from Molly, sir, that she is in her bedroom, having a sewing day. She's only been down for luncheon.'

'And what of Miss Jones?'

'She came through the hall when I was on my way to open the front door and went up the staircase.'

'How did she look? Being here has to be very unsettling for her.'

'It is of course only my opinion, sir, but I would describe her expression as sombre.'

'Understandable in the circumstances,' said Mrs Tressler.

'Quite so, madam. May I send Mrs Norris to escort you to your room and ascertain that all is as you wish it?'

'Thank you, Grumidge, but that won't be necessary. Please tell her I'd enjoy talking with her later. I always enjoy our moments together. Both she and you always contribute to the pleasure of my visits.'

'Thank you, madam; I will pass along your

message.' He inclined his head and left the drawing room.

'What a treasure he is,' said Mrs Tressler. 'Is his relationship with that very nice girl, Molly, who helped take care of you after that ill-suited nanny left, progressing satisfactorily?'

Ned laughed. 'Your hidden depths are amazing. Granny the acute observer! Yes, I think there'll be a happy outcome. What would you like to do this afternoon after settling in?'

'Either read or do my needlepoint. Perhaps Miss Jones will come down after a little while and we can converse while you are out continuing your search for Rouser.'

'Are you sure you won't feel I'm abandoning you?'

'Go!'

Mrs Tressler spent an hour taking a bath and then dressing in clothing that had been unpacked for her by Molly. She returned to the drawing room and rang for tea. Florence brought it in to her.

'It is good to have you back at Mullings, Mrs Tressler.'

'And to see you again, Mrs Norris. Please do sit down.'

Florence thanked her before doing so.

Mrs Tressler expressed the hope that all was well with her and spoke generally for a few moments before bringing up the subject of Ned. 'Knowing how close a bond there is between the two of you, I'm sure you've been concerned about this tangle he got into with Miss Blake. I'm sure she's an exceptional young lady, but quite unsuited to his personality and interests.'

'My feeling, Mrs Tressler.'

The older woman smiled. 'Then I'm happy to be able to put your mind at rest.' She explained what had transpired at The Manor, and after a little more conversation Florence returned to the kitchen for her own cup of tea with Mrs Mc-Donald. She meant to ask her if she had seen Sylvia Jones on her return from taking out the hermit's meal and perhaps going on into the village. She was slightly surprised that Miss Jones had not sought her out again, as she had seemed eager to converse. But Mrs McDonald forestalled her.

'Better sit down for this one, Mrs Norris!' The effect was that Florence froze in place.

'What's happened? A third catastrophe?'

'Well, I don't think it can be put in those terms, but the butcher's been round with a worrisome piece of gossip. It seems his Aunt Nellie heard from someone that sometimes goes to the Dog and Whistle – wouldn't say who, not a regular, mind – that he saw a stranger come in a couple of days back and go up to the bar and talk all confidential like to George Bird.'

'What of it?' Florence's heart was beating unreasonably fast.

'Whoever it was said he could've spotted the bloke as police a mile off. Not the sort in uniform, you understand, but one of what's called the plain-clothes sort.'

Florence sat down. 'What ever would the police want with George?'

'That's what I said, but I'm more than a little

329

bothered, Mrs Norris. That sort of rumour could be bad for a decent man's business.'

'I don't think it would have any effect on the regulars, or at least most of them, who think the world of George. I'm sure any of them catching wind of the story would tell him what was going round and he'd explain about the man, if there was anything to his putting in an appearance ... such as his being an old acquaintance wanting to borrow five pounds. That would account for the secretive air, wouldn't it?'

''Course it would,' Mrs McDonald passed her a cup of tea, 'but I can't help thinking about Mr Bird, coming over queer on the green that morning. It seemed like he was under the weather, but what if it was worry did it?'

Florence stared at her.

'All I can come up with is something to do with the pub. Oh, don't get me wrong, Mrs Norris, I don't mean him acting illegal ... more like finding there was to be a change in the licensing rules, or whatnot, that'd make it hard for him to keep going. What if that weren't a policeman but a...'

'A brewery official,' Florence concluded for her. 'You may have the right of it there, Mrs McDonald. It's useless to speculate, however.'

She could focus on little else for the rest of the day while going about her duties. She could not dismiss the thought that George's collapse might well have been brought on by worry, even a sudden shock. Of course the cause might have nothing to do with the pub ... perhaps someone he was fond of had been taken desperately ill, or was in some other kind of trouble. The person who instantly came to mind was his godson, Jim. That young man meant as much to him as Ned did to her. She'd heard, through the way things get about in a village, that his courtship had ended. She remembered vividly that last afternoon with George and his speaking about Jim's parents objecting to his girl for many reasons – one being her name, which to their minds was silly. George had thought it was along the lines of ... 'Fudge'. Yes, that's what he'd said. What if Jim had gone into a depression because of the break with her, or with some other young lady, or because he had not succeeded as an artist? What if...?

The questions could have continued going around in her head until she was dizzy, had she not pulled herself together. Even so, there remained an oppressiveness to the day, not fully accounted for by the darkening skies or the massing of thick, furred clouds and rumbles of thunder which failed to bring the refreshment of rain.

Ned came into the housekeeper's room before going up to bed that night at ten, and Florence filled him in about what the rest of the family had been up to. His aunt had only just returned; Lady Stodmarsh was not yet back; Miss Jones had been overly animated at dinner as if endeavouring to put on a brave front; Madge Bradley had quacked gamely on as was her wont about irrelevances; and his uncle had nodded off over the cheese and biscuits.

331

'If my grandmother weren't one to take things in her stride, Florie, she'd think it all very odd.' He stood looking drawn and heavy-eyed; he had risen at five that morning. 'I have to say, I feel there's a blight on the house.'

'Oh, dear,' said Florence, producing a rueful smile, 'you sound like Mrs McDonald and her forebodings. You may feel much restored after a good sleep.' Had she been forthright she would have confessed to her feeling that a net had spread itself around Mullings and was being drawn tighter by the minute into a knot that even the nimblest fingers would have difficulty unravelling.

'Perhaps I'm just on edge, Florie. I'm leaving the door to the study open in case Rouser returns.'

She promised to advise Grumidge, whose final task of the day was making sure all windows and doors were secured, to leave that one alone.

'I don't care about burglars, so long as Rouser can make it inside. Goodnight, Florie.' Ned trailed his way despondently upstairs.

The following morning he was to hope desperately that there *had* been a break-in. Regina had been stabbed to death in her bedroom, and if her killer were not a stranger then he, or she, had to be an occupant of Mullings.

TWELVE

The bloodstained body was discovered at seven in the morning by Molly when she was taking up Mrs William's usual cup of tea. She noticed that Lady Stodmarsh's bedroom door was open and looked in. Molly made no outcry, but with her usual good sense sought out Grumidge, who followed her back upstairs to observe the scene from the doorway. He located Ned, broke the news and awaited further instructions.

The first requirement was obvious – to telephone Doctor Chester and Constable Trout. This done, Ned told Grumidge to speak with Florence, and subsequently inform the rest of the staff. While Grumidge attended to these instructions Ned awakened his grandmother, explained the situation and asked her to rouse the family and Miss Jones.

Mrs Tressler, although her countenance evidenced shock, did not indulge in exclamations. Within ten minutes Doctor Chester and Constable Trout arrived and were escorted upstairs by Ned.

Ned left them to get on with their work and joined the others, except for William Stodmarsh, whom his wife said could not be roused from sleep, in the drawing room. They all appeared to

333

be in a state of disbelief, moving woodenly to seat themselves and stare blankly ahead, but as Ned spoke of the blood on the front of Regina's nightgown that suggested she had been stabbed in the chest, their faces came to life. Miss Jones's grew fear-stricken, Madge Bradley's tearily bewildered and Gertrude Stodmarsh's ponderous from brow to jowls. She was the first to speak.

'There's no getting around it; we'll all be under suspicion. Each of us heartily disliked her, with the possible exception of you, Mrs Tressler, but, forgive my saying so, her removal eases life enormously for your grandson. For one thing he is now free to marry Lamorna Blake. I am not saying this to frighten you, or Ned, merely to suggest you both prepare yourselves for extra grilling.'

'You're right, Aunt,' Ned remained standing, 'I am the likeliest of all to have killed her. I may even have been overheard by one of you when I was on the telephone the other day expressing a wish to do so. As it happens, my grandmother was present yesterday at The Manor when Lamorna and I agreed not to marry, but that could go against me. The police may decide it was a put-up job to shed my motive.'

'Surely not.' Madge clutched at her throat. 'Everyone knows how sweet-natured you are. The entire village would swear to it. How can we question that the villain was a burglar who entered by manipulating a door lock or breaking a window and that Regina awakened while he was robbing her bedroom?'

Ned passed a hand over his brow. 'There would have been no need for a forced entry. I left the study door open for Rouser in case he came back, but that does not alter the need for us to prepare ourselves for questioning. Trout said a county inspector is already on his way and should be here in the next half hour.'

'I can't believe any of you have a tenth as much to worry about as I do.' Miss Jones's voice came out high and thin. 'None of your resentments can equal mine. Lying dead is the woman who treated my mother with brutal inhumanity and denied my existence. Talk about burglary all you like, but when did one last occur at Mullings, if ever? I arrive and...' She buried her face in her hands.

Mrs Tressler surveyed her in the manner Florence had observed on earlier occasions of an unrufflable school mistress. 'There's a first time for everything, including burglars, dear child.'

Sylvia's eyes grew wild and she vehemently shook her head. 'I don't believe it was a ... a vagrant! It has to have been someone from inside Mullings! It isn't fair to blame a stranger!'

'Not fair?' Madge gripped her upper arms with her hands, 'I'm afraid I don't understand such a statement. Not that I wish to criticize. We're all at sixes and sevens.'

'To put it mildly!' Ned grinned sourly.

'Oh, yes,' Madge continued, 'but it is impossible to properly express the consternation, the sense of horror ... the trepidation! Perhaps I am wearing rose-coloured glasses, but they have enabled me to deal with travails of the past. I cannot accept, I refuse to do so – or I would go mad – that any one of us is capable of murder, however trying we may have found Regina.'

'I hated her,' said Sylvia Jones.

'I hated William for years, until I learned the unpalatable truth. Eating too much of it brings on nothing but indigestion.' Gertrude Stodmarsh heaved her stout body off her chair. 'I have found peace and contentment helping out with the flowers and other activities at the church in the last couple of years, and finally happiness in spending time with Miss Hendrick. Dear Henny! Always so uplifting!'

'Miss Hendrick is the vicar's housekeeper,' Ned explained, for Sylvia's benefit. 'Perhaps you should telephone her, Aunt, and encourage her to dissuade Mr Pimcrisp from tottering over here to brighten our darkness with visions of hell's fire. I can't say I'd blame him for not wishing her happy-ever-after, if only because of how she connived to entrap my grandfather. But the inevitable warnings about our being headed for the same fate if we don't abandon worldly pleasures, such as going for a paddle at the seaside or soaking up the sun in a deckchair, would be a bit thick.'

'Naturally I wish to talk to Henny,' said his aunt. 'Sharing my thoughts with her has become a necessity, but I'll wait to telephone until I have wakened William. Much as I would not regret his sleeping out the day, he has to be up and dressed before the inspector arrives.' Gertrude made for the drawing room door, then turned on reaching it. 'I wonder if he will be from Scotland

Yard. I know Henny will be pleased, even delighted, if that is the case. She is very keen on detective stories, always has one on the go.' Gertrude's gaze was focused elsewhere as she patted her gray hair, of which every strand was immoveable. She did not appear to have dressed in careless haste as Madge seemed to have done – even to the point of putting on the same frock she'd worn at dinner last evening. An edge of petticoat showed below the navy hem; Ned found this oddly touching.

He gave Sylvia Jones a mischievous look, intended to lighten her mood, and, intentionally mimicking the mode of speech of his erstwhile father-to-be, Sir Winthrop Blake, exclaimed, 'Upon my soul! Can we fasten on Miss Hendrick as a suspect? May she not have crept over at dead of night, broken into the house by way of the open study door to exact revenge upon Regina for the slights voiced against Aunt Gertrude and herself at dinner the night before last?'

Miss Jones didn't appear to absorb a word.

Madge gabbled into the void, her hands twisting into a cat's cradle. 'Wicked indeed, to suggest they harboured unnatural feelings for each other. I've never believed such women exist; the idea has to come from the same archaic outlook that led to people being persecuted as witches.'

'There I must disagree with you,' said Mrs Tressler evenly.

'Oh, dear!' Madge was now turning her fingers into sailors' knots. 'My knowledge of history is not all it should be...'

'Neither is mine. But we have two lovely ladies living together in my village that I've no doubt share the bond of which we speak. There are those who may disapprove, but I'm not amongst them. If you will forgive my saying so, Ned,' Mrs Tressler looked up at him, 'your aunt could only be described as harbouring unnatural feelings were she in love with her husband, but happily that is not the case.' She turned back to Madge. 'I think it says a lot about you, Miss Bradley, that you should give any thought to what Regina said to anyone other than yourself at dinner that evening. Ned told me it was a brutal attack.'

'So hurtful, accusing me of foisting myself on Cyril.'

'I'm sure you did nothing of the kind,' Miss Jones murmured drearily.

'You'd have thought I got a proposal out of him at knife-point. Oh, dear! What a stupid thing to say.' A flush crept up Madge's throat, accentuating her bleached face.

'Not at all,' responded Mrs Tressler. 'We should all be frank, especially when being interviewed by the police. I intend to tell the inspector I was surprised Regina didn't throw it in my face that on two occasions I had to be locked up in a lunatic asylum. I shall also divulge something else that may cause him to believe I am subject to relapses.'

'Are you going to tell us what that is?' Sylvia Jones looked and sounded a little stronger.

'No, my dear.'

Madge was unknotting her fingers. 'I must telephone Cyril before the dreadful news reaches him. May I use the one in the study, Ned?'

'Of course.'

'Always so tremendously kind!'

'Are you going to ask him to come here? I'm sure you could use his support.' Voices carried down from the upper hallway, Doctor Chester's amongst them.

'Oh, yes, but I mustn't be selfish. It would be too hard on his nerves. If the police wish to speak with him they can do so at his house. I shall be quite firm with them about that.'

Footsteps could be heard on the stairs within moments of Madge's departure. It was neither Doctor Chester nor Constable Trout who entered the drawing room, but Gertrude Stodmarsh. 'William has suffered a stroke,' she announced without visible consternation. Sylvia Jones joined Mrs Tressler and Ned in their exclamations of shock and concern. 'It happened when I told him Regina had been murdered. He sat up in bed, pointed a finger at me and opened his mouth. All that came out was dribble before he slumped sideways. I have to think he believed I was confessing. Whether he was aghast or pleasurably shocked that for once in my useless life I'd done something worthwhile, I'll have to wait to find out until he recovers. Doctor Chester is not optimistic. He is going to have him taken to the cottage hospital.'

'Why on earth would Uncle leap to such a conclusion?' Ned went to help her into a chair.

Gertrude declined to sit. 'That is easily answered. William accused me of killing his mother after she died.'

'*What?*'

'Not in the usual sense of murder, but to him it amounted to the same thing. He insisted I had gone up to her bedroom to tell her I wanted a separation and to ask if she would speak with my father-in-law about helping me out financially. I had intended to do so and he knew it, but I found her asleep and did not attempt to waken her.'

Before anything else could be said, the doorbell rang, heralding the awaited detective inspector. They sat in tense silence until Grumidge ushered the policeman into the drawing room and introduced him as Inspector LeCrane. If LeCrane was impressed by the size and elegance of the room, he gave no such indication. He was tall, with a narrow face dominated by a long, beaky nose, which would have done the suggested species of bird proud. Ned put him in his mid- to late-forties. No visible gray in his dark hair. Madge returned from the study. He eyed her as she came in, and then swept the other four with a glance. Ned was standing, wishing he was just a couple of inches taller. What was the correct form in greeting an inspector? Should he shake hands, or might doing so be taken for an attempt to curry favour? He decided to risk it, upon introducing himself.

'Ned Stodmarsh, sir.'

'Inspector will do, Lord Stodmarsh.' The voice was cultured, suggestive of a public school education, the tone conversational. 'Will the remainder of you kindly identify yourself as to

340

names and your relationship to Regina Stodmarsh?' Even as Mrs Tressler and Madge Bradley did as requested, his gaze strayed to Sylvia Jones. Ned hoped this was merely a sign that he admired blondes. The girl was making a brave attempt at not showing alarm. In fact, Inspector LeCrane did not submit her to a particularly penetrating stare when it came to her turn. Indeed, his expression became benign.

'And you are Miss...?'

'Sylvia Jones. Regina Stodmarsh was my maternal grandmother.'

'My sympathy. This is a bad business, but, based on information we have on hand, I'm optimistic we'll be able to get to the bottom of it quickly.'

'What information?' Gertrude Stodmarsh asked. It had been the question on four other pairs of lips. Mrs Tressler leaned forward in her chair, Sylvia Jones back in hers, Madge Bradley sat rigid and Ned stood looking intrigued.

'I'm not prepared to say. Could queer things for us if it got back to the wrong quarter. This isn't to say that someone living under this roof isn't either the murderer or an accessory. I'm leaning towards the latter, but I've gone down the wrong track before and may be doing so again. I brought with me my sergeant and two constables collected from other villages on our way here. Sergeant Wright is upstairs talking to Constable Trout and the doctor. So I'm not going to linger overly with you. When I go up Sergeant Wright will come down, ask you some questions and then explain how we intend to proceed with

341

our inquiries.' Inspector LeCrane looked to Gertrude Stodmarsh, who visibly had something to say.

'Yes, madam?'

'I'm Gertrude Stodmarsh, Mr Ned Stodmarsh's aunt by marriage. My husband William has suffered a stroke. It happened when I told him Regina had been murdered. Doctor Chester has sent for an ambulance to take him to the cottage hospital; it should be here any moment and I wish to accompany him.'

'I'm sorry to hear of his condition.'

'We are not and never have been a devoted couple, but duty must. Surely you could send one of the constables if you think it necessary to put me under watch.'

Inspector LeCrane would have made a perfect butler; nothing could be gained from his voice or facial expression. 'They are both needed here, Mrs Stodmarsh. One will be stationed at the foot of the front staircase, the other at the base of the back ones; the reason being that nobody will be permitted to return to their bedrooms until they have been searched, by Sergeant Wright and Constable Trout. As for your situation, Mrs Stodmarsh, I see no difficulty in allowing you to go to the hospital with your husband and remain with him as long as you wish. You can be interviewed there. I request that everyone else remain in the house. The grounds are also off limits. I regret the inconvenience, but it is as it must be. An attempt to flee would help rather than hurt the investigation. Only a guilty person would attempt to flee.'

342

'I'm not of a build suited to fleeing, Inspector,' Gertrude interjected. 'The best I could manage would be a trot, and I couldn't keep that up above thirty seconds.'

Inspector LeCrane's mouth inched upward at this stolid reply.

'Am I allowed to telephone a friend to let her know what has happened? I had intended to do so, but my husband's condition intervened.'

'Regrettably, Mrs Stodmarsh, I have to stipulate that no one use the phone, I'm sure you will all understand we cannot risk a message being conveyed to a confederate.'

'What a horrible word!' Madge gasped. 'Oh, dear! I do see the sound thinking, but I never thought ... I do hope it won't go against me that I phoned Cyril ... Cyril Fritch, my fiancé, to let him know what had happened, so he wouldn't hear it from someone else, and reassure him that I'm holding up well, which isn't quite the truth, but I did not want him to feel he had to rush over. He has very sensitive nerves.'

'Nothing to be done about that. Anyone else? Good.' He turned to Ned. 'May I impose on you, Lord Stodmarsh, to notify your staff of that prohibition and explain to them the reason they may not leave the lower levels. Also advise them to prepare themselves for being summoned for questioning.'

'Certainly.' Ned had been hoping for an early chance to speak with Florence. His concern for her chafed at him.

The inspector requested Gertrude to go with him and they were heard mounting the stairs.

Within moments there came a murmuring of voices, which included Doctor Chester's and possibly one of the constables.

'Interesting – his assertion that he has an outsider in mind for the crime – one who may have a cohort at Mullings. If so, that would seem to rule out a tramp,' said Mrs Tressler.

'He could have added that last part, Grandma,' suggested Ned, 'to make sure we all toe the line in following instructions.'

'But how comforting for it to be a stranger!' Madge clasped her hands to her chest – a less complicated gesture than her intricate knotting of them.

'I don't see why!' Sylvia Jones sounded on the verge of hysteria as she leaped to her feet. 'And I don't believe it! Someone in this room is the killer and I can't bear to be cooped up in this room with any of you any longer!'

'You don't need to be, child,' Mrs Tressler went over to her. 'The inspector did not restrict our movements on this floor.'

'No, he didn't. I think I'll go to the sitting room where I waited the other evening to find out whether Regina would see me or not. I don't mind if you come with me.' The platinum hair was at odds with her look of vulnerability.

'Thank you, I'll be glad to do so.'

Ned went with them down the hall and left them at the sitting-room door. He was about to continue towards the back stairs when he heard familiar barking from behind the study door. On opening it he received a rapturous greeting from Rouser, tail wagging a mile a minute, to which he responded with equal joy. The day brightened enormously. It didn't matter where the dog had been. He was back. 'Come along, old fellow,' Ned patted his side, 'let's get you some breakfast.' Rouser woofed approval.

At the base of the back stairs stood the constable assigned to guard them against access to the floors above. Ned had noted the man's colleague on duty by the front staircase. They had his sympathy; he couldn't imagine anything more tiresome than standing still for ten minutes, let alone facing the prospect of doing so for hours. He was expressing this solicitous view when Grumidge appeared in the passageway. After bending to pat the dog and congratulating Ned on its return, the butler offered the information that he'd left the study door to the terrace open so the police would find it in the same state as during the night.

'I trust I did right, sir.'

'Absolutely,' Ned glanced at the constable, who nodded agreement. Whether or not he had the authority to do so would be between him and the higher-ups. Ned passed along Inspector LeCrane's instructions to Grumidge, and then asked where he would find Mrs Norris.

'In the kitchen, sir, with Mrs McDonald.'

'How is everyone else holding up?'

'Seemingly well, except for Annie. I fear she will fall further apart at the thought of being questioned. Mrs Norris would have sent her up to sit with Jeanie, who is still resting her injured ankle, had the constable permitted.'

'Just doing my job,' rejoined the man.

345

'Commendable.' Ned clapped the man on the shoulder. 'But we can't leave a young woman to starve, can we? Someone has to take up her breakfast.'

'There you have me, Lord Stodmarsh,' the face under the helmet lengthened, 'puts me in a right quandary, that does.'

'Don't let it get you down. I'll explain it to the inspector or his sergeant.'

The constable nodded. Probably the only physical exercise he would get for a while.

'What about breakfast for yourself and the family, sir?' Grumidge inquired.

'I imagine we are at the mercy of the inspector's schedule there as in so much else,' replied Ned cheerfully, 'although I shall risk being handcuffed for giving Rouser his without requesting permission.' He stepped into the kitchen with the dog at his heels in time to hear Mrs McDonald say to Florence, 'I don't condone murder, but this one couldn't have happened to a nastier person and I'm not about to shed any crocodile tears.'

'No point in being hypocritical,' agreed Ned. 'I can't work myself up to a tinge of regret. See who's back where he belongs!'

Both women exclaimed over Rouser. A sheen of tears showed in Florence's eyes. 'What a relief! I wonder how long it's been since he's eaten. He must have his bowl filled immediately.'

While Mrs McDonald was thus occupied, Ned put an arm round Florence and kissed her cheek. 'I've some reasonably good news, Florie, dear.

346

The inspector indicated there may be a quick arrest. Even more encouraging, he has something up his sleeve that suggests to him Regina was killed by someone outside the household. He seems to have a particular person in mind.'

Florence took this in. 'I wonder,' she said slowly, 'if he suspects the ornamental hermit?'

'I hadn't thought about that, but if so it might explain the inspector's thinking that whoever it was may have had an accomplice at Mullings.'

'Well,' Mrs McDonald rejoined them, 'that's a fly in the ointment if ever there was one, Mr Ned. If it's true I've got to think someone made use of a crazy old man to do the deed for him or her. And my betting, though I took to her fine, is on Miss Jones as the most likely person; though in my book that makes her the murderer and him the accomplice.'

Florence disagreed. 'I don't believe it. I'm sorry, Ned. I think her arrival came in very handy as a pawn for a hand waiting for some time to make a move on the board.'

'Whose hand?' he asked, hollow voiced.

'I'm unwilling to say. I could be wrong.'

Ned's mind whirled, but he knew he mustn't press her. 'Will you open up to the inspector?'

'I must, though he'll probably dismiss my reasoning as nonsense.'

Mrs McDonald stared at her. 'Well, I never! Put shivers down my spine, you do! Still, I have to say, if anyone has their eyes and ears open to what goes on here it's you. So I wouldn't be surprised if you have the right of it.'

Ned endeavoured to console himself with the

certainty that his grandma was in the clear. Anyone else would not be devastating to the point of abject misery. He remembered to tell Florence and Mrs McDonald about his uncle's stroke, which he'd failed to communicate to Grumidge.

Each voiced shocked distress.

'As if this day couldn't get worse!' Mrs McDonald proclaimed.

'How is Mrs William doing?' The anxiety on Florence's face increased.

'She's been granted permission to go with him in the ambulance. As I told Grumidge, the rest of us will be restricted in our movements for the time being. Better get back to the gruelling. I'm sure the inspector will request a space to set up operations. If it suits him, which I'd think it should because there's a telephone there, I'll put the study at his disposal. I imagine I'll be the first summoned for questioning.' He shrugged expressively and left with Rouser at his heels.

On returning to the drawing room Ned discovered his grandmother and Sylvia Jones there, presumably ordered back by Sergeant Wright, who turned out to be a thickset, muscular man, with the broken-nosed countenance of a boxer. Presently he was dashing a pencil across the page of a notebook with a ferocity that suggested he would have preferred to be wielding a gun, ready to order Mrs Tressler, Madge Bradley and Sylvia Jones to put their hands up if they so much as squirmed in their seats. He did not bother to rise. Clearly he wasn't wearing kid

348

gloves.

'And you are?' He glanced around at Ned who responded cheerfully.

'Your host, Edward Stodmarsh. Ned to family and friends, which I gather is not likely to include you, Sergeant. Welcome to Mullings.'

'Better for you, Lord Stodmarsh, if you don't go throwing your upper-crust weight around. Save that for those that have to bow and scrape, which doesn't include me and Inspector Le-Crane. To us you're just another subject for questioning. First name?' As if he didn't already know.

Mrs Tressler, who in contrast to Madge Bradley and Sylvia Jones did not exhibit signs of being cowed, lit up as she beckoned Rouser. 'Ned, what a delightful relief. When did Rouser get back?'

'I heard him at the study door when I was going down the hall to give Grumidge and Mrs Norris the inspector's instructions about none of the staff being allowed upstairs until their rooms had been searched.'

Sergeant Wright stared sourly at the dog. 'Where's he been? Holiday on the French Riviera? Wouldn't be Southend or Blackpool, would it?'

'Missing.'

'Since when?'

'The night before last.'

Sergeant Wright made a display of scratching in his notebook. 'Not that it matters; I'm merely showing a friendly interest, to let you know I'm really a softie deep down.'

349

'Anything, even a dropped pin, can matter.' Inspector LeCrane spoke from the doorway.

'As you always say, sir.' The answer came unabashed, though the Sergeant did choose to rise for his superior. 'Haven't barely started with Lord Snodgrass, but made some general headway with the ladies.'

'He's been entertaining us very pleasantly,' Mrs Tressler assured the inspector.

'Oh, indeed!' Madge Bradley's words did not match her pallor. 'We regretted ... felt so rude ... not being able to offer him a cup of tea, but I for one was afraid to pull the bell rope in case it was restricted along with the telephone.'

Sylvia Jones sat silent, brown eyes wide and unfocused. The Sergeant's jerk of the head at her could have been a thumbing gesture. 'Young lady's attitude hasn't been what you could call cooperative. Did get out of her that she showed up here unexpected a few days ago. Claims to be Regina Stodmarsh's granddaughter, but admits to never having set eyes on the old lady before. Getting anything else out of her's been like yanking teeth. Could be,' he added sarcastically, 'she's shy, making her not the type of platinum blonde we usually come across.'

Sylvia Jones showed a flash of spirit. 'Have you received commendations for bullying, Sergeant?'

Inspector LeCrane remained in the doorway, his expression neutral. 'Hopefully I can put you more at ease, Miss Jones. Here's an update for all of you. Mr William Stodmarsh and his wife have been taken to hospital.'

'We heard their departure; the sounds of a stretcher being carried downstairs would be impossible not to notice,' said Mrs Tressler.

'His recovery is to be wished for his sake, along with the opportunity to question him as to what he may know or surmise. Doctor Chester has provided his initial findings. Photographs of the scene have been taken and fingerprinting is under way.'

'What sort of knife was it?' Despite his extreme lack of affection for Regina, Ned's stomach churned.

'The sort found in numerous kitchens for chopping meat. We may learn more from the post-mortem, but the cause of death is not in question. Lady Stodmarsh was stabbed repeatedly.'

'In a frenzy of rage?' Madge Bradley cupped her face with her hands. 'Oh dear, that doesn't seem to fit a stranger, does it? Which means that it must have been someone who knew and hated her!' Her eyes flinched away from Sylvia Jones, while avoiding those of Mrs Tressler and Ned.

'Not necessarily. Equally likely it was a matter of making a thorough job of it to ensure no chance of recovery. The body will shortly be removed and the search of Lady Stodmarsh's bedroom for evidence will continue. Meanwhile if you haven't yet breakfasted I suggested you do so soon. I would like to begin seeing each of you in private in not much more than an hour. Is there a room I may use for that purpose, Lord Stodmarsh?'

Ned offered the study as planned. 'I'll take you

351

there.'

'Thank you; sounds ideal.' His gaze circled. 'Any further questions?'

'How long before we're allowed to enter our bedrooms?' This was Mrs Tressler.

'Reasonably shortly for those of you where we discover nothing of significance; this may be true with all of you, but that waits to be seen. Sergeant, I'd like you to get started on this at once, assisted by Constable Trout.' He made way for the man to head past him into the hall before continuing.

'One of our primary objectives will be to search for bloodstained clothing, including both day- and nightwear. In doing so we will scour not only the bedrooms but all other areas of the upper levels where such items may have been hidden. Does anyone have on what they wore last evening?'

'I do,' came Madge Bradley's stricken response. 'I just grabbed for what was at hand ... my dress and petticoat lying over the chair. I never thought, didn't consider that they might need to be checked, but now, of course, I see ... It's all so ghastly.'

'I regret the imposition. We'll need a woman in attendance when you change. Constable Trump is a married man. I'll request him to phone his wife and ask if she would be agreeable to come here and assist you. A couple more things, Lord Stodmarsh.'

'Yes?'

'Is there a chambermaid who could tell if any apparel is missing from wardrobes or other storage places?'

'There are two – Daisy and Gladys.'

'I'll have Constable Trump fetch them when I speak to him about getting in touch with his wife. Finally, for now, did Lady Stodmarsh have a lady's maid?'

'She's had several,' Ned told him, 'sacking them each in turn under one pretext or another. A new one is – was – expected next week.'

'That's unfortunate. We need to know what of value was in that room, with particular emphasis on her jewellery.'

'Perhaps I can be of help there,' Madge Bradley volunteered nervously. 'Between maids she sometimes had me assist her in dressing for dinner, getting out what she wished to wear and performing other small tasks. I did not mind in the least. I know myself fortunate that little else is required of me in return for being able to continue living here.'

'The jewellery?'

'That was kept in a safe behind a panel to the left of the fireplace. She never had me open it, nor showed me how to do so. Nor did I see her do so. She rarely wore any jewellery except her pearls.'

'How frequently was that?'

'Nearly every day – if not always.'

Ned backed her up. 'That's correct, Inspector.'

'I am only at Mullings at few times a year,' contributed Mrs Tressler, 'but during such visits I've observed the pearls to be a constant of her apparel.'

Sylvia Jones winced.

'It must be difficult, Miss Jones, to hear your grandmother spoken of in the past tense. Miss Bradley,' he turned his head, 'did you assist Regina Stodmarsh in preparing for bed last evening?'

'No.'

'Would you know what she did with the pearls after taking them off?'

Madge Bradley nodded, hands knotting. 'She'd put them in a silver-topped tortoiseshell box on her dressing table.'

'Never in the safe?'

'Not in my presence. I recall being surprised the first time I saw her do it. I supposed them to be quite valuable. They had a beautiful sapphire clasp.'

'I'd state,' said Ned, 'it would be in character for her to enjoy daring someone to steal them, including Miss Bradley, in the hope of mounting a head on a platter. It was the sort of vicious gamesmanship she relished.'

'I did wonder ... Thank you all, that should be it now.' Inspector LeCrane inclined his head and left them to their own devices, which consisted of five minutes of sinking into silence.

By ten that morning they had breakfasted and learned that the body had been removed from the house. Ned was the first to be summoned to the study. The inspector rose from the chair behind the desk, waved him to another angled towards him and reseated himself.

'I hope not to keep you long, Lord Stodmarsh.'

Ned felt much as he'd done when asked to

354

present himself at the headmaster's office and assumed a severe reprimand, but answered equably. 'Not to worry, it's not as though I'm going anywhere.' Rouser had come in with him, but no objection was made. The first questions levelled at him were perfunctory in nature, delivered in an almost desultory manner. How long had Mullings been in his family? Where had he been educated? How did he currently occupy his time? They then became more directed.

'Did you hear any sound of a disturbance in the night?'

'No.'

'How would you describe your relationship with your step-grandmother?'

'I loathed her.'

'Any recent altercations?'

'Yes. I may have been overheard saying I could murder her.'

'Perhaps you will be so good as to fill me in on the whys and wherefores.'

Ned discovered he did not need to brace himself to make his disclosure. However, before he could answer, the telephone on the desk rang and the inspector, with a murmur of apology, lifted the receiver.

'This is LeCrane.'

Ned heard a burbling at the other end that extended in length to that of a many versed poem without interruption from the inspector, whose expression had altered strikingly. At last he spoke.

'Seems we've been barking up not one wrong

355

tree but two.'

Pause.

'I'll get on to that at once. I'll phone within a couple of hours, whether or not we meet with success.' He listened again. 'There is a lake. We'll have to concern ourselves later if necessary. Meanwhile I'll stay put and attempt to get what I can without alarming the party here into taking off. As for the other, I think it best not to make an immediate arrest.'

More burbling from the other end of the line.

'Yes, of course – those premises will be kept under constant surveillance by two constables. I'll instruct that any attempt to leave is reported back to me by one of them, while the other discreetly pursues. Meanwhile we may get lucky coming up with something damning within these walls, but somehow I doubt it. We would seem to be dealing with a mind that's thought of all contingencies, except – thank God, the one that counted.

'Sorry for the interruption, Lord Stodmarsh.' LeCrane might have been apologizing for breaking off to make a sandwich. A further delay occurred when the study door opened and Sergeant Wright came in, walked over to the desk and handed the inspector what looked to Ned like a woman's handkerchief sachet.

'You may find the contents interesting, sir, although from going through them I'd say they could be the result of an active imagination. Apart, that is, from a letter also contained.'

'Would you mind leaving us for a few moments, Lord Stodmarsh?' Inspector LeCrane requested. 'I would appreciate you remaining in the hall, as I will wish you to come back in. And I'd like you to keep your dog with you.'

Those moments turned into close on ten minutes. It was the Sergeant who then summoned him, also returning to the study. The sachet was not in view.

'Lord Stodmarsh, I have a request of you.' The inspector looked down at Rouser. 'We'd like to borrow your dog for a scouring of the grounds, in particular the woods.'

'A search for what? The knife?'

'A body. That of the curiously named "Ornamental Hermit".'

Ned's interest switched to shock, vividly bringing out every freckle on his whitening face.

'Whatever makes you think he's dead?' He waved an unsteady hand. 'No, don't bother answering that. You must have your reasons and I'm not sure I'm ready to hear them yet. As for Rouser, I doubt he'd go with you without me.'

'No reason why you shouldn't accompany Constable Trout and Sergeant Wright.'

Ned cleared his throat. 'Would you prefer I not mention this to other members of the household?'

'Better not to create further panic until we have more by way of answers to offer. Besides, I wish the search to begin immediately. Sergeant?'

'Yes, sir?'

'Kindly explain to the other two constables that they are freed from their present duties and advise them of what is now required of them.

They will continue with their new responsibilities until informed otherwise.'

Forty-five minutes later Florence was surprised when Grumidge returned from his summons to the study to say Inspector LeCrane wished to see Mrs McDonald next. She had expected to be the second member of the staff to be interrogated. Mrs McDonald also looked puzzled.

'Well, that's out of order, Mrs Norris.' She attempted a chuckle. 'Hope it's not because I'm a major suspect.'

Florence answered encouragingly, 'I don't think you have the least cause for worry. It'll be routine questioning.'

Grumidge concurred. 'I imagine it'll be much as it was for me, Mrs McDonald, nothing more alarming than inquiring whether I'd seen or heard anything yesterday, or before; and anything that might have suggested Lady Stodmarsh's life was in danger.'

When they left, Florence went into the housekeeper's room. A letter from her cousin Hattie Fly had been placed on her desk. She was tempted to open it to draw comfort from Hattie's voice on paper, but it was as much as she could do to sit down. She was gripped by intense fatigue, which numbed both body and mind. Up to this point she had been so fully occupied in calming down the staff, having the most difficulty with the hysterical Annie, and attending to her duties, that there hadn't been room for thought beyond absorbing the inevitability of Regina Stodmarsh's murder. Now, when she should have been endeavouring to sort through events, she was capable of nothing but staring blankly into space. The minutes ticked by until she heard Mrs McDonald return. There was no mistaking her weighty tread, and Florence rejoined her in the kitchen.

'How did it go?'

'Well, I'm not in handcuffs, am I?' came the breezy reply. 'And I'll hand it to the inspector that he set me at ease right off. It was like Mr Grumidge said, Mrs Norris; he wanted to know if I had anything to tell him about yesterday. Of course what leaped to mind was Mr Ned being so upset when he came down in the morning and found his dog had disappeared, and then Jeanie's tumble on the stairs after going to fetch down Lady Stodmarsh's breakfast tray.'

Florence's thoughts quickened. 'How did he respond?'

Mrs McDonald was putting the kettle on to boil. 'He wanted to know if the dog had taken off before. I told him: Never! Then he got into what'd been the thinking on how it had happened and I said that somebody must have left the house during the night and accidentally let him out.'

'Did you tell the inspector that Rouser had been shut in the study?'

'I did when he asked me where he would've been, and it seemed that whoever it was who had gone outside must have opened that door for some reason or other. How about a cup of tea, Mrs Norris?'

'That would be nice,' said Florence, though

sure she wouldn't be able to take a swallow.

'Do us both good.'

'Was that the end of the inspector's questions?'

'No.' Mrs McDonald reached for cups and saucers. 'He went back to Jeanie's fall and how she said it happened. So I told how she said she was pushed, but that was as maybe seeing as she isn't always truthful. He then wanted to know if there were any repercussions besides her sprained ankle. And I said how it meant she couldn't take out the hermit's midday meal. He asked who did so and I explained how Annie got all worked up that it would have to be her and how nice Miss Jones was about going instead.'

'I see. Was that all?'

'It was, other than the inspector thanking me very nicely for being cooperative. As though I'd've dared be anything else. I have to say he struck me as a man that won't let the grass grow under his feet, like the London police seem to've done – the man that knifed that old lady still being at large.'

'I don't know anything about that.'

Mrs McDonald placed a cup of tea on the table in front of Florence. 'It's been in all the newspapers.'

'I'm ashamed to say I rarely look at one.'

'Worst of it is that it's different from Lady Stodmarsh; she seems to have been a kind old girl. She'd taken in this young artist fellow, given him a roof over his head while he was getting ready for a showing, or whatever it's called for his painting,' Mrs McDonald blew into her cup, 'and that's how he rewarded her –

360

knifing her to death in her sitting room.'

The kitchen tilted under Florence's feet. 'Did the papers give his name?'

'Well, let me think ... I've got it – Arthur somebody.'

'Did they give a middle name?'

Mrs McDonald considered before coming up with a reply. 'James, if I remember right.'

Florence felt as though her insides were being hollowed out.

'Why so interested, Mrs Norris? You don't think that it could be him that got in last night looking for something to steal to help in his getaway? The mistress's bedroom would be the place to look for something valuable and easy to carry. And if Lady Stodmarsh awoke ... well, goes without saying. Maybe I'm giving way to wishful thinking; it would be such a relief to have everyone at Mullings cleared of suspicion.'

'Yes. Very convenient.'

Grumidge came in to say Inspector LeCrane would see Mrs Norris now. Florence was never sure afterwards how she made it to the study. So much had slid devastatingly into place: George's collapse on the green, in all likelihood on opening the paper – she remembered that, unlike her, reading both morning and evening editions was part of his daily routine; his refusal to see her, seemingly so contrary to his generous nature; and Mrs McDonald saying yesterday that according to rumour a plain-clothed policeman, or someone resembling such, had shown up at the Dog and Whistle a couple of days earlier.

'Good day, Mrs Norris. Please sit down,' said

361

Inspector LeCrane.

She did so without thought or feeling, unable to respond verbally.

'I need only keep you for a very short while. What questions I have mainly relate to this.' He pushed the handkerchief sachet forward on the desk. 'I hope you do not object to it being removed from a drawer in your bedroom.'

Florence stared at him, some semblance of normal feeling returning.

'You recall what it contains?'

'Yes. Notations I made in the aftermath of the first Lady Stodmarsh's death, along with a letter I received from a friend.'

'George Bird, publican of the Dog and Whistle?'

'Yes.'

'No handkerchiefs?'

'I put those in a new sachet my sister sent me the following Christmas.'

'Anything else in this one?'

'An anonymous note.'

'Saying?'

'Which one of them did it?'

'Just checking your recall, Mrs Norris. Did you show it to anyone?'

'No,' said Florence quietly.

'Not even your friend, George Bird?'

'I didn't want to burden him with my suspicions. I feared having to keep them back from him would put constraints on our friendship and stopped seeing him.'

'No contact of any sort with him since?'

'None.'

'You didn't take the note to Constable Trump?'

'If you've read what I wrote about that...'

'I have.'

'Then you'll see it was a difficult decision to make. In the end I decided it wouldn't be taken seriously – the implication was clear to me, but there was no reference to murder and no threat was made. As you'll have read, I felt sure it was written, not out of any knowledge, but from spite by a nanny who had been dismissed for drinking. Also, I had no concrete evidence to back up my suspicions.'

'And you were loath to place innocent persons under suspicion?'

'Yes.'

'Your being devoted to the family, especially to young Ned Stodmarsh?'

'I know him – have done so since he was a small boy.'

Inspector LeCrane leaned back in his chair. 'How do you now regard your decision to remain silent?'

'I've yet to delve into my feelings.'

'Then let me offer you some reassurance, Mrs Norris. I think you were right in believing the murderer would decide it was too risky to strike again and would not have done so had a scapegoat not appeared at an opportune moment.' Inspector LeCrane nodded towards the door. 'That will be all for now.'

'Thank you.' Florence had just risen, her legs steadier than they had been when she'd sat down, when a constable entered, followed by Ned with Rouser at his heels.

'Positive news to report, sir,' said the taller of the policemen. 'We discovered the body of the so-called ornamental hermit in a ravine close to the woodland path. He'd been covered by dead leaves. It was the dog that alerted us to the spot. We also found these near the hut.' He held up a string of pearls. 'Constable Phipps remains at the scene, awaiting further instructions.'

Inspector LeCrane looked to Ned, his expression as laconic as it had been during his questioning of Florence. 'I thank you for your cooperation and suggest you conduct Mrs Norris to a place where she can recover from this further shock.'

Ned put an arm round her in the hall. 'My God, Florie! This gets beastlier by the hour. Why the desire or need to kill that pathetic creature who may have done nothing to hurt anyone, beyond scaring them a little?'

'That has to be thought through. I'm all right, Ned. I'd like to go and sit at my desk and hope answers work their way into place. How are you after so grim an experience?'

'I was prepared. We'd been told what we were looking for. I'll come with you.'

'No. You have to pass on this news.'

'I refuse not to see you to your desk.'

When he left her, Florie closed her eyes and decided it might help to empty her mind of horror momentarily. She reached for Hattie's letter and read it through, picking up speed as she went along. She then refolded it, returned it to the envelope and drew in a deep breath. After doing so she sought out Grumidge and asked if he'd request Miss Jones to do her the kindness of coming to the housekeeper's room for a talk.

'Certainly, Mrs Norris.'

Florence turned her chair to face the door, drew another chair forward and angled it towards hers, then picked up the envelope again. Several minutes later she rose as the white-faced girl entered. She must have guessed what was coming. Shutting the door behind her, she leaned back against it, eyes riveted on what Florence was holding.

'From Miss Fly?'

'Yes, my dear.' Florence guided her to the chair. 'Don't look so frightened. Hattie writes very fondly of you and I value her opinion over most others. I think you and I should put our heads together.'

'I don't see how that can help.'

'I have faith it will. May I call you Toffee?'

'If you like.' The girl sat utterly listless.

'I'd like to begin at my end. A few years ago I was friendly with George Bird; that ended when ... something happened that caused me to regretfully cut off contact with him. I'll tell you about that later. During our times together he spoke often and with deep affection of his godson Jim. At our last meeting he mentioned that Jim had a young lady, from the sound of her a lovely girl, but his parents didn't approve of her any more than they had of his attempting to earn a living as a painter. Their reasons for disliking the girl unseen included her having a name they thought silly and affected. George couldn't remember what it was, only that it was something such as "Fudge". Hattie writes of her lodger, who went off unexpectedly with the possibility of not returning for an uncertain length of time, as "Toffee". It seemed just too close to be a coincidence. And there's the surname being the same.'

'I was sure she'd write – you're such an important part of her life, but I hoped I'd be gone before a letter came.' The response was bleak.

'George also mentioned that Jim's young lady had a platinum streak in her brown hair.'

'I had to bleach the rest, not because I thought you'd know about it, but because I was afraid the police had me under watch and might have me followed. It wasn't hard for them to find out about Jim and me. Even though things have been over between us for some time, as he said it was unfair to keep me waiting perhaps for years until we could afford to marry, it had to occur to them he might try to get in touch with me, to borrow money to help in his escape. I tried my very best to throw them off my trail in coming here.'

'I didn't know about the murder of the old lady until half an hour ago when Mrs McDonald mentioned it. I don't read the papers,' Florence told her. 'Did you come to this area principally to see George, to find out if he'd heard from Jim, or might even be hiding him?'

Toffee nodded. 'Neither proved the case. That lovely man is distraught but fighting against giving the game away. There is also the fact that I really am – was – Regina Stodmarsh's grand-daughter. And my first name is Sylvia. My father named me after my mother, but wished he

366

hadn't. He found it too painful, so he called me Toffee for the colour of my eyes. I discovered Regina had remarried and what her new surname was from the pure chance of going to lodge with dear Miss Fly. She never told me anything revealing about life at Mullings, apart from a few bare facts, and that was one of them. As I told you, I wanted my mother's pearls – they belonged to me by right – so I could give them to Jim if I were blessed enough to find him. And yesterday ... I did.'

Florence stared at her in amazement. 'When ... where?'

'In the ornamental hermit's hut, when I took out the tray of food because that girl Annie was too afraid to do so. It took several good looks for me to realize it was Jim. He was disguised by a false beard and hair, both of them long and gray. But I'd know his eyes anywhere ... I love him more than words can express and the only comfort left to me is that he told me he still felt the same about me. I hadn't argued when he broke things off between us, because I was afraid his explanation about our not being able to marry for ages was an excuse – that really he'd grown tired of me. I've never exactly bubbled over with confidence.'

Florence's thoughts ticked away with increasing speed. 'How had he come by the beard and hair?'

'He wouldn't say; only that it was not from George. There'd be no reason not to tell me if he'd bought them at a shop.'

'For the purpose of posing as the ornamental

hermit?'

'I suppose the police might say he knew of the man's existence from George and somehow got him out of the way.'

Florence hoped her face did not reveal the dread she was feeling. Then came a relieving memory. Inspector LeCrane had spoken of Lillian Stodmarsh's possible killer waiting for a scapegoat before striking again. 'Did you visit Jim again yesterday?'

Toffee shook her head. 'I told him I'd get the pearls in the middle of the night. He asked me not to, but I was determined and slipped into her bedroom, leaving the door ajar so there'd be some light. I hadn't taken two steps when I saw she ... she was dead. I raced out and went to warn Jim that he was liable to be suspected of her murder too. He was gone.'

'The false beard and hair?'

'Also gone.'

'I think,' said Florence, 'I can hazard a guess where they came from. When I first came to Mullings as a girl of fourteen, the housekeeper at that time, a Mrs Longbrow, mentioned that Edward Stodmarsh, Ned's grandfather, enjoyed amateur theatricals, which were performed in this house. He later mentioned to me that he had acted the part of Prospero in *The Tempest,* and that old costumes were stored in trunks in the attic.'

'Then that means,' gasped Toffee, 'that someone at Mullings provided them and helped him to hide out as the hermit, so that when Regina was murdered...'

368

She got no further. The door was opened by Inspector LeCrane.

'I trust you will both excuse me. Miss Jones, I would like you to accompany me to the police station, for no alarming reason. I have someone waiting there who is anxious to see you. And to allay further concerns, that person is not, nor will be, placed under arrest.'

Florence saw the girl's face light up with a wonderful vivacity. 'Come with me,' Toffee grasped her hand as they both stood, 'I want you to hear whatever else he has to say.'

Inspector LeCrane said, 'I hope to return in a couple of hours to find the family assembled so I can update them on how matters stand. I would appreciate your being present, Mrs Norris. Coming, Miss Jones?'

That was at three o'clock in the afternoon. At precisely five Grumidge ushered Inspector LeCrane once more into the drawing room. Gertrude Stodmarsh had not returned from the hospital; recent news of her husband was not good, and she did not expect to return that night. Miss Hendrick was with her. Inspector LeCrane surveyed the expectant faces fixed on his. Ned was standing. The others sat.

'As I told you this morning, I expected to make a speedy arrest. As it happens, the obvious suspect at that time has been positively cleared. We are, however, well on our way to closure. Mr Cyril Fritch has confessed to the murder of Regina Stodmarsh.'

Madge Bradley swayed, emitting a cry of

369

anguish.

'He claims his reason for committing the crime was that he has been embezzling money from the bookshop where he works to support his mother's excessive spending and feared discovery when his employer, Mr Craddock, sells it. Mr Fritch knew you were due for an inheritance, Miss Bradley, on Lady Stodmarsh's death, which would enable him to return the money.'

'I don't ... won't believe it!' Madge Bradley was weeping, tears dripping through the fingers covering her face.

Inspector LeCrane smiled thinly, 'Neither do I, Miss Bradley, but I think he'll stick gamely to his version, until we have him sit in while we question you about the death of Lillian Stodmarsh.'

'What rubbish is this?' Her hands dropped and Florence saw the vicious glitter of hatred in her eyes that she had witnessed once before, but this time it didn't flash almost too quickly to be absorbed. She then made the obvious mistake. 'You've no proof.'

'Perhaps not what might be termed hard evidence, but enough of the circumstantial sort to request an order of exhumation from the Home Secretary. But more importantly, sufficient evidence to have Mr Fritch decide you're not worth hanging for.' Inspector LeCrane nodded towards the two constables hovering in the doorway. 'Take her away, chaps. You can fetch me later. I'd like to stay for a cup of tea if it's on offer.'

THIRTEEN

Florence had not been so mesmerized by the scene which had just unfolded that she had failed to see the startled look on Ned's face change to one of anguish on hearing what the inspector had to say regarding Lillian Stodmarsh's death. He stared blankly after the figure being escorted from the room and stood as if frozen, even after they heard the front door closing, followed by the sound of a car being started and then driven away into silence. Florence longed to go over and put her arms around him, but she knew it was not her place to do so with Mrs Tressler present to offer comfort.

'My dear Ned,' said that lady, rising from the sofa, 'why don't I walk with you to another room, such as your study, where you can have the peace to allow the shock of what you've just heard sink in? I'll then leave if you wish, or sit without saying a word, unless you wish to talk.'

'Thank you, Grandma,' his green eyes held both gratitude and love behind the blur of tears, 'but I'll stay here.'

'If you're sure?'

He nodded and she returned to the sofa. 'I need to hear all that Inspector LeCrane has to reveal.' He turned to the long, lean figure, now occupying a wingback chair beside the fireplace, angled towards the other seating. 'May I offer you something stronger than tea, Inspector?'

Florence had never been prouder of Ned, witnessing the steadiness of his voice and stance.

'That is very obliging of you, Lord Stodmarsh,' was the response. 'I'll pretend I'm off duty, which in a sense I temporarily am, and accept, if I may, a whisky and soda.'

'It sounds like you've earned one.' Ned provided a handsome crystal glass, shimmering with amber fire, and settled himself down next to Mrs Tressler.

'I really had very little to do with solving one murder and discovering that it had been preceded by another.' Inspector LeCrane sipped his drink with obvious enjoyment. 'That's not self-deprecation. It's a fact. Credit goes to an unforeseen circumstance, which I will come to later, and the contributions of Mrs Tressler and Mrs Norris.'

Ned looked at each in turn, but neither his grandmother nor Florence said anything or showed surprise, and he decided this was not the moment to question the inspector and break his train of thought.

'On receiving the telephone message this morning alerting me to the stabbing of Regina Stodmarsh, I was ninety-nine per cent certain the murderer would prove to be Arthur James Leighton, who has been on the run for the past several days. He had fled the scene when discovered with a bloodied knife in his hand, standing over the body of an elderly woman in London who had taken him into her home. She had done so because she wished to assist him in pursuing his ambitions as an artist.'

Enlightenment dawned on Ned's face, but again he refrained from interjecting.

The inspector sat very much at ease in the wingback chair. In relaxation he had an elegance well suited to that of his surroundings. He might have been discussing the vintage contents of his wine cellar, or relating some anecdote about a peer of the realm who happened to be a member of his club. 'It did not take the police involved in the London case long to seriously consider the possibility that Mr Leighton might make his way to Dovecote Hatch.'

'Jim,' said Ned, 'godson of George Bird at the Dog and Whistle.'

'Precisely. He had been named for his father, Arthur James Leighton, but his parents called him Jim from the start. They were, of course, interviewed, and their home watched, but their statement that they were estranged from their son was confirmed by neighbours – putting them lower on the list of likely bolt holes the younger Mr Leighton might have in mind.'

'But were they otherwise helpful,' inquired Mrs Tressler, 'in directing you to Mr Bird – suggesting their son might seek sanctuary with him and providing his address?'

'That was so.' Inspector LeCrane finished his drink and set the glass down on the piecrust table by his chair. 'One prefers to believe they were doing their duty, as viewed from lives of unflagging respectability, and not acting out of

373

jealousy of the closeness between their son and his godfather. The negative aspect of police work is it inclines one to become cynical.'

'I'd call it a ratty thing to do, whatever their motive,' flared Ned. Florence was heartened by his becoming caught up in the information Inspector LeCrane was providing. 'Did the detectives who talked to the parents get the impression they believed in Jim's innocence or not?'

'It's in the report that they insisted he had been brought up to be a good boy but feared he would get into bad company and be led astray when he insisted on following his dream of becoming an artist. My mother said much the same thing when I told her I wanted to become a police-man.'

'George will have had faith in him all the way, and will go on doing so however dark things look presently,' Ned said, looking at Florence. 'Just as you would with me, Florie, if I were in his shoes.' Ned's eyes returned to LeCrane. 'From how George spoke of his godson it was clear he was not only frightfully fond of him, but thought highly of his character – his decency.'

'He did, Inspector,' said Florence.

'I believe, Mrs Norris,' said Mrs Tressler, 'that you and Mr Bird have it in common that you each accepted a formative role in a boy's life and fulfilled it to the crucial betterment of each.' Before Florence could answer she addressed LeCrane. 'Are my grandson and I correct in thinking that when Mr Bird was contacted he vehemently asserted his godson was incapable

374

of murder?'

'That was his position when we sent a man round to the Dog and Whistle. Mr Bird said he had learned of the murder from his morning newspaper and he denied having seen or heard from Leighton since.'

Florence could not hold back a question. 'Did the detective find him credible?'

'Yes. He said Mr Bird struck him as the sort of man who'd refuse to lie under any circumstance – that if he and his godson had been in touch his response would have been a refusal to answer the question.'

'So it would.'

'But that did not mean Dovecote Hatch was no longer kept under surveillance. The hope remained strong that Leighton might make for it. This theory was strengthened when a man sent to track his former girlfriend's movements succeeded, despite,' LeCrane's lips twitched, 'her attempts to throw the London chaps off the scent by disguising her appearance and taking a circuitous route that would have done any career criminal proud. She was seen going into the Dog and Whistle, then huddled outside in conversation with George. After which she walked here. That was two nights ago.'

'Sylvia Jones!' An appreciative gleam appeared in Ned's eyes. 'What a trump girl! She had to still be in love with him despite his being the one who decided to break things off! What a relief that Lamorna and I became unengaged! I'll cheerfully wait for years, if needed, for Sylvia's sort to come along.'

'She's known as Toffee amongst friends and acquaintances.'

'Is she Regina's granddaughter?' Mrs Tressler inquired of the inspector.

'We have the birth certificates to prove it.' LeCrane's mouth twitched again. 'Her own and her mother's – the latter being for Sylvia Tamersham Stapleton, born at the ancestral home of the Tamershams on the correct date. And now we come to that sorry individual, Cyril Fritch.'

The three other people in the room waited expectantly.

LeCrane leaned back in his chair. 'As I mentioned, he had been embezzling from his employer from quite early on in his employment. He did so, he says, to quell his mother's nagging for money, well beyond his slender needs, for holidays and other social events. His job at the bookshop included not only doing the bookkeeping but, when needed, serving in the shop. He would sell a rare costly book without noting the sale in his records. He kept the receipts with the pathetic intention of most embezzlers of returning the money. He was near his wits' end when Madge Bradley displayed an interest in him and eventually, under her guidance, found himself proposing to her. He did not for a minute believe she loved him, which he says was a relief. What he assumed to be her reasoning was that she wanted a husband, any husband, as a means of negating the stigma of being left at the altar. The light he saw at the end of the tunnel was a distant one. Madge would not come into her inheritance from the Stodmarsh trust until

Regina Stodmarsh's death, which could be years away, and in the meantime Madge had nothing beyond her yearly allowance. Then the worst possible happened. Mr Craddock decided to sell the bookshop, which would necessitate a stock-taking that would reveal the unaccounted volumes.'

'I can't help feeling sorry for him,' interjected Ned. 'For a man of his nervous disposition the shock must have been untenable. I'm amazed he didn't cut his throat!'

'He said he thought about suicide but hadn't the courage for it, and decided instead to throw himself on Madge's mercy. By now he knew her well enough to be sure she would not wish to see him publicly disgraced, because of its reflection on her, as a woman who had again shown faulty judgement in a man she had agreed to marry. So, on the rainy evening of Sylvia Jones's showing up, he wheeled his bicycle around the corner of the Dog and Whistle and, using his key to open the gate, entered the woodland. He was not seen to do this because the man assigned to watch the pub had his eyes glued to its door, having seen Sylvia Jones go inside shortly before.'

LeCrane paused, but no one said anything, and he continued, 'Fritch declares he was in a pan-icked state. He had dithered so long in leaving that he was likely to be late for his arranged meeting with Miss Bradley in the summer house. Regina Stodmarsh always made his presence at Mullings an unpleasant experience, even when he came here to work on the book-keeping.'

377

'He's not exaggerating there, Inspector. She was beyond beastly to him. As to a pattern of dishonesty, I don't believe he fiddled the accounts here. I went through the expenditures with him once a month and verified them, not out of a lack of trust but because I wanted to learn as much as I could, about the costs of running the estate.'

'Also, he would have been a fool to dig himself in deeper,' LeCrane pointed out. 'The reason Mr Fritch had delayed in setting out was that his bicycle lamp wasn't working and he was distracted in trying to fix it by the barking of the dogs from next door. When he failed in his attempt the obvious thing was to walk, but by then he was late, and if he were to have any time with Miss Bradley before the dinner hour, it pressed upon him that none should be wasted. Therefore, as I said, he wheeled the bike on to the path where he mounted it and set off, somewhat unsteadily because visibility was reduced by the rain and the surface was slippery. He had not gone far when he veered sideways and plunged into a ravine, felt the impact of a thud, and was flung off the bike. He assumed he'd hit a tree, but when he got up and unsteadily blundered a few steps, there was a flash of lightning and he saw the recumbent form of an old man with long gray locks and a beard.'

There was a punctuating hush before LeCrane proceeded. 'Horrified, Fritch tried and failed to rouse him by importations and grabbing at his shoulders, knowing as he did so that the man was already dead. The rock that the back of his head had landed on was wet with something far darker than rain. A vision of a doomed future flashed before his eyes. Regina Stodmarsh would be enraged at the loss of her eccentric antiquity, but that paled in comparison to the rest. Yes, it had been an accident, but one caused by illegally riding a bicycle without a functioning lamp. Facing the shame of a trial would be torture for him. He would be sent to prison – where meek, nervy men are the sort hardened, vicious criminals most enjoy tormenting. Beyond that he could not think, other than to go on trembling legs to a telephone box and call Madge Bradley.'

'She must have gone,' said Ned, 'because she came into dinner barely on time, which to my knowledge had never happened before.'

LeCrane inclined his head. 'She met him where he'd told her he'd be, bringing with her a torch. They would manage matters together, she told him calmly. From which we may take it the real Miss Bradley had stepped out from behind the curtain. None of the flustered, self-deprecating murmurings she must have felt it necessary to acquire in order to gain sufficient sympathy from Edward and Lillian Stodmarsh for them to provide for her every need and comfort at Mullings.'

'I didn't like her at the beginning and not much at the end,' said Ned. His mouth tightened and the rest of his face closed down.

'What were her instructions to Mr Fritch, Inspector?'

'The first was that they get rid of the bicycle.

The front wheel had been twisted out of alignment.'

'I remember her mentioning at dinner that it had been stolen. How very clever!' Florence suppressed a shiver.

'They would have to count on Fritch not having been observed wheeling it into the woods, but that was a safe enough bet considering the rain and the extremely short distance between his house and the gate, which had taken only moments to unlock. She was saying that the best place to dispose of it would be the lake, when they heard a rustling followed by something, or someone, thrashing about in the undergrowth coming from opposite where they were standing.' LeCrane broke to add an aside. 'You will have noticed I've stopped saying, "Fritch said" ... or "Fritch revealed under questioning", but that is always a given. At that moment,' he continued, 'Fritch turned witless with terror, convinced there was a person close enough to have spotted them through a gap in the trees, if only as two shadowy figures. Miss Bradley told him to stay where he was and crossed the path, torch in hand, to almost instantly disappear from view. This was quickly followed by the sound of voices, hers and what sounded like a man's.'

'Jim!' exclaimed Ned, Mrs Tressler and Florence in unison.

LeCrane raised an amused eyebrow. 'I may have forgotten to mention that Fritch, in his agitation to telephone Madge Bradley, had left the gate unlocked on leaving. After what was to him an agonizing wait, which he later calculated as about five minutes, Miss Bradley returned with the sodden young man who had not shaved in close to a week and appeared to be dropping on his feet. She explained succinctly who he was and why he was in the wood. His name was Jim Leighton, on the run from a murder charge of which he was innocent, having foolishly panicked knowing the cards would be stacked against him. He had come to Dovecote Hatch to try and speak with Mr Bird, his godfather, about what he should do, but on his way up the village street, he had seen a man outside the Dog and Whistle who looked to him like a detective. So he turned down a side street that came out closer to the pub than he'd expected, saw the gate to the woods, and found it unlocked.'

'You now have us in suspense, Inspector,' said Mrs Tressler. 'It is Mr Leighton's fate that matters to us. How did they decide to make use of him?'

'Again, credit must be given to Miss Bradley's quick thinking, Fritch being of course useless, apart from the one contribution he stammered out, of which she immediately saw the value. He remembered that as a boy Leighton had been in one of his English classes when he'd taught at a grammar school and, unlike his classmates, had not made fun of him. Miss Bradley seized on this tidbit as a means of making it seem more credible than it might have done, that she and Fritch would be willing to help him. Such a nice, kind boy could not have become a murderer.'

'Go on, Inspector,' urged Ned. 'We're all ears.'

'Here was her proposal – that he hide out for a

few days in the hut usually occupied by the ornamental hermit, whom he knew about from his godfather. She told him that they had a short while ago found the poor old man wandering about in the woods, and being worried about his hacking cough had persuaded him to go with them to Fritch's house – which he had to himself since his mother was away. They said they had tucked him into a warm bed, given him a hot soothing drink, and had just been on their way to inform Regina Stodmarsh of their actions – dreading the onslaught of her response to their interference. Now, they could have a temporary reprieve to the benefit of themselves, and Jim Leighton would play the part of the hermit.'

Ned winced. 'Of course, he swallowed it hook, line and sinker. What bloke wouldn't in his place, probably faint from hunger and fatigue? Followed them like a puppy, I bet!' He paused, his green eyes darkening.

'Exactly,' responded LeCrane. 'We'll get to Rouser very soon. Perhaps I should state here, Lord Stodmarsh, that I strongly suspect that had not such a perfect scapegoat been found in Jim Leighton, Miss Bradley would have selected you for the part. She was clearly primed for murder in that wood. I cannot doubt that her delay in disposing of Regina Stodmarsh long before came from the caution of self-preservation. The death of a second mistress of Mullings in short succession was bound to raise some eyebrows, leading to scrutiny, however innocently it might seem to have occurred. Your discord with Regina Stodmarsh over her refusal to release funds that would enable you to marry Lamorna Blake would have done nicely for a motive.'

'That doesn't make me any less sorry Jim got the brunt,' Ned growled.

'No, I didn't think it would. On reaching the hut, Miss Bradley explained they'd need to find him the appropriate disguise, since a maid would bring food twice a day, although she was not allowed to speak to the hermit.'

'But Jeanie wouldn't have been fooled,' said Florence. 'She'd been out there too often and had none of the superstitious fear that would have had another girl ducking blindly in and out.'

LeCrane once more inclined his head. 'Again, one of you is ahead of me. The disguise was no problem. Miss Bradley was well aware of the amateur theatricals put on at Mullings by Edward Stodmarsh in his youth. He'd once mentioned to her that he had played the role of Prospero in a long gray wig, attachable waist-length beard and coarse robe. She'd later looked for these amongst the attic trunks and found them. She said she would return during the night with these items, and something for Leighton to eat. Before leaving the hut she stressed that they were depending on him to honour his part of the bargain. The next objective was to hide the hermit's body where it could be readily dis-covered when the time was right, which meant not before the police showed up to investigate Regina Stodmarsh's murder. The second body would lead them to the hut and, hey presto!, there would be Jim Leighton peering out through hair and beard. An outcry ahead of time would ruin everything – hence the need to remove Rouser, with his Labrador scenting abilities, in case he should either be taken for a walk or let loose in that area.' LeCrane glanced at Ned.

'I took him out there every day, even when we spent much of it at Farn Deane,' Ned responded. 'Where did they put the hermit?'

'In the ravine by the path, which meant only having to drag him a few yards from where Fritch had collided with him on the bike. It contained plenty of dead leaves and broken-off branches, making for only a few minutes to cover him up. Another death to be blamed on Leighton. It would be assumed he'd knocked the man down, and there was the bloodstained rock for confirmation.'

'I cannot believe that Fritch was such a fool,' mused Mrs Tressler, 'that he did not know at that point what Madge had in store for Regina; otherwise it wouldn't have mattered if the hermit were found the next day.'

LeCrane nodded. 'Fritch claims that, in addition to his being the one who committed the murder, it was his idea in the first place. He returned to his home and Miss Bradley to Mullings, arriving, as has been said, virtually at the moment the gong rang for dinner. The rest followed smoothly. She collected the costume from the attic, a small amount of food and a container of lemonade from the kitchen, and took these to the hut where Fritch was also waiting. Afterwards they collected the bicycle and between them heaved it into the lake.'

Florence looked perplexed. 'Something woke me around two in the morning, and when I looked out of my bedroom window I saw a figure standing by the lake, before turning and then seeming to disappear at the edge of the woods. I assumed while you were speaking earlier, Inspector, that had to be when they threw it in the water. Perhaps it was the sound of the splash that awakened me.'

'More likely it was a bark or two from Rouser. Fritch says it was around that time when she brought him down the woodland path where they met halfway. Someone else looking out of a window at around two o'clock thought they saw a person enter the gate, but decided even if he were right it would be Constable Trump. What I think you may have seen, Mrs Norris, was Miss Bradley in an excess of caution peering into the water to reassure herself that the bicycle had not resurfaced. The next morning she pushed Jeanie down the back stairs and all was in train for the grand finale – the murder. When the horrifying news was broken she was well into her character part of the dithering, well-meaning cousin who feared above all else making a nuisance of herself. A nice touch was saying after getting off the phone from Fritch that she'd dissuaded him from coming over out of consideration for his nerves. What she'd told him was to release Rouser.' LeCrane smiled thinly. 'No doubt about it, she is a very clever woman, and yet she complacently overlooked the fact that there are other clever women at Mullings in the persons of Mrs Tressler and Mrs Norris.' He looked to the former. 'We come to the navy-blue dress she was wearing and claimed to have worn yesterday. Enlighten us about your observations in that regard, if you would be so good, Mrs Tressler.'

'Yes, of course, Inspector.' She turned to Florence. 'You may not have had occasion to notice, Mrs Norris, that when she came down this morning the hem of her petticoat was showing.'

'I did,' said Ned.

'I didn't,' Florence smiled at them both.

'I naturally thought it was because she had dressed in a hurry,' continued Mrs Tressler, 'but that was made nonsensical when she said she had on the dress she had worn yesterday, in which case the lengths of dress and petticoat would remain the same. The dress did appear to be identical – the neckline was quite distinctive – and then I remembered that yesterday I'd thought it an inch or two too long for her. Also, that she spent almost all of yesterday in her room sewing. And the answer slipped into place. She'd been making a replica dress so that when her room was searched, no bloodstained clothing would be found or noted to be missing. She need only strip off her underclothing, including the petticoat, remove her stockings and shoes and – knife in hand – tiptoe down the hallway to Regina's bedroom. Then, deed done, speed off to the lake and dispose of both pieces of evidence in a tied sack weighted down by a heavy rock. Prior to returning to the house she could walk a little way further into the water, wash herself, and then go into the summer house, allow herself time to dry off, and return in a garment, such

386

as a raincoat, that anyone might accidentally leave behind and later retrieve. I am grateful, Inspector, that you bore in mind the compressed version I gave you this morning.'

'It is to you, Mrs Tressler, and to Mrs Norris, that I am indebted. I have never been more ably assisted on to the right path. Our tale of infamy is drawing to a conclusion. Fritch said the knife used was a discarded one from his kitchen – his mother was always losing things that had to be replaced – and that he had tossed it into the woods. He also stated he had snatched up Lady Stodmarsh's pearls before hastening from the bedroom and dropped them not far from the hut, to cement the story that Leighton had broken into Mullings to steal something he could sell and had awakened her in the process. I have no doubt they were handed over to Fritch by Miss Bradley, possibly in the summer house.' Le-Crane nodded appreciatively at Mrs Tressler.

'What I don't understand,' said Ned, 'is that, given how she seems to have thought of every-thing, it didn't cross her mind – as it might those of the police – that if Jim were presumed to be the killer, he would also be expected to have fled the scene immediately following the murder.'

'A good point,' acknowledged LeCrane. 'Fritch said she had thought of that but she assured him we'd be too ecstatic on getting him to overthink anything. What even so capable a murderess could not have foreseen was the im-pact on Jim Leighton when Sylvia Jones entered that hut yesterday afternoon. Miss Bradley had no way of knowing she was his former girlfriend

387

and had come to Mullings on the desperately thin chance of discovering where he was so she could help him. This meeting would ruin all Miss Bradley's carefully laid plans. Miss Jones gave Leighton what money she had in her purse. Very shortly after she left, promising to return, he took off through the woods towards the rear of the property and climbed atop a stack of logs in order to scale the wall. He was spotted carrying a bundle and heading for the railway station, where he took the train departing for London at 3.35 p.m., and was tailed continuously to the police station which was handling the earlier murder case. It was noted that on his way there he dropped the bundle in a waste bin. This was picked up and proved to be the wig and beard rolled in the robe. At a little after five he was telling the desk sergeant he had decided to turn himself in after discovering that Sylvia Jones was at Mullings in Dovecote Hatch and not wishing her further involvement. Other than that he refused to say more. By ten at night he had not budged. The night was spent in a cell.'

'But when you came in, Inspector,' Florence felt compelled to break in, 'when Toffee ... Miss Jones and I were talking and you asked her to accompany you to the station; you said there was someone waiting there who was anxious to see her, and that person was not, nor would be, placed under arrest. That has to mean Jim has been cleared of killing that old lady.' She included Mrs Tressler in her look of intense relief.

LeCrane appeared as delighted as everyone else. 'Oh, how the best laid plans fall apart! One

388

could almost feel sufficiently sorry for Miss Bradley to hope she doesn't hang – which I happen to think a barbaric proceeding. Early this morning the wife of the old lady's nephew entered the police station in question and produced a pile of bloodstained clothing belonging to her husband that she'd found hidden in the coal shed. The wife then went to the police station door and beckoned her husband inside. He said he was glad to be found out, the strain had become too much. His reason for killing his aunt was that he'd gone into a frenzy when she refused to let him have the couple of hundred pounds for which he'd asked. He'd pretended to leave, waited until she dozed off and then stabbed her with a knife taken from a kitchen drawer. His escape was made by way of a side alley and could only have preceded by fifteen minutes Jim Leighton's arrival on the scene.

'And of course,' added LeCrane, 'you'll want to know what happened to him next. As a sergeant was breaking the good news to Jim and was about to say he was free to leave, the telephone rang. The voice at the other end informed the sergeant about the murder at Mullings, which was bound to be of interest in that quarter because of the connection to Leighton. The sergeant immediately related the conversation to Jim. Fully aware of the motive that could be assigned to the girl he loved, our Jim began to talk.'

'My dear Inspector,' exclaimed Ned joyously, 'I suspect you are a romantic.'

LeCrane's smile was enigmatic. He rose from

his chair. 'And now I must regrettably leave you all. I have abandoned Wright long enough to the wretched business of offering hospitality to Miss Bradley. Much as I may despair of Fritch's conduct, I do not think he should be the one to face the higher consequence of their adventures. I think learning of Miss Bradley's other excursions into crime from the notes you made at the time, Mrs Norris, will decide Fritch against redeeming himself by one ennobling gesture.'

EPILOGUE

Very little of substance was said between Mrs Tressler, Ned and Florence after Inspector LeCrane left that evening. It was clear to both women that Ned was not ready for the conversation to tend towards his late grandmother's death. The exhumation of her body would to him be an agonizing violation, and it was unlikely that LeCrane had mentioned the possibility only to give Madge Bradley a jolt. Florence soon excused herself to return to her duties. Ned had protested, but Mrs Tressler had said there would be plenty of time to talk in the morning, and if Mrs Norris felt as tired as she did, it was close on time for bed.

Mrs McDonald was agog for news, but Florence told her only that Miss Bradley had been arrested. Any further information must come from Lord Stodmarsh or Mrs Tressler. It was the first time she had referred to Ned that way. It had always been Mr Ned, but this no longer seemed appropriate now that he had matured so much.

She did not expect to sleep well, but did so. The next morning Ned sought her out as she'd known he would, but he simply looked at her with wordless gratitude followed by a hug and then was gone. She knew him too well not to understand. Shortly afterwards Mrs Tressler entered the housekeeper's room where Florence was at her desk.

'Please do remain seated, Mrs Norris,' she said as Florence started to rise. 'I won't stay long; there will be plenty of time for many talks in the future. I do hope you will be pleased that Ned has asked me to come and live here.'

'I'm delighted, Mrs Tressler. Your continued presence is exactly what he needs. And of course I wish for your happiness also.'

'I have always liked you, Mrs Norris, and had the utmost trust in your judgement, so be assured that I fully understand why you did not take your early suspicions of Madge Bradley to the police. You would not have been believed, any more than I would have been. I warned Lillian when the rest of the family went to church on the Sunday of her death, that I was afraid for her safety. I'd seen such looks of hatred in Madge's eyes when resting upon her, increasingly so after Lillian gave Edward the puppy and his delight in her thoughtfulness. His love for her was so evident.'

'I glimpsed that same look, but it was gone too quickly for me to hold on to and I didn't recall it until I visited my mother. She was wearing a navy dress. I wonder if Miss Bradley used pills prescribed for her after being left at the altar, something in the nature of valerian, maybe?'

'Very likely,' replied Mrs Tressler, 'I had a bottle of those with me. My doctor thought I should have them in case I ever feared a return of my old symptoms. But when here I put them in my bag, which I always kept with me. I didn't trust Madge Bradley not to go through my things. And clearly that was just as well under the circumstances. I'm convinced from what I saw in her eyes that her hate sprang from corrosive envy of a woman who was not only mistress of Mullings but was also deeply loved by a husband which she herself had failed to acquire. What in particular persuaded you, Mrs Norris, that Madge had murdered Lillian?'

'Annie was interrupted, and went into a screaming panic while preparing the hot milk, by someone who mentioned a mouse. Mrs Mc-Donald could not make head nor tail of it beyond a couple of words which were "wanted to return". I spoke to Annie the next day and got the full story from her. Miss Bradley had come into the kitchen to return a reel of cotton she had asked me for earlier in the week and then pointed across the room, crying, "There goes a mouse!" The whole thing smelled of a ruse to distract Annie, whose terror of mice is known above as well as below stairs. Returning the cotton was unnecessary, but if Miss Bradley had felt compelled, surely she would have brought it to this room, where I would have been much more likely to have been found than in the kitchen.'

Mrs Tressler shook her head. 'Such ruthless determination to destroy, whilst placing herself in a sympathetic light. I wonder if she imagined herself as wildly in love with that man as she did with Edward, for whom there was only one woman in the entire world. But she must have deluded herself he would turn to her as soon as would be socially acceptable after the funeral.' Mrs Tressler had one other piece of news to offer before leaving the housekeeper's room.

'Gertrude just returned from spending the night with Miss Hendrick at the vicarage after leaving the hospital yesterday. The report on William this morning is encouraging. He is recovering and Gertrude is hopeful that she and Miss Hendrick are fully prepared to cope with an invalid in the cottage with a large garden they plan to buy in the village. Gertrude told Ned she is sure everyone will understand why she does not wish to continue living at Mullings.'

Florence spent a good deal of time in reflection that day. The recent past would recede. Grumidge and Molly would marry, and unless they had children – which Molly had always asserted she did not want, having done her share with little ones as the oldest of twelve – Molly would make an ideal housekeeper when she retired. Perhaps it was too early to think about taking a new path, but Florence could not deny the restlessness inside her and the reason for it.

The next morning she left Mullings at eight o'clock.

Ned and Mrs Tressler were standing at the study window and saw her walk down the drive towards the rear Mullings gates that she had first entered so long ago.

'I know where our dear Florie is going,' Ned said to his grandmother.

'Of course you do, my dear!' They stood

watching until Florence turned on to the road.

Florence pictured George purchasing his morning newspaper and taking it with him to a bench on the green, no longer fearing its contents. But as she looked down the road, she saw him coming towards her, and from his joyous smile she knew there would be no need for words right now. A few moments later she looked up at him. A new start held no uncertainty when she walked arm-in-arm with an old friend.